About the Author

Mark Medoff has achieved international recognition as a playwright, screenwriter, and teacher. He won the Antoinette Perry (Tony) Award for *Children of a Lesser God* and was nominated for an Academy Award for the film script of *Children*. He received an OBIE Award for his Off-Broadway hit, *When You Comin' Back*, *Red Ryder*, and an ACE Award nomination for his HBO Premiere movie, *Apology*. Among his other screenplays are *City of Joy* and *Clara's Heart*. He lives with his wife and daughters in Las Cruces, New Mexico, where he is a Dramatist in Residence at New Mexico State University.

OTHER WORKS BY THE SAME AUTHOR

Plays

When You Comin' Back, Red Ryder?
The Wager
The Kramer
Children of a Lesser God
The Hands of Its Enemy
The Majestic Kid
The Heart Outright
Big Mary
Kringle's Window
Stefanie Hero

Screenplays

Good Guys Wear Black
When You Comin' Back, Red Ryder?
Off Beat
Apology
Children of a Lesser God
Clara's Heart
City of Joy

Dreams of Long Lasting

Mark Medoff

POCKET
BOOKS

New York   London   Toronto   Sydney   Tokyo   Singapore

First published in Great Britain by Pocket Books, 1993
An imprint of Simon & Schuster Ltd
A Paramount Communications Company

Simon & Schuster Ltd
West Garden Place
Kendal Street
London W2 2AQ

Simon & Schuster of Australia Pty Ltd
Sydney

A CIP catalogue record for this book is
available from the British Library
ISBN 0–671–715561–X

Typeset by Hewer Text Composition Services, Edinburgh
Printed and bound by
HarperCollinsManufacturing, Glasgow

To
The memory of
W. FRED SHAW
Who gave me faith

To
My Mother, Father, and Brother
THELMA, LARRY, and BUD
Who nourished it

And to
STEPHANIE
Who sustains it

All choice is error, the tragical mistake,
And you are mine because I name you mine.
Kiss, then, in pledge of the imponderables
That tilt the balance of eternity
A leaf's weight up and down.

J. V. Cunningham
'The Exclusion of a Rhyme'

I know
Of no more subtle master under heaven
Than is the maiden passion for a maid,
Not only to keep down the base in man,
But teach high thought, and amiable words
And courtliness, and the desire of fame,
And love of truth, and all that makes a man.

Alfred, Lord Tennyson
'Idylls of the King'

ACKNOWLEDGMENTS

Unlike the narrator of this novel,
I was blessed through my teens and young manhood
with extraordinary friendships;
I would like to mark here
the legacies
of a few who touched me with their spirits,
their love and intelligence and humor:
Sheila Wyle and Stephen Katz and June Levine Katz
Donald Sabin and Louie Hayes
Marcia Black Milkis and Paul Cohn
James Horland, Marsha Blacker Fishkin
Patricia Mideke Blum and Jay Kotzen
Barbara Cohn Keller
Betsy Lottman Schneider
Susan Davitte and Doris and Merv Fevrier
David Curtis and Gail Geiger
Arlyn Samuels Cypen
Vicki Eisler Holmes.

I would like also to express my thanks
for their support and guidance to
Gilbert Parker, Michael Peretzian, and Michael Carlisle;
and to note here my everlasting gratitude to my editor,
Jamie Raab,
who was indispensable to the journey of this book.

SUN OF GOD

1

When I see her, I know her from my dreams.

It's the fall quarter of my third doctoral year, and I've just gotten out of jail after laying siege to the Stanford Research Institute with several hundred other Stanford students.

Whatever led them to SRI, many of the people at the party this evening went to jail together and feel pretty good about it; consequently, by the time I step through the door after compulsively finishing a research paper not due until the day after tomorrow, most of the gathering is wasted.

The notable exception is the woman of my dreams.

She's dressed in the tacitly approved uniform of the day: rough-out boots and denims (hers are prefaded and probably cost twice as much as mine to look twice as worn), a muslin shirt, and an abundance of jet black hair. Whereas mine hangs in wild red ringlets (the so-called Izro), hers is perfectly straight and neatly restrained by a beaded Indian headband, manufactured, it's my guess, by one of the famous tribes of Hong Kong.

I'm trying at this time to look stoned, though I'm not. Pot, hash, hallucinogens, uppers, downers, are ferocious competitors for control of something for which I am already competing ferociously — myself — and so in a show of greater maturity than I am accustomed to practicing, I gave them all up one day several months ago and simply fake it now. Therefore, tonight I am just noticeably ripped on a joint I haven't smoked.

When I first lay eyes on her I nevertheless *feel* like I'm hallucinating, because here is this person with her eyes, clear and resolute, fixed on me, this person who, unless you're a member of a distant culture, a Ubangi, say, and measure a woman's beauty by the size of the crockery in her face, you can't help but notice instantly is one of the two or three best-looking women you've ever seen in your life.

This person whom I recognize immediately from my fantasies of what she will look like when she finally shows up in my life.

And who descends on me here in this doorway and utters four syllables that change my life.

'Guacamole!'

For a moment I'm confused, imagining in the din that I have heard her incorrectly or that she has spoken to me in a language I have forgotten I invented years ago just for this long anticipated meeting.

Then it occurs to me that she's not disclosing her identity to me at all but enunciating the war cry of this new, politically febrile generation – Kierkegaard! Lennon! Guacamole! – and I am prepared to follow her wherever she's leading.

Guacamole – fuckin A, he's my guy!

Finally I understand she's referring to the tray she holds at her waist, on which a battalion of wafers are arranged regimentally, slathered with a fetid-looking green stuff.

With a gravity that seems totally out of keeping with the subject matter, she asks, 'Have you had your ration of guacamole yet?'

Ration of guacamole?

Pretending not to have heard her clearly, I reach into the firestorm of my hair to palm an ear, buying time while I goggle through the gauzy muslin shirt at the silhouette of her breasts encased in an unstructured pale pink brassiere beneath.

Using my deep voice, the one intended to sound like I haven't slept since the Kennedy assassination and smoke a couple of packs of non-filter Camels a day, I say, 'Didn't quite catch that.'

The place is a sheet of noise; she leans in close as if against a wind. Her breath smells of cloves. 'I don't know how it happened, but we're running low on guacamole.'

Her voice has an almost masculine timbre to it, along with an accentless crystal clarity. 'We're requesting that everyone limit themselves to two.'

Gravity entices the muslin some inches from her sternum, and I devise a crick in my neck that allows me to gaze past my nose into the cleavage packed behind the pink fabric.

'If you've already had your deuce,' she says, 'please don't cop someone else's.'

The vernacular – 'your deuce, cop someone else's' – doesn't fit, and I take a swig of my Olympia and a gentle, professorial tone that seems my only weapon in holding my own against this vision from several thousand of my wet dreams. 'Most of us,' I remind her, 'just got out of jail after taking it upon ourselves to endeavor to save the United States from the fate of the Roman Empire. And you come to me in a confrontational mode about whether I plan to eat more green stuff than I have coming or would ever desire?'

I say this with a careful lack of self-righteousness that cannot be more self-righteous. She is to know I am being facetious and that I can really string words together.

'Well, I'm *very* sorry,' she says, 'but I had something extremely im*port*ant to do or I would have *been* there.' She exhales a nor'easter of cloves across my face. 'Now could you *please* just inform me whether you want some of this dukey or not. Others are waiting.'

'No, thanks. I ate before I came. Brown dukey. From a package.'

She has eyes so fiercely green, so flagrantly fired with sparks of yellow, that I think at first there must be some error in the way nature equipped this portion of her face. These eyes have a life of their own, as if deep within strings of Christmas lights twinkle. She accents these eyes with a heavy black line streaked like smoke across the upper lids and a white base that circles above the hillocks of her cheekbones and grows thick through the eye sockets perpendicular to a Romanesque nose, a nose just technically imperfect enough to excuse her for all her life from accusations of being merely another perfect face.

She turns her back on me with an intensity that I sense has to come from practice or madness; it is a turn that says it is her commitment to serving this green dukey alone that keeps her from making a scene in my face I'll never forget.

Later, buzzed on Olympia but pretending to be flying on two reds someone shoves into my hand and which I thumb surreptitiously into a Boston Fern, I put a wedge of tomato across my front teeth and try to weave close enough to amuse her; she senses me, however, and when I'm almost close enough to flash tomato teeth at her, she glides away with a tray of mashed bean dukey and is out of reach, leaving me to flash my teeth at pothead Edie

Weinberg, a revolutionary from Beverly Hills, and send
her into gales of disquieting laughter.

'Oh, Pontius Pilate!' cries Edie, befuddling me completely, but unleashing hilarity in the potheads around
her, who go into cardiac arrest savoring my tomato teeth
and her cries of, 'Oh, Ponty, Ponty, Ponty Pile!'

I gear up for a getaway.

Shoving her tallboy of Olympia at one of the guys
who is deeply attached to her Bonneville convertible
and the copious amounts of cannabis she buys with
Dad's regular donations to the Movement, Edie clings
to my arm with iced fingers and whispers with sudden
sobriety into my ear, 'I want you to come over to my
pad *very* soon and eat my moo goo gai pan.'

'But no MSG this time – promise?'

Edie thinks she's made sense and I've made sense,
and she winks, nods – agreement has been reached, a
deal struck.

I promise to call *real* soon and slip into the bathroom,
where there's a group smoking a corncob of hash with
the solemnity of cuckoos at a religious rite.

'Jaker,' someone hisses from distended lungs through
a clenched throat, 'take a hit, dodoface. Dynamite
bush.'

'Can't handle it. Just consumed a five-megaton tomato.
I'm flying!' I flash tomato pulp at them, igniting outsize mirth.

'Jake, Jake, Jake!' one cuckoo practically weeps, so
amazed is he by my incredible sense of humor.

If I had a bag of vegetables and this crowd as a steady
audience, I could have my own TV series.

I am more acutely aware than usual how bad most
of my brothers and sisters of the Movement smell. I am
simultaneously ashamed that I cheat and slap shaving

lotion into my pits in lieu of the virtually outlawed deodorant.

I am also thinking how unattractive my brothers and sisters look. Walking cultural compost heaps: the hair, the headbands, the dashikis and muslin shirts and heavily symbolic jewelry and granny glasses. Glancing in the mirror, I am reminded how exactly like them the person staring back at me looks.

And I am appalled not to know the answer to the simple question that flits through my mind: *How did this happen without my participation?* The lack of an answer from the person in the mirror with the flaming red, shoulder-length Izro and roistering beard makes me laugh, not at anything humorous, but at the ludicrousness of that person I see; the cuckoos around me smile knowingly (people in the Movement smile knowingly at each other a lot), and so I smile knowingly in return and flip out my wang to take a whiz.

Perhaps this is my greatest accomplishment as a revolutionary: learning to take a leak in a crowd.

I wash my hands and draw a couple of looks. Though I've learned to take a leak in a crowd, I haven't learned not to wash my hands.

After our first evening of pointless sex, following one of these self-congratulatory bashes, Edie Weinberg accused me of being hopelessly bourgeois because I washed my hands after taking a leak at her place. 'Like Jesus, Jacob, you just got through *eating* me, for chrissake, man. Like what do you think you were lapping up down there?'

When I did not assay an opinion, Edie Weinberg chortled triumphantly, 'Urine!'

Outside the bathroom, I glimpse the woman of my dreams in the kitchen, lining a tray with little dukey sandwiches. She's with the guy whose apartment we're in, a very short guy named Howard Bellman wearing very tall boots. At this moment Bellman is deranged by unknown pharmaceuticals, a shot of tequila in one hand, the woman of my dream's ass in the other. She politely removes the hand from her ass, takes a belt from a bottle of RC Cola, and slips into the sea of bodies with her tray of little sandwiches.

I notice that every guy in the room feels obligated to do as I did and try to say something so clever as she floats in and out of reach and earshot that he will win her forever with a passing remark.

And it strikes me that someone who looks like her must be constantly under siege by guys like these – *us* – and I have an uncharacteristic desire to apologize to her for my own, if not their, shallowness.

But she seems so much more convincing at what she's doing than I am at what I'm doing that I can't imagine successfully peddling her my penance.

So I go stand in a corner.

From where I observe the incident that confirms for me that the woman of my dreams is, in fact, who I'm trying to convince myself she actually is.

Sluicing through the troops with her tray and her solicitations to sample what's on it, she suddenly slams to a stop like she's been struck a blow. I follow her eyes to the door, where a young woman I've seen around the Movement has entered. I've heard the young woman has a degenerative muscle disease, and though she's on crutches at this time, she will over the next ten or so years move into a wheelchair, then to a bed, and finally a coffin or urn.

I've watched this young woman cross the hundred yards of White Memorial Plaza many times, and her locomotion is most memorable for two reasons: it's tortuous and it's determined.

The woman of my dream's demeanor alters perceptibly for only an instant.

What happens in that split second is that the lights in her eyes go out for as long as it takes her hand to fly to her breastbone, desperately holding something within that threatens to bust out. Her chest heaves once, and then, like that, it's over, the lights are back on, and she sets the tray down and is on her way toward the door to greet the young woman with words I can't hear and the kind of loving embrace that happens between friends who have not seen each other in a long time.

Why did this confirm she's who I'm trying to convince myself she is? Because, if I had given consciously adjectives to the woman I've seen for years in my head, 'beautiful' and 'subservient' would have no doubt led the list. In that split second, I knew to add the word *compassionate* to the list of imperatives.

When she wends her way to me later with a tray of little tofu somethings, I want to communicate my feelings to her, but I know anything I say will sound like a come-on.

So I remain silent and reach for her tray.

But she retracts the tray and cocks her head at me. 'What?' she asks.

'Excuse me?'

'The way you're looking at me.'

'How am I looking at you?'

'Like you want to say something to me.'

I shake my head. 'You must have me confused with someone else. Perhaps the only thing in the world I *don't* want to do is say something to you.'

She smiles. She's heard it all – come-on and counter-come-on.

She holds the tray beneath the shelter of her breasts. I prong a cube of the tofu something with a toothpick from a shot glass on the tray.

'You don't see a lot of redheads with brown eyes,' she says with clinical detachment. 'You're not Irish.'

'Nepalese,' I say.

'Jewish,' she says without judgment. 'No one has the combination of chutzpah and restraint Jews do. I've seen you speak at several demonstrations. You shouldn't work so hard at being someone you're not – you'd be more appealing.'

Having looked straight into me, she glides away, to the next group. I wonder if she has bruising insights for each person she serves or just me.

I want her for my very own too much to stay here and not have her, so I go next door to my apartment, where I turn out all the lights, crack the door slightly, and settle down on the floor in the dark with a flashlight and translate some Old English for the day after tomorrow's class (I finished translating tomorrow's assignment yesterday), while keeping an eye on Howard Bellman's door.

It's an hour and a half before all the guests are gone, and I'm convinced she belongs to Bellman and that he is, even as I await her celibate exit, porking her to within an inch of her life.

I am about to get up, go in the bathroom, and whack off when she exits, an apoplectic, blitzed Bellman careening after her toward the stairs to the basement parking garage.

'*You* wanted to play waitress! So don't blame me because people treated you like you were what you were pretending to be, shitface!'

'Oh, ouch – shitface; boy, do you know how to hurt a person.' She swings around on him. 'And I wasn't blaming you, Howard. You have no conscience, so how can you be blamed for anything? I was making an observation about the way people viewed me.'

She heads for the stairs.

'Just shut the hell up and get back in here! Now, Masterson, you ignorant twat!'

'Ignorant twat – ew, ouch.'

As she doesn't accede to this command, Bellman grabs her. She shakes loose. And I'm on my feet as she descends the stairs, Bellman stumbling perilously after her in his stacked boots. Halfway down into the garage, Bellman leaps, landing on her back, taking her to the cement. As she struggles beneath him, her eyes land on me at the turn in the stairs; they are notably without fear.

Bellman follows her eyes to me. He jolts her to her feet. 'What do you want, Jake?'

'I want you to let her go, Howard.'

'What? What'd you say?'

I walk down a couple of steps so I'm close enough to touch Howard Bellman but still several feet taller than he. 'I said let her go.'

Howard Bellman snorts at the implicit threat to let me know just how frightened he is. He has the woman of my dreams in a headlock, and I can no longer see her eyes at all. 'Mind your own fucking business, Landau! Go on, get the fuck out of here! *Now!*'

I figure if I really want to turn this into a show, I can put Howard Bellman on his ass. But something about this woman makes me play it straight.

I descend the last two steps and stand on ground level with him. At six feet I still tower over Howard, even with his boots, by five inches or so. Trying not to make it sound like the movies, I say to Howard Bellman, 'Take your hands off her, Howard. Now.'

Howard Bellman despises being cowed by another man perhaps more than anything that's happened to him in recent history; yet I suspect he senses that if he doesn't let go of her, I'm going to hit him, and if I hit him, he figures I'm going to hurt him, and after a moment he snaps his hands free of her, giving her just enough of a shove to let me know he's not *totally* giving in to me just because I scare him.

To the woman of my dreams I say simply, 'Go on.'

She still has no fear in her eyes; what I see there, actually, is disdain. For me.

'What a guy,' she says. She whistles appreciatively. 'Next time, mind your own business. Someone like him could never hurt me.'

And she disappears into the recesses of a giant old black-and-gold DeSoto.

Howard looks at me with wasted, malicious eyes, then wheels on her, shrieking, 'Is this an exit, Tits? Huh? You vacate the premises and I swear to God I'll . . .'

Unable to conjure sufficient punishment, spittle flies without accompanying language from Howard Bell-man's mouth, and he makes a sound like someone gargling, then finally manages to bounce a resounding, 'Fuck you, cunt ears!' off the block walls of the parking facility.

She laughs a wonderful laugh, deep and free and full of chimes.

He staggers to the laundry room, throws the light switch, and disappears inside as the woman of my dreams starts the old DeSoto and engages it in unhurried forward flight.

As the car is about to pass me, I step into its path and turn my palms down in a sign for 'Stop.'

The big DeSoto seems to stop in sections. Its engine rumbles restively, its driver fixes me with her luminous eyes. In the back of my mind, I'm planning to say something of such enormous impact that she's going to park her car and return with me to my apartment for life. But when words leave my lips, they are these: 'I'd head for a gas stop and have somebody take a look at your right rear tire.'

'How can you see my right rear tire,' she asks without malice, 'when you're on the left side of my car?'

'X-ray vision,' I tell her.

'Are you the Nepalese Superman?'

'His Jewish accountant.'

A hint of amusement crosses her eyes. But it's late and she's had about all the fun she can stand for this evening. There's only time left for this:

'Tell me right now,' she says, 'what you wanted to say to me before, or I promise I'll never have anything to do with you no matter what you might ever say to me or how many times you might come to my rescue.'

'I saw you see the young woman on the crutches,' I tell her.

The yellow striations in her eyes illuminate the basement. 'That was private,' she says.

'Nevertheless, I saw it and I stopped just wanting to fuck you and knew you're the woman I've waited to meet all my life.'

She cocks her head, as if getting a different, and better, angle on me, and says, 'I have to admit that's pretty good.'

Beneath her foot the Neanderthal DeSoto galvanizes its many parts into motion, and she's gone.

In the laundry room, Howard Bellman is systematically engaging each of the washing machines into a sloshing rinse cycle, all the while babbling with fierce unintelligibility.

What did that mean, that 'No'?

I begin shutting the washing machines down. 'Time to hit the sack, Howard.'

'Leave those machines on!'

I continue to shut them off.

'That's an order, Landau!'

'Let's go, I'll help you upstairs.'

Like a cornered criminal, he throws himself up against the last sloshing washer. 'Get *away* from me,' he screams. 'You *touch* this machine – '

I reach around him, shut the machine down. As it winds to a stop, so does Howard. Suddenly enervated, he allows me to take him by the arm and to assist him back upstairs to our floor and into his apartment, where he drops onto his couch amid the rubble of the celebration and sleeps as he lands. Just inside his bedroom doorway, an insensate couple lies half-naked, evidently taken by unconsciousness en route to making love there. It's not until I'm almost back out the door that I notice the female member of the couple has her index finger in the anus of the male.

Locking myself into my own apartment, I am momentarily empathic to my parents' separately expressed concerns, noted in our occasional correspondence, for my safety here.

2

After my first arrest, my mother, a child of Russian immigrants who fled the Bolsheviks in 1915, this woman I never knew to espouse any political point of view in her life stronger than the opinion that John Kennedy *looked* like a president, writes me that 'revolutions are not led by Jews, Jacob. Jews just become their martyrs.'

It saddens me that I'm startled to think my mother capable of such a well-turned notion, and in some distant, cluttered reach of my mind I think: *I really ought to get to know this woman sometime*.

In a response that I realize even as I write it only a twenty-six-year-old, overeducated smart-ass could compose, I reply: 'Re your letter – Jews and revolutions: Moses, Judas Mac, King Dave, Barry Spinoza, Big K. Marx, Henry Greenberg, S. Koufax.'

I would teach her to be intelligent with me.

My father, though, is a different story.

Morris Landau and I represent a fusion and a fissure that is not mine to totally comprehend. The former Warsaw and Lyons surgeon/scientist, now a shoe salesman whose mother died in a pogrom when he was seven and whose father died in Auschwitz, condones each arrest, as long, he notes, as I understand that release is not guaranteed. 'There is,' he cautions me, 'the stink of fascism in the air over America.' And he admonishes me, 'If they attempt to kill you for your beliefs, trust me

– and I know how difficult that might be – but you must kill them first. Or at least with you.'

I am, needless to say, ashamed to admit to Morris Landau, to the former Dr Motke Londovnik, the shallowness of my beliefs because – instinctively, at least – I know that few things in my life will ever be as important as finding a way to return to my father his pride in me.

3

The woman of my dreams was right about my trying to be someone I think I'm convincing people I am that I'm not.

At my first demonstration, two years ago, when a speaker is needed, as if disembodied from the act, I watch myself step forward and hear myself speak, maintaining passionately a point of view I don't know until that moment I hold; but I sense this is a time of great historical moment, and a dream of immortality more powerful than my fears of success and memories of past failure thrusts me forward.

Since then I continue to hang to the outside edge of those vying for leadership, sporadically making speeches most noted for their reliance on wide-ranging and erudite quotes from other sources and references to other revolutions, but vacillating, finally, between competing all out for a top spot and waiting to be thrust into one through the popular will of others.

A sizable setback in my confidence comes when, following what I consider my finest and most literate peroration, a young Government assistant professor points out to me that I attributed a quote by Karl Marx to Allen Ginsberg. 'They look alike,' he says, trying to soften my embarrassment. 'I always confuse Whitman and Ginsberg myself.'

He is only the reflection of other people's ideas, and even then the schmuck can't get his sources straight.

The woman of my dreams knew me on sight.

So neither leader nor follower – and as throughout my life since age fifteen when last I knew exactly what I wanted to be – I am someone in the process of becoming someone I never quite complete becoming before I wander onward toward not becoming the next someone.

I'm not surprised then that the day after the party at Howard Bellman's, without regret or conviction, I simply walk away from the Movement.

The direction I choose has to do with nothing more compelling than where I parked my car this morning.

4

Freed from an obligation to save the world – or at least to end the war in Vietnam and promulgate racial equality at home – I can dedicate myself totally to wondering, as I have for two days, how I'm going to locate the woman of my dreams.

The obvious way would be simply to go next door and ask Howard Bellman who she is and where to find her, but I don't want him to know I want to pursue someone who doesn't seem to want to be pursued.

As I pass the Theater Arts Department, the problem of her whereabouts is solved.

Her hair is no longer black, but a tapioca blond, and she sits on the steps, a bottle of RC Cola in one hand, those green eyes fixed on a play script in her lap.

'Boy, am I sorry to see you,' I say, shading my eyes against the sun, which isn't shining in them, an instinctive move I imagine somehow gives me protection in case she doesn't remember me. 'How you doin'?'

Without anger or relish, she says, 'Nepalese Superman's Jewish accountant.'

'You dyed your hair,' I tell her.

'Yep.'

'Well, if you're waiting for me to tell you whether I like this color or not, I do. Though not as well as the black.'

She cocks her head, getting that other, probing angle.

'So,' I say, 'perhaps at this juncture I should inquire what you're doing. What *are* you doing?'

'Learning lines.'

'Actor?'

'Trying.'

'Big role?'

'Pretty big.'

'What play?'

She takes a pull on her RC and turns the script toward me.

'*Taming of the Shrew*, huh?'

'Yep.'

'Kate?'

'Yep.'

'Kinda horseshit humility calling that a "pretty big role," isn't it?'

She smiles. 'Yeah.'

That's all: Yeah.

'I'd like to see you perform.'

'All you gotta do is flash your student ID, they give you a ticket, you grab a seat, I come out and try to electrify you.'

She indicates the box office behind her in the foyer of the building. If she glances back down at her script, I'll take it as an indication I shouldn't continue; if she looks back at me, I'll proceed.

Her eyes land on mine.

Without crowding her, I close the gap between us. 'You any good?' I ask.

'Yep.'

The eyes don't waver. It's simple: she believes in herself.

'Big future in Hollywood?'

'My goals aren't orientated to big bucks, if that's what you're implying.'

'Oriented,' I correct reflexively. 'Not orientated. There's no orientated.'

'Uh-oh,' she says. 'Going to try to reduce me a little, are you?' She takes a belt of the RC. 'What are you – an English professor?'

'Worse – a candidate to *become* an English professor.' I want to tell her something I wouldn't ordinarily admit, want to confess that wielding the language like a weapon is something I do to protect myself from rejection, being found out, the usual psychological bullshit.

But before I can mobilize myself for honesty, she says, 'Well, this has been great for my ego, but I have to study my lines and I'm sure you have other people to judge this afternoon.'

Given my leave, I remain for this: 'Last night at Bellman's, you were pretending to be subservient because as an actress in transit you were trying to understand the flip side of Kate.'

Her head snaps up, her eyes slice through bone, and my brain sizzles.

'Lucky guess,' I say.

And walk away, resisting successfully the desire to look back to see if she's watching me make my exit, certain she is.

5

I get a haircut, shave my face clean, and discard my wire-rim glasses the day I go see *The Taming of the Shrew*.

As Kate, this person, this *actor*, whose name the program says is Leslie Ann Masterson, is quite simply stunning.

In Kate, in three hours, there are more views than most people display or permit themselves to display in weeks and months, perhaps for some people in a lifetime: anger, passion, resistance, reluctance, hurt, self-righteousness, remorse, and still something larger underneath it all, or more accurately, surrounding it all like a just discernible protective skin – something steeped in compassion.

But more. Something, which at the expense of using a word that my compatriots and I have managed to trivialize in the last few years, spiritual.

She reminds me up there of someone more substantial than anyone I ever dreamed about.

I want very much to go backstage to tell her that in case nobody's told her before, she has a shitload of talent; but afraid of embarrassment, I head for my car, only to turn around and trot back toward the theater before she has time to change and disappear, then escalating my trot to a dead-out run as I see across the distance that actors are streaming out the stage door.

I almost collide with her as she leaves with Howard Bellman, who, needless to say, played Petruchio – thank God, not as well as she played Kate. (The *Stanford Daily*, in a refreshing shot of bigotry, considering the doggedly ecumenical times, snidely accuses him in its review the next day of confusing Petruchio and Shylock, referring to him as 'Petschlock.')

My breathing is out of control, and the effort to control it only makes it worse. 'Just want to let you guys know I thought you were terrific.'

Barely glancing at me, Howard Bellman mumbles something full of false humility, and Leslie Ann Masterson clearly enunciates a 'Thank you' before she allows him to guide her down the concourse of giant date palms on currents of graduate school egomania.

Effectively humbled, I bow my head. See a good-size rock. Impulsively pick it up, cock my arm, aim for Howard Bellman's skull.

'You came,' Leslie Ann Masterson calls.

She faces me from the shadows of a massive mission building thirty yards away.

'Yes,' I say, 'yes, I did.' The hand behind my head, coiled in anger, changes course and intent and smooths the back of my newly scissored hair.

'And you cut your hair and your beard off.'

'Yes,' I confess, 'yes, I did.'

'I couldn't see that red hair in the dark, and it took me a minute to recognize your voice.'

'I was using my deep voice,' I tell her.

She steps into the glow of a street lamp on the concourse, and I can see she's smiling. She has big, straight, perfectly spaced teeth, and I realize that because of their fullness, she can't smile with her mouth closed. When she smiles, she gives you the whole constellation.

Bellman presses at her elbow, indicating his desire not to let a lot of cement grow under their feet; yet she resists.

I advance toward them, hand extended. 'I hope you won't think this is silly, but . . .'

She looks at the rock in my outstretched palm.

'It's a vitreous uvarovite rock,' I tell her, winging it, 'found only in certain parts of Ethiopia, I'm told. Because of its volcanic origin, the natives consider it a great source of power against one's enemies, and especially useful against pompous Jews bearing gifts.'

Howard's countenance wonders whether a) I'm talking about me or him and b) whether there could possibly be an ounce of truth in any of this.

'I'd like you to have it – please.'

Though this is absolute bullshit, the part of me that wants to give her something, that wants to communicate respect to her, speaks with absolute sincerity.

She cocks her head, getting that angle on me, wondering if this *is* absolute bullshit or, like Howard, whether it's possible I'm telling the truth.

'That's very nice of you,' she says.

'Not really. Because the fact is if you refuse it now, it also carries a curse on all the short people in your life.'

Howard sighs wearily. 'Oh, Christ, Landau.'

She takes the rock, her fingertips brushing my palm, her little finger briefly hooking mine as she retracts her hand with my gift. 'Thank you.'

'Keep it next to your skin and all your wishes will come true.'

'Oh, Jesus H. Christ!'

She gives in to Howard's hand at her elbow. Yet two steps farther out of my life, she resists again and steps back into the light on the walkway, as she might if this were a play. 'By the way,' she calls without rancor, 'I looked up orientation. There's an oriented and an orientated.'

'But,' I say without rancor of my own, 'orientated is a neologism.'

She flicks her eyes into the dark, then back at me. 'A what?'

'A usage,' I tell her, 'that achieves acceptance only through decades of incorrect use.'

Howard Bellman mumbles something toward her ear – I catch only the word *cocksucker*.

Leslie Ann Masterson glances at him, looks at me. 'I'll never use "orientated" again,' she says. 'I promise.'

'I'd really appreciate it.'

The teeth peek out between her lips, refract the light, and in Bellman's charge she glides into the trees and night beyond the theater. His voice, remonstrating with her, denigrating me, recedes into silence as I watch them disappear.

Going to an opening night party, no doubt, there to be treated, I hope, with the respect her talent deserves.

I drive home to discover the opening night party for *The Taming of the Shrew* taking place next door to me in Howard's apartment. I sit down in my doorway with Faulkner's *Light in August*, waiting for Leslie Ann Masterson to appear in his doorway and invite me in, but she doesn't and I can't concentrate on Faulkner, so I get an Olympia and wander down to the pool.

Where I discover Leslie Ann Masterson sitting on a chaise longue, her only companion a bottle of RC Cola. The attitude of her body tells me she's been crying.

'We can't go on meeting like this,' I say behind her.

So far away is she that my voice startles her. She

manages a small laugh and turns to me, and do I imagine this, or does she seem pleased to see me?

'Are you following me?'

'Just checking up on my rock.'

She pulls her jeans leg up over the top of her boot. 'In the top of my sock. Next to my skin.' In the muted light bouncing off the pool from the horseshoe of apartments rising around us, I see her blush. In this era in which the act of cunnilingus can be flippantly compared to lapping urine, it's startling to see someone blush.

Age twelve, sixth grade, about to attend my first boy-girl party.

'Women,' my father tells me, 'are not in fact born of Adam, not from his rib,' he says.

'Where are they from?' I inquire of him with great curiosity as I stand squeezing my buttocks together in abject fear of the very thing I hope he will demystify for me in one fatherly sentence.

And says my pop, 'Beats the hell outta me, Jakey, beats the unholy hell outta me, boychik.'

'Did you get my rock on a dig in Ethiopia,' she asks, 'or was that a bunch of baloney?'

I like the way she says 'my rock.' I sense that, in fact, in passing from me to her, it has in some mysterious fashion given up something to her totally that does make it hers.

'Actually,' I tell her, 'I picked it up off the ground in front of the theater. I was going to bounce it off Bellman's skull for making me feel like a living, ambulating putz.'

I turn my hands up in resignation to whatever punishment she cares to mete out.

But she laughs and indicates the lounge chair opposite her. 'Like to sit down?'

'Why not?'

She sticks out a hand. 'Leslie Ann Masterson.'

'Yes,' I say, 'I know.'

Her fingers are narrow and slight. But when the hand is gone, there's warmth.

'You going to tell me your name?'

'Jacob Landau.' And then, after a moment's debate, I add, 'Who cut his hair and removed his beard for you.'

She fixes me with those eyes. There's no doubt in them: I am not the first male to have acted in extremis for her; not, in all likelihood, among the first one hundred.

'And got contact lenses?'

'No. The glasses were just decorative . . . Party boring?' I ask.

'Oh, I don't know. Theater people pretty much cover the same territory whenever they're together. My performance, my method. Your performance, your method. And of course, how insensitive the audience was to our collective brilliance.'

A tulle fog is settling in, and the edges of the world have begun to recede. We've become an island. She puts the big glass bottle of cola to her mouth. I can hear it effervesce against her teeth.

'Why were you crying?' I ask her.

'I wasn't,' she says.

Without weighing the risk, I let my hand go to her hair, almost white in the opaque light; do it not, I think, only because I want so much to feel some part of her in physical contact with some part of me, but because I sense in this moment how difficult the life ahead of her is going to be if she's really as talented as I think she is.

She seems both very old and very young, simultaneously at the end and beginning of life.

'What do you dream of, Jacob?' she asks.

The question startles and threatens me. 'Oh, you know, the usual: an automobile that requires no more than periodic maintenance and a life free of contagious social disease.'

She smiles, though neither of us thinks what I said was particularly witty.

'Immortality at a young age,' I tell her, 'lasting mercifully throughout life.'

She rotates her head in the palm of my hand – a reward for telling the truth – and a gesture that urges me onward. 'Tell me what your dream of immortality is,' she says.

I suggest the utter inconsequence of such a thing with a dismissive wave of my hand.

'Couldn't be any dumber than dreaming of becoming an actor. What do you dream, Jacob?'

I feel her hands come down lightly on my jeans at my knees.

'Come on, you're dying to tell me to see if I laugh in your face.'

There is about her a receptivity that makes not telling her impossible.

'Golf.'

'Golf.' She repeats the word without prejudice, at once verifying that we are speaking the same language and at the same time reaffirming her desire to hear what I have to say.

Our faces are only inches apart.

'Once upon a time, I dreamed of being a great golfer,' I tell her. 'The best.'

'But you don't dream that anymore.'

'No.'

'What happened?' she asks.

'Found out one day in adolescence that I'd never be able to putt worth a shit in the clutch.'

'So what do you dream now?'

'To be a fine teacher,' I tell her.

She stares at me, into me. Doesn't believe me. 'You may want to be a fine teacher,' she says. 'I mean, who wants to be a bad one? But I don't think that's your dream.'

'Actually, I'm between dreams right now.'

She lifts one hand and puts her index finger to the corner of my mouth, directly on a place I've suspected from childhood harbors some secret I know somewhere in me I want very much for someone to unlock.

'Don't be afraid,' she says.

She leans closer to me, and my hand on the back of her head comes forward with her, sliding down the back of her skull. Just behind her ear, I feel the ridge of a scar. My index finger traces it to the hairline at the nape of her neck.

'My brother,' she says, her eyes locked to mine, 'hit me with a baseball bat when I was thirteen because his friends had become more interested in watching my breasts grow than in playing baseball with him.'

Our faces are virtually touching. The fog has closed us in. 'First inkling,' I ask, 'that you'd been blessed and cursed?'

'One of 'em,' she says.

'What were the others?'

She shakes her head. A door starts to close.

Hoping to prolong my view inside, I press my mouth to her forehead, square my lips to the ridge of her hairline. Her hair smells wonderfully of herbs – coriander, perhaps, or sweet basil.

She takes my hands in the skeletons of hers, and

with a lament she says, 'I'm very sorry to have met you.'

'Thank you,' I say, 'the feeling is entirely mutual.'

And we follow this shared lament to the other's mouth.

6

I awaken to find Leslie Ann Masterson naked in my
kitchen, scrambling an egg concoction that utilizes
virtually everything in my refrigerator that isn't plastic
or metal.

Surveying her from the cover of my covers, I photograph her breasts, their thimblelike nipples, her porcelain ass, photograph the whole of her mentally for recall
in my impotent old age.

Then creep into the kitchen of my studio apartment,
my penis preceding me. There I fall to my knees and bury
my face in Leslie Ann Masterson, my fingers harpooning
her buttocks, garbling nonsensically into the hair, the
plateaus of flesh, the redolence.

We throw ourselves on the floor, naked, and eat Leslie
Ann's 'eggs à la refrigerator.'

I have coffee, she has my last Dr Brown's Cream Soda
with lots of ice.

'You talk,' she says.

'You pick a subject,' I suggest.

'How come you don't have thousands of freckles like
most redheads?'

'No idea.'

'I see. Is everyone in your family redheaded?'

'No one. Depending on whether my mother was mad
at me or dreaming a life of extraordinary fame for me on
any given day in my little-boy-hood, she would tell me I
was either adopted, thereby explaining my bad behavior

by bad genes, or she and my father had found me, after the fashion of Moses, in the famous bullrushes of Miami Beach.'

'Tell me about girls.'

'Na.'

'Come on.'

'If I tell you the truth, will you be disappointed?'

'Could be. But if you lie, I'll know and I'll make you start from the beginning again.'

And so I tell her the truth, more or less. Basically this:

From the age of twelve I do not merely desire the female body – at first to gratefully kiss it, touch it, nibble it, and stick my fingers into it; then to lick it, suck it, fornicate with it – but crave it. The sight of certain female forms, personalities totally unknown, can cause my throat to emit, even against my wishes, a little guttural cry that bemoans the fact that I am not at that moment entwined in some form of sexual activity with that particular amalgamation of flesh and hair and bone I might glimpse for only a moment stepping onto a Greyhound heading in the opposite direction, about to disappear from my life, with its delectable cargo, forever.

Until I am fifteen, I tell her, and become drunk for the first time with another boy on the golf team, a night of firsts in which I discover that I am not alone in this craving, I have assumed I am afflicted with a sickness that I alone suffer in the world. I have no confidant my age, and I don't dare confide this sort of thing to my father, then my constant companion. And golfers, adolescent ones, anyway, do not talk sex in the locker room. For the most part, in fact, they don't talk. Instinctively, in this very individual sport, every other competitor is your enemy.

'How old were you when you first did the deed?' Leslie Ann wants to know.

Bound by the restraints of the late Fifties and early Sixties, I tell her, combined with my mother's esoteric threats of blinding, deafening, castrating social diseases, my father's couched pleas for circumspection, I confess to her that I am a twenty-one-year-old college senior when I have intercourse the first time. My guide is a Gainesville hooker old enough to be my grandmother, and she gives me the clap.

Arriving at Stanford to avoid the draft after two years working in my father's shoe store, I am utterly amazed, I tell her, at the sexual practices my generation has begun to practice in my absence.

'You think it's good?' she wants to know.

No. But am I going to single-handedly hold back the tidal wave of rabid promiscuity disguised as freedom sweeping the campuses of America?

'No,' we say in tandem.

I laugh. She doesn't.

Is she passing judgment? Can't tell. But one thing is certain: she's listening with monastic concentration.

How, she wants to know, did I get into literature?

My father and my mother want me to study dentistry (in my mother's case) or law (in my father's; he cannot get past Mengele where dentistry is concerned), but at the University of Florida, I date a Yugoslavian 'beatnik' who lures me into literature with her assurances that I am by nature a poet – kindred spirit, according to her, to Arthur Rimbaud. As it turns out, the greatest similarity between Rimbaud and me is that we both stop writing poetry when we're nineteen.

When I graduate, it is nevertheless with a BA in English.

At home, nothing is said about my decision to study literature. A prefab rationale is available: my father has instilled in me from an early age a love of books and ideas. One bag we carry to every golf tournament is filled with my schoolwork and with novels he wants me to read and which I almost invariably love as he feeds them to me. (When I return from winning the North-South Amateur to my eighth-grade English class and turn in a 'free choice' book report to my teacher on *Notes from Underground*, tears spring to her eyes. 'Oh, Jacob,' she says. 'You . . . I . . . oooh.' This seemed wonderfully inarticulate to my pop and me, coming from an English teacher.)

And so I find myself, after four years of college, with a degree with which, in terms of a life's work, I am qualified to do virtually nothing.

Except, in search of more of the same and to avoid a life in the shoe business, to go to graduate school where I can prepare to spend the rest of my life talking about other men's work, honoring the labor of people who will remind me daily that I am less than they and haven't grown up to be what I really want to be.

The light coming in my windows has changed, become less hospitable. It's midafternoon. I've been talking for hours and have been listened to with an intensity that has mass.

'Good story,' she says. 'Thanks for telling me.'

'Thank you,' I say, 'for listening.'

She lays my fingers into the palm of her hand and studies them. I bit my fingernails when I was playing golf, and though I stopped that habit many years ago, I'm still self-conscious about anyone looking at my nails. I remove the hand from scrutiny by taking hers and pressing it to my lips.

'Now,' I say, 'you tell me your secrets.'

'I had a boyfriend in high school,' she says. 'We didn't have sex. I had two lovers in college. Another here. And now you. I've wanted to be an actor since I was five or six and maybe before then, except I can't remember back past five or six. I had a pretty uneventful childhood and hope to have an enormously eventful adulthood with just enough pain to keep my work fresh and growing.'

She puts the glass of iceless, diluted Dr Brown's to her lips, and I'm certain for a reason I can't explain that she's lying to me.

Door closing.

'I talked for thirty-seven hours, and you cover the same period in your life in thirty seconds.'

Her eyes flick about my face, making heat where they touch. 'In the theater everything's compressed,' she says.

'What happened that you won't tell me?'

She shrugs. 'Boring things,' she says.

Not to me, I want to say. *I want to know everything! I can take it all!*

'Jacob,' she says.

I raise my eyebrows, anticipating, welcoming more. But that's all there is. Just my name.

Like a benediction.

7

We make love in the bathtub, sending a tidal wave over the side, irrigating the linoleum and five feet of carpet in the living room.

We throw down towels to sop up the mess, then fall down in it and make some more.

Finally – a long time later – we get back in the bathtub. We wash each other. We get out and dry each other with the sheets off the bed, as all the towels are wet from mopping the floor.

Then it's dark outside and she's dressed and ready to leave and I ask her not to go.

'I have to,' she says.

'Why?'

'Because I'm in the doorway. It definitely has the feel of an exit.'

'We can close the door,' I suggest, 'and you can stay.'

'My clothes are rancid.'

'Wear mine.'

'They'll be too big.'

'I'll have them tailored.'

She laughs. So do I.

'Sunday's the day I make up for indulging my theater habit the rest of the week,' she says. ' I have to do laundry, go to the grocery, the gas station.'

'I'll miss you,' I say.

'I'll come back,' she says.

'Pretend you left and you're already here.'

She looks me in the eyes, and some veil – whether the last one or one of thousands, I can't guess – drops away and she says, 'I don't want you to get tired of me.'

I hoot. That's a good one – get tired of her – that's a hot one! '*That*,' I tell her, 'is beyond the realm of possibility – trust me.'

'I'm about as close to trusting you right now as I'm ever likely to get,' she says without subterfuge, 'but men always get tired of me.'

Far, far away I know there is a warning here that I should at least mark, if not heed; but, quite simply, I am not thinking with the part of me that reasons, just the part that lusts, the part between my legs from whence the dream of her originally sprang.

Howard Bellman opens his door with an unidentifiable piece of lunch meat in his beard and stares blankly first at Leslie Ann and then at me. He blinks rapidly twice in what, for someone as stuporous as he, has to pass for a cataclysm of disbelief.

'Good afternoon, Howard,' I say with neighborly conviviality, and point helpfully at his beard. 'You got some dukey in your beard there.'

And I close my door, leaving Leslie Ann Masterson to choose for herself, even though the mere thought of never being with her again is, after a missed putt at the United States National Junior Championship at age fifteen, the second greatest agony I've felt in my twenty-six years.

8

I have the students in my Intro to Lit class turn their desks into a circle so they're looking at each other; and though I have a desk among them, I spend most of the period on my feet, moving behind them, prodding response and debate, returning occasionally to my home base when I need to see where I am in the progression of my methodical notes.

We're discussing Tennyson this morning, 'Idylls of the King,' and I am leading them on a merry chase from the poet to the Bible to Nietzsche's nihilism, Jung's archetypes, Camus's *Stranger*, to Erich Fromm's idealized utopia, and back to Tennyson by way of Bernard Malamud's novel about the holy grail, *The Natural*.

At one point, floating past the windows that open onto the Quad, I catch the faint odor of a newly familiar scent, and while one of my sophomores attacks what he divines as my atheistic reading of Lord Tennyson's poem, I peek over the edge of the thick limestone casement and see the top of the head of someone sitting on the portico floor, an open notebook on her lap, an RC Cola beside her, taking notes.

I want to touch her head, to let her know not just that I know she's there, but how tender it seems.

But I don't. Because now I wonder if she's viewing me less as a lover than as an audience. Me the performer now, she the critic.

I try to continue as if she weren't there. It feels that, at best, I impersonate myself.

When class is over and I exit onto the Quad, she's gone. Clearly she doesn't want me to know she was there.

So when I head off to meet her for lunch, I tell myself I'll pretend not to know.

As I approach her on the patio outside the Student Union, I am taken again by the way she listens. There are a young man and woman in conversation behind her back, and I can tell she's not just taking in their conversation, but expropriating it for whatever future use she might care to make of it.

I keep my distance.

I want to view her as who she is when I'm not there to see her.

She's massaging something in her hand, and it's not until the couple behind her moves away that she shifts and I see that what she's stroking in her hand is the rock I gave her.

From behind, I lean down and put my lips to her hair, breathe the smell of herbs.

She reaches behind her and squeezes my knee, then turns her face up, offering me first that ebullient smile and then her mouth. Her tongue touches my lips.

I sit across the small metal table from her. 'Anything good?' I ask, indicating the now departed people behind her.

'Were you spying on me?'

'Yep – spying on you spying on them. Busy day of eavesdropping, huh?'

There's no apology in her eyes, no defensiveness, when she asks, 'How did you know?'

'I smelled Tabu.' Trying not to appear as anxious for

her approval as I feel, I ask, 'What'd you hear?'

'God, lots of interesting stuff. You really cover some territory in an hour, don't you?'

I relax under the relief of this stroke. Until some enzymes and synapses hook up in my brain and I know the stroke is not only a stroke.

'What bothered you about the territory I covered?'

'You were talking about that beautiful poem like it was an inanimate *thing* of some sort.'

'Inanimate *thing* . . . ?'

'All those literary and philosophical and psychological references. It was like you were explaining a detail map of a foreign country.'

'What are overeducated fools like me supposed to do if we can't impress people with the breadth of our knowledge?'

She takes a hit on the cup of cola between us, crushed ice shifting like fine, crackling bones. 'Once art is decoded by you experts, people like me can't ever just feel it again. And you weren't only trying to expand their vistas, were you?'

'What else was going on?'

'They scare you.'

Warning sirens go off along my spinal column: *Threat! Threat! Threat!*

'How do you mean, "scare me"?'

'Na, you don't want to hear this.'

'True. But I don't have the intestinal fortitude to resist, either. So go on.'

She pushes the cup of cola to the edge of the table, clearing a battleground between us. 'You talk a little bit above their heads, so they know you know more than they do and so occasionally they have to ask you to explain yourself so they can really understand what it is you're trying to tell them as you take them further and further from a spontaneous response to what you've assigned them to read.' She brings the cola back, takes a hit. Ice shifts, bones snap. 'Are you mad?'

I am, but not as mad as I expected to be. 'A little.'

'Tough,' she says, but takes my hands between hers. 'But I like the way you stand.'

Okay, now the good stuff.

'How do I stand?'

'You don't know?'

'No.'

'God.' She stands up, spreads her legs, and puts her hands on her hips. 'Like this.'

'Looks like I'm taking a dump in the woods.'

'What can I tell you?'

'Why do I do that, you figure?'

'D'know.' She gives me a shrug that I've begun to realize indicates her basic lack of interest in analyses and definitive reasons for actions, habits, the origin of the universe, and so on.

She smiles her smile.

'Did you wear braces?' I ask her.

'Nope. They just came out this way.'

'Amazing.'

'And I've never had a cavity. Did you wear braces?'

'No. I wore steel girders.'

Laughter like chimes.

Extraordinary.

9

I attend each of the last five performances of *The Taming of the Shrew*.

Each performance, I am more taken by Leslie Ann Masterson's talent. There is a wholeness to Kate that is greater than the sum of Leslie Ann's (at least discernible) parts.

Something else: Around Leslie Ann, as her performance grows nightly, the others pale, so that finally, on the last night, I feel that I'm watching a professional carrying a cast of amateurs. In this way, her abilities weaken the production, and it is not nearly as good as it was when she was less.

Backstage there's a coolness toward her because she's better than all these other people who aspire to the same notoriety and future success – the immortality – that Leslie Ann seems to have locked up.

When I tell her this on the way to the car closing night, she slaps my face and explodes at me: 'Don't you think I *know* that! What am I supposed to do? Be *bad*?'

My face stings with a peculiar blend of outrage and pleasure.

'Oh, God, Jacob,' she says, clutching my face in her two hands, 'I'm sorry, I'm sorry.'

'Okay,' I say, 'it's okay.'

Her hands leave my cheeks and go to her mouth. 'I'm sorry.'

'It's all right, Leslie Ann. Let it go.'

She takes my hand, leads me on toward my car. She hooks her index finger into the back pocket of my jeans. 'You were going to hit me back.'

'No, I wasn't.'

'I saw your left shoulder tense.'

'That was my hand endeavoring to work independently of my brain. I would never hit you.'

'But your hand might.'

'Na.'

'Are you sure?'

'Positive.'

'Okay.'

'Are you relieved or disappointed?'

She slides her whole hand into my back pocket, turning it inward, her palm against my buttock, and she cocks her head at me. 'Relieved,' she says.

I can't say why, but I know at this instant she's been hit a lot in her life.

And just past that realization there lurks an intimation of catastrophe.

10

Twice a week Leslie Ann conducts a scene-work lab in the afternoons with first-year under-graduate acting students.

I ask if I can watch and, before she can say no, remind her she eavesdropped on me.

They meet in a rehearsal hall/dance studio, and Leslie Ann seats me on a chair at the students' backs; in other words, I'm facing her. I could never have done that; I'd want her behind me where I couldn't watch her watch me.

The twelve students do prepared scenes, two actors to a scene. Leslie Ann watches, moving silently along the edges of the room, taking notes, that way of listening and focusing just as evident here with these freshmen as it is with me alone.

When each scene is finished, she critiques.

I'm fascinated by her refusal to intellectualize about the scenes, her refusal to give them credence as things that derived from the intelligence of their authors; she recognizes the existence of the scenes only by virtue of their visceral and emotional qualities, and once she's broken them down into a sequence of feelings, instincts, unnamed sensory data, she then admonishes the students to forget the individual 'beats' and chides virtually each student in his or her turn to 'cut out the acting, quit pretending. Have the courage to just *be* what's inside. You follow? Let everything conscious, all the intellectual googaw and analysis, pass through your consciousness as fast as you can and then forget it and just *do* it!'

And I am fascinated, too, by the specific manner in which she does the chiding. It's not mean, but it's not in any way patronizing. She doesn't say something's good that she thinks is bad; yet she is very clear about what she thinks is wrong, and it always has to do with false behavior.

'Acting's just about behavior,' she says at the end of the class. 'Action! Reaction! Being! You think authors sit around and intellectualize about what they're going to write before they write it or *as* they write it or even when they're *through* writing it? That's what critics and English and drama professors are for − I guess. To explain to us dumbdumbs what our behavior means. I don't care what it means! I *am* my behavior! That's it!'

The class is over long before it seems two hours can have passed, and Leslie Ann brings the students together into a huddle. In the short time I've known Leslie Ann Masterson, I've never seen her sweat − even at the end of a performance. Someone as beautiful and talented as she, of course, shouldn't be burdened with something as mundane as sweat, but now her armpits are soaked, her upper lip spackled with moisture.

In the huddle, she and her students hug each other, and I hear a passionate injunction whispered to them: 'No fear,' she says.

As the lab breaks up, each student comes to Leslie Ann and thanks her. She touches a cheek here, squeezes an arm there, has something direct and private to say to each.

Inevitably I compare what I've seen here to what I envision in my mind's eye of my own teaching. I am always conscious of putting on a show, of creating a persona – the aggressively masculine and widely knowledgeable, droll young Ph.D. candidate who is always suspicious that the students who bother to come to the front of the room after a class to say 'Good class today' or to otherwise commend me on stimulating them, do so with an ulterior motive: they suspect I can be flattered toward leniency in grading, helping to insure them a finer future – higher GPA, stronger résumé, weightier graduate school, better job.

I dab the sleeve of my workshirt to her face and bend my face to her workshirt to sniff at her. Indeed, she smells faintly of her perfume and distinctly of body odor.

'Don't smell me,' she says, 'I stink.'

'I find it reassuring. I'd begun to suspect you were an extraterrestrial.'

She looks at me from a distant place.

'What?' I ask.

She shakes her head.

Door closing.

She slips her hand into the back pocket of my jeans, heads us for the door, and says, 'So, let's have the review, Professor.'

11

The next weekend, she takes me camping in Yosemite.

When she suggests the trip, she does it with such enthusiasm that it's impossible for me to refuse.

Yet when she wakes me at five in the morning, herds me through a shower, a bite, and into the car, she seems withdrawn.

'You okay?' I ask as we embark.

'Oh, yeah,' she says. 'Take the freeway north.'

She navigates and squints against the early morning sun burning through the fog. She doesn't wear sunglasses because, according to her, 'they get between people's faces.' Ten, fifteen years from now, she'll have little creases like the spokes of a wheel emanating away from the hubs of her eyes.

We're heading into the mountains. The temperature's dropping. The bucket seats in my Volkswagen are separated by the gearshift and the hand brake. My heater's been broken since '66, and Leslie Ann leans across the open space between us and grips my arm, puts one hand in the armpit of my down jacket, slips the other into the side pocket, presses her cheek to my shoulder.

'How you doin'?' I ask congenially.

'Great,' she says into the horizon.

'How 'bout a medley of the best of Screamin' Jay Hawkins?'

'Never heard of him.'

'Never heard of Screamin' Jay? Who'd you listen to in the early Fifties?'

'Frank and Ella.'

'Frank and Ella? Why?'

She goes away. 'That's who was on their phonograph.' She comes back, remembers me beside her. 'Sing me,' she says.

I put my arm around her.

She makes herself smaller, cuddles tight.

And I sing her.

12

The plan is to fish for our dinner. She purchases the licenses and selects the rental poles and lures, and because she assumes a Jewish kid from Miami Beach couldn't possibly know anything about fishing, she educates me ('The great challenge in fishing is to catch the biggest fish with the thinnest line').

I don't even consider spoiling her enjoyment by telling her the truth – that I was practically born to the rod and reel.

Ensconced behind a clump of bushes along the bank of a rushing stream, out of sight of the fish, facing the sun so that we don't cast our shadows on the water, I whisper, 'Who taught you to fish?'

'My father.'

'That's nice.'

'For a while,' she says – the statement without prejudice, unadorned.

'What happened?'

'Sshh, let's not spook the fish. There's the primary current – see there?' She points, imitates the movement of the water. 'You want to try to land your line upstream there, at the edge of the secondary current, right behind that brush pile. Go ahead, give it a try.'

'You show me.'

Barely moving her upper body, she sends the tiny lure with a flick of her wrist through the sunlight, landing it with feather lightness beside the brush pile, takes up the slack as the fly glides unbitten downstream.

I visualize us decades from now, old and gnarled, at the confluence of a primary and secondary current somewhere, casting flies upstream.

'Now you,' she says.

I land my lure an inch or so from where she landed hers.

'Uh-oh,' she says. 'No fair – you've done this before.'

'Sheer, inexplicable beginner's luck,' I say, and kiss her shining, makeupless face.

We each catch two rainbow trout, and she insists on gutting and cleaning them herself with a serrated knife her father gave her when she was six.

We grill the trout on sticks over an open fire, basting them with mustard butter.

Afterward we walk the woods until the sun is gone.

And then, feeling as happy as I've ever felt in my life, we climb into the two sleeping bags she's zipped together into one downy labiate envelope, and we make love so sweet I want to cry.

13

In the morning I awaken to find her dressed and whipping up Denver omelets on the open hearth.

My back aches from the night on the ground, I have to pee but am too cold to leave the bag, and the odor of food combined with the odor of *me* wafting up out of the sleeping bag into my face is repulsive.

'Isn't this unbelievable?' Leslie Ann asks. She includes into the ebullience of her embrace everything within sight, sound, and smell.

'Great!' I agree. 'Just great.'

And it is.

For anyone who appreciates rusticity, disdains the superfluous comforts of modern life like toilets, showers, mattresses, and central heating.

In short, this is ideal for people unlike me, who for all my life has despised camping and remembers that now.

My parents sent my sister, Susan, and me to camp for a couple of years before the whole family became slaves to the junior golf circuit. I hated it: the outdoors, the metal army cots we slept on, the dearth of hot water . . . To my father, who really couldn't afford the tuition – this doctor who wouldn't be called doctor, who could make four, five, ten times what he made selling shoes if he were willing to doctor again – camp made his children as good as the children of wealthier Miami Beach parents.

'My father's a doctor, too,' I hurl at a rich little

Birmingham kike named Norman Erlichman when I'm seven and in my first year of camp.

'Is not!' says Erlichman.

'Is too!'

'Not!'

'Too!'

'*Not!*'

And at this historic crossroad, where the language can be reduced no further, I discover a new and wondrous emotion: terror of being hit, hurt, maimed. Physical disgrace. For Norman Erlichman appends himself to me like a centipede, and both my counselors fail to arrive to rescue me until he has made me say ten times that my father *isn't* a doctor.

Freed finally by adult intervention, I yowl that my father is going to sue his father for everything he's worth!

Outraged anew, Erlichman leaps onto the upper bunk in which I erroneously assume I have achieved safety, and, his fingers around my throat, he informs me through frothing lips, 'If you sue him, I'll kill you! I'll come to wherever you are and I'll choke your eyeballs out and mash 'em with my tennies!'

So, okay, I tell Erlichman, so there won't be any suit – fine!

Soon thereafter, Norman Erlichman is elected captain of the junior bunk blue color war team. By acclamation.

I am the last person chosen.

By the red team.

Rusty the Pusillanimous Weakling Landau.

'What's the matter?' Leslie Ann Masterson asks, slipping my omelet onto a paper plate.

'The matter? You jest.'

I leap out of the sleeping bag, fill my lungs with mountain air, and head for the omelets.

'You really know what you're doing out here, don't you, lady?'

'Should,' she says. She puts my plate on the wooden picnic table beside a cup of steaming coffee and sends this personal missive my way: 'My father left my brother and me right here overnight, at this campsite, when Evan was five and I was seven.'

'Alone?'

'Oh, yeah.'

'Were you terrified?'

'If you scream for about three hours, is that terror?'

'Why'd he do that?'

'Passage, he said. To succeed at each passage was to build up strength for what lay ahead.'

'Which was?'

'The essence of life on earth, Jakey, according to my daddy: the shitstorm.'

14

We spend the day at the road races at Leguna Seca.

We sit on the infield grass inside the serpentine track, and the cars fly round and round. Leslie Ann explains to me the mysteries of these wondrous, ear-damaging machines, the secrets of their drivers' strategies and way of life. She was in a play once about a race car driver, she explains.

Her research, clearly, was exhaustive.

But the noise is so extraordinary that she gives up, and we watch the race, her hand in the back pocket of my jeans, palm warming my tush, my hand on the flesh of her hip, and I pray silently for the salvation of my eardrums.

Hours later – days, maybe – the banshee cars stop, and we have our picnic lunch on the infield grass in blessed quiet.

And she says she lied about why she knows so much about auto racing.

I used to love the way the three contestants on 'To Tell the Truth' would look at each other while we waited in our living rooms with baited breath, certain we had separated truth from lie, and then one would fake a rise, then another, and finally the real person would stand and Bennett or Arlene or Dorothy would moan or roll his or her eyes because he or she had been duped. Effectively had.

Deceived.

I used to think it would be great to be on 'To Tell the Truth' but not be the real person. To be able to pretend to be someone else, see how well I could presume someone else's life.

'My father,' she says, 'was involved in auto racing. He died at Le Mans in fifty-eight.'

Heart attack, I would have figured. Korea, even. But Le Mans?

'I'm sorry,' I say. But some mean tensile lightning rod in me somewhere takes a jolt. Instinctively I am jealous of her (dead) father. 'What happened?' I ask.

'He was standing on the pit wall with my stepmother, and – according to her – he leaned over to kiss her and lost his balance. He was hit by one of the Ferraris coming in to take on fuel. He broke his neck, fractured his skull, and threw a massive embolism that killed him before they could get him to the hospital.'

She stares past the silent racing cars being tended in the pits, toward a vanishing point past which, it seems, in moments like these we review the past.

'What was he doing at Le Mans standing on the pit wall in the first place?'

'He manufactured shock absorbers and he owned Team Cherokee. Ever hear of it?'

Anybody who read the sports pages – whether an auto racing fan or not – could not help but know at least the basic facts about Team Cherokee. 'It was owned by a Cherokee Indian, I thought.'

'My father.'

Her father was an auto-racing Cherokee who died at Le Mans?

'So you're a Cherokee Indian?'

'Half. My mother's parents were Swedish.'

Where to next?

'How old were you when he died?'

'Ten.'

'But your father was standing on the pit wall with your stepmother, you said.'

'Mm.'

'So your father had obviously remarried.'

'He married this charming German woman. Supposedly she was one of the "good" Germans who chose to leave Germany. Personally, I think she was Eichmann or Mengele or one of those guys and had a sex change operation.'

I'm not sure if that's supposed to be funny or not.

She's not smiling.

I don't laugh.

'The cherished Magda taught history at San Francisco State then; she teaches at the University of Hawaii now.'

'Did your parents divorce?'

The question lingers in the air after the words fade into silence.

'No. My mother died when I was eight. She . . .'

And now her response hangs, incomplete, and the sob that rises up out of her fills the acreage around us.

Door closing.

No – slamming, sending shock waves through the air.

I reach to take her in my arms, but she recoils.

'No,' she says, 'please, I'm all right, let's just don't talk about any of them and I'll be just fine, okay?'

Okay?

No! I have a thousand questions.

Her mother died when she was eight, her father when

she was ten, she grew up in a house without a natural parent . . . ?

She grips my hand, mashes it to her mouth, using it to restrain further sound.

15

In my apartment, in the middle of the night, I reach for her and find her missing. I open my eyes and see her silhouette against the window, watching the sparse, three A.M. traffic on the freeway beyond.

She feels me beside her but doesn't look at me.

'I'm sorry,' she says.

'About what?'

'Lying to you. What do you want to know?'

'Whatever you want to tell me.'

'My father,' she says, 'was the son of a medicine man. He was an artist, a sculptor. He was also' – she scans a list of words in her head, chooses two carefully – 'a passionate and a reckless man. He was the token Indian here at Stanford in the Forties. He played football and drove stock cars on the weekend. He met my mother. She was the daughter of a scientist at Los Alamos, one of the atomic bomb scientists. After the war, my father and my grandfather, the artist and the scientist, the Indian and the super Wasp, went into the race car business by way of a revolutionary shock absorber. My father and my mother loved each other . . .'

She takes a deep breath. She is trying not to replicate that sob of this afternoon.

'. . . very much,' she says. 'My mother was perfect. Perfect mother, perfect wife, perfect human being. My brother, Evan, and I grew up in a house filled by her warmth, where she touched us and encouraged us to

draw and act and carve things out of wood and . . .'
Leslie Ann shrugs. She blows air through pursed lips.
Tries to maintain control.

I know not to touch her, that to do so would stop her
because she would then be able to focus on repelling my
sympathy.

'And then my mother died.'

'How?'

Her teeth clamp on her lip, and in her eyes I see a
pain so dense I cannot name it.

Her soft breath rushes past my cheeks with these
words: 'She killed herself.'

And now it's my breath that, unbidden, rushes from
my chest. 'Why?'

She dissolves in furious, racking, spastic sobs against
my chest.

'I don't knoooooooooooooow!' she cries. 'I don't
knoooooooooooow!'

16

Without calling it this, we are pretending to be married.

Leslie Ann plans meals for the week and makes a list in her meticulous script so that we have only to shop once (except for an every-other-day pickup of a half gallon of skim milk and the occasional trip for fresh tuna for sushi).

I don't know what it is exactly that is so satisfying about pushing a cart in the grocery store or carrying the little arm basket through the farmers' market with her.

About returning to my apartment and putting things away in the cupboards and refrigerator according to the order she has imposed on my kitchen.

Mincing and dicing and chopping together. Parboiling and grilling and baking.

Eating and sleeping.

Soon she is spending each night in my apartment, in my bed. In the mornings, she smoothes the linen, folds the blanket and makes the bed into a couch once again – in a sense disappearing the conjugal part of our relationship, this after she makes my breakfast and sends me off to teach my Freshman Comp or Intro to Lit class. Then she tidies up everything that can tolerate tidying before going off to her room in the graduate dorm to replenish her supplies and on to the theater.

She begins to bring clothes for several days at a stretch; begins to seriously take the Ajax to the tub and sinks and bathroom floor; she does the laundry as fast as we dirty a load, supplying the quarters and commentaries on the eccentricities of the various washers and dryers; and when I so much as became even mildly tumescent, she has me in her hand or in her mouth or encased deep within her body.

At last she is never absent.

Though, at first, she seems tentative, as if it's only her body which lives here; not unhappy, but distrustful almost of her ease, our ease together, in this place. I reassure her that this is good – us – in this place. Relax, I tell her, you're safe.

And I see her try and begin to succeed.

The apartment comes alive with an afghan her mother made when she was born, with her theater posters and books and cookbooks and blender. The half-empty medicine chest is filled by her cosmetics and perfumes, her deodorant and Q-tips and cotton balls and astringents, her diaphragm in its neat, pink case (birth control pills make her sick). The drawers and closets give up space to her clothes and to her strange shoes (two pair of each to accommodate one size seven foot, one size eight. 'Why not throw out the pair you can't wear?' 'I keep thinking I'll meet someone with the same problem, but on the opposite feet.'). My rock 'n roll and classical records blend together with her Sinatra and Ella and Big Band albums in an alphabetical row on the floor without benefit of labels – mine, yours. The air and chairs and walls and towels become infused with our commingled smells.

The place becomes ours.

We become Jacobandleslieann.

17

I have never lived with a woman. As a kid, past the age at which I start playing golf, I never have friends sleep over. Past that age, I never sleep over at my friends' houses.

Being a loner becomes both a necessity and a form of protection that endures, however unfortunately, until Leslie Ann's arrival in my life.

Why the following syllogism is true I don't know, but I postulate it as the truth nevertheless: a) My father ran from the Nazis; b) I did not; therefore, c) I become a golfer and a loner and have no friends.

Even Aristotle, I suspect, would be puzzled.

I remember a discussion with my father when I was a freshman at the University of Florida, in the first consumptive throes of intellectual awakening. I came home for Thanksgiving, armed with the Holocaust as viewed by my non-Jewish World History professor. I spun a long, looping sociopolitical web of intellectual cause and effect around my father going back to Abraham.

To which my father responded, 'Why make what is simple so complicated? The human being is a hopelessly flawed organism. It acts without thinking, or thinks it should do one thing and does another. It hates and it fears, and usually it hates out of fear. As for Abraham, he was an idiot and the second Nazi – willing to sacrifice his son at the whim of Nazi number one, his hedonistic, arbitrary, lunatic of a God, who deep down he probably hated because the great Yahweh scared the pants off of him.'

My mother was scandalized. At least through my sister's bat mitzvah and my bar mitzvah, there had been the pretense of appropriate religious faith in the house, though both my sister, Susan, and I long suspected, for my father, at any rate, this was a charade so that his children wouldn't grow up to be God-less heathens. For my mother, religion was an insurance policy. What was the point of not believing?

'Morris,' said my mother, 'what a way to talk. Now, tonight when I should be sleeping, I'll have to pray for your forgiveness. What's the matter – do you have indigestion or what? Say you're sorry.'

To which order my father responded by unleashing a belch of Talmudic proportions.

As a little boy, I love team sports. Instinctively I think I respond to their familial nature, the interdependence, the right one has, in a sense, not to stand out individually but to be less than the sum of one's parts on a team.

In the fifth and sixth grades, I am pretty good at basketball. I am also at the age when my abject fear of being beaten up (in place since that day at camp I got stomped) is in full flower because the bully of the Hebrew school van, Allan Adelman, is tormenting me because I am available for it.

The first few times I arrive home with tales of terror en route to my religious training, my father is largely silent, allowing my mother's motherly pacifist advice to hold sway.

Then, the last week of school, I come quaking into the house following Hebrew School. My mother sings to the Victrola when she prepares dinner; she selects a singer, she says, to suit the meal. She is listening when I return this evening to my forty-five of Frankie Laine singing 'Mule Train.' Whatever she is coalescing in her big stew pot is being whisked with such brio that it seems unfair to disrupt her with the latest installment of my Allan Adelman saga at this time.

Available is my father.

Now, my father is a massive man, not quite as tall as I, but heavier by fifty pounds even today. At five ten and two thirty, he looks like a bear — because of his shape, yes, but also because he is covered with fur from head to toe, front and back, and because he wears on his face a nose broken 'many times,' which spreads from its flattened bridge to its flattened base like a trapezoid. ('How'd it get broken so many times, Poppa?' 'How? How do noses get broken?')

As a boy I remember him towering over me and my delicate wisp of a mother with her fine Semitic features. This particular day he hunkers massively at the sink in the half bath downstairs, washing and washing his hands, as if he were still the Warsaw surgeon, but in fact trying to eradicate from the whorls and gullies of his fingers the smell of human feet.

I slip into the shadow of his protective mass — 'Allan Adelman pulled my pants down in front of Candi Garfunkel and Deanna Kugel!' — and then I drop dramatically to the floor and there writhe in fury and humiliation, hoping that my histrionics will impel my father to wrathful retribution in my behalf.

But what my father does is straddle me — I think I'm looking up at some mythical forest monster, this gigantic, hairy, mash-nosed thing — and he goes crazy, or as crazy as I ever see my father go, before or since.

'Jews!' my father screams. 'Jews Jews Jews!'

In the kitchen my mother stops singing 'Mule Train,'

though Frankie Laine continues on the Victrola in the living room.

'Listen to me, you, Mister Jew!'

Listen to him? I'm certain, as is my mother ('Sshh, Morris, the neighbors!'), that everyone on the South Beach is listening to him, from Biscayne Bay to the Atlantic, from First Street to Lincoln Road.

The decibel level, however, is on the ascendant.

'Jews have no guts!' screams my father. 'Jews are inherently frightened, sniveling, groveling cowards! Faygelehs! Gutless meshugges! Who leaves nations at the whims of idiots? Who dies by ones and tens and thousands and millions? Individuals and families and communities and nations? Who? Jews!'

My mother has raised the volume on Frankie Laine and begun closing windows. Another forty-five has dropped on the turntable. Frankie is now warbling the plaintive and ecclesiastical 'I Believe.' It occurs to me that, by rights, my mother ought to be at her pot, stirring ardently, piously, whatever it is she is preparing for the sustenance and enjoyment of the three nudnicks who live with her in this house.

My sister has crept down from her room – where she does nameless sequestered things in the afternoon – to hear this never-before-heard voice in person.

'You!' He's talking to me. I can tell because from above he has grabbed me by the shirtfront and lifted me up with one hand so that I am practically nose to nose with him. 'You must become a golem.'

I am scared shitless and witless by this behemoth. 'A what, Poppa?'

'Never mind.' (The golem, I will learn later, is an apocryphal hairy, person-eating monster who, if I were going to describe him, looked exactly like my angry father looked that day.) 'You must become a monster as monstrous as those who would humiliate you! Who would torture and torment and slaughter you!'

'But he's Jewish, Poppa – Allan. Allan Adelman is a –'

My father shakes me violently, snapping my neck, sending a signal through my entire neural network, igniting my entire body in the sensation of electrocution. 'Oh, sure, a Jew who beats up other Jews – that's easy. Who can't do that?' He jolts me again to insure there's no mistake whom he's addressing now. 'You! You must learn to defeat the Adelmans of the world or you will be helpless in the world outside this shitty crappy stinking shitty little town!'

I had never in my twelve years heard my father utter a profanity before, unless in Yiddish, thereby making it unavailable to me for literal translation.

Frankie Laine sings 'I Believe' into the neighborhood, bespeaking musically his faith in the basic decency of mankind and the rightness of the world.

'All right, you, you're taking boxing lessons this summer.'

'Boxing lessons?'

'What did I just say?'

'Boxing lessons, you said I'm taking –'

'Good, you have good ears, your hearing is good. That's important; at least you can hear your enemies coming. Now, you must learn what to do *after* you've heard them.'

For all his enormous size and for all I assume he suffered at the hands of his gentile Polish brethren, my father has never struck me as a man who considers striking another human being as an acceptable form of human behavior, let alone becoming a monster.

'Where am I going to take these boxing – '

'Where? Where they teach the coloreds and the Cubans and the nudnicks from Hialeah who steal people's cars and rob grocery stores!'

'Where's that?'

'If I knew, we would be there in two minutes,' said my father. 'But, believe me, I'm going to find out.'

My father realizes now that he has gone somewhere I have never seen him go, and he releases me, smooths my shirt, looks at my mother. '*Gevalt*,' he says, 'I'm hungry enough to eat the *tuchus* out of a golem.'

Vastly relieved to have my father back to 'normal,' my mother and my sister laugh uproariously at that one.

I don't.

Because I am lost in deep thought. What I'm thinking is this: *Boxing? With coloreds and Cubans and nudnicks who steal people's cars and rob grocery stores!*

I'll get killed!

And so, my father discovers that not ten blocks south of his shoe store on Washington Avenue stands the Fifth Street Gym. Where boxers are trained.

And to where I am excused three times a week that entire summer from my duties as stock boy in the store so that I may learn the art of self-defense.

To my practically orgasmic delight, I find myself at first surviving against the sixteen coloreds and Cubans and hoods from Hialeah, then excelling against all but the three fastest and strongest (one of whom is almost certainly psychotic).

The fourth toughest kid in his boxing class – Jakey Landau!

When the summer ends, I tell my father I want to train for the Golden Gloves and be the next great Jewish boxer. The Barney Ross of the Sixties.

'Never mind Barney Ross,' says my father. 'For you, the boxing is finished. You use it only to smash in the face anyone who threatens you because you're a whimpering Jew. Before it is over entirely, though,' he says, and his huge, hairy paws grip my shoulders, seeming to consume them in his fists, 'you must punch in the mouth Allan Adelman with all your might exactly one time.'

Without so much as a thought, I demur. A boxing ring is one thing – gloves, headgear, rules, adults ready to rush into the fray should it get out of hand. 'Punch him?'

'Yes,' says my father.

My head whips back and forth: oh no . . . oh no . . . oh no . . .

My father's head goes up and down to the same rhythm mine goes side to side: oh yes . . . oh yes . . . oh yes . . .

'I *can't*, Poppy.'

And then an amazing thing happens. My father's eyes become glassy, I think he is about to cry, and he says, 'For me, you will do this – you must.'

There is only one word to accurately describe the sound of that plea: desperation. My father is desperate for me to comply with this mandate.

So it is the first day of Hebrew School and we are on the way to Temple Beth Sholem in the van from Biscayne Elementary. Allan Adelman, assuming that life for a bully will go on always as it has before, slips onto the seat beside me and resumes his ritual debasement of Rusty, the redheaded, pusillanimous pansy pussy fruitcake. My heart flaps its gigantic wings furiously within my chest, sending gale-force winds into my thorax, to my jaw, to my cheeks and temples and eyeballs.

I have planned to say something cool to Allan
Adelman, something out of a cowboy movie, something
like 'I wouldn't do that if I were you, Al'; but I cannot
imagine that sound is available from my throat, what
with the beating of those wings, and so without so much
as a sportsmanlike warning, I drive up out of my seat
and ventilate Allan Adelman's cruel mouth with a left
hook that would have been the envy of anyone in the
Fifth Street Gym, including Marvell Sanderson, Flavio
Querido, and Doakie Polisandrioti, the big three.

Allan's father calls my father that night to threaten a
lawsuit. My father dumps on Mr Adelman one of the
memorable sentences of my childhood: 'I would cherish
the opportunity,' says Morris Landau, 'to engage you
face to face before the American judicial system as
witness to my son's rightful vengeance.'

That is the last physical harassment I endure from
Allan Adelman or anyone else for a long time. I realize,
however indistinctly, that when you pretend you're
tough, others – who might actually be stronger physically – more often than not give you a wide berth.

My new image of myself affects most immediately my
name and my basketball playing.

About my name: I order people to stop calling me
Rusty. Rusty is the wimpiest, it seems to me, of all the
names that could be associated with being redheaded.
Call me JD, I suggest, combining the first initials of
my first and middle names in homage to a phrase much
in vogue at the time that seems, if not specifically, at
least generally, to befit my new toughness – juvenile
delinquent.

About playing basketball: Now that I'm tough, I find
I like setting picks and ripping the ball off the boards
with flying elbows and setting other people up. I like

the roles of enforcer and playmaker. Like my teammates thanking me for making them look good. Like making things possible.

And then toward the end of the sixth grade, we move into my mother's dream house, a nice little three-bedroom home on Normandy Shores, right on Fairway Drive, literally across the street from the tenth fairway of the Normandy Shores golf course.

Throughout my early years, I have the sense of my father as someone who is trying to stop being a survivor of the pogroms, trying to stop being the remaining relative of a family that otherwise perishes in the concentration camps. I sense him trying to be what he calls a 'regular Jew.' Part of that regularness, when I am twelve and we move to Fairway Drive, is my father's taking up of golf, to his mind the perfect Regular Jew sport.

Another part of my father's efforts to be just a Regular Jew is to do things he associates with being just a Regular Dad.

And so, in the summer between the sixth and seventh grades, when there is no basketball and the Little League baseball season has ended, he invites me to take a series of six golf lessons with him.

(I am an aspiring catcher in baseball – 'My son,' my father enjoys saying, 'has an arm like a launcher of a hand grenade!' Thus my confidence that I could dent Howard Bellman's head nicely with a rock.)

'Six lessons of golf,' my father informs me, 'that are costing me plenty, so don't do me any favors, boychik, if it's not something you want to do.'

I know that I should, even that I must, do with the former Dr Motke Londovnik whatever he invites me to do with him, so in August of that year, 1958, I walk across Fairway Drive with my father holding my hand (something he does with my good wishes until I enter high school because it seems important to him).

We walk to the driving range just east of the ninth tee, where, by the end of that first lesson, we learn two things: 1) that my father's belly and chest are so capacious that his range of motion precludes anything remotely resembling a normal golf swing; 2) that I have hidden in me, waiting like some dormant beast to consume all of us, a gift: I can swing this wooden stick with a hard bulb on one end at a rubber ball and make it go straight and far. And what's more, I can hit it short distances into a small, a very small, hole, with such unnerving accuracy that the pro at the Normandy Shores golf course begins by the end of our six-lesson cycle to imagine for himself the vicarious fame that comes with fostering the career of an immortal.

We're on the way home after lesson six. My hand with its sparse auburn hairs is swallowed in my father's hairy black bear's paw. 'So?' he says.

'I don't like it that much, Poppy.'

I tell him this after the pro offers to take me on for free, on one condition: I will dedicate myself totally to the sport, forsaking all else.

'Don't like it?' my father asks. 'What's not to like about a blessing?'

'I don't know,' I say. 'I feel . . . lonesome, kind of.'

'Lonesome! Is this a *vitz* – are you kidding me? Who's going to be with you every lesson, every hole, all the way?'

My father wants very badly for me to be something he views as not-having-anything-to-do-with-being-the-child-of-a-Jew-Hitler-hated.

But, oh God, I don't want to forsake all else. I want

to play basketball with my teammates at Nautilus
Junior High and at Beach High and go on to Duke
or North Carolina and then into the pros and win *team*
championships! I want to lift weights and go about
six six, two forty, and be a rebounder and enforcer in
the NBA. Me and Russ, the Dipper, Luke Jackson –
enforcers all. And I want to kiss girls and eventually
put things into the various openings of their bodies!

Ah, but in golf there seems to be something for my
father. Maybe he relishes the right to come out of those
distant basketball and baseball bleachers and walk
beside me for the rest of his life across lush green grass.
Or maybe he's trying to warn me that I must never, ever
make the mistake of trusting a group of people around
me, that I must never, ever count on anyone but myself.

I didn't know. I'm not sure still.

Because to this day my father has never let me know
who he is really inside that massive body.

I know little more than that he and his doctor-father,
Mordechai, tire of the Jew hating in Warsaw and are
living in 1938 in Lyons, the father an internist, the son
a surgeon. Sensing what is about to happen in Europe,
my grandfather arranges for my father to emigrate to
the United States. A year later Mordechai is to follow
– both have been accepted onto the staff of Brooklyn
Presbyterian Hospital – but just before Hitler invades
Poland, Mordechai returns to Warsaw to doctor the sick
and the persecuted and the dying. Following the Warsaw
ghetto uprising my father's father is sent to Auschwitz
and never heard from again.

And Motke Londovnik, my father, never practices
medicine again.

And so, fourteen years ago, I take up golf and forsake
all else.

Even though I am positive – despite the fact that the pro, a Cuban Jew named Pablo Brilliante, promises to teach me golf for free and give me my clubs and balls and shoes for free – that I will never see my father because he will have to sell millions of pairs of shoes in order that I can go to junior tournaments all over the country.

But I'm wrong.

My father leaves the store at three every afternoon and picks me up at Nautilus Junior High, drives me home, and, hand in hand, walks with me across Fairway Drive to the driving range and my lesson with Pablo Brilliante.

Or to the first tee, when I begin playing rounds with Pablo Brilliante.

And finally, to Tallahassee and Charlotte, to Columbus and Trenton and Colorado Springs, to Atlanta and South Bend and San Diego and Las Vegas and Dearborn.

Where we are often the only Jews in clubs usually restricted only to non-Jews with white skin and Protestant backgrounds traceable to the *Mayflower*.

And where I come in twenty-fourth and then fifteenth, ninth, and then first, first, first, first, first, first, first.

And then, at age fifteen, to Seattle, where I lead the United States Junior Championship by four strokes with three holes to go.

And where I lose.

And then to Palm Beach, where I walk off the course after I three putt from under ten feet for the third time in the tournament.

And at last, and finally, to Bethesda, where they carry me off, suffering what the tournament doctor says is not a heart attack, but something with the same symptoms, something he gives the lofty name 'protracted anxiety' – a fist in the chest that he tells my father accusingly is a manifestation of tension 'deeply alarming in a boy so young.'

My father, this giant of flesh and sinew, weeps.

My golfing days are over.

And that is as close as Motke Londovnik gets to being a Regular Jew or me to having a teammate again.

Until now.

18

My mate awaits me on the patio of the Student Union with the young woman on crutches.

When I sit down, I feel I'm interrupting something they don't finish because they don't want me to hear its conclusion.

'This is Darlene Delvecchio,' she says. 'This is my Jake.'

'Of course,' says Darlene, 'I've heard you shpeak. Haven't sheen you at any of the meetings for a while.'

I pretend there's nothing abnormal here.

'No,' I say, 'I haven't been attending.'

'No,' she says, 'I notished.'

'I lost interest,' I tell her, trying not to stare oddly at her pretty, cherubic face perched atop a body obviously in revolt.

She prods her bush of corn yellow hair away from dense chocolate eyes, almost as if she were saying to me, 'You want to stare oddly at me, let me give you the entire face.' 'I know what you mean,' she says, 'or I think I do – I mean, I shouldn't shay that, because I don't know you, but I think I would, too – lose interest – it's gotten sho shelf-indulgent – but I don't have anything elsh to commit myshelf to, sho I shtick with it.'

'I've been telling Darlene that she should get into advocacy for the handicapped.'

Leslie Ann looks at me. Her look says, 'Now it's your

line, darling.' When I don't pick up my cue, she feeds me another.

'Don't you think, Jacob, the way people are rebelling against the federal government and against privileged classes, that's going to be a whole big field in the very near future – advocacy? What's your opinion?'

I feel like I'm on Jerry Lewis's telethon or I've just been introduced at a minority political rally.

I've never heard Leslie Ann sound disingenuous before.

Both women seem anxiously to await my response.

In a tone inordinately patronizing, I say, 'I agree, yes indeed. In fact, you know, Darlene, Les and I were sitting around the ashram just the other night and I was saying – or was she saying? – one of us was saying – Who said this, darling? That what with the current inclination toward decentralizing federal government authority and the general antagonism toward elitism abuilding in the land, advocacy for minorities of all colors and hues, and for handicaps of every stripe – not to mix my metaphors – is going to become the vogue and make the first and loudest *kvetchers* famous, if not rich. Who said that, dear? Did you or did I?'

They are both looking at me like I'm nuts.

'Or did I read it?' I ask. 'Maybe I read it. Or did I just make it up?'

In Leslie Ann's eyes, I see hurt.

'I'm kidding,' I say quickly. 'It just sounded like you were giving me an intro to a commercial, so I sort of responded like I was an actor doing . . .'

I'm sure I have offended Darlene to her handicapped core, and I am about to launch into a more fulsome apology when she smiles.

And then laughs, the laugh coming out in a little burst,

then breaking off, then continuing in another burst, as if it were on tape and a piece were spliced out, leader tape put in, then the laugh resumed.

'Very funny,' she says, meaning it. 'People treat me like a shoufflé. Thank you for treating me like I'm normal.'

She tosses her hair in a way that is very sensual, her dark eyes flicker against my face; the combination, though perhaps not intentional, seems flirtatious, feminine, normal; and I wonder if this sensuality, this flirtatiousness, is really current or a throwback to a time prior to this affliction.

'Darlene just started her MA in the grad Journalism School,' Leslie Ann says. 'She wants to be a theater and film critic.'

'I was going to be an actress,' Darlene says, 'but this friend of mine always got the roles I wanted.'

Leslie Ann pats Darlene's hand. Darlene's hand leaps out and imprisons Leslie Ann's – and some unspoken reverence leaks from Darlene's eyes, a reverence that Leslie Ann doesn't want. She pats Darlene's hand now with her other hand and frees the first. 'Tell Jacob,' says Leslie Ann, 'what you were telling me about what's going on in France in the theater right now.'

But Darlene Delvecchio doesn't speak. She only stares at Leslie Ann. I wait, anticipating that she's gearing up to respond to this latest of Leslie Ann's conversational intros, but then I sense she hasn't even heard Leslie Ann's cue line to her.

'Darlene?' Leslie Ann says, cueing her again.

'Oh, pardon me.' She shakes her head, banishing the images she was seeing wherever she'd gone. 'I'm shorry, Maggie, what were you shaying?'

Maggie? We're in big trouble here.

'I said I thought Jacob would be very interested in

what you were saying about postabsurdist theater in France right now.'

'Oh!' says Darlene, turning back to me with hope writ large on her face. 'Would you, Jacob, be intereshted?'

'Theater in France? Not really. Any other choices?'

Leslie Ann's mouth drops slightly open – front teeth, semismile. She is not pleased by my lack of coopera- tion.

'Sure,' Darlene says, 'anything – you pick.'

'As I'm pretty uncomfortable here,' I tell Darlene, 'I'd like to hear what you're doing on crutches, what you've got, how long you're going to live – all that. Then we can move on to theater in France if you really want to.'

Darlene whispers to Leslie Ann, but obviously for my ears, 'Is he always sho awfully glib?'

With mock disapproval, Leslie Ann nods.

All three of us are being extremely cute.

Darlene has multiple sclerosis, she tells me, has had it for five years, without reason or explanation. Her body is a mess, but her brain – except for the slurring of speech – and her eyes – so far – are fine.

Her hands, she shows me, are fine until she tries to pick up a pen and write or a fork and feed her- self.

She picks up her fork; it's steady as a rock. She loads it with chef's salad; still a pillar of dependability. But as she guides it toward her mouth, some perverse jokester takes the helm of her arm, her elbow twitches, her wrist goes spastic, and the salad flies, landing on me, Leslie Ann, and the guy at the next table, who swings around angrily, sees what he's dealing with, and politely offers the salad back.

'Thash all right,' Darlene tells him, 'keep it, I have more.'

He nods his instantaneous, total forgiveness and retains a treasured bit of salad.

Darlene looks at me. I'm in danger of manifesting my current feelings in laughter.

'How humiliating,' she says, but she's with me – about to burst into laughter.

Unable to contain ourselves, we try to cut loose and at the same time restrain ourselves; consequently we both spew spittle in the other's direction.

Then we're both in rollicking hysterics. Darlene's laugh is so powerful that her disease can't interrupt it this time – a cackle like machine-gun fire.

The guy at the next table looks at us.

'They're not laughing at you,' Leslie Ann assures him.

'Yesh, we are!' howls Darlene Delvecchio.

Uncertain what to make of this, the guy smiles and has the grace to return to his lunch and his open notebook.

'Want to eat?' Leslie Ann asks.

'Schtarving,' says Darlene.

Leslie Ann takes the fork and begins to feed Darlene.

I lean toward Darlene. 'So, you were saying.'

She leans toward me, bracing herself on her elbows. Chews. Talks.

Her shoulders, from five years on crutches, are somewhat overdeveloped, squarish, a table set for the presentation of her lovely head.

'I could,' she says, 'live a normal number of years or I could go into rapid decline anytime. I could even go into remission and it could all dishappear.' She shrugs. 'That's about it.'

'Can I catch it?' I ask.

'Not from me,' she says.

'Good deal,' I say. 'Let's be friends.'

She really has a very wonderful smile, a wonderful strength, and I like her in spite of the fact that I'm supposed to.

At ten to one we head for class, starting away from the patio across White Memorial Plaza.

'Don't wait for me,' Darlene says. 'It makes me crazy when people try to walk with me.'

Leslie Ann says she'll see Darlene tomorrow, and then she walks me toward my office, sliding her hand into my back pocket, her palm to my buttock through the denim.

I don't know where to start.

I encircle Leslie Ann's shoulders and kiss her temple. I can feel her heart beat against my lips.

I jump in here: 'How come she called you Maggie?'

'Maggie was my nickname in high school, just someone some of my friends thought I used to be.'

'You and Darlene went to high school together.'

'Yep.'

'She wanted to be an actress, too, but you got all the roles.'

'Something like that.'

'"Something like that." How 'bout putting it in the proper perspective for me, then, so I have it straight.'

'She wanted . . .'

She looks at me, wonders whether to say the words that are attempting to come over her lips.

'She wanted to be me,' says Leslie Ann.

'In what way?'

'She thought she was too well adjusted to be a good actor. She used to tell me, "I need to carry your baggage so I have some." She wanted to go to undergraduate school with me and room together. Fortunately, her parents made her go to Wellesley. I hadn't seen her

until she walked into that party that night. I felt . . .
Oh, I don't know, Jacob – it's stupid!'

'No, please. Please, please, please.'

She shakes her head once, with finality.

'You felt like somehow you'd given her multiple
sclerosis because you'd been blessed with greater talent
and horrific luggage.'

She looks at me. Grudgingly she nods.

As if this next sentence logically follows the last, she
says to me without altering the cadence or tone of our
conversation, 'I think you should make love to her.' She
kisses me quickly – 'I'll see you at dinner, I love you' –
and she takes off at a trot toward the theater.

'Hold it!'

'Think about it!' she calls, and accelerates into her
dopey girl's run – her odd-size feet splayed out, her
knees extruded into other people's space, forcing them
to accommodate her.

19

In the costume shop Leslie Ann had lined a huge purse with plastic, and we went once a week to the Hunan restaurant on University Avenue for the all-you-can-eat kung pao squid night. When the waitress turned her back, we slipped all of Leslie Ann's serving into the purse, I scooped half of mine onto her plate, and by the time the waitress returned, we were calling ravenously for seconds. A couple of times around and we had a free Chinese dinner at home the next night.

Across our small dining table tonight, we eat leftover kung pao squid with chopsticks. There's a flickering candle between us.

We have this conversation:

'Why did you say that?'

'Say what?'

'You know what.'

'You were flirting with her.'

'I wasn't flirting with her.'

'Oh, Jacob, you were, too. But I'm not mad. She's still very pretty, she has that incredible vitality – why deny you find her attractive?'

'Why do I feel you're pinning this on me when something else is going on here?'

'What do you mean?'

'I don't know. Perhaps you can tell me.'

'I asked her.'

'Asked her what?'

'If she'd like to make love with you.'

'You *asked* her if she'd like to make love with me?'

'Yes.'

'Why?'

'It seemed like the right question at the time.'

'And when *was* this right time?'

'A couple of days ago.'

'A couple of *days* ago?'

'Are you going to repeat everything I say?'

'Let's find out. Under what conditions did you happen to ask her that particular question a couple of days ago?'

'I've started going to her room in the morning to help with her cares.'

' "Help with her cares"?'

'That's what they call what has to be done for her – "cares." '

'Since when?'

'Since when do they call them "cares"?'

'Since when have you been going there to perform them?'

'I don't like the way you said "perform," Jacob.'

'Since when have you been going there to do whatever you do?'

'Since about a week ago when she came to interview me for the *Daily*. I told you she came to interview me.'

'You told me you were interviewed, you didn't say by whom.'

'It was Darlene.'

'So I gather. What has to be done for her in the way of "cares"?'

'She has to be bathed and dressed – she can pick up the soap and pick out her clothes, but as soon as her brain thinks she wants to wash herself or get dressed, it starts throwing stuff around. You were at lunch.'

'Yes, I was. Flying salad – I remember.'

'And her bag has to be changed.'

'Bag?'

'She has erratic kidney function.'

'She pees without warning.'

'Right.'

'Who does her "cares" when you're not there?'

'She has a woman who lives with her. I'm going to spell her for an hour or so in the mornings.'

'Why didn't you tell me?'

'I didn't want you to think I was doing it for the wrong reasons.'

'What would the wrong reasons be?'

'That I was using her to make myself feel better. Or performing. Or that I just want to expropriate her life and pain for future use on the stage. *Is* that what you think?'

'No. I think you're doing it because you're a compassionate human being and can't stand to see people suffer.'

'Are you sure?'

'No.'

'Me neither. Because I know I'm taking notes.'

For the first time since we've known each other, I'm annoyed at her. Irritably I say, 'How could you not take notes? You're not only an actor, you're a human being!'

'Why are you yelling?'

Her eyes mist. She fights tears.

'I'm not yelling. Is that why you're crying – because I'm yelling?'

She shrugs.

'Or because you're questioning your motives?'

She shrugs.

'I'm sorry,' I say, 'I'm not mad, I don't mean to yell.'

I shove my kung pao squid around on my plate. She puts her feet between my ankles. I squeeze them reassuringly.

'Let's talk about something else,' she says.

'No. How exactly did the subject of my *schtupping* her come up?'

'I raised it.'

'Kind of an unsolicited offer? Wouldn't it be nice if someone porked you and I'm living with this guy, he's clean – that sort of thing.'

'She said she knew who you were, that you always worked so hard at being cool when you weren't really – '

'Nice that you both agree on that.'

' – but that there was something dopily appealing about you.'

' "Dopily appealing." Gee, that fills me with warmth. Let me at her!'

'She meant it as a compliment.'

'I feel great. What about fidelity and constancy, Leslie Ann?'

'I'm giving you permission.'

'Permission? You're pimping for me. Do you feel *that* responsible for her condition?'

I mean this question somewhat seriously, somewhat glibly. I am somewhat surprised to get a deadly serious answer to it.

'I used to pray some terrible disaster would befall her.'

'What do you mean?'

'When we first started competing for roles. I prayed that she would be in a car accident and defaced. And deformed. Sometimes killed. But usually just . . . just deformed. And I'd move into her house to take care of her. So I could live with her parents, who were . . . who were nice.'

She looks at me as if she earnestly expects me to serve up some terrible sentence for these terrible crimes.

'Leslie Ann, everybody prays that their competitors will have car accidents. In my case, at *least* car accidents.'

'But now . . .' She shrugs, her lips press hard against each other. 'She was so . . . Oh, I don't know why I want you to do it, Jacob. I just think it's important.'

'You want to watch?'

The lack of embroidery around the question startles her.

'See, you do think I'm doing it for the wrong reasons.'

'Watch or no watch?'

The candlelight flickers across her face, making the yellow stria in her eyes look like a dozen tiny bonfires, ebbing and flaring.

'If I say yes, you'll think less of me; if I say no, you'll call me a liar.'

'You're in a definite no-win situation. You want to watch?'

'Of course I want to watch, but that would be a bit much, don't you think?'

'And perhaps even somewhat disease related.'

She leans across the table, out of her chair, in my face. 'Stop making me feel like I have to analyze everything, Jacob — it's not fair!'

She slams herself back down on her chair.

'I'm not having sex with Darlene Delvecchio,' I tell her.

'But it interests you.'

'Good-looking cripple – how could it not?' I ask.

'It couldn't,' she says, cocking her glorious head at me. 'So can I watch?'

20

The profile on Leslie Ann in the *Stanford Daily* by Darlene Delvecchio is a flattering portrait of a portion of the person I live with and have seen onstage.

What triggers action are these two paragraphs: 'Leslie Ann Masterson was born and raised in Santa Fe, New Mexico, but attended Balboa High School in San Francisco where, at that time, her stepmother taught European History at San Francisco State.

'It was at Balboa High that she became a cherished enigma.'

Something tweaks me, something unsaid combined with what she'd said to me the day before when we had lunch with Darlene: 'Maggie was my nickname in high school, just someone some of my friends thought I used to be.'

She seemed to have no close friends now. Why would she then? And people without close friends had nicknames that were pejorative or rendered out of envy – Dumbo, Honkerface.

Tits.

From my office, I call Balboa High in San Francisco. I tell the secretary who answers that I'm trying to track down the cousin of a buddy of mine killed in Vietnam (I figure I need some heavy ammo to get any information). The secretary is properly sympathetic and asks me the student's name.

'Her name's Leslie Ann Masterson. She graduated in 1965.'

It's half a minute or so before the secretary comes back on the line; in the very instant prior to her transmitting the words down the peninsula to Palo Alto, I am confident what they'll be.

'I'm sorry, but we have no record of anyone by that name.'

'Oh, shoot,' I say contritely, dropping into a folksy drawl, 'I got the wrong cousin here. Wait a minute, lemme see here. Oh, yeah, here we go. How 'bout Maggie Masterson? Margaret.'

I wait.

'No, I'm afraid not. The only Margaret I remember in that class was Margaret Jewel Carmine.'

'Oh, man, I'm really confused. Here it is – other side of the family – here it is, it's here. Margaret Jewel. Where's she now – Margaret Jewel – you got any idea?'

'Oh, yes. Margaret Jewel's in graduate school at Stanford University. In Palo Alto, California. Now I'm sorry, sir, but I'm afraid I've helped you as much as I can.'

'Yes, you have, and I wanna thank yawl a whole heckuva lot.'

The rest of the morning, until I meet Leslie Ann for lunch, I wrestle with whether to call her on this or let it go.

Aren't I a big fan of Sartre?

Oh, yes.

So doesn't a person have the right at any time to change her life?

You bet.

'Who was Carmine?' I ask her as I slide my lunch tray onto the table.

She looks at me a moment, a forked grapefruit section frozen between her plate and her mouth.

'My stepfather,' she says.

'Not the Cherokee Indian fishing sculptor shock absorber king who may or may not have been shoved by your Nazi stepmother in front of a Ferrari at Le Mans?'

'Who have you been talking to – Darlene?'

'No. I called your high school.'

'No, you didn't.'

'Yes, I did.'

'No.'

'Uh-huh.'

'Uh-uh.'

'Yep.'

'Oh, Jacob, why?'

'To get some clarification on who you are.'

'You think *they* know who I am – at my high school?'

'I was just trying to start with your real name.'

'My real name, Jacob, is the name you know me by. And if it's not, then you don't know me. Do you think you know me?'

'I know you now.'

'Isn't that when you want to know me? Now.'

'Yes.'

'And into the future?'

Men always get tired of me.

'Yes.'

'Then leave my past alone. I've told you everything I want to tell you!'

She puts the grapefruit section in her mouth. She stares across White Memorial Plaza and doesn't chew. Now, she does. Eight times. She swallows.

And says, 'My stepmother remarried. His name was

Carmine. He adopted my brother and me. I wasn't that crazy about him. When I became twenty-one, I changed my name. Okay?'

'Why didn't you just tell me all that when you told me everything else?'

'Because, Jacob, I guess I didn't want to or it just didn't come out.'

She slides another grapefruit section onto her spoon and into her mouth. 'You didn't say hello or kiss me,' she says around the fruit.

'Hello,' I say, and lean across the table to kiss her.

She passes the grapefruit section from her mouth to mine.

21

The week before Christmas, I hear Leslie Ann – whom I have never heard use a word of profanity – use some.

Coming up the stairwell from the garage and about to open our door, I hear her voice from within scream, 'That's not fair! That is not fair, Magda! It's not your place to decide something like that! Don't you dare hang up on – ' Then I hear the receiver slam violently once, twice, three times against the body of the telephone.

I open the door to find Leslie Ann on the couch.

'You father-fucking, cocksucking piece of shit of a ball-busting cunt!'

She slams the reunited phone parts onto the lamp table beside the couch and looks up to find me just inside our door.

'I really hope you weren't talking to Mother Teresa or Lucille Ball,' I tell her.

'The wicked stepmother.'

'You okay?'

'Not really.'

'What's the problem?'

'My brother flunked two of his courses at NYU, so she won't pay his tuition next semester. She doesn't pay his tuition, his deferment's withdrawn, and he'll get drafted. We have money in trust, but we don't get it till we're thirty, and she won't lend it to him. She's not even related to us, for Godsake! She got stuck with us because she coveted my father. She lost him and inherited us. Why can't she just give us our money and get out of our lives! Fucking slut of a Nazi whore bitch!'

Leslie Ann says she's going to have to go to Hawaii for at least part of Christmas break and talk to the woman face to face. She says she would invite me to go with her, but blood is going to be let that can only flow without the encumbrance of a loved one's presence. She hopes I understand.

I assure her I'll be fine, not to worry, I'll be waiting when she gets back.

When we discussed back around Thanksgiving whether either of us would go anywhere over Christmas without the other, it was clear neither of us wanted to be without the other, and as neither of us wanted to go 'home,' we wouldn't separate.

'Doesn't your family want you to come home, though?' she asked then.

'I told them I'm going to be very busy with my dissertation, and they accept that because we don't know how to talk about everything we know we should but can't because we don't know how to start.' I laughed. 'What'd I just say?'

She didn't laugh. She knew what I'd just said even if I didn't – which I did – and she was prepared to feel sorry for me.

'Would you like to invite your brother to come out and visit us?'

She shakes her head. 'You're my family. Let's just be alone, take long walks, cook a lot of wonderful food, and you'll make me laugh.'

The night before she leaves for Honolulu, we open our Christmas/Chanukah presents.

We take the two wrapped gifts from underneath –

actually, beside — the Wandering Jew in the window we're using for a Christmas tree/Chanukah bush, which Leslie Ann has decorated in a riot of color with jelly beans and gum balls. I open mine first. It's a picture of Leslie Ann as Kate, hands on hips, mouth open in a cry of rebellion against Petruchio. On it she's written: 'J, I love you! LA.'

Then she opens the first edition of Rimbaud's *A Season in Hell* I shoplifted from a rare bookstore in Mendocino one weekend when we moteled as Mr and Mrs Motke Londovnik.

22

O n Christmas I watch football, and when that palls I putz around on my dissertation, which is about four months ahead of schedule, even with the arrival of Leslie Ann in my life.

Dutifully, I call my family. We have one of our information-packed, emotion-spare conversations.

'How's the dissertation?' my father wants to know.

'A pisser,' I tell him.

'I'll bet,' he says. 'Don't let them make tougher criticism on yours than they do on the goyim, you hear me?'

I don't tell them about Leslie Ann. I want to, but I know they'll ask me questions I either won't want to answer or to which I won't *have* answers.

Leslie Ann and I have agreed not to spend money on overseas calls. And though I would break the rule tonight, I realize she's left me no number in Hawaii.

But she has left me notes. One I found under the bolster on the couch when I made the bed last night – 'Think of me last before you sleep.'

Another taped to the shower head this morning read: 'You'll have to wash your own equipment. But no self-abuse, please. Save it for me. Merry Christmas and know I'll be missing you.'

At the small Italian restaurant in Menlo Park we love because the pasta is cheap and homemade, I eat alone Christmas night, content to work on a paper on

Frederick Goddard Tuckerman ('Behold! the autumn goes,/The shadow grows,/The moments take hold of eternity;/Even while we stop to wrangle or repine/Our lives are gone – /Like thinnest mist') and imagine Leslie Ann sitting across from me, her ankles between mine the way she likes to sit.

In fact, I've never minded eating alone. Did it all through college. Came, really, to prefer it, I suppose.

I don't like seeing other people eating alone, however. Inevitably, I figure it's either an error – they've been stood up – or, worse, they have no friends or mates.

When I notice the man at a far table, alone, it's a moment before I realize he's my adviser in the English Department, Dr Jeffrey Kaplan, a Chaucerian in his mid-thirties who has always treated me with contempt, for fear, I've assumed, of accusations of a conspiracy among Stanford's Jewish minority. When I submit my dissertation proposal on Gertrude Stein and her circle, he terms it a 'masturbatory exegesis in irrelevance' but says he'll support it 'because somebody has to write those theses.'

Seeing him eating alone makes me regret hating his guts.

I decide to slip out without his seeing me so as not to embarrass him; but as I head for the door, his head comes up from his plate and rotates my way. He's been waiting.

'Ah,' he says.

'Well,' say I.

'Ç va?' he asks.

'Fine, fine,' I say.

'Good,' says he. 'How are the holidays treating you?'

'Nicely,' I say. 'You?'

'Ah, well, the continual confusion, you know – Chanukah or Christmas, Christmas or Chanukah.'

'I know what you mean,' I say, as if finding someone else suffering the same profound dilemma is a quantum relief. I have no idea what he means. My family is about as religious as the Himmlers. It was at Leslie Ann's insistence that we turned our Wandering Jew into a symbol of the season and exchanged gifts.

'Sit, sit,' he says.

A message sealed in a bottle is tossed into a stream not far away, and a gentle tide sends it sashaying downstream my way. 'Well,' I say, my mind's eye flicking at the bottle, trying to discern from too great a distance what the message says, 'I should probably get back to . . .' I glance at my wrist.

I don't wear a watch.

'Sure,' I say, and sit. And then, anticipating what the message in the bottle bobbing my way might indicate, I ask Dr Jeffrey Kaplan, 'Mrs Kaplan out of town?'

'Who?'

'Oh, I thought you were married to . . . I thought I met her at the annual – '

'No.'

The bottle rolls up at my feet.

'So,' I note, 'angel hair with pesto, eh?'

'Yes,' he says.

'Piñon or walnuts?'

'Oh, piñon, piñon.' He smiles. '*Cela va sans dire!*'

He laughs. So do I. I have no idea what he said. I managed to pass French as one of my required doctoral languages only by taking a crash course and promptly forgetting most of it and certainly the part that included the words he just used.

'So what about you?' he asks.

'Linguine with white clam sauce,' I tell him.

He smiles indulgently – the professor at the student.

'I meant, how's it going? How's the dissertation coming? Haven't talked to you, I'll bet, in a fortnight.'

Fortnight? Did people really fail to communicate in that period of time?

'Fine, good,' I assure him, 'everything's progressing apace.'

Apace? Jesus, it's catching.

His hand reaches for me, clutching his napkin. 'Come here,' he says.

I deflect my cheek and snap-lock Dr Jeffrey Kaplan's wrist in my fist, yanking him half up out of his chair.

He gasps, whimpers, snatches his wrist free, wraps a hand around it.

'I'm sorry,' I say. 'Did I hurt you?'

'Well, yes. Good Lord. You have something on your cheek.'

I brush at my cheek.

'You'd think I – No,' he says, looking at my other cheek, and somewhat more cautiously, the napkin shifted to his other hand, he reaches across the table and dabs at the correct cheek. 'For goodness sake – there,' he says. 'A bit of scallion from your clam sauce.'

The napkin smells of sweet basil and pine nuts and is moist against my cheek.

'I should have just left it there. I mean, after all, it's not my reputation, is it?'

Dr Jeffrey Kaplan puts his napkin back in his lap and begins to work his wrist, letting me know that it hurts pretty bad.

I am supposed to say to Dr Jeffrey Kaplan, 'Let me see,' and take his wrist, massage it, make it better.

When I don't, Dr Jeffrey Kaplan says, 'I was just finishing up.' He continues to rotate his wrist, using it subtly to suggest I owe him the favor he is about to ask, for being generous enough not to charge me with assault. 'I was going to go back to my abode,' he says, 'and listen to some Brahms, make some cappuccino. Like to fall by, play some whist?'

'Oh, gee, wouldn't that be great. But the thing is, my friend, my girlfriend, is coming back from Honolulu and I have to pick her up in – ' I crane my neck to get a look at Dr Jeffrey Kaplan's watch (no idea what it reads). 'Oh, Jesus, I'm just going to make it if I rip out of here right now.'

'Coming *back*?' asks Dr Jeffrey Kaplan. 'Unless I've entered a time warp, vacation has just begun.'

'Big fight with her mother ten minutes after she got there. San Francisco to Honolulu, seven hours, and the minute you hit terra firma you're fighting about whether it's legal to go braless in Polynesia – you believe that?'

He doesn't, of course, but clearly we're at the parting.

'Well,' says Dr Jeffrey Kaplan, 'perhaps some other time,' and he turns his eyes dismissively back to the several remaining strands of his angel hair pesto and prongs with his fork at the single piñon nut awash in olive oil in the corner of his plate.

Back in the apartment, I feel guilty about Dr Jeffrey Kaplan, for lying, for being shallow, even for being in bed alone. I miss Leslie Ann in our bed. Her leg tossed over me, her hands drawn in to her chest, her face pressed into my shoulder.

I get up, wander around the apartment. Open Leslie Ann's underwear drawer, rub a pair of her blue satin panties across my face. Get an erection.

As I refold the panties and put them back where they belong, something catches my eye under a slip on the far side of the drawer, wrapped in a chamois cloth.

I take it out of the drawer, unwrap it.

It's made of wood, carved by hand in minute, clean strokes, and painted. It has a distinctly religious feel to it – a human figure, a foot high, several inches in diameter; a girl with black hair peeking out from beneath a head covering, a scarf; tiny hands are folded prayerfully at the figure's waist; the eyes are hollowed orbs, painted green with flecks of yellow. Someone's vision of the young Leslie Ann Masterson, of Margaret Jewel Whatever-Her-Real-Last-Name-Was?

I turn the figure over in my hands. On the bottom side of the base, the piece is signed 'W.B.M., '54.'

In 1954 Margaret Jewel was six years old. The figure could well be a six-year-old girl. And W.B.M. could be her father, the Cherokee sculptor, Blank Blank Masterson.

The effigy seems to be a religious figure. Saint. Martyr.

There is a feeling in the eyes of the figure, a twist to the mouth that projects great what?

A line from the Bible comes at me from somewhere: 'The peace of God, which passeth all understanding.'

Her eyes are different today from the eyes in this statue.

And in a moment's insight, I know the pain I saw in Leslie Ann's eyes the night she told me her mother died, the pain I could not name.

Not just loss, not just sorrow.

Remorse.

What had she done, what does she think she did, to contribute to her mother's suicide?

And now I know what the other thing was I saw in her onstage that first night I watched her do Kate.

There was compassion, yes, and there was something incredibly spiritual, oh yeah.

But there was something *haunted*.

23

In the pantry the next morning I find this note from Leslie Ann: 'I knew you'd get hungry eventually. Darlene is here alone. Just give her a call – that's all I'm asking. She's losing the feeling in her vagina. I love you.'

Now *that*, I think, is a note!

What is the appeal to having sex with a really attractive cripple? Not sure, but there definitely is one.

Perhaps in the abnormality of it alone lies the attraction.

Okay, so Darlene's here alone with a numb vagina. What am I going to do about it?

Just give her a call.

My adrenaline goes to afterburners as I dial Darlene's number. I think about hanging up after five rings and telling Leslie Ann I tried but she wasn't there.

On the sixth ring I get the woman on the phone who performs Darlene Delvecchio's 'cares.'

She tells me Darlene's in the hospital.

I find her on the second floor of the Stanford Medical Center, propped up in bed reading in a room with a woman who's whimpering politely in pain.

When I loom around the half-drawn curtain between the two beds, Darlene squeals. 'Oh, no, don't shee me!'

She starts patting at her hair with one hand and smoothing her hospital gown with the other. 'Why didn't you tell me you were coming?'

'I wanted to surprise you,' I say, 'and catch you looking like shit.'

'Well, congratulations, you did. Don't come in, but do.'

I step around to the far side of the bed, take her hand, squeeze it, pat it.

The woman in the next bed expels gas loudly. Darlene and I look at each other – we have established the right to laugh together at things we shouldn't. We bite our respective lips.

'She just had her gall bladder out,' she whispers. 'It fills you with gash, and it hash nowhere to go.'

'But finally,' I whisper to her, 'it hash to go shome-where.'

'That's right,' she says, 'and when it does, you wish you were dead.'

We'd really like to laugh but manage not to.

'I like it that you can mimic the way I slur my speech,' she says. 'That's shweet.'

She ducks her head, smooths the textured cover of her book, rattles her eyes off my forehead.

'I don't need to be here. My care attendant just didn't want to have to deal with me; her boyfriend came, and she wants to shtore up all the sex she can before he leaves and she's shtuck with me again.'

I'm not sure if I imagine it, but it seems the subject of sex causes the rhythm of Darlene's breathing to change.

'What happened to you?' I ask.

'My intestines went on the fritz. If they don't shtraighten out, I'm gonna need a new care attendant. She's obviously not into other people's poop.'

'Shurprishing,' I tell her.

'Well, God, it's only old food.' She laughs. The disease bangs on the Stop button. Darlene obeys.

'God, it's nice that you came,' she says. 'Maggie told you what we talked about, didn't she?'

'Yes,' I say, 'she did.'

'Ay!' She turns her head away. 'I'm sho embarrassed.'

'Don't be. I'm flattered that you found me appealing because I'm such a shlub.'

'I didn't say you were a shlub. I just think it's cute that you try not to show your vulnerability.'

'I find you appealing, too.'

'I'm sure.'

'I do.'

She looks me in the eyes. 'Do you shwear?'

'I shwear.'

Though seeing her now, I feel anything but sexually interested, and am therefore fascinated to hear myself say, 'You know Rubens's painting *The Toilet of Venus*?'

She cackles. Again, the disease spitefully interrupts. 'Oh, God, I remind you of a toilet?'

'It's a woman with her maid and a cherub holding up a mirror to her beautiful face. Red lips, yellow hair, and a truly remarkable ass.'

Her breathing begins going a little haywire.

'You okay?'

She glances toward the woman moaning in the other bed, she lowers her voice still more: 'I'm fine, don't worry, keep talking.'

'That's it.'

'Oh, no, I'm just getting . . . I think if you keep talking I might . . .'

She puffs through her pursed lips, her eyes roll back in her head. I put my hand to her forehead. She grabs it and presses it to her breast.

Beneath my hand, it's too wide, too soft. It's not a breast I care to touch.

And yet, I am getting an erection.

My penis is behaving. My brain can't keep pace.

'Pull the curtain,' she says.

The woman in the other bed continues to cry in a low, continuous gurgle. She looks at me as I start to close the curtain.

'Hi, how you doing? I'm just going to close this a little so we can . . .'

The woman nods, she doesn't care.

'I'm scared,' Darlene says.

'Don't be.'

'What if the nursh shows up?'

'She'll have to wait her turn.'

Darlene cackles, nods, clutches my hand back to her breast. 'What should we do?'

'What do you feel like?'

'I shtink, I'm dirty.'

'Doesn't matter.'

'Yesh, it does. Could I just do you?'

' "Do me"? Ish that a euphemishm of shome short?'

'Don't make me laugh,' she says, her words crackling together. 'I don't want to lose my place.'

'I'm sorry.'

I step close to the bed and unfasten the top of my jeans, unzip my fly. She rolls onto her side as I push my pants down half a foot and my springloaded penis flies up.

A man's mind, I have to marvel, is a wondrous thing.

'How'd it get big so fast?'

'Somebody called your order in ahead.'

She laughs. The disease wallops the laughter to a stop. She pants. 'I told you not to do that. If they hear people laughing, they'll get shuspicious.'

She curls steady fingers around me. Her breathing

becomes stentorian. So does mine. The woman in the next bed evacuates a rush of gas that sounds like a decelerating Austin Healey.

'What are you *doing* over there?' she inquires, her voice slack, distant.

'Nothing,' calls Darlene. 'Talking.'

And she begins gently, firmly, to stroke me.

'I hear funny breathing,' the woman says dreamily.

'Oh, my God,' Darlene whispers in wonder. 'Look, I'm doing it!'

And then her hand erupts in crazed convulsion.

If the spasm were one that unleashed her hand in an up-and-down direction, we would have been home free; but it doesn't have regimentation or sexual release in mind; whatever mind it has chooses chaos.

For a moment I'm certain Darlene Delvecchio is going to rip my cock out by its roots.

'I can't let go!' she whispers in a panic.

'You're doing something evil over there!' the woman in the next bed affirms, her gaseous bowels booming one off the walls like some nebular decree.

'No, we're not!' hisses Darlene.

No, we're two cartoon characters in a pitched battle, my cock and Darlene's hand sprinting and squirting this way and that. I chase her hand; with my member hostage, the hand takes evasive action. I pursue. It evades. Finally I catch up with it, capture and grip it fiercely in mine, bringing it still and peeling the fingers away from my throbbing, whiplashed organ.

Uncoupled from me, Darlene's hand goes limp and she begins to cry. 'Oh, I'm sho shorry, I'm sho shorry.'

'Sshh, no, it's all right, it's okay.'

And then, in spite of the fact that my penis feels like it needs to go to Intensive Care, I begin to laugh.

'Don't!' Darlene cries.

The woman next door unlooses a sonic boom. 'Stop that laughing,' she howls. 'Don't you know there are human beings here in pain?'

And Darlene can't keep her emotions straight, either, and she begins to cackle, firing a couple of hundred rounds of ammo through the room.

We both laugh so hard that I start to piddle and she pops her urine bag and soaks her sheets and the woman in the next bed is farting and screaming for the nurse.

Suddenly the room is full of help.

But we don't need it.

There's piss everywhere.

But we don't care.

24

I awaken in the middle of the night to find Leslie Ann
kneeling beside the bed, one hand laid gently against
the side of my head. The bathroom light is on, the door
half-closed.

'You came back.'

'I'll always come back,' she says, 'as long as you want
me and I can get a flight.'

'You promise?'

'Yes.'

'What if you stop loving me?'

'Then I won't come back.'

'This was a better deal before I asked that question.'

She presses her hands to my chest; her palms are
damp. 'I missed you,' she says.

'Not as much as I missed you.'

'You don't know that.'

The heat from her hands sends a current to my
feet. After just these few days, I am reminded what
the loss of her touch would mean now that I've felt
it.

'What did you miss about me?' I ask her. 'Make me
feel adored.'

'I missed your bulk,' she says, and in her long cotton
skirt and peasant blouse she climbs on the bed beside
me, pulls her hands into her own chest now, and I wrap
my bigger self around her.

'No limbs over the edge,' she told me when I asked

her about the way she sleeps. 'There could be wolves under there that would eat your arms.'

'How were things with your stepmother?'

'I think we have one basically unsolvable problem.'

'What's that?'

'We despise each other.'

'Did you tell her you were living with a person of the Hebrew persuasion?'

'Would I miss that chance? She asked if you had money and whether you were studying to be a doctor or a lawyer.'

'Sounds like she has a certain stereotype in mind.'

'I'm kidding.'

'About what?'

'She didn't say that.'

'What'd she say?'

' "Don't bring him here." Did you find my notes?'

'Yes.'

'Did you like them?'

'I rated several very highly.'

'Did you give Darlene a call?'

When I don't answer, she lifts her head and inspects some part of me deep behind my eyes. 'What'd you do?'

In the light from the bathroom I can see her eyes studying my face, looking for messages in the arrangements of skin on bone.

Sensing I should lie, I tell her the truth about what happened with Darlene.

When I'm finished, she says only, 'I've got to take a nap.'

'That's all you're going to say?'

She nods and tries to give me the full constellation of teeth, but it doesn't work.

She turns away from me and, in a moment, seems to sleep.

When I wake at nine, she's sitting on the edge of the bed, naked, shining from a bath, holding the carved figure of the little girl.

'You put it back almost the way it was.'

'I wasn't pillaging your drawer.'

'Just confused about whose drawer is whose?'

'I went in there to smell your underwear.'

It takes her a moment to grasp that. 'That's disgusting, Jacob! I put my underwear in there to . . . to be quiet.'

I touch her cheek. She presses my hand hard to her silky skin.

'I don't think I wanted you to make love to Darlene.'

'I didn't.'

'You tried.'

'I thought you wanted me to.'

'I thought I did, but I didn't. And I wanted you to know that, even if I didn't.'

'Well, I didn't know that, but I also didn't make love to her.'

'But not for the right reason! Stop using the language to confuse things!'

'Fine. Let's be clear. You're jealous of what I did, even though I didn't do what you didn't want me to do.'

She stares at the carved statue, at the face. 'My father called me the Sun of God.'

Son of God? Uh-oh.

'Had his genders a little screwed up, didn't he?'

'Not son, as in boy-child, but sun as in the thing up in the sky.'

'As in light, illumination.'

'Yeah. He hated the white man for diluting the Cherokee religion with Christianity; yet he married

a white Christian and decided he loved the story of
Jesus and his relationship to his fathers – both Joseph
and Yahweh – if not what the religion had achieved
during its first several thousand years of operation. He
thought things could be changed by certain luminous
lights. Shepherds.'

'Like his child.'

'Yeah. But he disappointed me and I disappointed
him.'

'He disappointed you by marrying your stepmother.'

'More than that, Jacob. He disappointed me past
forgiveness way before that,' she says.

'When? In what way?'

'When he cheated on my mother. If my mother wasn't
beyond cheating on, then . . .'

'What?'

She shakes her head and grabs the afghan her mother
made off the floor, wraps it around her nakedness. She
fixes me with her haunted eyes.

Men always get tired of me.

'There was nothing wrong with my mother. Do you
understand what I'm saying?'

'I think you told me she was perfect.'

'I know every time I open my mouth to talk about my
frigging past, I sound like a lunatic, but she was. She was
the ideal. I want to show you something.'

She goes to her blouse and T-shirt drawer, takes out
a sheet of paper from beneath the T-shirts, and hands
it to me.

The paper is dated December 18, 1956. It's a list of
some sort.

1. Tricky – grooming.
2. Evan's track meet.

3. Wait for air conditioner man.
4. Get flowers for teachers and deliver.
5. Get drinks for tomorrow's parties and deliver.
6. Arrange chicken for Maggie's class.
7. Pick up Maggie's shoes.
8. Call about garbage pickup.
9. Pho-Tech – Christmas family photo.
10. Call Mrs Yamamoto.
11. Call club re 11 or 11:30.
12. Walgreen's Maggie's medicine.
13. Maggie's fitting at Paula's 3 or 3:30.
14. Make an attempt at desk.
15. Groceries very important!
16. Pick Tricky up.
17. Evan pickup 2:30.
18. Maggie pickup 3:10.
19. Greenhouse for geraniums and petunias.
20. TV table for Maggie.
21. Marinate hens.

I look up at Leslie Ann.

'How many people, how many mothers, would do all that in one day? And she had a list like that every day. So, what'd he want from her? Come on, you have an analysis of everything.'

'Maybe given his own feelings of imperfection, he couldn't stand her doing all she did, so he had to do something destructive to her.'

'Then why'd he keep pushing me to be like her?'

'D'know.'

'He loved me, I know he did.'

'But?'

She reads my eyes. The door is partially open. Open it farther . . . or slam it?

I sense – whether for the first time or just more acutely than any other time – that she wants to entrust me with all the truths of her life, with her*self*.

She wants to believe that I'm capable of loving her sufficiently.

'But,' she says, 'he beat me.'

Her eyes flick about my face, decoding my eyes, my cheeks, my mouth.

'He hit you?'

'That's right.'

Challenging me to doubt her, begging me to believe her.

'Your perfect mother permitted that.'

Flash! Fury in her eyes again.

Courting her trust, I've achieved the opposite.

'What's that supposed to mean?' She hurls the afghan aside. 'She didn't know! You think my mother knew?'

'How could she not?'

'How could she not? He only did it when she wasn't home. And only hit me where she couldn't see.'

'Where can you hit a child so her mother can't see?'

Her hands close into fists beside her head. I am impugning her perfect mother.

I raise my hands to ward off the blows that don't descend.

Because behind the anger, there still remains the desire to unburden herself.

'Inside,' she says.

'He hit you inside? How do you hit somebody inside? You mean he abused you with ideas?'

'Yeah, there was that. He said he wanted me to grow up to be someone who would "put him next to godliness." '

'So nothing you could do was sufficient.'

She nods.

'So he . . .'

'Hit me inside, Jacob.'

I shake my head. Why are we playing games? Why doesn't she – 'I don't under –'

'Not with his fist,' she says. 'Just with this.'

She unfolds one of the fists and holds the hand toward me. I start to reach for it.

Then she extrudes the middle finger at me.

The finger stares at me. Speaks its silent imagery.

'You were just a little girl.'

'I thought, but didn't know how to say: "How can I be pure, Daddy, how can I be perfect, if you do this to me?"'

In my family we may not speak, but never do I recall a hand being raised by a parent against my sister or me in anger.

I recoil against belief. I doubt! But doubt whom, what? Doubt that she's telling the truth? She's obviously capable of keeping from me anything she wants that I don't happen to trip over.

But no. Not doubting her.

Nothing seems clearer to me at this moment than that this woman wants me to be able to love her in spite of the fact that she may be badly damaged.

What I am doubting is that a father could do that to a child!

'How long did that go on?'

'Till he got tired of me.'

'When was that?'

'Just before my mother died. He just stopped talking to me, stopped everything with me. It was like I didn't exist. That's when he started with Magda.'

'And you don't think that's why your mother killed herself – because she found out?'

The accusation implicit in the question has been hurled before. Probably many times. By herself. But she can't stand it. 'No!' she says.

She looks so tired. The skin below her eyes sags away from the bone.

I pull her to me. She comes easily, tucks her hands in.

From inside my arms, she asks, 'Found out which?'

'Found out which what?'

Something goes out of her voice now, too. The force has evaporated. I can barely feel her breath against my chest. 'Killed herself because she found out which? About Magda or what he was doing to me?'

I stroke her head. The shape has become so familiar.

'I was thinking maybe your mother told your father she knew what he was doing, and so he stopped, but her guilt that she hadn't known sooner and done something about it was so overwhelming that she – '

'Maybe, maybe, maybe, maybe, okay, maybe!'

'Or maybe you're right,' I say, disbelieving it but saying it to give her an out, 'maybe she found out about the other woman and – '

'Yeah, well, the problem with someone who doesn't leave a note,' Leslie Ann says, 'is you can never be sure, can you?'

'She didn't leave a note?'

'Not one fucking word. And even if she had, how many people really believe other people's explanations of the truth?'

She untucks from the protectorate of my arms, walks into the bathroom, and locks the door. We never lock the bathroom.

I go to the door.

'Are you all right?'

'Yep.'

'What are you doing?'

I hear the tub faucets turn on. Hear the rush of water.

'Taking a bath.'

'Didn't you just get out of one?'

'Taking another one,' she says.

I understand that she's in danger. When she emerges, she seems fine. She initiates our lovemaking. Yet when I enter her and am rushing (I assume with her) toward orgasm, I look at her and she's staring at me with dead eyes.

I ejaculate immediately.

'What's the matter?' I ask.

She shrugs and goes to bathe a third time.

I press my face to the locked door. 'We may have something of a problem here, Les.'

From within the bathroom her voice comes at me, angry, admonitory. 'No, we don't,' she says. 'I'll be fine.'

And she does, in fact, come out of the third bath and kiss me sweetly on the mouth. 'See,' she says, 'all better.'

25

S he suggests we visit Darlene.
   I suggest we don't.

She says we have to go *because* neither one of us wants to.

When we get to the hospital, we're informed Darlene's been sent home.

Darlene's in her dorm room with the woman who does her 'cares.'

We take her to dinner, where Leslie Ann is just subdividing the huge antipasto when Darlene says, 'Jacob told you about the other night in the hospital.'

'Yes,' Leslie Ann says, 'he told me.'

She smiles at us respectfully. 'You're lucky that you can tell each other the truth,' Darlene says.

'I'm sorry,' says Leslie Ann. 'Not that Jacob told me, but that you couldn't control yourself and get what you wanted.'

Given the information Leslie Ann passed on this morning and her initial response to what I told her happened with Darlene, there is something extremely disagreeable about this conversation.

While I mull what, if anything, to do about it, I'm also aware that life at its more mundane continues.

Darlene has to be fed.

Something in me doesn't want to let Leslie Ann, who's doing the serving, do the feeding.

So I reach for Darlene's fork, prong some provolone,

salami, and lettuce. I get most of it into her mouth, but the provolone falls; without thinking, I pick it up with my fingers and put it to Darlene's lips. She takes the cheese and several inches of my index finger and thumb into her mouth, sucks the cheese out of my grip, bathing my fingers in the process.

'I'm shorry,' says Darlene. 'I didn't mean to do that. Oh, Maggie, I should go home – '

Leslie Ann unveils her abundant teeth in a disengenuous smile. 'Don't be silly,' she says.

'I'm sho embarrassed.'

Leslie Ann leans into the middle of the table and says quietly, 'For Godsake, Darlene, just say what you want.'

Alert!

Around us, the close air in the room, thick with the smell of garlic and oregano, pulsates to our three pounding heartbeats.

'I want a man inside of me,' says Darlene.

'Any man? Or Jacob? Or *my* man – who happens to *be* Jacob?'

Like me, Darlene is confused. She doesn't know how to read Leslie Ann's aggression.

'Why are you so mad, Maggie? You shent Jacob to me. Am I crazy, or were you offering to share him with me?'

'D'know. Do not know. And I'm not going to sit here and try to deduce an answer from the empirical fucking evidence. The point is you want to be fucked so bad you can't think about anything else in this fucking, ugly, stinking, piece of shit of a world. But you can't control your fucking shitty fucking filthy crappy fucking body! Isn't that about the size of it?'

'Well, gee,' I say, 'I'm stuffed. How 'bout you guys? Anybody want to take in a flick?'

Leslie Ann scoots her chair close to Darlene's wheel-chair and takes Darlene's cherubic face in her hands. The ferocity of Leslie Ann's grip twists Darlene's face grotesquely.

'Together,' she says to Darlene, but clearly speaking to me, too, 'we can control your body and make it happen.'

I cock my head at Leslie Ann, having claimed the gesture from her somewhere along the way.

'Together?' I ask.

'The three of us.'

'The three of us. A team working toward a common goal?'

'Say what you want to say, Jakey.'

'Thanks, Les. What I want to say is I'm wondering who's manipulating whom here. Is this the ultimate male fuck fantasy we're working toward – I boff Darlene while my inamorata watches? Are you doing this because you think *I* want it? Out of pity or compassion for the crip here? Or maybe because you told me things this morning you're sorry you told me? Or to further denigrate yourself because I was stupid enough to do what I thought you wanted me to do in the first place that you really didn't want me to do because you wanted me to prove to you you were worthier of my devotion than you think you are?'

I prong the crucifix of anchovies sitting in the middle of the remains of the antipasto. 'Any opinion, Les?'

'Can I select all of the above?'

'Hey, it's your neuroses on parade here. We'll permit you to – '

'Shtop it! Both of you, shtop talking about thish.'

We finish the salad in silence. And then take Darlene back to her room.

26

On the ride to our apartment, we don't speak.

Inside our doorway she says, 'Want to fuck?'

'Why?'

'Who cares why. You want to or not?'

We tear at each other's clothes in a confusion of disdain and desire, punishing each other with clawing, pinching fingers. There's no foreplay. She grabs me viciously in her fist, yanks me down by my root, and shoves me into her.

We pound against each other, our bellies making tensile *whaps* each time we slam the distance between us shut.

We grunt furiously – me, she, me, she – in a contrapuntal, bestial chant that bounces between our two faces, glued wetly forehead to forehead.

I feel her teeth snapping at my chin.

I lower my mouth on hers.

Our tongues drive at each other, then my mouth, hers, each tries to swallow the other's tongue. And in the midst of this kiss, pelvic bones walloping pelvic bones, we find ourselves staring at each other openeyed. I don't know what she sees in my eyes, but in hers I see such a depth of longing, of sorrow, that I am unable to do anything but stop – stop kissing, stop pounding, stop moving – and to stroke her face, to begin slowly anew to make love to her with love.

And she reciprocates.

Jacobandleslieann.

Yet, soon we lie rank with the sweat and spice of our running juices, and after some minutes of wondering what needs to be said to summarize or properly place the events of the day, she says, 'Want me to move out?'

'No.'

'Swear?'

'Yes.'

'How come?'

'Because I love you a lot more than I hate you.'

'Do you swear?'

'Yes.'

'Why? Don't you think I'm sick?'

'I think you're more complicated than I am, or than I thought you were. I think maybe that annoys the hell outta me because I always wanted to be the most interesting and neurotic person I knew, but what the hell . . .'

'That's really glib, Jacob. I can be out of here in twenty — '

'Cut it out!'

The words carom off the walls, and then it's still.

She presses close.

I crush her to me. Hold her head in my hand, feel against my palm the scar her brother put there many years ago because his powers were unequal to hers.

I want to say something healing to her, want to tell her how much I never want her to leave, how alive her passions, even her dementia, make me feel, how much I want to help her overcome whatever haunts her.

But I'm afraid I can't really do anything but injure her further.

STALKING THE TYGER

1

In the mornings we shower together. On a morning in late January, I'm soaping her armpits and singing 'Long Tall Sallie,' telling her with abiding passion that 'she got everything Uncle Tom need/Oh baby,' when she tells me that in the night I gave her a bunch of little pats and called her 'Pop.'

'I patted you and called you Pop?'

She shows me how I patted her – little sympathetic strokes on the shoulder.

I squirt shampoo into my hand, spread it briskly through her hair – it's her natural jet black again – and whip it into a froth of white foam.

I'm fascinated that I might somehow associate her with my father.

It's not that hard a leap to make in terms of the horrors and the burdens of their respective pasts, certainly.

Or the kept counsel.

I tilt her head under the rush of water. White water streams off her cheeks. I look down at the equilateral triangle of soft hair between her legs.

I try to imagine I am *her* father.

There was no hair there then.

Why couldn't he take whatever impulse drove him to touch her, to put his fingers in his child, and turn it on himself?

I put my palm to Leslie Ann's belly. Its slick surface fills my palm.

Children.
Fathers.
Pop.

I remember a night long ago, some golf tournament run by Protestants, my father and me ostracized, relegated early to our motel room, the TV on, me asleep, then not, awakening to the sound of my father going, *Ziiz, ziiz, ziiz.* My back to him, the sound of his bed moving just discernibly, certain that if I turn, I'll see my father, my very own Poppy, pounding his liverwurst as I have begun to do with religious zeal myself. I groan and do not turn. 'You okay, Poppy?'

'Fine. Fine. Something in my throat. Go back to sleep.'

It distressed me deeply that my father – a man! – a married man married to my mother! – permitted himself to do what I did out of necessity.

How badly did he need release that he was willing to seek it in a room his child also occupied?

Badly. He must have needed release badly.

Whom did he think of? My mother? Elizabeth Taylor or Sophia Loren – his favorite actresses?

Or my sister, maybe.

Or me.

What is not fair for the imagination to entertain?

In the morning I awakened to find my father sitting on the edge of his bed staring at me. If I had not known better, I would have thought he'd been crying.

Did Leslie Ann's father only put his fingers in her vagina? Or did he put other things in other apertures?

I can see myself as an SS officer and as a father who whacks off in a bed next to his son and as a father who abuses his child, and I am for the first time in my life certain I could participate in the murder of millions.

I kiss Leslie Ann's nose. 'Done,' I say.

The Sun of God opens her eyes and cocks her head at me. 'What?' she asks.

'Pop, huh?'

She nods and takes the soap and begins to lather me up.

'You'll have to gain about a hundred and fifty pounds.'

2

While we finish the dishes after dinner that evening (she washes, I dry) Leslie Ann tells me she decided she's going to have Howard direct her in a studio production of Ionesco's *The Lesson*.

I assume she's going to play the malleable, whining female student who is abused and then murdered by the professor.

But, no, she says, she doesn't want to play the traditionally female student; she wants to play the traditionally male professor – as a woman, but with all the inherent masculine implications in the script – and cast the student as a young male. The professor, she and Howard decided, would be a Nazi, the student an Orthodox Jew.

'So much violence,' she says simply. 'I want to see if I can feel what the attraction is.'

Sounds simple. Reasonable. I suspect it's neither.

She takes the dish towel, dries her hands, dabs at something on my chin, folds the towel, replaces it precisely over the handle on the oven door.

Then cups my scrotum through my jeans.

Neural chaos ensues: blood rushes to that part of my body, muscles contract, adrenaline surges.

'I want to draw your penis so I have a road sign.'

'Draw?'

'Trace. Then I want you to describe what it feels like.'

'Describe what it feels like to have a penis?'

'Does that seem a peculiar question for a woman to ask, Jacob? Or is anything I ask you or say to you or do from now on going to seem peculiar so that I have to question everything I ask and say and do from now on?'

My scrotum still rests in her hand.

'What was the question again, dear?'

'Describe the heft.'

'The heft? Like baseball bat versus flashlight versus wiener?'

The chimes ring out.

'Yeah,' she says, 'stuff like that. When it's big, does it make you feel big? What keeps it standing out there? A boner's not really bone, right? It's muscle. I mean, if there were bone in there, it would break, right?'

'Indeed. There'd be a lot of young gentlemen roaming about with their ding-dongs in splints.'

Her face plastered with a grin, she leads me by the crotch to the end of the dining table she uses for a desk and opens the large, cloth-bound notebook in which the actor writes. 'Put it here,' she says.

I do as I'm told. Lay my erection lengthwise against one of the unmarked pages of her ledger.

'Gee,' I say. 'I'm disappointed it fits on the page. I hope that's an eight-and-a-half-by-eleven sheet of paper.'

'Talk,' she says as she immortalizes the outline of the Landau member in her book.

' "The Truncheon in My Pants," ' I say. 'By Jacob Landau.'

3

When she comes home several days later, she's wearing a yarmulke. Needless to say, I ask her why, though instinctively I know it has something to do with my calling her 'Pop,' which led, at least in part, to her decision to do *The Lesson.*

'The student I'm going to kill is Orthodox. Isn't your father Orthodox?'

'When he was a kid. Not anymore.'

'When he was, didn't he wear a yarmulke all the time?'

'Or a hat.'

'So wouldn't this kid?'

'Yeah.'

'I want to go to an Orthodox service.'

'You'll have to sit in the women's section.'

'What women's section?'

'The section for women.'

'They separate men and women?'

I nod.

'It's 1971!'

'To you. To them, it's still three thousand years ago when a bunch of guys hanging around with Moses figured that women were more impure than men because they spew all this gunk out of their genital regions every month and therefore ought to sit in the back of the synagogue with something between us and them that makes them invisible.'

'Are you serious?'

'No, I'm making it up.'

She considers her options. The actor makes choices. 'Okay, so I'll dress like a man.'

'Women are forbidden to wear men's clothes.'

'You're kidding.'

'I don't kid about religious matters.'

'I thought Judaism was supposed to be so intelligent.'

'No. All religions, in fact, have managed over the centuries to achieve approximately the same level of imbecility.'

She snaps off the yarmulke and chucks it on the table. 'Okay, so I'll sit in the back. But I want to eat kosher. Would that be *legal*, you think? Would that meet with Moses's ap*prov*al?'

'I'll check with his office.'

She digs out pen and cloth-bound notebook, sits erect at the dining table, turns past the page on which my erection is enshrined, and looks at me, pen poised, all the teeth out. 'This is *neat*,' she says. 'Okay, what can we eat, what can't we eat?'

'Well, you can't eat meat and milk dishes at the same meal.'

'Okay.' She writes.

'Got to let six hours pass between a slab of beef and a bowl of cereal.'

She nods. 'Okay.' She writes.

'Got to have two sets of cooking utensils and vessels.'

'Really?' She looks at me, she plots. 'Okay, I'll borrow some of Howard's stuff. Go on.'

'There's food that's clean and there's food that's unclean. Kosher and *trayf*.'

'*Trayf* – that's the word for unclean?'

I nod. I spell it.

'Oh, that's good, that's a good word. What is it when a word sounds like it is?'

'Onomatopoeia.'

'Which doesn't sound at all like what it is, in case you never noticed.'

Her enthusiasm is infectious. I have to put the back of my hand to her cheek. She squeezes my hand between her cheek and shoulder, then leans away.

'Don't distract me. So what can we eat that's not *trayf*?'

I turn a dining chair around backward and hunker close to her. 'We can eat four-footed animals that chew their cuds and possess a cloven hoof.'

'Mm, yum-yum, makes me want to start making up menus already. What exactly are we talking about?'

'We cannot eat apes, monkeys, or the mythical Prince of Darkness. We cannot eat goat, gazelle, pygarg, or antelope.'

'What a shame – I was hankering for a nice pygarg steak.'

'You and many others. We cannot eat rabbit or pork or camel.'

'Too bad. Right behind pygarg, I love a good piece of camel.'

'Just for your information, although I would be the last one to question the factual veracity of the Bible, the camel *is* a cloven-hooved beast that chews its cud.'

'So we could have camel.'

'We'll have to ask a kosher butcher. If, in this heavily Jewish area, we can find one before the turn of the century.'

She unleashes all her teeth at me. 'I've already found one.' She jumps up, snaps her notebook shut, plants a delicious, sopping wet kiss on my mouth. 'Let's go shopping!'

4

From kosher, we move onward.

She comes leaping and bounding into the apartment one afternoon wearing an oversize jumpsuit – white, the voluminous sleeves and bottoms rolled up what looks like dozens of times to give a semblance of fitting. I assume she went to spend the day in jail, charmed criminals and defenders of the law alike, and somebody gave her the jumpsuit off his body as a going-away present.

But I'm wrong.

I'm working on my dissertation. She cries, 'Eeiiyah!' and plops down on the corner of my desk.

'I consulted a karate expert,' she says. 'The professor kills his students by choking them. The sensei taught me how to kill with my hands.'

'Skipped all that Eastern spiritual bullshit and got right to the heart of the matter.'

'The way he explained it, even killing can be very spiritual.'

'Boy, that's a relief.'

'His philosophy is if you're fated to kill, then you must love the doing of it, and that carries over to whatever your fate is in any aspect of your life.'

'*Amor fati.*'

'What's that? *Amor fati.*' She digs her notebook out of her shoulder bag, which she dumped on the floor beside my desk. 'Is this going to be good or are you just showing off?'

'Showing off?'

'Because you're jealous.'

'Of what?'

'That he gave me this' – the outfit – 'and that I know something you don't?'

'One karate lesson – how to kill – and a pair of pajamas that would be large on the Buddha?'

'I see it in your eyes. Maybe you'd like to remind me how smart you are and how dumb I am or he is or we are together. *Amor fati* – what is it? – and don't say "Skip it," that'll really piss me off.'

'*Amor fati* – love of your fate. A central idea in Nietzsche. You must embrace every fact and act of your life. Man is his own God.'

'Yeah, well, maybe Nietzsche got it from some little yellow Oriental whenever the hell it was Nietzsche walked the earth.'

'Certainly possible – he was a very great lover of vegetable tempura.'

She sighs. 'Please don't be clever all the time. Sometimes just be ordinary.'

'I am a little jealous,' I confess, 'yeah.'

'Thank you. Can I show you what I learned?'

'Do I get to live?'

'Unless I make a mistake.'

She demonstrates the techniques passively, distantly, as if she doesn't trust herself to demonstrate them actively for fear of actually killing me.

I have to hug her. Find it impossible not to.

She comes home several days later and tells me she went to a shooting range in San Mateo and fired a .32-caliber handgun. She smells of gunpowder. She wants to know if I've ever owned a gun.

I tell her I haven't.

She says we should have one in our home.

'Why?' I ask her.

'The challenge of not using it on each other,' says she.

She charms her way into an autopsy in the county coroner's office. Female strangulation victim, then run over by a car, driven by her lover, the strangler.

'You can see the finger marks. It looks like someone painted her neck with violet paint.'

I doze off on a Saturday afternoon watching a Forty-Niners game. I pass through consciousness for some seconds and assume I'm dreaming that she sits in her corner behind the dining table with a paring knife to an exposed nipple, running the blade around the thimble of flesh, which she stretches outward with her free thumb and index finger. She lets the nipple go. It snaps into place and I sink back into sleep.

When I awaken, she's making dinner and I'm sure I wasn't dreaming.

I cross the apartment, stand behind her in the kitchen, put my arms around her, kiss her neck, and let my hands roam gently over her breasts.

Two nipples.

5

The female Student in the graduate school production of *The Lesson* becomes a boy in a yarmulke, an at first pompous, posturing, and finally babbling, inane, insane young male who is helpless and hopeless against the autocratic, brilliant, and mad female Professor in her Nazi uniform.

Leslie Ann reduces language and reason and feeling to homicidal rubble and in her totally enlightened madness apotheosizes lack of feeling, lack of regret, lack of morality.

She is simply Evil as behavior.

She has cut her hair to the edge of her scalp and bleached it white, sheared her fingernails, and applied makeup that makes her occipital orbits look like abysses. She wears my old rimless glasses.

After the first performance, backstage, still in costume, she is surrounded by her adoring freshmen and by other graduate students and professors from the department, these paying homage with the old grudging respect and transparent envy, but with something more now.

Awe.

That she went somewhere most of them don't have the talent to – or, given the talent, wouldn't dare – go.

When she sees me, she excuses herself immediately from the others and comes to me. 'Did I do it?' she asks.

'It was the scariest, most sexually charged thing I've

ever seen in my life. I was hyperventilating and had a hard-on throughout.'

She throws her arms around me. My skin explodes in goose bumps when she touches me, and quietly, against my cheek, for my ear only, she says, 'No wonder your father can't speak about it and my stepmother lies. No wonder my father stuck his fingers in me. No wonder I permitted it.'

6

Neither of us brings up the topic of what we're going to do when we graduate in May.

My assumption is that Leslie Ann will go to Los Angeles or New York and become famous.

I don't have an assumption as to what I'll do.

But when the Modern Language Association meeting in San Francisco arrives with its annual week of hysterical job seeking, I ask her if she wants to go in with me while I interview.

It takes her a moment to digest the question. Then she says, 'I almost forgot,' but doesn't say forgot what. We both know. 'Who are you going to interview with?'

'Loyola Marymount and NYU,' I tell her. 'Both have openings in my field.'

I cannot tell by the usual bellwether – her eyes, the angle of her head – what she makes of the implicit selection of only two schools, one in Los Angeles, the other in New York.

'Sure,' she says, 'I'll go with you.'

Driving in, she says, 'If you're going to teach college, you should stay here or go to Harvard or Berkeley, somewhere where you'll be challenged to do your best.'

'They won't offer me a position here. Graduate schools don't hire their own graduates.'

'Does Harvard or Berkeley have an opening in your field?'

'Harvard does,' I tell her.

'Then that's where you should go.'

There is no subterfuge that I can discern; yet is she truly unaware of what's going on here?

'Everybody with an ego will apply to Harvard.'

'So why shouldn't you?'

'Because I'd hate to be rejected ... And because Harvard's a long way from you.'

The acting is superb, or still she's really not following me. 'What do you mean?'

'I mean, if I'm in Boston, that's a long way from New York or Los Angeles.'

Now she understands. 'Oh,' she says.

What has she been thinking all these months about our future?

We drive in silence. Then she looks at me directly – she would never avert her eyes to say something important – and says, 'You can't decide about your future based on what I decide about mine.'

'Why not?'

'Because what you do with your life is just as important as what I do with mine.'

The time has come to simply utter the Question.

'Do you want us to be together?'

'Sure.'

'And said with gusto.'

'Of course I want us to be together; but we're just starting our adult lives. How could we expect to stay together later if we stay together now for the wrong reasons?'

'I understand what you're saying, but if I think I'll be just as happy at Loyola or NYU as Harvard, why can't I try for one of those places?'

'You can.'

'Thank you.'

'I didn't mean it to sound like that. It's just that I don't know where I'm going when I graduate.'

'Where would you go besides New York or Los Angeles?'

'You know how many actors my age there are in New York and Los Angeles?'

'They're not you.'

'They're similar.'

'No. You're unique.'

'And every one of them has someone who loves them telling them the same thing.'

Approaching the exit to Candlestick Park, I swerve to the side of the freeway, onto the soft shoulder.

Leslie Ann grabs my wrist. 'What's the matter?'

I rip my wrist out of her hand and take her by the forearms. 'Leslie Ann, you're one in a thousand. One in ten thousand. You're the Hepburn, the Bergman, of your generation.'

'No, I'm not.'

'The hell you aren't!'

For the briefest moment fear twists her mouth, and she flinches from the sound of my voice as if it were a blow to her face.

She turns away, stares at the freeway stretching out in monotonous repetition ahead. 'I don't know if that's enough, Jacob.'

'To be the Hepburn or Bergman of your generation wouldn't be enough? What would be enough?'

She shrugs. 'D'know.' And she takes my hands from her forearms and squeezes them to her cheek. 'But I know you can't wait for me to figure it out to decide where you're going.'

7

There are hundreds of other MA and Ph.D. candidates in the hotel, moving like draftees from room to room (suite to suite in the case of the better proprietary universities), their vitae under their arms, their ties perfectly tied around their necks, sweat stains creeping into the armpits of many a suit jacket.

'Everyone's wearing a tie,' Leslie Ann says as we make our way down the hallway to the Loyola Marymount suite.

'That's why I'm not.'

I'm wearing what we call my 'dress' jeans (the ones without any holes yet), loafers with no socks, a ten-year-old button-down oxford-cloth shirt, and a sport jacket purchased the same day as the shirt at the same store.

'Are you trying not to get a job?' she asks.

'Certainly possible.'

I knock.

'Break a leg,' she says.

She pats me on the *tuchus* and settles onto the hallway floor to wait and watch the line of overeducated hopefuls moving from hope to hope.

I am reminded again that the thought of spending the rest of my life teaching college English is abhorrent, and so my interviews sound fatuous to me. It's only when I leave the second audition that the enormity of what rejection at this meat market will represent hits me – even though both Loyola and NYU assure me that I'll hear from them within six weeks, and each hints that I stand an excellent chance of winning their top-of-the-scale, tenure-track assistant professorship.

'That's wonderful,' says Leslie Ann.

'I'm sure they give the same assurances to everyone else who comes drooling and blathering to their doors.'

I'm heading for the lobby and an exit.

'Humor me,' she says, 'and go to the Harvard interview. Please.'

'I don't have an appointment. They'd be scandalized if I just showed up. And if we're not going to be together, Les, it doesn't matter where I go. It doesn't matter, frankly, *if* I go.'

'That's not fair, Jacob – to make me feel responsible for your life.'

As we're crossing the lobby to head for Chinatown and dinner, I am hailed by name by an enormous man in a three-piece western suit and cowboy boots.

'Who does he look like?' Leslie Ann whispers. 'He looks like someone.'

'I was hopin' I'd catch you before you left,' the cowboy says in a high, raspy voice, his eyes helplessly bouncing off me to linger on Leslie Ann, then wrenching themselves back to the business at hand. 'I'm a little disappointed you didn't sign up to interview with me.'

I glance at his name tag, trying to identify him so it doesn't look like I'm doing it in case I met him sometime and should remember.

'It's all right, I'm pullin' your leg,' he says with bibulous goodwill. 'You don't know me. I'm a former colleague of your beloved adviser and mentor at the University of Florida. He knows someone at Stanford who told him you were comin' out this year. He told me and I hunted you down.'

Beloved adviser and mentor? Who would that be? I can list the beloveds in my life on a couple of fingers. I did have an adviser at Gainesville, and I did take several courses with him once I settled into the English Department . . .

Froman? Freidlich. Frolech!

'Of course,' I say, paying my respects to his friend, my ol' mentor, 'Dr Frolech.'

'Who?'

'Dr Freidlich was my adviser. Good man.'

The cowboy's red-rimmed eyes are dubious at best. 'Freidlich?'

'Freyermuth!'

'Dr Donny Freund was your adviser – least, accordin' to him.'

'Of course! Donny Freund! Dr Don!'

I remember him vaguely now. Terrible teacher. As an adviser, who knows? I remember no advice, surely would have accepted none at that time in my life had any been offered.

I can feel in the pressure of Leslie Ann's hand in mine that she is prepared to become mirthful here and that we've settled this just in the nick of time.

'Your brain's prob'ly fried,' says the cowboy, 'from all the fun you've had today gittin' grilled by a buncha pompous assholes 'bout neorealism and postmodernism and the resta that hyphenated crap.'

Leslie Ann cocks her head at the cowboy.

I do, too.

'Tell you what. I promise not to grill you 'bout nothin'. But how about we have a drink. Whudduyou say, I'll just grab my gear.'

Before I can vacillate my way to an answer, he waddles back to the couch where he left his briefcase and suit bag. He must have been waiting for me on his way out.

'Jingles,' I whisper to Leslie Ann.

'Who?' she whispers back.

'Jingles.'

'Jingles!' She's got it.

In fact, the big gentleman looks a great deal like Andy Devine as Jingles in the old 'Adventures of Wild Bill Hickok' show. And seeing him as Jingles, I feel a rush of warmth for him. Wild Bill Hickok had a great influence on me in my cowboy days. I liked wearing my guns backward, the way Wild Bill and Jingles did. Anybody could wear his guns frontward. And my mother insisted I looked a great deal like a redheaded Guy Madison, whom the ladies at the cabana considered 'some kind of guy, that Guy,' and it was she who named me Slickguy Menscheim, an extremely uncowboylike name, I thought, but one that she seemed to relish using. (It became easier to swallow when my father explained to me that Menscheim, in translation, meant Heroman.)

'Been waitin' around this lobby for three hours,' Jingles says as he leads us into the bar, 'tryin' to get a lead on who you were, where I was going to intersect you. Stanford person described you by your lady friend here.' He winks at Leslie Ann. 'Couldn't afford to stay here like the regular scholars – too damn expensive. Stayed at a little dive down on the Embarcadero, met some strange damn people, I'll tell you.'

Leslie Ann is etching Jingles onto her memory for life.

When we're seated he says, 'I'm Dr Joel D'Amico, head of the English and Speech Departments at the University of New Mexico.'

'New Mexico,' says Leslie Ann.

'Yes, ma'am. Ever been there?' Dr Joel D'Amico hunches toward Leslie Ann, happy for an excuse to gaze on her.

'Grew up in Santa Fe.'

'Then you know it's God's country,' he says. And forcing his eyes from her to me again: 'Tell the truth, Mr Landau, haven't you always wanted to go to New Mexico? Cowboys, Indians? The Old West.'

'Well,' I say, 'New Mexico and Iceland – sort of a toss-up.'

Dr Joel D'Amico laughs a high-pitched, big fat guy laugh.

It's one thing to be too afraid of rejection to interview with Harvard, quite another to settle for New Mexico.

'Is there a professional theater company in Albuquerque yet?' Leslie Ann asks Dr Joel D'Amico.

The big cowboy has drained off his vodka martini before I've even put my glass of wine to my lips. 'Nope, sure isn't.' He says this with grave disappointment. Because, of course, he'd love Leslie Ann to come to New Mexico – with me or without me – just so he could see her around town occasionally and fantasize about her. 'But we got a fine Drama Department at UNM,' he says. 'That your field – theater?'

'Yes,' says Leslie Ann, 'I'm just finishing my MFA.'

'Well, I can sure take your name and have 'em contact you if there's a position comin' free next year.'

'That would be terrific.'

The enthusiasm of the one seems to infect the other, and now they are both reaching for paper and pen.

Leslie Ann opens her purse to get out the little notepad she carries for just such life-altering occasions.

'Les, Les, whoa, hold it!'

Both Leslie Ann and Dr Joel D'Amico stop in midreach and give me their undivided attention.

'You're going to go to New Mexico to teach drama?'

'Maybe.'

'No.'

'Why not?'

'Why not? Because,' I say through my teeth, 'you are destined for other things.'

She takes her hand out of her purse, flips it shut. It's as if we're in a movie and she's lost her head and I've had to slap her and now she's come back to her senses and the film can continue onward to its logical – though heartrending – end in which the two star-crossed lovers part.

Leslie Ann folds her hands in her lap, then unfolds them and takes hold of my nearer kneecap.

Becomes still.

'Welp, little lady,' says Dr Joel D'Amico, 'you change your mind, you know where to find me.'

Leslie Ann nods contritely.

'Now then, Mr Landau, here's what I can do for you, amigo. We've got a new president who thinks the Old West is going to be the new academic frontier here in the next coupla decades. So he's told us department heads to go on out and hire us some guns from reputable institutions.'

Dr Joel D'Amico's second vodka martini lands and disappears into his huge fist.

My father. He reminds me also of my father. Was that the initial unconscious attraction to Wild Bill and Jingles? Jakey and Morrie the Bear?

My father would play 'Guns' with me on the beach off the First Street Pier years before we moved uptown.

He'd put one of my cap guns into the waistband of
his abundant bathing shorts, and the two of us would
have a gunfight with outlaws, killing hundreds of them
before my pop suddenly took a bullet in the gut and did
a staggering, twirling death on the sand, pretending to
be dead, then coming back to life to say, 'Snakey' (to
my mother I was Slick Menscheim, to my father I was
Jake the Snake – Jake the Good Snake, as he noted
when he gave me the monicker, 'that doesn't bite them
he shouldn't, but eats rodents by the dozens') 'Snakey,
tell Hymie he may've got me, but good, in the person
of you, Jake the Snake, will prevail in the end.' (Hymie.
My father thought Hymie was a good Bad Guy name for
a western.) Then my father would die, then come back
to life to say in his best Polish cowboy accent, 'If you
could give him that message, Snakey, I would appreciate
it very much.' Then he would die for good.

He who grew up among real gunfights and lived to
cavort with his son on the sand would appreciate it if
I would tell the scum of the earth that in the end good
will out.

What strikes me now is the certainty that my father
did not then and I suspect does not now believe for a
single second that good will prevail.

To say nothing of my ability to be its advocate.

Dr Joel D'Amico has continued talking about the
virtues of New Mexico and he has perused my academic
file and letters of recommendation and he is saying
this now: 'I'll match whatever any other school offers
you. I'll put you on three-year tenure track; I'll pay
movin' expenses; and I'll guarantee you the year you
get tenure, you want it, you become head of the
department. After that, I can pret'near promise you,
six years of departmental administration, they'll throw

you an associate deanship; that tickles your fancy, from there, needless to say, you can start peekin' around at deanships and academic vice-presidencies. Time you're fifty, you're ready to go after a presidency somewhere. On toppa that, I'll teach you to eat red chile and drink tequila.'

He salutes me with his vodka martini and drains it.

Deanships? Academic vice-presidencies? Presidencies?

We're talkin' grown-up here, folks.

We're talkin' down the road.

A career in academe.

Middle age.

The future.

We're talkin' death, amigo.

8

On the way home after dinner my body begins sending signals that a more attentive person would take as the first hints of an impending, intensified rebellion from within.

The fist that seizes my chest is the same fist I came to know on the golf course ten years ago. The blow radiates out from my sternum and reverberates along my brain stem, setting off thousands of electrical shocks in my upper body. The pressure seems to increase with the gnawing fear that I don't want to be anything like what I'm on course to become.

And so, it is on the ride home that evening that I do some deep breathing and, when the fist has let loose, tell Leslie Ann Masterson that I'm writing a play for her.

I'm not sure what I expect her reaction to this announcement to be. Surprise . . . gratitude . . .

Disdain . . .

She has her arm across the back of my seat, her hand on my neck; a moment ago her fingers were gently stroking. Now her fingers are still, her eyes are on the freeway, and it seems that she remains like that for minutes, miles.

In fact, it's only a few seconds before she asks simply, 'What about your dissertation?'

Endeavoring to appear as if I agree that lack of interest is the way to approach something I want approached in just the opposite manner, I say, 'Finished for all intents and purposes.'

'What's it about?'

'The play?'

'Of course.'

'Rather not talk about it just yet.'

And now she looks at me. In the amber light from the dashboard, I see in her eyes not so much a question as to my motive here as a deep flicker of disbelief that I can pull it off. That, at least, would explain the seeming disinterest.

'Okay,' she says, 'but you better hurry. I'm gone in three months.'

Gone in three months.

With a recklessness that comes from hurt and anger, I tell her, 'I've almost finished a first draft.'

But now I can see out of the corner of my eye her chest going up and down, and I realize she's not disinterested at all. She not only believes my lie, but she's not surprised to hear it.

She's not surprised I'm writing a play.

Which I'm not.

But will be within the hour.

'Howard has a slot in March for his thesis directing project,' she says, and I can hear the nervousness in her voice. 'I know he's looking for a new play, but he doesn't like anything any of the playwrighting students have done.'

I assure her, 'He'll like *Who Stalk the Tiger.*'

'That's the title?'

'What do you think?'

'Good sound. What's it mean?'

Winging it: 'From the Blake poem.'

'What Blake poem?'

'Tyger, Tyger burning bright! . . .'

'I don't get it,' she says.

'Everyone,' I explain, as if I've given this a good deal of thought, 'thinks he can stalk the tiger – the beast, the opiate, the obsession within – and once caught, cohabit with it; but only the most gifted, the truly fearless, those who are truly willing to face death, can capture and control this powerful and fearsome metaphoric beast. It takes most people their whole lives to admit to their limitations.'

'How many characters?'

'Three,' I say.

'Love triangle,' she presumes.

'Is that bad?'

'Certainly not.'

'Love triangle,' I confess.

'Tell me one thing about my character.'

And I hear my mouth announce, 'She has multiple sclerosis.'

And beside me, Leslie Ann's fingers grip my arm and in her voice there is both relief and triumph. 'Oh, Jacob, I knew it! Have you ever . . . have you ever . . . just *known* a thing was going to happen but for a long time you started to think it wasn't and then it did but you were terrified it wasn't going to be what you dreamed it would be if it did but then it turns out it *is*?'

I look from the freeway to her and I begin to laugh because I'm so relieved that she's so happy.

And she begins to laugh and she clutches me around the neck and we almost take a flyer into an eighteen-wheeler parked on the soft shoulder and buy it before we get to see what our new future holds.

9

It's midnight when we get home, but while Leslie Ann removes her makeup and washes her face, I go to my desk and roll a piece of typing paper into my Corona.

I stare at the sheet of paper. How do you write a play?

First you set tabs that are different from those you use to write a dissertation.

Then?

Then somebody says something or does something and somebody else responds and you're writing a play.

Simple.

Independent of me, my fingers poise above the keys.

And then they type D-A-P-H-N-E and write for her this line: 'I want to do something unforgivable to the person I love most in the world.'

Amazingly, someone named W-A-R-R-E-N answers, 'I'm the guy can help you get the job done.'

When Leslie Ann comes out of the bathroom, I tell her I'm going to write for a while.

She says she's not sleepy, either, and since I've finished my dissertation, can she read it?

Absently I push it across the desk at her.

Over the next ten hours I stop to pee twice and at some point eat a sliced kiwi that appears at my elbow.

I'm dimly conscious of Leslie Ann sitting on the floor in her corner behind the dining table, her head bent to Gertrude Stein and company, and that the pile of pages in her lap diminishes and grows beside her on the carpet as the pile of clean white sheets to my left diminishes as pieces of it pass through my typewriter and grow on my right.

I don't stop typing until it's time to dress to teach my Comp class in the morning.

By then she has finished the two hundred ten pages of my dissertation.

While I shave she says, 'It was very powerful.'

I am soaring on the rampaging actions and images in my head. I think she's talking about the play.

'How do you know?' I ask her.

'I just finished it.'

'How could you? Oh' – I'm disappointed; for a moment I think I've finished the play and she's passed favorable judgment on it – 'you're talking about my dissertation.'

'What'd you think I was talking about?'

'My play.'

'I haven't read it.'

'I know. You're saying my dissertation is very power-ful. Good. Great.'

I could care less.

'Can I tell you something?'

'Absolutely.'

'It troubles me.'

'That's good.'

What'd she say? What troubles her? My dissertation troubles her?

'Why – what?'

'You don't want to hear this.'

'Of course I want to hear it. What? Tell me – but fast, I have to go.'

'You rip those people to shreds.'

I am trying to remain focused on the various fictional balls I threw into the air these last hours, to keep them revolving and intersecting. I don't want to talk about my dissertation!

'I don't rip them to shreds. I analyze their work and the impulses of the times. I laud them and I – '

'Jacob,' she says, and it strikes me distantly that in the months we've lived together, neither of us has ever interrupted the other. We have always let the other finish his or her sentences.

I watch her in the mirror as I continue shaving. In the doorway she's shaving with me, unconsciously moving her face in a miniature version of my movements as I tense this acreage, then that.

'I know I don't know these people the way you do, but Stein, Hemingway, Picasso – these people were pioneers, weren't they? I mean, they were fearless, reckless, extraordinary people, right?'

'More or less.'

'Okay, but what I wonder is if because you're afraid you can't do what they did, you've ripped them to shreds under the camouflage of scholarly criticism. You've cut them down to our size.'

The airborne balls crash around me. I know immediately that she's right. For a year and half I didn't know, and in an instant I do.

I also know that she shouldn't say 'our' size.

It's my size we're talking about.

I have spent a year and a half writing something that is merely indicative of everything that's wrong with me.

I take a towel to my face, disappear behind it. *What do I do – erupt in righteous indignation, bury her under a persiflage of language?*

'Maybe I'm wrong,' she says.

I pat my face.

'Maybe I don't understand the purpose of scholarly writing.'

The purpose of scholarly writing is to hide one's envy of the thing being written about in a scholarly manner.

Pat pat pat.

'I'm probably wrong,' she says.

Pat pat pat pat pat.

'Am I wrong, Jacob?'

A direct question. Have to come out from behind the towel.

'No,' I say, 'you're right.' I make myself look my accuser in the eyes. 'So what do I do about it? Do I junk the piece of crap and spend another year here writing another one or rewriting this one?'

I snap the towel into the sink and bolt from the bathroom, compounding my guilt with petulance.

I look at the manuscript piled in perfect symmetry on the dining table. I've sensed for at least a year what I haven't had the guts to know: I hate my dissertation! I thought all along it was because I believed Stein, Hemingway, et al. were pitifully overrated and I was unjustly stuck living with these blowhards in the service of future generations of literature students.

I grab the manuscript off the dining table and hurl it against the wall. The two hundred ten pages spread about the room, a blizzard of eight-and-a-half-by-eleven-inch snowflakes.

'Oh, Jakey,' says Leslie Ann, managing to make the words both remonstrative and sympathetic at the same time.

She gets on her knees and begins to scoop the pages together, tending the wounded from a wreck.

I go to a neutral corner, stand facing her.

'Somebody has to write things like this to help other people put the truth in perspective. Right?'

I don't respond.

'Just think of it like you've written something in which you've successfully portrayed a point of view you no longer hold. Let it go. It's done.'

I slide along the wall, out of the corner and away from her to the closet.

By the time I'm dressed and ready to go out the door to teach my class, educate young minds to my view of world literature, my manuscript sits stacked once again in lopsided symmetry on my desk.

'Jacob,' she says.

She wraps a corner of her T-shirt around her index finger and cleans shaving cream from the rim of my ear.

The sweet pinkness of her brassiere peeks out from under the T-shirt.

'Look at me.'

I do.

'This is important.'

I nod.

'One thing's for sure. You can write. I always figured you could. But you have to go deeper. To where real feeling, real truth, lives. Go there, Jakey.'

Her look reminds me of what I see when she looks at Darlene Delvecchio the night I meet her at Howard Bellman's, the moment at which I fall in love with her.

It's a look of infinite sadness for a cripple.

'No fear,' she says. 'Please.'

The 'please,' it seems to me, is less plea than threat.

10

I don't know why I follow Leslie Ann on her weekly shopping excursion Saturday.

Part of it has to do with feeling under siege by this play I'm supposedly writing and part of it has to do with the fact that Leslie Ann seems agitated and doesn't want me to go with her today.

'I need a break, a little air,' I say with my new artistic weariness, indicating the pile of pages beside my typewriter.

'You don't have time for a break,' she says. 'You need a little air, open the window. You've got to show it to Howard soon or he's going to have something else.'

Instant adult: 'You're right.'

She's distracted. Glances at her watch, kisses me, hustles out the door.

I peer around the corner of the stairwell in the garage, watching the big DeSoto lumber out onto the street.

Then leap into my V-dub and tail her onto the freeway.

I love her driving, though I hate being driven by her. She drives exactly the speed limit.

'Why?' I asked her the first – and last – time I let her drive on our Saturday shopping trip.

'Why would they set speed limits if they didn't want you to drive them?'

She drives first half an hour to San Jose to buy vegetables at the farmers' market, the closest farmers' market to us with vegetables Leslie Ann considers guaranteed free of pesticides. She talks to the cucumber farmer for twenty minutes; gives equal time to the cilantro lady, though the cilantro lady must say something really funny because Leslie Ann unleashes a beauty of a laugh midway through the stop.

She drives twenty minutes back to Mountain View and the only Japanese butcher from whom she'll buy the fresh tuna for our sushi. We argue not long ago when Leslie Ann, holding a handful of the man's sliced maroon fish meat toward me, proclaims the gentleman an artist as great as any I can name. I look respectfully at the sliced flesh and fiber and tell Leslie Ann she's full of shit. Titian's an artist, I proclaim. Tennyson's an artist. You're an artist. A Jap who slices fish, I tell her, is a butcher.

Leslie Ann does not bend.

From hiding I watch the man chop the head off a fresh tuna and pop the eyeballs. He offers one to Leslie Ann, keeps the other for himself; in sync, they chew fish eyeballs as the man begins to trim and slice.

Our dinner in hand, she strolls down the block, singing something quietly to herself.

She takes a stool in her favorite health bar, where she shoots the breeze with the vitamin 'counselor' and has what I assume is a 'carrot blitz' – a favorite treat, available only here, concocted from a secret Middle Eastern recipe she suspects without fear contains the thyroid secretion of some unnamed mammal.

And now she glances at her watch, presses her fingers to her temples. Squeezes. She has remembered, perhaps, whatever it is that's making her uneasy today.

She leaves the health bar quickly and, actually exceeding the speed limit by two miles an hour, drives back to an office building in Palo Alto. By the time I slip into the lobby, she's disappeared. The complex houses many people – dentists, doctors, and lawyers; four public welfare agencies; a caterer.

I go back to my car and wait. Eventually she comes out. She cocks her head at the sky for a long time, her gaze fixed and unmoving.

She gets into the antediluvian DeSoto and drives to a place in Sunnyvale it never occurred to me might be there, a place with a big sign out front that says 'Big Vince Carmine. Ford/Lincoln/Mercury.'

Margaret Jewel Masterson Carmine Masterson parks her car at the outskirts of the used car lot and sits.

Waiting.

It's noon and no more than a minute before a big, handsome, curly-haired, gray guy in his late forties I assume is Big Vince himself walks out of the showroom and gets into a flashy little Mustang, which, given Big Vince's good size, he appears to be wearing around his waist. With him is a woman about thirty in a miniskirt that starts – or stops – about half an inch from that little inverted shelf that makes women's asses the extraordinary things they are.

They pull out, Leslie Ann behind them, me behind her.

Big Vince drives several blocks to a Howdy Burger Drive-In and fires into a space with a recklessness and a squandering of rubber meant, no doubt, to sell a Mustang or two. Leslie Ann slips into a space several over, me into one several spaces from her, a battleship-size Imperial and a little Nash Rambler between us. Big Vince revs his engine and gives his horn a shove, unleashing a shrill whistle used once upon a time to let a girl know of a boy's lascivious interest in her. For yet another moment, Big

Vince has the attention of every prospective car buyer in the joint.

Leslie Ann watches Big Vince Carmine, and I watch her watch him. All this watching, I sense, has something to do with Leslie Ann looking at the sky.

Big Vince orders, giving the carhop a shameless pat on her haunch as she turns to make her exit. I didn't think there were guys who actually did things like that outside the movies. The same carhop addresses Leslie Ann, and if I'm not mistaken, Leslie Ann asks the carhop what Big Vince ordered. Leslie Ann shakes her head – Big Vince must have ordered some real crap. I try to read Leslie Ann's lips; I think she orders an iced tea. When the carhop comes to me, I order a Coke, a Howdy Burger Supreme, and a large fries, then guiltily change the order to an iced tea also. The carhop isn't thrilled to have two of her valuable lunchtime spaces held down by a pair of iced teas. I'll leave a buck and a note telling her to pray Leslie Ann doesn't look at the sky again.

Leslie Ann gets out of her car and casually – never so much as glancing his way – strolls past her stepfather's Mustang and into the ladies' room. Moments later she exits the ladies' room, strolls past Big Vince again, and gets back into the DeSoto.

Then she snaps her fingers as if she's forgotten something, gets out of the DeSoto, and strolls past Big Vince and into the ladies' room again.

She exits the ladies' room immediately, but instead of strolling past Big Vince for the fourth time, she stops, puts her foot up on Big Vince's bumper, and ties her rough-out boot.

Ties her rough-out boot?

It doesn't have a shoelace.

I'm either watching a great actress putting on a terrible

performance or there's something of great consequence
going on here in the life of a human being, about which
I am more than a little bit apprehensive and totally
ignorant.

Just as I was ignorant of the fact that her stepfather
lives and works within spitting distance of us.

Now Leslie Ann sort of gives Big Vince's bumper a
little jolt.

How can he fail to notice her?

How? By being totally intent on what's going on below
eye level in the front seat of the Mustang, an area to which
the head of Big Vince's companion has disappeared.

A blow job at the Howdy Burger? Surely not!

Leslie Ann finishes tying her laceless boot and continues back to the DeSoto.

I slip out of my VW and creep behind the five cars
separating me from Big Vince Carmine's Mustang,
crouching low behind Leslie Ann's tank. When I reach
the Mustang, I half rise as if I've injured my back and
hobble past the passenger side of Big Vince's little car,
peering down into the front seat, where, sure enough,
the woman's head rises and sinks pneumatically around
Big Vince's wang.

And here comes Leslie Ann again, strolling for the
ladies' room. I hunker down and scamper behind the
Mustang, waiting for Leslie Ann to pass so I can return
to my car.

But Leslie Ann doesn't pass. Instead she pretends to
recognize her stepfather. 'Why, Big Vince,' she says as
if this were really a coincidence of some size.

'Huh?' says Big Vince, and I can feel the car
shift as the woman whips up from Big Vince's
lap, belting her head pretty good on the steering wheel.

'Found it,' she says, going with the old you-couldn't-see-me-because-I-was-looking-for-something-on-the-floor gambit.

I can tell Leslie Ann is at the driver's window now.

'What a coincidence,' says Leslie Ann. 'I didn't know you ate here.'

Big Vince's answer, meant to be an affirmation of the popularity of the Howdy Burger, is something like 'Ohrgridp!'

'How's Mrs Carmine?' asks Leslie Ann.

'Fine, fine, good, great,' says Big Vince. 'She's just . . . she's . . . great.'

'That's good,' says Leslie Ann.

'She's great,' says Big Vince.

'Tell her I said hey,' says Leslie Ann.

'I will,' says Big Vince. 'I sure will, Maggie.'

'I'm just parked right down there,' says Leslie Ann.

'Well, I'll be darned,' says Big Vince.

'I'm just having an iced tea,' she says.

'How do you like that,' says Big Vince, and does not invite Leslie Ann to join him and the blow job artist who isn't his wife.

I want to jump from hiding and scream: 'Can't you tell she needs something from you, asshole!'

Something, it occurs to me, she obviously doesn't think she can get from me.

The carhop arrives with Big Vince's order. She glances at me crouched at the back of Big Vince's car. I pretend to be inspecting the tarmac for cracks.

She's seen stranger things. She lets it go.

'Welp,' says Leslie Ann, 'here's your order.'

'Here it is!' says Big Vince. 'Drop by the dealership sometime. I never see you anymore.'

'I will. I'll drop by first chance I get.'

'And be sure to tell your friend and mine next time you talk to her that I'm doing great – you want to do that for me?'

'I will, Big Vince,' says Leslie Ann. 'I'll tell her.'

'You do that for me and I will be forever in your debt.'

Dismissed, Leslie Ann doesn't move. 'Did you happen to see me,' she asks, 'in *The Taming of the Shrew*?'

'Shoot, you know now, Maggie, I had your little announcement right on my desk there, and wouldn't you know, every night I thought I was going to get over there, something come up at the dealership, and would you believe, I never did get there.'

'Oh, well,' says Leslie Ann, 'I know how busy you get.'

'Car business,' says Big Vince.

'How's your golf game?'

'Single-digit handicap – finally.'

'Oh, that's great, Big Vince.'

'I knew you'd be proud.'

'Welp,' says Leslie Ann. 'Bye-bye, Big Vince.'

'Ciao, Maggie, you take care.'

'Oh, I will, don't you worry. I know how you worry, and I don't want you to, okay?'

'Well, you know me, but if you say so.'

What person, what *situation*, can take someone like Leslie Ann Masterson, an extraordinarily gifted actor, an oracle and seer, and reduce her to a blithering, infantile idiot?

Leslie Ann heads for the DeSoto, and I stand up and walk to the blow job artist's side of the car. On the back seat are a serious set of golf clubs in a serious leather golf bag; the towel hooked to the bag looks damp. Big Vince must have played this morning.

Big Vince and the B.J. artist follow Leslie Ann's exit. As Big Vince reaches for the B.J. artist's neck to return her to her appointed round, I lean in the window.

'How you guys doin'?'

Instinctively the B.J. artist says, 'Jesus and Mary,' and crosses herself. She knows who I am.

'What can I do for you, young man?'

I flip my wallet open to my student ID card, an official- and ornate-looking document. 'Todd Felker, private investigator,' I inform them, and flip the wallet shut.

'Oh, shit,' says the B.J. artist. I have confirmed her worst fear.

'Just wanted to let you two clowns know I nailed you.'

The big DeSoto lurches and belches away from the Howdy Burger, and I start casually away from the Mustang.

'Wait a minute there, buddy boy!' says Big Vince.

I get into my V-dub, logging Leslie Ann's direction.

Big Vince lumbers out of the Mustang. 'C'mere!' he calls in what's supposed to be a good-natured command. 'Lemme see your badge, I didn't see any badge!'

As I back out, Big Vince appends himself to my window. 'Whoa, whoa, whoa, hey, hey, hey, pal, young fella, what's the hurry?'

I disengage the clutch. 'What's on your mind?' I ask Big Vince.

He sticks his formidable head into the front compartment of my V-dub, and it occurs to me that this guy might very well be able to do sizable damage to me should he, say, get his ham hocks around my neck. But this is good – the adrenaline pumping feels good, the fear is titillating.

'You got photos?' he wants to know, nailing me with a blast of Sen-Sen breath.

'Photos?' I say. 'I got oil paintings.' And I floor it, throwing Big Vince off my running board and almost taking his head with me.

'Son of a bitch!' Big Vince screams.

My heart is pounding. I check myself out in the rearview mirror – glimpse Big Vince with raised fist receding behind me – and give my visage in the mirror a big smile.

Leslie Ann heads through the foothills to the ocean, pushing the old battle wagon to its limit, smoke streaming from its tailpipes like vomit.

What is it not to be willing or able to share your problems and darkest secrets with other people?

I have wondered many times if my father has ever told my mother the whole truth. He's always seemed to treat her with great respect; she's always seemed to treat him, for all his size, like a . . . puppy.

Did his respect for her come from her response to his agonies or from admiring her strength in living with him all these years without knowing him?

Leslie Ann parks the DeSoto on a cliff and climbs down to the beach where we have come a half dozen times to collect mussels.

I climb down after her. She's sitting on the sand, her hands burrowing down deep. I know she's feeling the grains, the mass.

I walk up behind her, drop to my knees, and take her in my arms from behind.

'Hi,' I say.

She's startled by my touch, recoils from it. Then is pleased to see me. And now frightened. 'What are you doing here?' she wants to know. 'What's the matter?' –

as if I might be in trouble and so intersected her here for help.

'Finally had to take a break. Don't punish me, okay? Great minds think alike, I guess.'

An almost maternal tenderness spills out of her, and she pulls my head to her shoulder. 'You okay?' she asks.

'Absolutely.'

The soft back of her hand moves along my jawline. 'You sure?'

'Yep. What about you?'

'Me? I'm great. Need to bounce any ideas for the play off me?'

I take her hands, dust them. 'Actually,' I say, 'I was thinking about buying you a new car for graduation.'

'Why?'

'Can't go off to become famous in an old DeSoto.'

'Where you going to get the money?'

I shrug, squeeze her tightly around the waist, joining us back to front. She presses her head back on my shoulder.

Stares out to sea.

Tell me! Tell me what it is that made you look at the sky. Tell me what you feel about your unloving, insensitive stepfather having his cock sucked by some woman who isn't your stepmother or his wife, tell me all that remains to be told, and bind yourself to me for all time.

'What have you been doing?' I ask when she takes no more than that nibble at automobiles.

'Oh,' she says, 'I just did the shopping and felt like coming here for a minute.'

And she's silent, breathing the sea air deeply.

And it occurs to me that she can't share her agonies

with me because she's afraid if she does, I won't be able to love her.

The same might be true of my father.

What was done to each of them – or what each of them did – must be, or seem to be, unforgivable.

How do I deal with that?

Later that afternoon Leslie Ann is ironing while I translate Old English, and through my bookcases I catch a moment I'm not supposed to catch: she has a look on her face that I can only call *loving*. My first thought is she's simply ruminating on one thing or another. But then I sense that this loving look is directed at whatever it is she's ironing. The look on her face takes on a slightly different shape. Still loving, but touched with sadness.

I shift and lift on the desk chair.

Stretched across the ironing board is one of my T-shirts.

Sensing my movement and my eyes from behind the wall of books, Leslie Ann comes back from wherever she was and smiles at me, embarrassed.

'What's the matter?' I ask.

'Nothing,' she says, and begins to iron again, with all too apparent lack of interest in the T-shirt.

'Why were you looking at my T-shirt like that?'

She peers through the bookcases at me. She thinks only momentarily of trying to float a lie and then just tells the truth. 'When I'm ironing my clothes, they're just clothes, but yours are you.'

I get up and go around the bookcases. Her face is constricted in an effort not to let the tears that are welling in her eyes run down her face.

'I can never escape me, but you could. I could lose you. Or I could be with you all my life, but someday

you could die and I wouldn't be with you anymore.'
  What's this about?
  I hold her so tightly that I hear vertebrae adjusting.

11

Three days later I hand her the first draft of *Who Stalk the Tiger*, a three-character play about someone like who I imagine Leslie Ann could be if she were Darlene Delvecchio and someone who I imagine I could be if I hadn't met Leslie Ann and someone who I imagine someone else I can't identify and I hope I never meet could be.

In a hundred and thirty-six pages, the three of them make a shambles of each other's lives, the play ending with all three alone, any chance of reconciliation or commitment among them destroyed by the machinations of their pursuit and denial of each other.

She says she doesn't want me to watch her read, so she closes herself into the bathroom. I prostrate myself on the floor outside, peering through the crack at the bottom of the door. I can see her legs and the elastic of her pale blue satin panties at the edge of her khaki shorts. I can see those delicate fingers make a pile of pages that two hours later finally includes all the pages I wrote.

She tugs at the edge of her panties and stands up.

I roll away from the door just before it opens. She stands above me. I pretend to be sleeping.

I want her to get down beside me, like she does in the morning, and wake me with soft voice and mouth against my ear. But she nudges me with her foot.

'Oh, hi,' I say sleepily, expanding my acting repertoire to include not only a man who just wakes up but who also has a bad taste in his mouth from being asleep. 'What do you think?' I ask, as if the answer to that is, at best, of marginal interest.

'The female character – Daphne – stinks. The rest: good.'

'What do you mean the female character . . . Just *good* – the rest?'

'When I say good, I mean good. The rest of the play is good.'

Spoken thus, judgment is immutable, and one weight lifts from my chest as another descends.

'How good – the rest?'

'Depends on how much better it gets in phase two.'

'Which is?'

'Taking what's good and making it better; taking what's bad – Daphne – and making her at least good. Going to take guts.'

'You think I don't have the requisite guts?'

'I didn't say that.'

'What's wrong with Daphne?'

'The implication that she initiates all this havoc because of something that happened in her past, without ever divulging what it is, is a copout. It also sounds like you don't know and you're pinning everything on something that never gets explained. The play shouldn't turn on this muscle disease that may or may not turn her into a vegetable or kill her.'

'I see. Anything else?'

'Yes. The big thing. She's a heterosexual male's view of a woman. She's explained, narrated, summarized. Gotta get to the female inside you to find her.'

'What's that mean?'

'Just what I said. You want to write a female character, put the female in you on the job and then just let her

behave like you let the men behave; let her act and react.
You don't think you can do it, just write men. Let's go
next door and give it to Howard.'

She's on her way to the door.

'Wait a second! *What* female in me?'

'Writers – good ones – have to be androgynous. You're
afraid somebody will think you're queer if you let the
woman loose in you. Let's go.'

She heads for the door again.

'Wait a minute!'

She waits.

'You think he'll like it – Howard?'

'Have to let him read it before we can find that out,
won't we?'

No indulgence. The woman who decides the fate and
genetic makeup of novice playwrights is not the woman
who irons my T-shirts.

12

We knock on Howard Bellman's door. He opens it, is eating a bowl of fruity, yogurty, grainy mush. His mouth is full and, as always, a little bit of whatever it is adorns his beard.

'How you doin', assholes?'

'Got your thesis play yet, Howard?'

'Couple of possibilities – what's it to you, Nips?'

It does not please me that he calls her Nips and Tits, but I am here on a mission of high self-service, so having kept silent this long, I am not about to speak at this particular juncture.

Leslie Ann holds my manuscript out in both hands, title page up. 'Read this.'

He looks at it as if it's some unidentifiable *thing* that in no way stimulates his interest. 'What is it?'

'What's it look like?'

He knows what it is.

He fills his face with the stuff in the bowl and gurgles, 'Who wrote it?'

He knows who wrote it.

'You know who wrote it,' she says.

Howard Bellman looks at me, looks at my script, looks at Leslie Ann, chews.

'Read it now. We'll be home. Wipe your mouth.'

She drops the script on his doormat and walks back into our apartment, leaving me momentarily alone with

Howard. He bends over unwillingly to pick up the only copy of my play.

'I'm really excited,' he says, and closes his door in my face.

13

An hour and eighteen minutes later, our bell rings. I get up to answer.

Leslie Ann whispers, 'No, I've got it. You pretend to be asleep like you did with me, but be more convincing.'

'You think I wasn't asleep?'

'You want to argue about it now?'

'No.'

I compose myself on the couch, going through three poses before she opens the door and I'm forced to go with the one I'm in – a kind of 'Thinker Meets Dead Body' impression that Leslie Ann shakes me gently out of moments later.

'Howard's here, Jakey.'

'Oh – gee, must've dozed off. Where is he?' I try to locate Howard in the vast reaches of our closet-size studio apartment. Accomplishing this, I invite him to approach His Eminence the Playwright: 'Come in, Howard, please, come in.'

Howard cocks his hip at me in front of the sofa, holding my play on the palm of one hand like a small, dead, fetid rodent, but then says quietly, and if not quite reverentially, certainly earnestly, 'This play . . .'

My heart pounds so hard my eyeballs swell.

'This play is an unmitigated piece of shit.'

I am fifteen again. That putt is on its way, turning over and over on its way uphill against the grain, destined to end up short, right! Then something fulminates in my chest as it did several weeks after that missed putt when they had to carry me off the course in Bethesda with what was not a heart attack.

Now, eleven years later, that pain threatens the boundaries of my body, my hands turn to fists at my side.

To Howard's side, Leslie Ann stares out our window at the freeway and says quietly, 'You're a goddamn liar, Howard.'

The whites of Howard Bellman's eyes disappear almost entirely behind his eyelids as they narrow at her. 'Fine,' he says, 'so actually it's pretty good.'

He fixes on me now without subterfuge. 'Answer yes or no to the following questions: You afraid to hear suggestions that'll send you running back to the typewriter in a rage at me every day for the next five weeks?'

'Yes,' I say.

'Afraid to have other people roaming around your psyche complaining endlessly that what you've written isn't sufficient?'

'Yes.'

'Afraid to have hundreds of people come in and acquit or dismiss you with an adjective or two?'

'Jesus, yes.'

'Afraid to ultimately fail?'

'More than anything.'

'Good. Now go get a notepad and a pencil, and sit your ass down at the table. We're going to kick this puppy around till its tits bleed.'

Notepad and pencil in place at the dining room table, Leslie Ann and I sit forward, Howard sits back. Howard sits forward, I lean back, Leslie Ann remains still.

'First thing,' he says, 'no three-act plays. Can't get

today's braindead audience back from two intermissions. They're used to TV, paying attention for eight minutes, then getting a snack, taking a piss, talking about the abundance of pointless issues on their functionally illiterate minds. They want their culture compressed, obvious, easy. Gotta cut thirty pages outta this sucker and build one big act break.'

'Cut thirty – '

'Just shut up. Don't argue, don't defend, don't explain – nobody gives a damn what you think, what you intended, what you can't possibly live without, what glorious metaphors and symbols and themes are contained herein – especially me!'

Beneath the table, Leslie Ann's hand comes reassuringly to my knee.

'Do yourself a big favor,' Howard says, 'and don't fall in love with any of this crap. You'll never miss a cut. You do – it'll show up in a later draft, you'll write your way back to it, it'll refuse to die. Next: The character modeled after me is one-dimensional; you obviously don't understand the sociopathic personality.'

'What character modeled after you?'

'What character modeled after me do you think, Peckerhead?'

Leslie Ann looks at me curiously, as if she knew all along and she's wondering if I really knew and am pretending not to, or if I really didn't know that the character like someone I couldn't identify is Howard Bellman, thus making the triangle some subconscious fantasy horror story involving the three of us (plus Darlene).

'Fine,' I say, 'I'll study you.'

'See that you do. I don't like being misrepresented or underrated. Just don't expect me to show you the truth.'

In some peculiar way, I feel warm toward Howard Bellman for the first time.

'Leslie Ann says Daphne's no good,' I tell him, 'that I don't understand women.'

'Nips is full of shit. She just doesn't want to play a crippled cunt.'

'Daphne's not a crippled cunt,' I say.

'She's not a crippled cunt,' says Howard, 'we got no play.'

'How do you figure?'

'We gotta pit Nips and her disease and me against you. You're reasonably intelligent, honest, naive, uncommitted – in other words, Everyschmuck. Nobody's going to want to admit they're you. I'm your flip side. Secret: Make me a multileveled demon, one the audience finally has to reject, attractive though I may be. And leave her a crippled cunt. Everybody says they do, but the truth is nobody really has any sympathy or admiration for this so-called liberated woman everybody's babbling about, even other so-called liberated women, and everybody hates people wobbling around on crutches trying to be noble.'

'That's ridiculous,' says Leslie Ann.

'Shut the fuck up, Tits!'

As if Howard hasn't spoken, let alone insulted her, Leslie Ann says, 'If it's clear the playwright doesn't respect my character – '

'Am I directing, Nips, or are you?'

'You.'

'You want to be in my thesis project, Miss Nipples?'

'Yep.'

'You sure? Because there are only half a dozen other coozes would jump at it.'

'Oh, please let me be in it, Mr Bellman.'

'Then trust me. Shut your mouth and be a cunt.'

Leslie Ann's fingers remain easily on my knee under the table. I connect her ease with Howard's vulgarity to the night I met her, to her lack of fear of Howard in his drunken rage.

On the other hand, maybe it's a relief to her to be disparaged.

To me, Howard says, 'And if I'm offending you by offending her, Landau, that's tough! She's an actor. She's a piece of meat. She thinks her brain matter is required to get this thing on. It isn't. Like it or not, everybody's got to trust me to know where *you* want to go with this thing, what *you* may not even know you intended to write, and then to let me drive everybody there. You don't like where that is once we get there, you can always go back to what you handed me today. And there are no rules, no restrictions, no riders. I do what I need to do to get the work done.'

He offers his hand and thrusts his face upward at mine. 'You in, you out?'

14

I am reeducated to 'playing' team sports, but in this team sport it seems it is the chief role – or 'obligation,' as Howard puts it – of my teammates to remind me that no matter what I do to improve my play, I've got to do more, or other people, audiences and critics, are going to come into the theater and they – my teammates – are going to be humiliated because I haven't provided them with what they need to soothe and satisfy those audiences and critics.

I tell Howard not to put that kind of pressure on me.

He tells me to go fuck myself.

Leslie Ann gives tacit support to his point of view.

So he and the actors fight with me, debate with me; they lacerate and accuse and cajole and, according to Leslie Ann, love me.

'Love in the sense,' she says driving home one night, 'that we – you and me and Howard and the guys, these people depending on you – all of us bring the best of ourselves into the rehearsal and leave all those things that can get in the way of the work outside. That's why I don't hang around with other people in the program any more than I have to. I don't want to know all the personal things about them that would diminish them when I meet them as these grander people we get to pretend to be on the stage. All that matters in the room is the work. Your play. Our exploring and refining and personifying the stuff of your imagination.'

It sounds great when she says it, but I am bloody from hours of this 'love,' and I am damp and smelly from flop sweat, fearful that I am not equal to the task.

She buries her face against my chest. 'Oh, God, don't you just love it?' she asks.

'Oh, Jesus,' I lie to her, 'I do.'

And I do. I love being at the center of Leslie Ann's world.

But I don't *just* love it. I *almost* just love it. But falling just short of that, what's left is loathing.

Because despite the real feelings of camaraderie, of teamwork, of shared purpose, the hugging and massaging and sharing of health food products and yoga exercises, I am not only always under siege to make things better, but quite simply I am, no kidding around, the person on whom all these people are dependent for success.

There is no way they can be any better than I make it possible for them to be.

Yet I have the feeling this process simply isn't as important to me as it is to her and them and as they all assume it is to me.

And if it isn't as important to me, why isn't it?

Because it's not fit work for someone on the edge of adulthood? Because it's make-believe and not real life?

Don't know. But as a means of deciding, I have the opportunity to compare the two.

15

Real Life vs. Theater Experience:

HOWARD: This eats the big one, this reason – that she wanted to be a dancer and she broke her ankle at fifteen and didn't have the strength and parental support to come back, and now she's got this disease? It's boring, it's a cliché, it's fucking television.

ME: I agree.

HOWARD: That's it? Just like that?

ME: Yeah. (To Leslie Ann) What would be a good incident from her past to affect her present?

LESLIE ANN: You're the writer. I'll just end up giving you something personal. I want to be your view of her filtered through me. Not mine filtered through you.

I want to use her father's abuse of her, of course, but don't want to just come out and say so.

And then a murky notion strikes me, murky because I have no premonition about what I might hear should I find a way to get an honest answer.

Or maybe I just want an excuse to play golf.

In any event, the following morning, Thursday, I sit across the street from Big Vince Carmine's house just before dawn.

That day at the Howdy Burger, Big Vince told Leslie Ann he has a single-digit handicap. You don't maintain a single-digit handicap by not playing. The towel on his bag was still damp at noon that day. He must have played before work. If I'm right, he'll play this morning, and if not this morning, tomorrow morning.

('Doing?' Leslie Ann mumbles when she feels me slide from beneath her leg a few minutes past five this morning.

'Take a drive. Think. Want to make some changes in the Ping-Pong scene.'

'Mm,' she says, and leans her lips my way for a kiss.)

At five-thirty Big Vince Carmine, a symphony in polyester, gets into his Mustang and, with me on his tail, drives to the university golf course.

While he's getting his bag out of the trunk and putting on his cleats, I precede him into the clubhouse, show my student ID, check out a set of rental clubs, and buy a box of three Titleist golf balls.

When I see Big Vince rounding the bend, I ask the young woman behind the desk, 'Any chance of picking up a game?'

As Big Vince walks in the door, she says, 'Well, all the early tee times are threesomes and foursomes.'

Big Vince is shorter and wider than I remember, with a gut that was probably once muscle – an interior lineman, I would guess, once upon a time. He looks older today than the day at the Howdy Burger – maybe it's the pastel polyesters, maybe the fact that a young woman sucking his cock in the front seat of a sporty little car made him seem younger, taller, leaner. By his accent, it can't be all that many years ago he left Brooklyn.

Still, I can see there might have been – might still be – a gruff, uncultured charm to him that would appeal to women, even Teutonic History professors susceptible to cocky, primitive tough guys.

Big Vince leans his bulk over the counter and puckers

up. 'You going to gimme a kiss or do I gotta commit suicide right in front of your eyes?' Big Vince raises an imaginary knife over his heart.

'Morning, Big Vince,' the young woman says, and makes fleeting contact with Big Vince's lips.

'Mm-mmph!' Big Vince says. 'That really hit the spot.'

'Where're P.B. and Sweet Lou?' the young woman asks. 'You're going to lose your time.'

'One claims illness, the other business. You believe that?'

The young woman shakes her head in commiseration. 'Well, this gentleman is looking for a game.'

Big Vince takes a look at my jeans, my sneakers, my rented bag.

Up close there is a grainy quality to his face, as if despite the bravado his is a face that has been fiercely tensed tens of thousands of times in his life. His chin is trebled, and his dark eyes, unless I am reading this into them, are haunted just like Leslie Ann's.

'How you doing?'

'Fine. Looking for a game,' I say.

'Just for fun?'

'Fun, money, conversation – you name it.'

'How much you got on you?'

''Bout fifteen bucks.'

To the girl behind the counter, Big Vince says, 'Did he say fifteen or fifty?'

'He's a student, Big Vince,' says the young woman in my defense, and gives me a warning look behind Big Vince's back that tells me my fifteen bucks are in grave danger should I play Big Vince Carmine.

'I can write a check for more,' I offer.

'How do I know you got it in the bank?'

'You don't. But I do.'

'Do, huh?'

'Yep. Doesn't matter, though, because I won't lose.'

'Won't, huh?'

'Uh-uh.'

Big Vince reaches for a scorecard and pencil. 'Play for a hundred?' He heads for the door.

I feel more than merely brazen here, more than merely titillated by the ability to startle and maybe rattle Big Vince Carmine. I guess what I feel is purpose. And so I say to Big Vince, 'Play for a thousand.'

He looks around at me from the doorway. He's about to laugh, but my countenance must successfully convey to him that I'm dead serious because he asks without a hint of geniality, 'What's your handicap?'

'No handicap. Play you straight up – scratch. What's yours?'

'Twelve,' says Big Vince.

Do I ask the girl to confirm he's lying, or do I just proceed from living recklessly to living dangerously? Have to decide fast, can't appear to . . .

'Twelve's fine,' I tell Big Vince.

And I walk through the door Big Vince is holding open. I feel him linger behind my back. I know he must wink at the counter girl and that she frets now for my very life.

This poor student came in wearing jeans and tennies and he believed Big Vince has a twelve handicap and Big Vince took him for a thousand dollars! I don't even know where he got the rope, but he's . . . he's hanging from the tree over the water hazard on number five.

Big Vince Carmine flips a quarter. 'Heads,' I call.

'Heads it is,' he says, and gestures me to the tee box.

Elevated tee aimed across the entry road of the course to a long par five.

Fairway bunker on the left at about two-twenty, another on the right at about two thirty-five.

Two choices: Lay up with a two iron or, after a decade without a club in my hand, take the driver and try to play right to left *over* the left bunker, leaving a three wood to the green and a possible eagle.

I take the overly whippy, rented driver from my bag.

Out of the corner of my eye, as I tee up my ball three-quarters of an inch out of the ground, I can see Big Vince Carmine watching me with interest, flicking a finger toward a nostril of his abundant nose. But then, standing over the ball, though he remains where he is in fact, he disappears from my view, and as if I were fourteen again, the world goes away and I am in a void, and there is only my body, the club, the bit of earth out of which that little white ball protrudes.

The drama of the moment precludes taking even so much as a single practice swing. I put myself in the trust of muscle memory. My head and shoulders turn slightly right, my stronger, left eye fixing the ball. My hands start away slowly inside along the ground, my hips and shoulders rotate as my arms lift the club skyward; my wrists break at the top, the club parallel to the ground, pointing, I know, directly at my target, and now, my right side coiled to explode, I pull down passionately, driving my hips through the ball, sending it rocketing away, into the morning, ferocious and true, from the present into the distant past.

My God, it's a beautiful sight, ascending slightly to my right and then, at two hundred yards, beginning to draw back, landing just over the left-hand bunker and rolling another twenty yards down the left center of the fairway.

'Fuck,' says Big Vince Carmine, bringing me into the present again.

He sinks his tee, sets his ball, and pushes a long power fade deep into the woods to the right.

I fantasize as we go around the course that, inevitably, we will come to the eighteenth green and I'll be faced with a putt like the one I missed at age fifteen, but in good part because of the presence of this man's stepdaughter in my life, I'll nail it into the back of the cup, no question, to beat Big Vince Carmine for a thousand dollars.

But it doesn't happen that way.

Because I shoot a workmanlike four over par seventy-six and Big Vince shoots an ninety-one. Real handicap or fake – doesn't matter – I beat him by three strokes.

The lack of drama, the lack of uncertainty, is a little disappointing. To be able to come back and play so well so easily so long after I quit makes the game seem much less mysterious than I once thought it was.

'Fuck,' says Big Vince when I par out on eighteen. That has virtually been the extent of our conversation, Big Vince saying 'Fuck' every time I hit a good shot or he hits a bad one. I've counted the number of times he's said the word just for the hell of it: the last one makes one hundred and five.

'Lemme write you a check,' he says without grace as we start up the hill from the eighteenth toward the clubhouse.

'Lose with dignity,' my father tells me. 'Less ability than another player on a given day is one thing. Lack of grace is something else. That depreciates us all.'

'You'll have to walk me to my car,' says Big Vince.

A forced march to the parking lot is the only punishment he has remaining to inflict on me.

'No.'

'No – whudduya mean, no? Whudduya want – a
presentation in the clubhouse?'

'I don't want your money.'

Big Vince is wary. He looks around – for what or
whom I have no idea. 'Whudduya want then?'

'I just want you to answer a question.'

'Question.'

'Yeah.'

'Why?'

'Because I need it answered.'

'What makes you think I know the answer?'

'I just know you do. Will you answer it?'

Big Vince Carmine laughs. 'For a grand – whether I
know the answer or not!'

I have no idea what I'm going to ask Vince Carmine.
Leslie Ann's real father stuck his fingers in her. Her
perfect mother killed herself, maybe because the finger
sticker had an affair with a Nazi. The Nazi married a
car dealer. Does an abuser marry an abuser marry an
abuser?

Certainly doesn't follow with any mathematical certainty, but what else do I have to go on?

So I take a flyer: 'Was it verbal or physical or did you
sexually abuse Maggie?'

Big Vince Carmine stops in his tracks like he's hit a
wall. He looks at me, cocking one eye like it's ready to
fire a payload. 'Who are you?'

Jesus, out of hunch and ignorance, I'm on to something
I'm pretty sure I'm not going to like finding out. Before
I can decide what to ask next, Big Vince says, 'I know
you,' and he dumps his bag. 'You're that private eye. I

knew there was something familiar. I thought you were investigating Bunny.'

Big Vince starts for me, the one eye cocked, sighting a gun.

'No,' I say, and I retreat, 'I was investigating you.'

'I thought her husband hired you. C'mere, where you going?' Big Vince Carmine continues toward me. 'Who hired you?' he wants to know. 'The Wicked Witch?'

'Who else?' I say.

'That Nazi cunt,' he says.

What could still be at issue between Leslie Ann's stepmother and Big Vince?

Money, maybe?

Fists cocked, Big Vince pursues, still sighting me with his cocked eye.

I tell him, 'Don't swing at me.'

'Oh, but I am, unless you tell me what she sent you to find out.'

'I used to box,' I tell him.

'Good,' says Big Vince, 'then I don't have to feel guilty about breaking your head 'cause, you see, I played three years of offensive guard for the Pitt Panthers.'

Big Vince Carmine is ready to do battle.

He makes a shoulder feint that's supposed to catch me by surprise and make me respond to my left so he can hit me from the right. The punch he launches at me would, were it to connect, remove my jaw from my skull. But I don't go for the shoulder fake. Instead I put all my marbles in Motke Londovnik's basket, so to speak, and call up from muscle memory something far more unlikely to return than my golf swing, and that's my boxing lessons from age twelve.

But, from a right forward stance, I actually manage to block the punch with my left forearm. On contact, I know the forearm will be blue, black, red, and swollen – a vivid memory of this moment for weeks to come.

And now, before Big Vince's off-balance weight lands on me and takes me to the ground, where he'll beat my face to a pulp, I snap a right uppercut to Big Vince's groin with all my might, gaining momentum and power from my hips just as if I were hitting a two iron. Big Vince says, 'Oof,' and hits the ground like a sack of wheat.

'Fuuuuuck,' wheezes Big Vince.

Remarkable! My first punch-up since Allan Adelman in seventh grade and a knockdown!

I am tempted to call for photographers to memorialize this moment for my father.

Short of that, in a show of false bravado, my scrotum tensed should Big Vince be faking it, I straddle his ample waist. 'What'd you do to her?'

Big Vince Carmine is holding his breath against his will. He'd like to breathe, but there's no breath available; it has all escaped through his aching testicles.

'I never did anything to her,' he rasps, 'she didn't want done.'

'What's *that* mean?'

Big Vince sucks air. He doesn't answer my question. What he says is this: 'And the witch knew that, too! She just couldn't stand that Maggie and me had something me and her didn't. Fucking Nazi cunt!'

'Just what did you and Maggie have?'

'She wants any more money outta me, I'll see her in court, buddy boy, or in hell, whichever comes first, before I answer that!'

16

The curtain line of Act I of *Who Stalk the Tiger* is amazingly apt in describing the way I feel on the way home: following an hour-and-three-minute onslaught of verbiage, Daphne finally screams at Michael, 'I'm so sick of words! Of talking and listening, analyzing and anatomizing, evaluating and dissecting! I crave physical violence!'

'Fine!' screams Michael, and he slaps her.

She slaps him back.

Pause. The lights start to dim.

He slaps her.

She slaps him.

Pause. The lights continue to dim.

She slaps him.

He slaps her.

'Jesus,' she cries as the stage becomes black, 'that hurts so good!'

Jesus, I think, *I've been craving violence. And it hurts so good to have succumbed to it.*

When I enter the apartment, Leslie Ann is hunkered on the floor in her corner, working on her lines, playing as she does with her big toe, a big plastic cup of RC and ice at her knee.

'Where you been, Jakey?'

'Inventing an incident for Daphne's past.'

'I made you a veggie shake.' She points toward the refrigerator. 'Stir it up real good. Whudduya got for me?'

I go to the refrigerator, out of her sight, to make things easier for her. 'What if she and her father had a really peculiar relationship when she was a kid?'

Her response is neutral. 'In what way?'

I stir my pureed veggie shake with a long teaspoon and keep my distance from her corner. 'What if, say, her mother was very abusive, physically, verbally, maybe both, okay?'

'Mm.' Though I can't see her, I know she's nodding, shoving it all into Daphne's history for a look-see even as I invent it.

'And out of her hatred of her mother, she allows herself to fall into a relationship with her father.'

'They become friends, you mean? United against the mother?'

'More.'

'How?'

'At first friends, but out of a shared hatred of the mother – the mother abuses the father, too, let's say – out of that shared hatred for the mother and a growing affection for each other, daughter and father become lovers in her teens. She's never told anyone about their relationship or how terrible her life was at home, but then when Warren attacks her for what she's doing to poor him, she explodes.' I emerge into her sight, sit on the far side of the dining table, and take a hit on my shake. She's watching me. 'What if her husband's abuse brings back the memory of her mother's abuse and the guilt of what she did with her father, so that she gets free not only of Warren and Michael, but of her parents.'

The woman is either the greatest actor in history or utterly without guile, because she seems to take what I'm giving her as something I've invented out of whole cloth.

'That's good,' she says.

'Is it?'

'I think so.'

I take a hit on the shake.

'Are those the sweetest turnips we've ever had?' she asks, indicating the pureed gunk in my glass.

'Mm,' I say.

'Physical abuse and verbal,' she says almost inaudibly.

'What?'

'Should be physical *and* verbal – the mother's abuse. Something very specific – not just general slapping around.'

'Like what?'

'Well, here's an endearing little thing Magda used to do to my brother: she'd slap him on the back of the head. She's short and it was an upward, glancing blow, and she'd startle him so, after a couple of months, Evan developed this habit of suddenly turning around when he thought he heard Magda behind him.'

'And a lot of times she wasn't there.'

Leslie Ann suddenly swings around, ducking, her eyes darting left and right. No one there. She laughs high in her throat, the sound clattering against the back of her teeth. 'I'm sorry, I don't mean to laugh.'

'You don't have to apologize to me.'

'Is that okay? If it's not, you change it however you want.'

'No, that's fine. So how does she first end up having sex with her father?'

Leslie Ann exhales through pursed lips, turns her palms up. 'Not easily, would be my first guess. But who knows? You decide.'

She takes a hit on her RC.

'I think he has to be the aggressor – the father. You think?'

'What if her father,' she says, 'actually did something to her like Warren threatens to do in scene five.'

(In scene 5 Warren threatens to ram his fist up inside Daphne, to rip her apart from the inside out, and then appears, in his fury, as if he'll actually do that, but Michael walks in before it can happen.)

'If her father put his *fist* in her?' I ask with a touch of incredulity.

She nods.

'Why would he do that? I thought they were friends.'

'He starts to hate her because he loves her so much, and because no matter what they say, what acceptable reasons they think they have for doing what they're doing, it's . . . it's sick.'

She takes a sip of my shake, nods a nod that confirms this is a terrific idea.

'Okay,' I say, 'fine.'

She nods. 'Good. Now let's talk about something else.'

'Sounds good to me. Pick a subject.'

'I'm pregnant, Jakey.'

17

I sit on the grass at the top of the giant amphitheater that sinks into the middle of the Stanford campus, facing the stage the mother of my child and I will walk onto in two months, adorned in cap and gown, she in a masters, me in a doctoral hood; the stage from which I, anyway, will descend as through a trapdoor into the everlasting hell reserved for those who achieve pinnacles they don't aspire to.

Below me, Leslie Ann balances on one foot on one of the grass terraces of the amphitheater, the other leg elevated before her, bent gracefully at the knee.

When did she study ballet? Somewhere back there — another story untold.

'What do you want to do, Jakey?' she asks, a backlit silhouette of a flat-bellied woman in the sunlight.

The ballet position, I realize, is meant to deflect me from how seriously she intends her question, how intensely she'll receive my answer.

Perhaps she expects me to be glib and is steeling herself for disappointment.

'I want two things equally,' I tell her. 'One: I want to marry you and have the baby and live a different life than I ever imagined. Two: I don't want to marry you because I don't think you want to marry me and I don't think I could stand to discover I can't live without you.'

She faces me in first position or second position — in

one of those positions – absorbing my answer through her pores.

'We're so unfinished, Jacob.'

She seems detached. Still I sense she wants this child.

Or more precisely, wants to want this child.

With me.

But is afraid.

And not just of me.

'You really want a baby now, Jacob?'

I want to be very clear with her. And I want to tell the truth. 'When you told me, I thought I would be revolted, but that wasn't what I felt. I felt . . . I felt very close to you.'

She climbs up to where I sit. Stands over me and stares down.

Into the remote reaches of her eyes, I say, 'I want the baby.'

'What's the attraction?'

'Something very powerful.'

She straddles my knees, peers deep, deep inside me and beyond. Then crushes my head to her chest.

Her heart beats against my cheek. 'You'd be a wonderful mother,' I say.

Her heart, against my face, quickens. She wanted me to say that, wants to believe I mean it.

I press her away from me, so I can see her face. 'I've seen you with your students. I can even step outside of us and see you with me. You'd be an extraordinary mother.'

Her head cocked, her veiled eyes pierce my skull. 'I think I could. I've dreamed I could.'

Clearly, she still requires from me a gesture of indelible certainty.

But, even as I try to convey to her with all the available conviction in my body that I believe what I said, I see something pass away there in the distance between us.

And she says, 'Oh, Jacob, I can't. I can't now. I can't.' She slides off my knees, puts space between us. Her hand goes to her mouth, cloaks her lips behind her palm. But the words come around, under and over. 'And I can't get married. I can't. Not yet.'

Out of arms' reach now. In retreat, her voice goes cold. 'In the most romantic sense, it would be nice to imagine that someone couldn't live without a particular someone; but my guess is, anybody can live without anyone when you come right down to it. Who's irreplaceable? Not me, Jakey.'

Once, how many weeks or months ago – those first days after she walked out of my simple-minded dream of what she would be when I met her – might I have argued with her? But she's right. Sure, I could live without her. Somewhere in me, I can even feel the desire to be without her now because she scares me and life somehow would be easier without her.

And a child.

Men always get tired of me.

'I'm going to have an abortion,' she says. 'Okay?'

Yet, no – no, it's not okay!

But why not? I'm not a Catholic. I'm a modern young man living in the midst of the Great Sexual Revolution.

It's not okay for a reason that tantalizes me just beyond words. I feel the reason, feel it emanating from her into me. My skin crawls, my brain is bloated with a feeling of desperation. Hers. She desperately needs this child to make her new.

When I don't respond, she says, now icily, 'Jacob? I'm going to get rid of the thing in my belly. Okay?'

I look up at the sun, ninety-some-odd million miles away, heating my face. I know to speak the right words. But do not know what they are. So: 'Yeah,' I say, 'okay, get rid of it.'

It seems a while before the words reach her. More seconds before she stares where I stare. Up. Out there.

And she asks if we can drive across town to the all-night grocery – she wants to put a twelve-bean stew on to simmer in the morning for tomorrow night's post-rehearsal dinner to which she wants to invite Darlene Delvecchio and she needs two leeks.

En route to the grocery store, we pass Big Vince Carmine's Ford/Lincoln/Mercury Dealership.

Pregnant Leslie Ann turns her face away, toward the Datsun place across the street.

18

The next evening in rehearsal, Daphne's crutches torn in a fury from her by Michael, Leslie Ann, in a fury of her own as Daphne, relives her childhood abuse by means of her own fist (the scene played with Leslie Ann's back discreetly to us), and my play explodes before me into something so powerful that I find myself locked on my seat, my breath suspended in my chest like some part of my life in limbo.

Beside me, Darlene Delvecchio weeps.

At the end of the scene, the actor playing Michael, the character like me, tries to embrace Leslie Ann, but she shrieks at him in a voice I've never heard come from her, 'Don't touch me! Don't touch me! Don't touch me!' and I bolt from my seat – almost rupturing myself on Darlene's crutches – afraid that what I've written and what Leslie Ann herself endured must have finally gotten close enough together that she's in real danger.

Howard leaps into my path, hisses in my face, 'Leave her alone or I'll kill you!'

I knock him aside and jump up onto the stage. As I'm about to take her into protective custody, she snaps a rigid index finger out at me, freezing me five feet away.

She stands stock still, her face away from me, and then she says peaceably, 'Okay, got it,' and she holds her hand out to me.

I think I want to take the hand and walk offstage with her. But I don't. And she stares at me. Cocks her head.

And walks offstage alone.

Everyone in the room applauds, not just Leslie Ann's guts, but it – the scene, the totality that is this thing.

My play.

Us.

19

O ver twelve-bean stew, Darlene does a verbal review of the play, the performances, the direction, extolling the virtues of all and making a dozen cogent remarks about what could be better, from what Leslie Ann's doing as a victim of multiple sclerosis to the script itself.

Leslie Ann takes notes for me because she can see that although I'm sitting with them and appear to be listening, I'm not all there.

The greater part of me is permitting some nameless bile that I want to direct at Leslie Ann to percolate in me.

Even though she reached for me afterward, I know in part I'm hurt because she pointed that finger at me when I went to her, thinking she was in danger, only to discover she was merely committing the experience to memory for future use, that she was only acting. I know in part I'm disgusted because we're even continuing to rehearse, to Make Art, when there's her pregnancy to deal with.

And I know I'm furious that she wants this baby and that I don't know how to say what needs to be said to make it all right to have that baby because she's right and we're unfinished and have no right on earth to have a child.

And yet, when we have taken Darlene home and are in the bathroom, she scrubbing her face, me brushing my teeth, I bring up the Thing in her belly and tell her I think she should have it and give it to me.

'What would you do with a child, Jacob?'

'You want a list or just a general answer like "I'd love it"?'

What am I doing? Taunting her? Tempting her with another opportunity to embrace this relationship I sense she wants: *Jacobandleslieannandsomebodyelse*?

A tremor passes across some fault line in her body. 'No.' She whips her head emphatically; she wants to be done with this decision. 'I couldn't stand knowing you had it and I had abdigated my responsibility.'

And now anger swallows me whole – or I permit it to. 'You don't mean abdigate, Leslie Ann. There's no abdigate.'

'Excuse me,' she says simply, neither snidely nor cowed, 'what do I mean?'

'How the fuck should I know?' With the ferocity of the words, I spit toothpaste into the sink. Words and white froth rebound around us, the toothpaste blasting countertop, faucet, and mirror. 'You mean abdicate or abnegate.' I rinse and spit white water. 'But since obviously you don't mean abnegate, you must mean abdicate.' I throw my toothbrush at the Gertrude Stein stein Leslie Ann gave me for Valentine's Day, in which our toothbrushes reside. It clatters away, bounces once, lands on the floor.

'You couldn't stand knowing you abdicated your responsibility. Okay, good, so make your point.'

'You sound like Howard, Jacob. It's not terribly appealing.'

'There's some Howard in all of us boys, Les. Eventually, I guess it must out.'

As I haven't stooped to retrieve my toothbrush from the floor, Leslie Ann bends toward it.

'Touch that toothbrush and I'll break your fingers.'

Those luminous eyes measure me out of a mask of soap. 'Why are you mad, Jacob?'

'Because I'm just goddamn sick and tired of students misusing the language, that's why!'

A laugh full of scorn boils up out of her belly. 'Oh, Jacob!'

I think I want to kill her for laughing at my idiocy, but I hear myself laugh as caustically as she before I can decide whether I want to or not.

Our laughter dies a swift death. She peers at me out of her soapy face.

'I'm sorry,' I say, 'excuse me, please go on. We were talking about the Thing.'

But are we? her look inquires. And if we're not talking about the Thing, what are we talking about?

'If we can't have it together,' she says, 'I just don't want it to be had.'

'And we can't have it together because you don't want a child or marriage. Yet.'

'I guess that's right.'

'Don't guess, Leslie Ann. This is one of those times that really requires certitude, don't you think?'

'When you say "Leslie Ann" like that, I know you're trying to be more mature than you are, Jacob. You don't have to be. It's all right sometimes if we're both the little kids and neither of us is the parent.'

She reaches a hand for my cheek. I recoil.

She fixes those eyes on me, freezing me where I stand. 'I want ... I want to be ... normal, Jacob. But I have to feel I can help you help me to believe I'm worthy ... or ... capable, that I'm capable ...'

A massive howl of frustration erupts up out of her belly. Her feelings defy language.

And since I feel the same, how can I fail to understand?

In my face, she cries, 'I can't do it! I'm not able! I'm having an abortion!'

And now the fist grabs my chest and throat and cracks me like a whip. I lurch against the wall, gasping for breath.

I see terror on Leslie Ann's face: Before she's able to kill the Thing, she's killed Its father. 'What?' she cries, hands gripping my shoulders.

I shake my head.

'Are you all right?'

I breathe deeply, breathe slowly.

'Jacob, do you need help?'

In response to her concern, I scream at her, 'No, and don't you expect me to help you find some butcher to murder my child!'

I plunge my hand to the floor and retrieve my toothbrush. Hurl it at the Gertrude Stein stein. It misses again. Clatters to the floor.

I leave it there for Leslie Ann to retrieve and sanitize.

20

By the next evening's rehearsal, the pain in my chest is arriving with such authority that it makes my ears ring.

We have our first full dress rehearsal of the play, after which I thank Darlene Delvecchio for the notes from last night and she tells me I have effectively dealt with most of her criticism but several remain and she thinks she has a fix on the biggest one, and something detonates in my head and I tell her to keep any more criticism to herself or I'm going to shove one of her crutches up her ass.

Stupefied, speechless, Darlene drags herself out of her seat and moves torturously up the aisle. I pretend not to give a damn until she gets as far as the lobby and then I cut her off.

'I'm sorry. Don't go. Come on, come back inside and tell me what I still need to fix.'

'I can't.'

'Yes, you can.'

'Are you sure?'

'Absolutely. I'm just feeling a little edgy.'

She's not convinced.

'A tad combustible.' I smile – I'm being winning. 'A might skittish.'

She smiles.

I bend to kiss her cheek, but she turns her lovely face just slightly so that our lips touch. I really wish she wouldn't do that!

Nevertheless, I stroke her cheek where a triangle of almost invisible down creeps out of her hairline.

I step to the door back into the theater. Hold it open. Darlene drags one leg toward me, then the other.

As she arrives at the door, I close it.

'You know a lot of doctors,' I ask her, 'right?'

'I'm on a firsth-name bashish with every doctor in northern California.'

'Know one who does abortions?'

Her eyes investigate mine for only a moment before she says, 'No. But I can find out.'

21

B ut it isn't necessary.

Because the following Monday, when there's no rehearsal, Leslie Ann has the Thing terminated.

And tells me about it afterward.

I arrive home from class to find her huddled on the bed, arms drawn in against wolves, wrapped in her mother's afghan. I've heard about morning sickness, and though it's afternoon, I assume in my naiveté she's simply nauseated. 'You okay?' I ask.

I sit beside her on the bed, put a hand to her forehead.

She looks at me with eyes that don't quite see me and tells me she went to a doctor that morning. 'It's gone,' she says.

My first thought is not about the no-longer child. My first thought is this: 'You went without me.'

'I didn't want to have to deal with your feelings and mine, too, Jakey.'

'Was it . . .' What? What do I want to know? Was it heartrending? Painful? Expensive?

'It was gone like that,' she says, and tries but fails to snap her fingers.

Gone like that!

Some slick, venulose matter that, given time, would come to look like an amalgamation of the two of us.

I stare at her closeted face, her unavailable self, and want both to stroke and to crack my fist into her face.

Who *is* this person? How did we, out of all the people in the world, come together?

And why?

I can think of only one answer: To learn something for future use.

This other human being, a stranger six months ago, with whom I made a fetus, a prospective other person, who is now . . . where?

And I'm not talking purgatory, heaven . . . I'm wondering what, really, they do with them. The Things they scrape and flush out of the women who come to be disengaged from what's growing inside them?

Garbage in the universe.

I am about to ask her questions aimed ultimately, I suspect, at making her feel as guilty as possible about what she did when she takes my hand from her cheek and touches it to her woolly lips. The feel against my knuckles is something new; her lips are always soft and moist, irrigated from some invisible inner spring.

'Jakey,' she says from far away.

'Hmph?'

'You hate me pretty good right now, don't you?'

'I think the truth is, Leslie Ann, I despise you pretty much right now. I despise the person I love most in the world.'

'I feel,' she says from wherever she is, 'the same about you.'

22

The expulsion of the fetus from Leslie Ann's uterus does nothing to stop the fist that with increasing disregard for my wishes rocks the walls of my chest, starts a carillon chiming in my ears and a pressure behind my face that threatens to disgorge my eyeballs from their sockets.

In my infinite medical, diagnostic wisdom, I decided it must have something to do with my digestive tract, and so if I don't eat, my chest won't seize and the fist won't strike – no frog eyes, no church towers. By the next weekend I've lost seven pounds. My eyes sit in place, but they are glazed and Wagnerian and my body is heading for cadaverous.

With apologies, Leslie Ann says she can't pamper me right now; she's in a play, a new one that is changing daily and which is going to be presented to a critical public in a matter of days.

We are having trouble speaking. We are having trouble living in the same apartment. We haven't made love, of course, since the abortion – but not, really, because of the abortion; we know other means of satisfying each other besides intercourse. We are suffering a lack of interest – or if not a lack, call it a reduction.

I watch her sit in her corner with the script, reading a new scene I've just written, a hand playing with her big toe. I am not reading Jane Austen as I'm supposed to for a class this afternoon.

She finishes. Finds me watching her.

'She wakes up on the couch to find Warren peeing on her?'

'What do you think?'

'Well, my first thought is I shouldn't just scream in your face that this is nonsense, but treat it seriously by saying something intelligent like we know real well the ambivalence Warren feels for her – therefore, we don't need sensationalist *crap* like this.'

'I think it'll be a good scene. Behavior rather than exposition.'

'Jacob, if you wrote this just to degrade me, that's not fair to the play or to the other people involved.'

'Good scene, I think. Doesn't work, I trash it.'

She looks at me, the eyes hooded beneath her hair, permed and gone wild for the role of Daphne.

'Okay. Take a leak on me.'

'The actor's not literally going to urinate on you, Leslie Ann.'

'A fake urination scene,' she says.

'Acting, Leslie Ann.'

'But I have to feel urinated on, Jacob, don't I? Oh yes indeed.'

The bile rises. I rise. And close Jane Austen; neither she nor her characters should have to listen to the sorts of things people are going to say to each other in the middle of the next century.

I move from my desk to Leslie Ann's corner.

'I just took a leak twenty minutes ago, but, sure, Les, anything for art. Lemme see what I can do for you.'

I whip out my hose and straddle her, aiming the little eye at her face. I remember the afternoon I awoke from a nap when she was preparing to do *The Lesson* to find her playing a paring knife against her nipple. As part of me would have been perfectly willing to see her slice her own nipple off, everything I'm feeling just now tells me I want to piss on her.

But some inner reserve or my bladder's own conscience refuses.

I slam my cock back in my pants, yank the zipper upward. 'Guess you're just going to have to imagine it, Les.'

'Oh, I don't think so,' she says.

She gets up, heads for the door.

I block her way. 'You're not going to ask Howard to piss on you, Leslie Ann.'

'Sure I am.'

And she goes around me and out the door and into the breezeway.

'Leslie Ann, come here!'

'Don't tell me to come here. What am I – a dog?'

She raps on Howard's door.

'Come *in* here,' I order her.

She glances at my eyes, she glances at my hands at my sides.

Why don't I raise my hands? I don't have to hit her. I can simply wrap my arms around her, pick her up, bring her back inside.

Tie her up. Tie her to the plumbing under the kitchen sink. Long rope. Hang her out the window. Naked. Sign around her neck: 'Piss on this woman – free!'

Howard opens his door. His eyes look like he just blew in through a dust storm. As there are no dust storms in our apartment complex, I assume he's just smoked a five-pound joint.

'Will you do me a favor, Howard?'

'It'll cost you.'

'It's for the play.'

'Discount rate in effect, then.' He looks into the general vicinity of where I stand. 'But what could you possibly require of me that the great Jaker can't provide?'

'He wrote a new scene. I need you to piss on me.'

Howard blows air through his pursed lips. 'Jesus, you know how many that makes today? Doesn't anybody just like to straight screw anymore?'

Leslie Ann glances once more at me. When I don't grab her, hit her, whatever it is she's wondering whether I'll do, she steps into Howard's apartment, leaving Howard staring goggle-eyed at me.

'Sounds like a great scene – can hardly wait for rehearsal.'

He closes his door.

Why didn't I stop her?

Do I *want* Howard to piss on her?

Would I love for the actor playing Warren to really piss on her before a packed house every night the play runs?

Several minutes later she returns to our apartment.

The sight of her wet hair, face, T-shirt, make me livid.

She goes into the bathroom, turns on the faucet in the tub, closes the drain.

'You know,' I tell her, 'I don't want to burst any bubbles, but you have some serious psychological problems.'

'But you're the picture of normalcy, right?'

'What would you say is your basic problem, Leslie Ann?'

She strips off her shirt and shorts, dumps them in the sink. 'D'know, Jakey. What's yours?'

'I'm serious, Leslie Ann. So don't tell me you don't know.'

She looks at me so that she can look away from me, dismiss me. She unhooks her bra, steps out of her panties, tosses them, the bra, in the sink.

'What do you figure your problem is – the major one, the one that most – '

She runs an index finger down her face, puts the tip of the finger to her lips. Puts her tongue to the finger. Looks at me. 'D'know, Jake.'

'I'm warning you, Leslie Ann.'

'"I'm so sick of words!"' she says monotonically, quoting the end of Act I to me in a much different tone from the one she takes onstage, where she hisses it like a cheetah. "'Of talking and listening . . ."'

'Are you, Les?'

'". . . analyzing and anatomizing . . ."'

'Tired of talk – huh?'

'" . . . evaluating and dissecting."'

'You crave violence? Huh? Hungry for a little violence. Boy, I am.'

I grab her by the hair. She doesn't scream. I spit in her face. She doesn't flinch. I twist the hair in my fist. She expels a rush of air – but it's not a scream, not even a protest. I jam my other hand up between her legs, lift with that hand, bang her with my hip, and together we crash into the tub. The water is barely an inch deep at the low end of the tub, but it's deep enough for me to flip her on her stomach and to immerse her face. She doesn't struggle. I shake her viciously, banging her head on the porcelain, then mash her face against the bottom of the tub. She doesn't struggle. The water from the faucet pours over her head. The level rises. Her ears are underwater. I hold her there. She doesn't struggle.

The hammer hits my chest.

I yank her up into the air. She gasps for breath.

So do I.

'Jesus,' she says utterly without relish, 'that hurt good.'

And in this atmosphere, the play opens.

The Other Thing is born.

23

The first ninety-seven public witnesses to my play are mostly students and faculty from the Theatre Department; there is, however, a small contingent of my fellow Ph.D. candidates from the English Department led by my adviser, Dr Jeffrey Kaplan, all of whom I'm confident will feel obligated to detest the play whether they do or not.

Doesn't matter, though, as absolutely nothing works anyway, and I find myself thinking, *It's only theater.* It's not like it's representative of anything important. Consequence, okay, but importance, no.

Who cares about the dissolution of a young marriage?

Who cares about some broad with a muscle disease?

Who cares about some young professor struggling for direction or some sociopath who wishes he could love but can't?

Who cares about all this fucking verbiage?

I crave violence!

When the fatuous piece of horseshit finally ends, Howard gushes that the performance is better than he dared hope and Edie Weinberg appears out from behind a pair of dark glasses and from beneath a babushka and whispers marijuana breath in my ear, 'I didn't imagine that you could be God.'

Jesus, talk about fatuous horseshit!

But I have the good sense of thank Edie modestly and

let it ride. She gives me the clenched-fist power salute and, as if backing away from a shrine, disappears into the crowd of well-wishers, mouthing, 'Call me, please, I miss our talks.'

Before it was my kosher salami, now that I've debuted as an artiste it's our talks.

From the corner of my eye I can see the contingent from the English Department squirting about aimlessly like a piece of mercury splintered against a slab of ice. One of the women, a Spencerian, clearly wants to come over to say something but is cautioned with a gesture to keep her ground by Dr Jeffrey Kaplan, who herds all the little pieces of mercury back into a whole, then detaches himself and wriggles his way through the crowd to me.

Finally, I think, *some well-deserved contempt.*

He shakes my hand firmly and leans in; clearly what he has to say is such that others are best not saddled with hearing it. 'Good,' he whispers. 'Interesting. Everyone thought so.' He pats me on the shoulder and wriggles back toward his charges, endeavoring en route to look as though my play continues to stimulate in him very deep thought. He shepherds the others out the door, a few dismissive hands raised to me in tribute as they disappear into the night, where I assume they'll spend the next hours ripping my play to shreds, mounting polysyllables and invective toward a crescendo of hatred and, finally, exhausted and relieved, able to go to bed and face me on equal terms again tomorrow.

How dare they disdain my work more than I do!

At the cast party Leslie Ann gets drunk for the first and only time since I've known her, and both hands stuffed in my back pockets, she clings to me, dancing with me, song after song.

'Want to know the sweetest thing you ever did?' she

whispers hotly against my ear. 'You started peeing sitting down. Like a girl. For me. So there wouldn't be no more pee spots on the seat and the rim and the floor. Isn't that right?'

I nodded my head against her cheek.

'Sweet, sweet, sweet,' she says. 'That's the pee scene you *should've* written.' She cocks her head up from my chest, views me through some dense prism. And then says, 'I wonder if where you'll go, you'll keep sitting down to pee.'

She thrusts away from me. Stumbles backward. I catch her. Hold her steady. 'I'm drunk,' she says. 'Take me home.'

Home.

Jacobandleslieann.

Unfinished.

We drop Darlene off. I accompany her up the walk to her room and her waiting caretaker.

'It's not as good as we thought it was going to be,' I say.

She waffles a moment between truth and lie, then says, 'No. Sheeing it in front of an audience, it was . . .' She shakes her head; some finer truth escapes her.

So it's true; my instincts are correct. It's not good.

I am relieved and I am mortified. Almost euphoric and, still, furious.

'Superficial,' I say. 'Inconsequential. Glib when it should have been serious. Ponderous when it should have been funny.'

'I should have helped you better,' she says.

'Oh no you don't! You're not blaming this on yourself. The failure's mine – I get to wallow in it.'

'You'll make it better.'

'Why?' I ask her. 'Good night.'

I head for the car and the unconscious heap of Leslie Ann piled onto the passenger seat.

The next day the reviewers for the *Palo Alto Times* and the *Daily* both lavish compliments on the acting, especially Leslie Ann's, and on the direction, and congratulate the Theater Department for supporting the work of a new writer.

Then each reviewer savages the play and the particular new writer the Theater Department chose to support. The reviewer for the *Times* hopes, for his reader's sake, that I have other vocational ambitions.

'How do you feel?' Leslie Ann asks.

We sit on the patio outside the cafeteria, the papers spread between us.

'I think I can safely say that I've finally experienced a humiliation worse than I felt when I missed that putt at fifteen. It's nice to move on.'

She puts her face close to mine. 'Want to stick your fist in me, Jakey?'

'Yeah,' I say.

'Why?'

'Because you wanted the play to fail.'

'I wanted it to succeed *and* I wanted it to fail.'

She presses one of my hands to her lips.

I'm not sure if the chill comes from my hand or her mouth.

The next night there are exactly eight people in the audience in addition to Howard and me. I don't know about him, but I know I don't want to be there and can't imagine why the other eight *are* there. I know better than to suggest the remaining performances be canceled, though that's my fervent wish. When I notice that one of the eight people in the audience is Big Vince Carmine, however, it strikes me that the attendees are composed of friends or relatives of the cast; that is, they are there out of duty.

Big Vince is with a trim, crisply dressed woman he obviously has no interest in whom I can only assume is the second (or at *least* the second) Mrs Carmine.

Big Vince nods off ten or so minutes into my play, wakes up to bring his hands together in a single applaud at the end of the first act, and conks out again at the beginning of the second. It is not until his stepdaughter tries to ram her fist up her vagina twenty feet away and the person I presume to be his wife elbows him that Big Vince fixes with any real interest on the evening's presentation.

I watch the Carmines leave the theater. They do not speak, but Mrs Carmine looks at her husband sympathetically, squeezes his arm to her, pats his massive back. She knows only that her husband has been embarrassed by a public act of his stepchild.

I am tempted to go after them.

But I remember the look on my father's face eleven years ago when I missed that putt (and when he stood frozen at the edge of the green and waited too long to come and lead me away), and so I go backstage, where I find Leslie Ann seated in a pair of bikini panties, her blouse held to her bare chest, accepting the good wishes of two male theater students.

When they've gone I ask her, 'Why are you greeting people like that?'

'They knocked. I thought it would be you.'

'Bullshit.'

She stares at me. 'If I wanted strangers to look at my breasts, Jacob, I wouldn't bother holding anything over them.'

'He left,' I say.

'Who?'

'Just in case you were expecting him to come backstage so you can offend or titillate him.'

'What're you talking about?'

'I think you know.'

'You think I know what?'

'Maybe I don't know enough to talk. Is that what you're saying?'

'I don't know what I'm saying except I don't know what you're saying.'

'Fine.'

The air around us peals in tensile silence.

Someone knocks on her dressing room door. Instinctively I know it's Big Vince, that he had to come back.

'There he is,' I tell her. "You going to put your robe on?'

'Him who?' asks Leslie Ann.

'It's me,' comes Howard's voice.

'It's Howard,' Leslie Ann says.

'I know it's Howard, Les. He just said it's Howard and he has Howard's voice. Put your goddamn robe on.'

She cruises my face. 'So who'd you think it was?'

'Big Vince,' I say.

The eyes do not waver, give nothing more away than what she assumes I know.

She lays her blouse aside. 'Come in,' she calls, and reaches for the robe just after Howard comes through the door, taking in her breasts, then starting to give her notes on her performance.

26

I knew you knew about Vince,' she says on the way home.

Some part of me is too weary of all this – both real drama and invented drama – to bother to respond.

She paraphrases: 'You were aware I knew you knew about Vincent, yes or no?'

'I didn't know you knew I knew, Leslie Ann, but if you say you knew, fine, you knew.'

'I don't want you thinking you were putting something over on me. That day you ended up on the same beach I was on, I knew you must have followed me.'

'No, you didn't know I followed you until this evening when you realized I knew who Big Vince is and figured I *must've* followed you that day.'

'That's wrong, Jacob.'

'Don't tell me that's wrong, Leslie Ann, I beg you.'

'What will you do – drown me again?'

I drive. After a moment she looks out her window.

'Did you talk to him?' she asks nicely.

'Yes.'

'Tonight?'

'No.'

'That day?'

'Yes. I played golf with him.'

'You played golf with Vince?'

'What'd I just say, Leslie Ann? Didn't I just say I played golf with him? Yes, I did, I did say that.'

She stares out the window. 'Beat him?' she asks.

'Yeah.'

'He's a pretty good golfer.'

'He stinks.'

She looks at me. I look at her. She looks out the window.

I drive.

'What'd he tell you?'

'That whatever was wrong when you were all together, it was your stepmother's fault. But I think that's bullshit. I think he abused you too. Right?'

'No.'

'I think he did, Les.'

'Then that would make you wrong, Jacob.'

'No, I don't think so. Because I think you can't get involved with anybody who doesn't end up abusing you. Isn't that what you mean by "Men always get tired of me"? Didn't Big Vince get tired of you being remarkable and gorgeous and neurotic and start to abuse you? How'd he do it? Physically? Verbally?'

'You're such a know-it-all. Aren't you? You're so insightful. *Aren't* you, Jacob?'

'Evidently not in your estimation, given your tone of voice.'

'Vince and I were lovers, you pompous schmuck.'

'No, you weren't.'

'Oh, yes, we were, too, you *putz!* You *momzer!*'

I hurl the wheel of my VW to the right. Leslie Ann flies against my side. I stand on the brake. The car smokes to a stop, and I almost take out a parking meter and a potted magnolia on University Avenue.

'Why?' I demand.

'Why what?'

'Why are you telling me this?'

'Because it's the truth. You're always asking me to tell you the – '

'This isn't the truth.'

'Why would I make it up?'

'You slept with your stepfather?'

'Yes!'

'Why?' I scream at her. 'Why did you *do* that?'

'I don't know,' she screams right back at me.

'Don't tell me you don't know, okay? I'm begging you not to tell me that.'

I try to become calm. I try hard. Because I do not want to succumb again to the extraordinary desire to become violent with this woman, because I'm pretty sure I'll do irremediable damage to her.

Downtown Palo Alto is a ghost town. There's no one here to stop me from doing whatever I might do to her.

'All right,' I ask her, 'when did this happen?'

'When I was seventeen.'

'Why'd you stop?'

'He got . . .'

'. . . tired of you.'

'– Found out.'

'Your stepmother found out.'

'No.'

'Who?'

'My brother.'

'Told him to stop.'

'Walked in on us.'

'And?'

'He tried to kill Vince. But I told him I had as much to do with it as Vince did.'

'So your brother said what?'

'He felt a lot of guilt because he never said anything to my mother about my father when we were kids.'

'Goddamn you, I don't know what you're talking about! Your brother knew what your father was doing to you?'

'He was in the TV room a lot of times watching TV, and my father and I were behind him on the couch.'

'And he never said anything.'

'Right.'

'Did you ask for help?'

'Nope.'

'Cry out?'

'Nope.'

'So how do you know he knew?'

'I saw the back of his *head*, Jacob!'

'So now he feels obligated to stop your stepfather from porking you.'

'Yes.'

'So you stopped.'

'We said we would, but we didn't.'

I want to *pound* her! I want to beat her to *death*! 'Why didn't you stop?'

'Because I do not know, Jacob.'

'Don't tell me that, that is *not* an acceptable answer. Why did you continue?'

'Because.'

She wants me to hurt her.

'Why did you continue, Leslie Ann? Please, tell me anything, but tell me something.'

And she explodes: 'Because I *liked* it, Jacob! Because Vincent was *gentle*! Because my stepmother was a cruel, malicious witch! Because I was lonely and angry and unholy! *Because* Jacob, *because*!'

'Suck him off in the front seat of his car?'

'Coupla times,' she screams in my face, 'sure! He taught me a lot!'

'When did it end?'

'When Vince couldn't stand it.'

'Otherwise you would've gone right on.'

'I assume so!'

She slams the dashboard. She kicks the floorboard. She presses her head against the paneling between the two side windows.

I reach across her, into the glove compartment for the tiny package of tissues she put there months ago, along with a penlight, a small pad and pencil, and a change purse with dimes in case I needed to make any emergency phone calls.

I hold out a tissue. 'Here,' I say.

She looks at the tissue. 'I'm not crying, Jacob.'

I fold the tissue neatly, slide it into my shirt pocket. 'Why didn't you tell me?' I ask her.

'Because I'm allowed to be someone else, Jacob. Because I'm allowed to be new.'

One of my hands, seeming to work independently of my body, reaches out to her. 'Les.'

'Yes.'

'Leslie Ann Masterson née Margaret Jewel Carmine.'

'Yes, Jacob.'

And then my mouth, seeming to work independently of my brain, says, 'No matter what, I love you. Only you in all the world.'

'That sounds good, Jacob, but I don't believe it. Who you love is who you want me to be.'

'Goddamn it, what do you want from me?'

'The same thing you want from me, I guess. More than you have to give.'

Though we know it's almost over, we don't actually say it.

And to take my mind off my anger and my regret (and to try to avoid any more public humiliation), I turn all my available energies to my academic life and lash myself through the last suggestions from my graduate committee on my odious dissertation and immerse myself in the literature of the world and the critical theories appertaining thereto.

As a result, at the end of May I pass my writtens and orals and see my dissertation accepted by my committee with all the appropriate hosannas.

Preposterous. I hate the dissertation and I don't want the degree.

Shortly thereafter I am officially offered positions at Loyola Marymount, NYU, and, of course, the University of New Mexico.

We attend the English Department graduation social because Leslie Ann convinces me that not going will look like the play's failure had precisely the effect on my ego it had.

We're barely in the door before the woman Spencerian says to me, 'I was sorry about the reception of the play, Doctor. I thought it had a good deal to recommend it.'

My peers revel now in calling each another 'Doctor,' pretending it means nothing but hoping they in turn will be called 'Doctor.'

I thank her for her backhanded compliment, want to commit a heinous crime against her, do not call her Doctor, and look for an avenue of exit.

The Commons Room in the English Department is full, and in turning away from the Spencerian, we come face to face with a very tipsy Dr Jeffrey Kaplan, who is looking Leslie Ann up and down.

She looks absolutely extraordinary in black vinyl boots that cling to her calves, a black crocheted cloche hat, and a black minidress with a red vest.

Dr Jeffrey Kaplan's gaze, however, seems to say something else, as if he knew we would turn and see him looking at her and he wanted to be sure we knew he didn't approve of her attire.

I introduce Leslie Ann to Dr Kaplan. Each expresses something akin to elation at meeting the other.

Then Dr Jeffrey Kaplan tickles his nose, an act that

would be considered nose picking if the finger were not moving so fast, and he says to his advisee via the conduit of his advisee's gorgeous roommate in a voice full of solicitude he obviously doesn't feel, 'Do you know how irresponsible it is for this boy to take his skills to North Dakota?'

'New Mexico,' Leslie Ann corrects him.

Dr Jeffrey Kaplan doesn't care; he's drunk and he has a point to make. 'North Dakota,' he says, 'New Mexico, what's the difference?'

He looks at me, conveying exaggerated anger. He exhales irascibly. 'A Ph.D. from one of the premier institutions of higher learning in the nation, and he wants to go to a fifth-rate degree factory in the middle of nowhere.'

'He's going to a very good university,' says Leslie Ann, flicking her eyes at me. 'He's going to Loyola Marymount or NYU.'

'*Au contraire*,' Dr Jeffrey Kaplan says smugly – there's no tricking *him*, 'word here is he's going to North Dakota – or wherever you said.'

'He's been offered a position at New Mexico, but he's probably going to NYU or . . .' It occurs to her to ask me, 'Are you going to New Mexico, Jacob?'

I nod, concealing my pleasure in letting her find it out here.

'Of course he's going to New Mexico,' says Dr Jeffrey Kaplan. 'Because he's not up to the pressure that a top position makes on the individual to maintain the superior level of achievement. Term after term. Year after year. I don't think Dr Landau has the balls. I think his little testes are just too tightly wrapped in his scrotie. Hmm?'

I step between Leslie Ann and Dr Jeffrey Kaplan, putting her at my back, forcing her to move to improve

her line of sight and forcing Dr Jeffrey Kaplan's eyes
onto mine. 'The truth is, Dr Kaplan, that I'd prefer
an assistant professorship someplace like the University
of New Mexico, where mediocrity will be sufficient
and where I won't have to sit around with a lot of
pompous faggots like you and engage in a lifetime of
intellectual whacking off because I can't get laid in the
real world.'

This said, I feel neither relief nor satisfaction. I feel
like I imagine an actor must feel delivering a line he
doesn't like in a play to which he's not committed.

Dr Jeffrey Kaplan sucks his lips together, stimulating
nothing more accurately than an asshole, and flicks his
eyes at Leslie Ann and says in a musical tone, 'Let me
make a suggestion to you, Dr Landau. May I?'

'Please.'

'Why don't you,' says Dr Jeffrey Kaplan, 'go suck a
big fat, syphilitic cock.'

This is getting better all the time. Two doctors of
philosophy, steeped in the Great Literature of the world,
bandying their intelligence back and forth.

But nothing can stop me now, and I say to Dr Jeffrey
Kaplan, 'Believe me, Dr Kaplan, if I thought it would
teach my esophagus a lesson, I'd be on my knees even
as we speak.'

And now the moment has arrived: *I spin Dr Jeffrey
Kaplan around by his shoulders and, with my foot, propel
him head first into the punch bowl, launching a cascade
of rubicund beverage and a riot of pastel petits fours in
all directions.*

Except I don't do that.

Instead I say to Dr Jeffrey Kaplan, 'I'm sorry, I don't
mean any of that. I think you're right, I'm feeling the
pressure. What I really want to say to you, Dr Kaplan,

is thank you for all your support and guidance during these past three years.'

Dr Jeffrey Kaplan's face thaws, he offers me an imperious hand and is about to tell me he, too, is sorry if he was a bit rough on *me*, but I'm on my way out of the room.

On the Quad, Leslie Ann whistles appreciatively as she catches up, matches me stride for stride.

'Your first adult act, huh, Jakey?'

She hooks her index finger into my back pocket. I knock it away and accelerate. She goes into passing gear, gets ahead of me, turns into my path, stops me.

'Are you really going to New Mexico, Jacob?'

'Yeah.'

She squints at me. The signal's not coming through clearly. I'm jamming her channel. If she asks me why, she figures either I'll give her a long convoluted answer that'll be at best partial truth . . . or I'll borrow 'D'know.'

So she touches my cheek and says, 'You'll have to let me know what it's like there.'

And I say to her: 'Leave me your address. I'll drop you a note.'

I must have slept because I awaken. It's night. I'm naked. In our bed.

Leslie Ann Masterson, naked, sleeps beside me, on her back, her hands loose at her belly.

Moonlight lifts the silhouette of her body into the space above the bed. My eyes follow the angles and swells from her forehead to her toes, and I touch the nearer nipple that punctuates the air like the mast of some humpbacked ship.

Blood roars in my head, seems to impel me to replace my fingers with my mouth and then my mouth with my teeth.

I hold the nipple firmly between my teeth, flick my tongue against it.

Leslie Ann Masterson stirs, whispers, 'You want, Jakey, you need?'

But I do not answer; instead, with the fluidity of a perfectly conceived piece of machinery, I bring my teeth together and behead the breast.

Her career is ruined and we are married and she has our child and together the three of us set sail for uncharted waters, heads high, eyes resolute, bodies honed (though short one nipple).

And now I awaken from what I did not believe was sleep. Leslie Ann isn't beside me. The sheets give off only the faintest scent of Tabu, of her. She's been gone a long time.

She has packed all her belongings – her clothing and flower vases and plants, her blender and her omelet pan, her spice rack and her treasure chest of vitamins and protein powder and yeast, her plays and her books about theater and acting – packed it all with incredible symmetry into her DeSoto.

She sits at the kitchen table sipping RC with a lot of ice. All of my possessions have either been sold, mailed to my parents' house in Miami Beach, or stand ordered by Leslie Ann and ready to be packed into my Volkswagen. The apartment stands stripped of my three years in it, her eight months, and seeing it this way, I feel indelibly how much she's brought to my life. How much I'm about to lose.

Our time is up.

I can't imagine not seeing her in the morning.

Not touching her.

Cannot imagine walking without her beside me, her index finger hooked into my back pocket.

I don't know how we got here.

I am suddenly on the verge of panic.

'I've been waiting for you to wake up,' she tells me, 'so I can help you put everything in your car.'

I want to beg her to stay with me or to take me with her.

Yet I would be too embarrassed to do that, and so I must not prolong this. Must not keep her any longer from what awaits her in Los Angeles (where she's decided to pursue her professional career). 'I can do it myself,' I tell her. 'You go ahead.'

'I have everything in a particular order.'

'I'll figure it out,' I assure her.

She nods, rinses her glass, places it in the remaining box.

She comes to where I lie still and silent and cadaverous in our bed.

'See you,' she says, and kisses the top of my head.

And before I can say anything more, she presses her index and middle fingers to my lips and, without looking back, walks out of my life.

DOCTOR SNAKE

1

In Miami Beach they welcome me home with cherry cheesecake from Wolfie's.

My sister, Susan, throws open one of the double doors, my father self-consciously manages the other, and between them, holding the cherry cheese, trying to restrain her pleasure so as not to appear happier than my father or sister, stands my mother.

Their joy is short-lived.

'Holy Christ, JD,' says my sister, Susan, ever the diplomat, 'you look like shit.'

'Hey, hey,' I reassure her, talking really to my mother, 'nothing to worry about.'

My arms are open, I wait to be enclosed in loving embraces, then to devour a piece of Wolfie's cherry cheese.

'Ma,' says my sister, 'look at terminal gauntness.'

Like those television moms of the Fifties, Florence Landau is always in a dress and heels, always looks her very best. Yet now tears spring to my mother's eyes and begin to excavate highways through her Max Factor. The cheesecake droops, wax from the single brightly burning candle in its center drips onto the fire engine glaze. My mother begins to cluck her tongue like a metronome beating four-four time, shaking her head to the same beat, as if my present condition is merely one more instance of inequity perpetrated by me on them: First *The Putt*, followed in lockstep by

The Degree in English, The Ph.D., and now *Terminal Gauntness*.

'You look,' says my sister, 'like absolute caca.'

I have forgotten the special way my sister has of making a point. Repeat it, is her policy, until people despise you.

My mother puts an end to further variations by my sister. 'Rusty,' she whispers, 'why?'

'I joined a religious order,' I confess solemnly, then launch into a little Hare Krishna dance, my fingers banging tiny, imaginary cymbals above my head. 'Hare, hare,' I sing, 'hare lama . . .'

'*Oy, Gut!*' says my mother.

'But don't worry,' I say, beckoning them to me, 'I quit the other day – gave back my robe, cut off my fetlock, sold my cymbals to a small Korean jazz group . . .'

My mother and sister sweep into my arms. My father hangs back.

'Hi, Pop.'

'Hello, Jacob.'

He slips one of those big, hairy hands that smell eternally of feet into the tangle of arms and fingers and squeezes my shoulder deeply, our eyes meeting and deflecting like insoluble substances.

2

I can't remember when I stop living in fear that my
parents will die and leave me, the older of two
children, with the responsibility of sustaining life. I
envision myself as a character out of Dickens. In my
updated version I run a deli sandwich stand on the
beach and lead my sister across miles of sand at night
with a Geiger counter, Geigering for dropped change,
ever trepidant in a world of jellyfish and Fagins. My
worst fear, of course – worse than the fear of my parents'
demise – is that I won't meet the challenge of survival if
it comes.

Around twelve I develop a concept of aging. My
parents are young, in their late forties. It will be a quarter
century before they exhaust their 'life expectancies'. I
relax a little. Discover boxing, intimidation, golf, girls,
masturbation, add them to the curse of intelligence,
and lurch into adolescence confident I can torment my
parents for years and still have plenty of time to make
amends before they buy the farm.

Suddenly it is a decade and a half later; my parents
are in their early sixties, and though they look tan and
reasonably fit, they are methodically and inevitably
exhausting those life expectancies.

I understand this at dinner tonight and know it's time
for the amends to begin.

I cannot divine, though, how to start the process
except by not resuming the old process by which I try

to make them feel guilty for many things that are not their fault.

We go to my favorite seafood house and eat Cherry-stones and Blue Points, lobster, drink a nice wine. And I do not tell them anything about two things: the tank regiment in my chest or the relationship I hold responsible for its encampment there.

Driving home along Collins Avenue, luxuriating on the backseat of my father's twelve-year-old Caddie con-vert, the top down, the humid sea breeze wafting across us, I marvel that I have not had a fist in the chest for three days, the exact amount of time I've been separated from Leslie Ann Masterson. To commemorate this mitzvah, I lay a fart down deep into the velour upholstery.

'Rusty!' my mother cries happily.

My sister rips off a beauty beside me, and my mother, my sister and I fill the night with laughter. At the wheel, intent first and foremost on engineering us safely from point A to point B, I can see the hint of a smile on my father's face.

'You're up, Ma,' I challenge my mother.

'Not me. I don't do that anymore.'

'Pop,' I say.

'Oh, sure,' says my mother.

My father shakes his head. 'I'm driving,' he says.

'He's a specialist,' says my mother. 'He can't drive and make a windy.'

'Okay,' says Susan, 'check it out,' and she fires off her specialty, the one I commemorated for all time as The Thrilling Trilling One Leg Lifter.

I go for the matched pair.

Having chastised my father for nonparticipation, my mother knocks out a deuce right behind me.

'All right, Ma!' cries my sister.

'I had to, what can I say,' says my mother to my father.

'So,' says my father, 'all right,' and he unleashes the one we came to know and love as The Big Bear's Bass Boomer.

Oh, yes! After three years of rarefied scholarship, after dabbling in the Revolution and Show Biz, after The Woman of My Dreams and our junked fetus, it is nice – hell, it is beatific – to be home in Miami Beach, blasting windies with *mishpukah*.

3

Susan comes to my room when our parents have called it a night. I'm glad she comes, not only because I realize, now that I'm with her, that I've missed her, but because I have been dwelling on whom I don't want to dwell on.

Is where? Doing what? With whom?

I make room on my bed and offer Susan a chocolate-chip cookie from the box I've brought up from the kitchen.

'Mom stocked up on about eighteen boxes of chippers for you,' she says, declining.

I kiss my sister on the forehead, leaving crumbs I wipe away, reminded anew that she is not an attractive woman, even with the Sandra Dee nose she got for her sixteenth birthday.

A great deal of speculation in our childhood was given over to the question of whether Susan would ever meet 'the right boy' and marry. She made the whole question of 'rightness' moot by eloping with a salesman from a dental supply house when she was eighteen. (That's as close, by the way, as anybody in the Landau family got to dental school.) She came home with a lifetime supply of dental floss when she was twenty and has been working at the store, pursuing a business degree at the University of Miami at night, and living at home since.

She hikes her nightgown above her knees and sits cross-legged on my bed. Her unfortunate breasts make simple dents in the inside of the thin material. She peers at me with her small, close-set brown eyes, eyes that lend an aura of mystery, I'm told, to my face but seem to conspire in Susan's with her pert, prosthetic nose and wide mouth to create a face without compatible parts.

As children I urged her to be the girl I rescued from evil when we played 'Jake the (Good) Snake to the Rescue,' but Susan insisted even then she wasn't pretty enough to be rescued. She chose, instead, to ride with the guys. Shana Rosenblatt or Trudi Bialenki, she decreed, should be rescued. And truth be told, it was a pleasure to rescue either of those adorable little persons from the clutches of Evil.

'We knew something was wrong,' she says now. 'Your letters were too happy. Pop almost let Mom fly out, so you know he was worried. But the accountant couldn't figure out how to write it off as a business trip, and about then you stopped writing for a while, so he decided in his wisdom that whatever was wrong wasn't anymore because you were ignoring us like you usually did. But whatever was wrong is still wrong, the way I figure it.'

I look at the bare walls and shelves of my room, a room that once was filled with the memorabilia of my first fifteen years but was stripped in a rage one night in July of 1958 and never restored or refurbished.

'I'm fine,' I tell Susan.

I try to remember the bookshelves stacked with golf trophies and cataloged advice on the sport, my walls lined with photographs of me swinging various clubs at various ages, standing importantly with the greats who came to play Miami and who were duly warned by my father of my impending arrival as he posed those at the top with their heir presumptive and snapped the Kodak.

'Bullshit them all you want, JD. They'll swallow anything that makes it easier for them to accept the fact neither of us is what they wanted us to be and that neither of them can figure out what they did to screw us up. But don't bullshit me.'

I don't remember her being this hard. What's her future going to be like if she's this hard now, at twenty-five?

'I was sick,' I say. 'I had some upper GI problems. Chest pains.'

I have the feeling not too many things impress my sister anymore. Chest pains impress her.

'Like when you were a kid?'

'Na,' I say, 'nothing like that, not that bad. They're gone, it was nothing.'

'Where'd they come from?'

'D'know – you call this number, couple of days they come in the mail.'

'From the Ph.D.,' she asks, 'or from a girl?'

'There was a girl in the mix.'

'A girl gave you chest pains? She must have been some girl.'

'She was passable,' I say. 'I figure if she was really good, she would've given me cancer or acne – something major. But, in any event, we're not together anymore, and I don't have the pains.'

'In love with her?'

My sister does not ask the question in a complete sentence; to do so would give credibility to something we have both craved but which – until now – neither of us has experienced.

'Was,' I say, giving it only that much credibility and putting it in a safe tense. 'But it's not fair to dump it all on her. Wasn't just her. It was other stuff, too.'

'For instance?' Susan adjusts her legs, sucking my eyes downward momentarily, where I catch a glimpse of her profusion of pubic hair as it flashes and disappears. 'The cunt of Godzilla,' as I once overheard her describe it to Shana and Trudi in a not infrequent teenage outburst of self-loathing. 'Hair gone mad!' she cried, inviting her two friends to explain to her why they had 'tiny little poofs' and she had 'this jungle.'

I slide my eyes to the carpet, thinking of Leslie Ann's silken, perfect equilateral triangle.

'I wrote a play,' I say.

'As in live and onstage?'

'My next-door neighbor was taking an MFA in directing. He needed something to do for his thesis. I wrote something.'

My sister's eyes are alive for the first time since I arrive home. As kids we grew up on the movies, on TV; there was virtually no live theater in the Miami area, unless you consider Sammy Davis, Jr., at the Diplomat Hotel live theater. But we saw a touring company of *Annie Get Your Gun* at the Dade County Auditorium when we were in elementary school, and though my father disliked it because he said he could smell the feet of everyone around us (my mother suggested if he hadn't bought the cheap seats, the smells would have been entirely different), my sister was hooked. She wanted to be a stage actor, and she dressed up and did after-supper shows for the family, took piano and dance lessons.

Until she got it in her head that unattractive people didn't make it in Show Business.

('Tell me one singing, dancing big name that's ugly!' she demanded.

'Jimmy Durante,' my father said, trying to be helpful.

'Oh, great,' said my sister. 'Oh, thanks.' Weeks later,

months, maybe, she came out of her room, her dreams of a life in Show Biz eighty-sixed.)

Now, a decade and a half later, she is titillated by the prospect of my taking up that old banner for her.

'Is it a good play?' she wants to know.

'No.'

'Is it really bad, or now that you have a Ph.D. are you trying to be humble?'

'It's really bad.'

'How hard did you try?'

She has always pretended to think more of me than I deserved to have thought of me. This new hardness in her wants to attack, to accuse me of not having tried hard enough, of having held back, protected myself.

'I gave it everything I had,' I said.

But for the first time, I wonder if I did hold back.

'So what about you?' I ask.

'Working at the store,' she says, distracted by the hints of the life I've led in my absence from her, 'hoping to finish my undergraduate degree by the millennium.'

'Why don't you go full-time, get it done, and go to law school?'

'What for?'

'You don't want to work in a shoe store all your life.'

'I'm waiting for something. Or maybe for some*body*.'

'Don't have anybody?'

'Lotta *anybodies*, JD. Anybody who doesn't have a communicable disease.'

I hold my arms open to my sister, who shakes her head, disavowing the need for succor; then, as I do not retract the invitation, she comes to lie down beside me, in the crook of my arm, against my chest.

Gimme some bulk, Jakey, toast me up.

'We really screwed up, Jacob. How'd that happen?'

'Beats the hell outta me, kid.'

'Me I can see. I was ugly and smart and I wanted to be pretty and dumb. But you ... Somehow, someone should've been able to figure out why you couldn't put that little white ball in that hole anymore. Pop'll never forgive himself that he couldn't figure out how to do the job himself.'

I stroke my sister's cheek and blink my eyes furiously against the tears that blur my vision of my bare walls.

'He sits in front of those golf tournaments Sunday after Sunday and projects you into the body of every one of those slick studs who wins one of those things.'

I flick a hand across my eyes. In the darkness behind my eyelids I see storms of electric light, and for a moment I glimpse amid the flashes the mementos of my lost dreams.

4

Knowing, say, that someone is in an area of approximately eight million people and you are twenty-three hundred miles away in a household that doesn't make long-distance calls, how do you proceed to locate that person if, for instance, you don't know her address, phone number, or the person to contact in case of emergency?

You don't.

What you do is you lie in bed, shaped like a croissant, and you miss and desire and despise that person and you imagine the unimaginable in the ways of vengeance, hoping against hope that by morning you will inure yourself to longing for and even thinking about that lost person.

Even though you're pretty sure it won't work.

Sometimes, I've heard, though thinking does no good at all, prayer is helpful.

Dear God That I'm Pretty Sure Doesn't Exist, please let me forget the only person in my life I have ever wanted to remember even when I'm dead.

When the phone rings at three-fifteen in the morning, I snatch the receiver off the hook before anyone else in the house awakens, so powerfully, I realize, have I been anticipating its sound.

'We have to be together,' she'll say. 'I'll go to New Mexico with you or you come here with me – it doesn't matter . . .'

'Hi, Les.'

'Hi, Jakey. I just wanted to make sure you got home all right.'

'Yep – sure did. Where are you?'

'Los Angeles. A motel in Santa Monica.'

She doesn't offer the name, I don't ask.

'Jacob?'

'Yeah, Les.'

'When I went down to the garage the other day to leave, I waited ten minutes for you to come after me.'

'I lay in bed for an hour, waiting for you to come back.'

I can hear her breathing. She always holds the phone very close to her lips, practically climbs inside.

'Well, I guess we showed each other, didn't we?' she says. 'Or something.'

'I think "or something" is close.'

No laughter, no snicker. Is she smiling? Sitting? Standing? Alone? In a kitchen, a motel, at a pay phone?

She sucks in a massive breath. 'I can't get a decent breath, Jacob.'

'The air,' I say.

'Or something,' she says.

The line crackles.

Outside my window, distant thunder rolls from the ocean.

'Does every couple who ever loved each other figure they were unique in all the world? The one true love?'

'Probably.'

'Why would you want to be together if you didn't feel like that, right?'

Lightning illuminates my room momentarily through my curtains.

'Howard asked me once why I wouldn't sleep with him. I told him we lacked the qualities to be tragic.'

Howard asked me once why I wouldn't sleep with him?

'You never slept with Howard?'

'We got naked once when we first met, but I stopped. I knew it was just . . . just fucking to him.'

'Why didn't you tell me that?'

Before she says it, I know she's going to say, 'D'know.' But she doesn't. She takes one of those breaths and says, 'Make you jealous, maybe; keep the tension.'

Do I believe her?

Why would she lie about that now?

'That day you wouldn't urinate on me? Remember?'

'I remember everything, Leslie Ann.'

'Howard didn't pee on me. I told him I was playing a joke on you. I went in his kitchen and wet myself with orange juice.'

'Why'd you do that?'

'You were so consumed with writing that play so you could be better than me.'

'I don't think that's quite accurate. I wasn't trying to be better than you, I was trying to be good enough *for* you.'

'Same thing,' she says.

Cryptogram from Hollywood.

'Remember Sunday night grape feasts? That big red plastic bowl full of seedless greens and purples. Just sitting in front of the TV, cuddled up, watching *Bonanza*. Remember the time you stuck a grape in your nose and bet me you could blow it farther across the room than I could?'

We both laugh.

Sunday night, cuddled up watching *Bonanza*. She

loved Lorne Greene. We used to joke that when she made it big, she'd do Cordelia and Lorne would do Lear. That, we agreed, would be a Shakespeare for our times.

Down the hall, I hear a toilet flush. My mother or father up in the night. I've heard that from a certain age on, you can't sleep through a night without having to empty your bladder.

Something to look forward to.

'How is it being home?'

'The first twelve hours have been very nice. Tell me about you.'

'Oh Jakey, there are thousands of me here. Just different names – Fawn, Dawn, Sheena, Shawna, Pam, Sam – same eyes, same hair, no fat, firm breasts, miniskirts. Can you go to an audition in anything today but a miniskirt?'

'Have you been to auditions already?'

'Oh sure. What was I going to do – sit around and think?'

'Tell me about the auditions.'

'Can I?'

'Of course. Anytime. You can always call me.'

'For as long as we both shall live?'

'Even longer if there are phones.'

Chimes.

I miss that laugh.

I miss the 'tension.'

The danger.

'Okay.' Wherever she is, I can see her get into her in-bed-talking position – on her side, legs tucked up, cheek on palm of hand. 'I've been to three so far. They were all B movies – they're the only things that have open calls.'

'Lot of raping, lot of plundering.'

'*Lot* of raping and plundering. So at each audition I read a really insipid scene – and then at each one I was asked if I'd consider doing a nude scene. When I said yes, I'd consider it, all three producers asked if I'd mind taking my clothes off now, adding hastily that there was a union representative in the room – like all these producers go to a class and memorize the same lines, you know. Union rep raises her hand. First audition, I asked what that means, having a union rep in the room. Smile, chuckle: That's to make sure we're not just a bunch of horny guys getting free looks at naked women. They all said they liked my reading and that not taking off my clothes wouldn't count against me. I decline, in that case, I said to each horny gentleman, to take my clothes off. Each nodded understandingly in his turn and said that I'd hear from him. I haven't.'

'They lied.'

'Yeah.'

'I'm surprised.'

'I know.'

Down the hall, my sister cries out in her sleep. A clap of thunder explodes closer now out my window. I move the curtain. Lightning flashes overhead, and rain begins to slap against the window. From here I can see the tenth fairway at Normandy Shores.

I don't like it that much, Poppy.

Don't like it? What's not to like about a mitzvah, a blessing?

'What's important, Jacob?' Leslie Ann wants to know. 'What'll it mean if I make it in the movies or TV or even on the stage? I've been to six movies this week and four plays. All I could think in all cases was that

I wasn't watching real life, I was just watching sicko actors working out their therapy on my buck.'

'You're just frightened and you're naturally questioning yourself. There's *never* been anyone like you.'

'Thank you, Jacob.'

Her voice catches. My chest heaves, my teeth clamp involuntarily over my lower lip.

'I miss you most at mealtime and bedtime,' she says. 'It's been a long time since I've eaten and slept alone. I wake up on your side of the bed. I miss your bulk.'

And then she sobs.

'Jacob . . .'

'Yeah, Les.'

'I know I made you get tired of me,' she says. 'Because in real life, I'm just so gutless.'

And she's gone.

Lying there, holding the droning phone, I think: *She's the beautiful and damned princess in the tower. I'm the knight errant. I unlock the riddle of her curse and I can have her for life.*

But I wonder if maybe I didn't try as hard as I could to unlock the riddle because I didn't want the burden of then righting things so the princess and I could live happily ever after.

True or false?

D'know.

5

From earliest childhood I hate going to the Fontainebleau Hotel Cabana Club from April through
September. I hate it because I know we can't afford
to have a cabana at the Fontainebleau, but because my
father thinks my mother needs a cabana there, he spends
money he doesn't have on making her (and us), in his
view, equal to Beachites he doesn't really think she (or
we) are equal to.

Much as I don't want to go, I know that first Sunday
I have to go for my mother's sake, so she can, with that
modesty that reeks of unbearable pride, reintroduce me
to everyone I haven't seen for three years as Dr Jacob
Landau, professor.

To my mother's chagrin, all anyone really wants to
talk about, however, is how I look as if I've come
not from Palo Alto, but from Auschwitz, Dachau,
Bergen-Belsen – pick your camp.

This is a frame of reference that has a Pavlovian effect
on my father, who does fifteen minutes on the Jewish
quota at American proprietary universities. I make no
effort to stop him. This, I know, is his idea of fathering.
'A Jew is at the top of the academic heap out there,'
he says, 'what do you think that's going to do to the
next fifty Jewish boys apply to that joint? Guess how
many're going to get in? Huh – who thinks he knows?
Philly? . . .'

Phil Dickson shrugs – quotas aren't his field. What he

wants to talk is Literature: 'Harold Robbins,' he says to Dr Landau, 'top five American authors all-time or not, Jakey?'

'Top five, Philly, top six, who's to say.'

'Better than Irving Wallace or not?'

'I think we're talking a lock there, Philly.'

Phil Dickson nods, gestures to Thelma Dickson, settling finally an argument that has obviously raged for years. 'So much,' he says to her, 'for that.'

By noon, the concentration camp references aside, my mother achieves a surfeit of pride and I am free to retire to a lounge in a corner.

I watch my father at a distance, this woolly bear in a bathing suit that rides below his great belly, wearing black socks and tasseled loafers, reading a book on mathematics. ('Why are you reading a math book, Pop?' 'Who knows?' he says. 'It was on sale. I bought it.') Occasionally I catch him glancing across the deck at me.

He wants to get up. I want to get up. We want to meet midsundeck and do . . . what? Lend accuracy to events we have pretended for years didn't happen as we pretend they happened? Know things about the other's hopes and fears and histories that the owner of those respective hopes and fears and histories doesn't want to inflict on the other because . . . why?

'Not too much sun,' he yells when our eyes lock for the fourth or fifth time and a response of some sort becomes mandatory.

'Don't worry,' I yell back, poking testily at my pale skin and nodding as if we have achieved some major accord.

My mother, sequestered beneath a landing strip-size sun hat, says something to him, and one of my father's massive hands slices the air in a gesture of dismissal. He lumbers to his feet and moves to a group of older men playing gin.

Takes a spectating position with his back to my mother.

Who looks at me and smiles, waves. I wave. She continues to smile at me. I break eye contact.

I wonder if my father has ever hit her with one of those hands.

God, the way he held my hand when we crossed Fairway Drive to the golf course when I was a kid.

No, he never hit her. He was not a hitter.

But I wonder if he ever strokes her anymore with one of those hands.

At the gin table he takes a napkin from under someone's drink and blows his nose.

A cornucopia of nose.

What was that from?

High school. English class. Describe something vividly in one paragraph.

I described Morris Landau's nose.

Compulsively I begin preparing lectures and syllabi and quizzes for the classes I'm scheduled to teach at the University of New Mexico come September when, despite all my intentions to the contrary, I will evidently walk into a classroom and become, at least in name, a professor.

I don't know how long Sandra Pollack has been staring – or glaring – at me before my mother – who never particularly liked any of the girls I dated *except* Sandra (who was unfailingly nice to her) – moseys over to whisper, 'Look who's looking at who from guess where?'

'Who?' I ask.

'Look,' she says.

'Where?'

'The opposite direction from the one I nod.' She nods to my right.

I look to my left, but the moment I look Sandra's way she pointedly ignores me, therefore enticing me to unload my lap of notebook and five-pound survey edition of Modern American Lit and, with a little pat on the tush from my mother, cross the deck to where she lies behind a pair of flying saucer-size shades.

Here is the jilted girl I dated before the Yugoslavian in all her Slavic mystery turned my head to hairy armpits, Rachmaninoff, and Rimbaud. Tiny, doll-like Sandra with her big hazel eyes and delicate cheekbones, small mouth, rounded chin. Her hair used to cascade to the middle of her back; now it lies solemnly just below her elfin ears, emerging brown at her skull, becoming teak and then walnut blond the farther it gets from her head. Her skin has the soft, golden-brown sheen of her eyes. Her fingernails and toenails are perfectly (and professionally) manicured and painted bright red (Sandra began to accompany her mother to the manicurist – for her own upkeep – at the official outset of her teens).

From a distance Sandra's face has a soft, angelic look; but up close there is a seasoned, almost severe look to her like so many of the girls I grew up with here – a set to their mouths and eyes that suggests they have gone places in life and endured tests they have not.

Sandra Pollack lies facedown on her chaise, her bikini top unhooked, her arms ramrod straight down her sides to preclude any side shots of her breasts, her face turned down, peering through the slats of the chaise at the hardbound book open on the deck below (my cynical sister once noted that no one at the Fontainebleau is allowed to bring a paperback).

I stand close to Sandra's head, silent (as I can't think of a really scintillating opener), anticipating that she'll recognize me by my feet, the big toes of which, in lieu of anything that would threaten her amateur status, she once enjoyed sucking.

I'm dying to see what she's reading. Robbins, Wallace, the hot lowbrow book of the summer, *The Exorcist*?

Tacked to the lounge, Sandra twists her head to me, shading her eyes against the sun that isn't shining in them, unattractively distending her mouth and popping the veins in her neck. 'Yes?'

Yes?

'Jacob Landau,' I say, hoping that by playing along a round or two I'll quickly launch this charade into the realm of the ridiculous.

By the vacant manner with which Sandra looks at me, I sense I may be in for a long routine here. Trying to leap some of the inevitable, I tell her, 'I know, I look like shit, I contracted periphrasis in the Tropics, what can I say, but it's me, your former future fiancé, how you doin', may I sit down and bridge a gap or two?'

She stares at me, trying to convince me she is actually trying to convince herself it actually *is* me.

It's been a long time since I played games like this. To test my recall of accepted procedure, I say to Sandra, 'Well, if gap bridging is out of the question, may I say that I've been observing you from across the pool, Sanny, and I felt it my duty to make my way over to tell you that all the precautions you took to unfasten your top and situate yourself so that you could both sun your entire back and preserve the fact that your breasts are embarrassingly, shall we say, *petite* was a sizable failure. I got a refresher course in your entire western tit, a bonus I had not dared dream I might achieve on my first Sunday back in Pastrami Land.'

With that I return to my corner. My mother winks at me. To her, this reunion looked good. Promising.

When my sister came home from her marriage with dental floss and no babies, my mother pinned her hopes for grandchildren on me.

I can feel Sandra Pollack boiling across the deck. I turn my attention to my notes, but momentarily she stands in front of me, her book pressed to her chest for protection. When I glimpse the title, I want to crush her head like a grape. Surely she doesn't expect me to believe she's reading *The Pentagon Papers*!

She says, 'I ought to smack you right in the mouth, JD Landau.'

Wanting to call a truce, to act like I imagine a twenty-seven-year-old Ph.D. should, I hear myself say nevertheless, 'You do and I'll punch you right in your reconstructed nose.'

Sandra knows from our previous relationship that a verbal battle with me in which there are no rules of decorum is not one she can do better than lose in a rout. With a Ph.D., she envisions me, I imagine, as unassailable. And so she stands before me projecting an attitude that says, 'As always, you hurt me. Apologize. Please.'

I have no interest, I realize, in Sandra Pollack – she could never replace Leslie Ann except in the most elementary, generic way – so I am a little surprised at the exchange that follows.

'So San,' my voice says.

'What?'

'How about dinner tonight?'

'You've got to be kidding,' says she, the long-ago and newly injured party.

'You're probably right, but how about some chow anyway?'

Behavior. Actions. Reaction.

Watch this, Les.

6

D on't drive that thing to take a young woman to dinner,' my mother says. 'Take the Caddy.'

My mother, for my father's benefit, will not dignify my Volkswagen by giving it a name.

'Sure,' he says, 'you want the yacht, take it. Here – ' And he digs the keys from the pocket of his voluminous madras Bermuda shorts, worn, like his bathing suit, over his tassel loafers and black socks.

During the two years after college I worked in the shoe store, a mean-spirited notion took up residence in my head: My father is overly sensitive about Germans. Many of them are perfectly nice. So when I was getting ready to leave for graduate school, I am certain I bought the V-dub – used, battered, in furious barter – to offend my father.

'I've really come to admire German engineering,' I said at the time. 'I've got to have something cheap and dependable.'

My father said nothing. Made no objection.

Jesus, what do we do to each other?

And why do fathers like my father wear Bermuda shorts with black socks and tasseled loafers?

With perhaps more gratitude than the gesture deserves, I say to him, 'Thanks, Pop, I'm telling you, that Krautmobile has been a piece a crap. Vapor locked five times coming through the desert on the way home. Unbelievable. Goddamn Krauts.'

I reach for the keys to what Susan calls the 'Jewcanoe,' hoping to allow my hand to linger a moment against my father's, but he tosses the keys through the air, forcing me to catch them.

7

I'm greeted at the baronial entryway to the Pollacks' five-bedroom, seven-bath, neo-Moorish-Mediterranean monstrosity on exclusive Sunset Island #2 by Sandra's father, who is dressed in white patent-leather slip-ons, double knit slacks, and a synthetic print shirt that clings to his expanding flesh like a tattooed second skin; he is awash in rings, a gold watch no thicker than a couple of dollar bills and an outsize cable-link, gold ID with 'Ernie' written in script. Behind him stands Sandra's mother, the image of what I think of as the Miami Beach housewife of opulent means – so smartly dressed in a double-knit pants suit, so fastidiously coiffed and made-up and accoutred in just slightly too much jewelry that I want both to fuck her and beat the shit out of her because she always looks better than my mother and has never worked a day in her life.

'JD,' says Ernie Pollack, crushing my fossilized fingers together, 'long time no see.'

'Mr Pollack,' say I, 'long time no see.' I have never been crazy about Ernie Pollack, who followed his son Michael's golf career as obsessively as my father did mine but who silently disparaged my father and openly chastised his son, Michael, because he could never beat me. 'Mrs Pollack,' I say, 'long time no see.'

'Hello, JD,' says Neddie Pollack. She almost masks her disdain for me and what I did eight years ago to her daughter, whom I could never be worthy of and

who should certainly have had the sense to dump me
before I defamed the entire family by dumping *her*.

'The Micker couldn't get over tonight,' says Ernie
Pollack with a toss of his hands that suggests life
can really throw up some cruel roadblocks when it
wants to.

'That's the way it goes,' I say, trying with religious
zeal not to think about what in God's name I'm doing
here with these people again.

'Give him a call first thing in the morning,' Ernie
Pollack says. 'He'll appreciate it.'

Knowing I won't and sure Michael Pollack would just
as soon I didn't, I assure Ernie Pollack, 'It's at the top
my list.'

'He can hardly wait to talk to you.'

'Double for me.'

I figure we've done about the requisite amount of this,
and Neddie Pollack must agree because she shoves on to
the next item on the agenda. 'JD,' she says, 'you've lost
a lot of weight.'

'Yes, Mrs P.,' I agree, 'yes, I *have* lost a lot of
weight.'

'You must have been sick,' she says.

'Yes,' I agree, 'yes I was. I *was* sick.'

'But,' says Neddie Pollack, warning me I'd better not
be if I plan to traffic with her daughter again, 'you're
not anymore.'

'No,' I assure her, 'no, now I'm well.'

Ernie and Neddie Pollack nod at this good news,
and when nobody spurs the conversation on to greater
heights, Neddie embarks on a new tack entirely. 'It's
nice to see somebody with short hair for a change, isn't
it?' she asks both me and her husband, whether looking
for a consensus or just an opinion I'm not sure.

I don't say whether I agree with her or not. Not simply because I feel disposed to aggravate the Pollacks, but because I'm trying to silence the voice in my head that has begun to cackle at me contemptuously.

'Isn't it refreshing, Ernie?' Neddie Pollack asks her husband when I fail to return the ball. 'Short hair for a change?'

'You know, JD,' Ernie Pollack says with abrupt, sweet intensity, 'I've known for eight years that the day would come when you'd show up at our door again to take our daughter to dinner.'

It's the first time I realize that for the half year Sandra and I were a serious item, it wasn't Sandra's father who initiated the contempt I felt for my prospective membership in their family.

As if, despite my claim of wellness, she were announcing the arrival of a disease, Neddie Pollack calls into the labyrinthine house, 'San, JD's here!'

'How about a drink?' Ernie Pollack asks.

The formality of it all – the getting dressed, the going to the girl's house, the entremets, as my mother used to call these moments between the young man and the girl's parents, precious few of which my mother experienced during my sister's adolescence; the waiting for the girl's entrance – all of it, gone from my life for as long as I've been gone from Sandra Pollack, is having a strange effect on me that, despite my cynicism and the voice cackling at me, I find difficult to resist.

I am giving in, I think, *to giving up Leslie Ann Masterson and all she represents.*

That dream.

And nightmare.

Ernie Pollack stands behind his teakwood bar and opens his hands. 'Name it.'

'A shot of vodka, a shot of Scotch, and a shot of bourbon,' I say.

The Pollacks turn small, rumpled smiles on me, the man willing to be amused, the woman not.

'I was just thinking about the first drink I had,' I tell them, 'right here at this bar with Michael when we were fourteen and anxious to grow up.'

'Fourteen?' Neddie Pollack asks.

'Nineteen,' I amend. 'We thought a mixed drink was a *mixed* drink.'

Ernie Pollack chuckles, his wife exhales carbon dioxide in the direction of one of the three Tiffany lamps in the room.

'Jack Daniel's, please,' I say, 'no ice, no water.'

Ernie Pollack cracks a new bottle of Black Jack. 'Well, JD, so you're an English professor now. Not many of our boys down here go into education.'

'No,' I agree, 'no, they don't. And I'm not sure I want to be one of the first.'

'You're not going to teach?' asks Ernie Pollack.

'I may,' I say, 'I may not.' This is news to me. 'You know, sorting my options.'

What options?

'Well, I'm sure there are many avenues a young man with your intelligence and drive and education could take.'

For the first time, I realize for a fact that *I don't have to go to New Mexico and teach*.

'And we hear you've written a book about Miami Beach,' Neddie Pollack says.

A book about Miami Beach? In a mere twenty-four hours, through the mysteries of gossip and parental pride, the play that failed or the dissertation that was vicious and pointless has become 'a book about Miami Beach.'

There's a nebulous fear not quite under wraps down at the bottom of Neddie Pollack's voice, however, that's irresistible, so, 'Yes,' I say, 'a modest little study of the mating ritual of the third-generation Jewish American of upper-middle-class background. The result of my research indicates – and this really boggled my mind – that Hitler was a cabana boy at the Fontainebleau in the late twenties, and *that's* what really started that whole Final Solution business and led to the invention in my generation of the so-called Jewish-American princess and the nascent fear that young Jewish men will be the ones to complete that Final Solution. Scared the hell out of me, I can tell you that.'

Only the cackling voice in my head laughs at that one.

Ernie Pollack hands me my drink with a look that says he's assuming that's a joke until he hears differently from the source.

Neddie Pollack, on the other hand, wants to know right now, 'Was that intended to be amusing, JD?'

'Well, Mrs P., yes, yes, it was.'

'Of course it was,' says Ernie Pollack. 'Ethnic humor is very popular nowadays.'

'It works a hell of a lot better,' I tell Ernie Pollack, 'in a roomful of gentiles.'

Ernie Pollack laughs a big phlegmy laugh, so that Neddie Pollack has to say somewhat too loudly, 'You know, JD, I always suspected you of being an anti-Semite.'

'Hello,' says Sandra Pollack as she sweeps into the room wearing a long walnut-blond fall that blends perfectly into the extremities of her own hair, white patent-leather low-heeled sandals, and a double-knit pants suit, the jacket open over a synthetic print shirt that hugs her tiny torso like a prophylactic. 'I'm sorry I'm late.'

'No problem,' I say, tossing off the shot of mash, 'next time I'll come later.'

8

As I engineer my dad's Caddy convertible out of her driveway, I say to Sandra, 'It's been a long time, Sanny, since I've seen a girl your age wearing grown-up clothes and hair that isn't her own.'

Sandra's eyes become glassy and she looks out the window of the big, fish-finned car at the incredible verdancy of Miami Beach.

'Are you sure you want to start up with me again, JD?'

I can see the tips of the bobby pins holding the hair that isn't Sandra's to the hair that is, and I feel a surge of tenderness for her and wish, for her sake, she *wasn't* about to become involved with me again.

I first became involved with Sandra at a time in my life when I desperately needed someone to think highly of me. She did. Why, I haven't the faintest idea. I was a sophomore in college. I had no career aspirations. I wasn't in a fraternity. I didn't drive a nice car. I had no extracurricular activities.

'I'm sure,' I say, and touch her hand with mine. For a moment she doesn't respond, but then she turns her palm up to mine and our two hands wind together with eerie familiarity.

Her hands are small, the fingers narrow and hollow feeling. Similar to Leslie Ann's.

But not hers, not Leslie Ann's, which worked in concert with the rest of her body to convey worlds.

Sandra's hand in mine seems only to convey anxiety.

But then Sandra's father never stuck his fingers in her, and neither parent, according to something she told me years ago, had ever screamed in fury at her, let alone struck her.

9

Over fried dumplings she says, 'Michael just finished his residency in gynecology.'

'I'm not surprised,' I say. 'He was always trying to look up girls' dresses.'

'You'll like him, I think.'

'I always did.'

'Not really.'

'So why would I now?'

'Because he's turned into a very nice man.'

'That's good. Because he was sure a *putz* the last time I saw him.' The last time I saw Michael Pollack, he was playing number one for the University of Florida golf team and told me that he was better then than I would have been, even if I'd had the guts to keep playing.

'Worse than the *putz* you were the last time I saw you?'

'No,' I say, 'not that bad.'

I didn't even have the guts or the dignity or the regard for either of us to tell Sandra face to face that I was dumping her for the Slav. Imagining I was doing something memorable – for whom, I'm not sure, because then (as now) I had no real friends or accomplices to show off for – I sent her a single white rose, accompanied by a card that said: '*Je regret.* JD.'

'The worst of it,' I tell her now, 'is I didn't even speak French. I stole the whole thing from some account

I heard of some famous French actor dumping his
girlfriend.'

She looks at me. The look says that I have just paid
some penance for that act, at last, by admitting to its
callowness.

'A lot of people who used to know you,' she says,
'were very impressed when the *Sun* ran that article
on you.'

*Hey, Pop, JD's on the phone; he's been arrested! Isn't
that fabulous? You gotta send money.*

The *Miami Beach Sun* ran a story under the headline
FORMER BEACH LINKS GREAT ARRESTED.

'I was very impressed that you cared enough about the
injustice of the war to try to do something about it.'

*Former Miami Beach golfing prodigy JD Landau was
arrested yesterday at the forefront of an antiwar demonstration on the campus of Stanford University . . .*

My mind reels against the endless fantasies I entertained as a boy about heroic homecomings – fantasies
that ceased on that afternoon when I missed first
the putt that tied the United States Golf Association
Junior Championship and then the putt that gave the
championship to the kid from California who blew a
two-stroke lead earlier in the day and had been sitting
in the clubhouse for a half hour, waiting to descend into
a lifelong agony from which I rescued him.

Sandra lays her chopsticks on her plate and presses
her face into her napkin.

'What's the matter?'

She shakes her head and replaces her napkin in her
lap. Smiles symmetrically at me. 'So, tell me – how was
the Chinese food in San Francisco? Fabulous, I'll bet.'

'The Chinese food in San Francisco is inedible. Whole
thing's a Chamber of Commerce conspiracy. All those

ostensible Chinks out there? Surgically altered Mongols, every one.'

The symmetrical smile breaks down.

Becomes real.

We both laugh – her laughter metallic and throaty, like mine.

After dinner – those several hours of weaving through her (I assume abridged) version of her past eight years and my editing of mine – we sit on the beach that runs from south of the First Street Pier to the jetty that marks the end of Miami Beach and the marriage of the Atlantic Ocean with Biscayne Bay. The water slides to within inches of our shoes.

Beneath the lights on the First Street Pier we can see fifty or so people fishing, as I used to when I was a boy and wanted to dream in private but out of doors and then again later, after that failure at the eighteenth hole, when I needed to get away from everyone and everywhere so I could feel sorry for and hate myself in tranquillity.

I unpin Sandra's fall from her own hair and kiss her. This old new mouth is an off fit with my own – too small, it needs to be stretched to accommodate my tongue, and it emits a strange taste that is neither the aftertaste of dinner nor the styptic bite of the Sen-Sen she supplied both of us from her purse as we walked down the beach moments earlier. It is something that lives in her mouth somewhere, that is almost acrid but not quite and that I've forgotten. I remember thinking long ago that the prospect of a lifetime married to that taste would necessitate asking her to do something about it.

Most of all, though, her mouth, her tongue, her taste, are not Leslie Ann's.

And finally Sandra Pollack asks, 'What happened to us eight years ago, JD?'

'I became confused,' I say, figuring that's a good all-purpose answer for any question having to do with my actions.

'Maybe what scared you was that I loved you for so long. God, I fell in love with you when I was twelve years old, riding in the cart with my father, following you and Michael around the golf course. Maybe it scared you that I believed in you even after you didn't. Maybe you resented the pressure you imagined that put on you to become something else that had about it the glory that being a famous athlete would have.'

Ah, analysis!

'Hey, I think you got insightful while I was gone.'

'I was always insightful. I just learned to hide it so I wouldn't scare you with that, too.'

The water creeps closer to our shoes, but we remain where we are, and I do feel threatened by her intelligence, by a feeling that what I always assumed was some advantage of mine over her had been just the opposite. Seeking an advantage now, I initiate another kiss into which she turns while simultaneously I cup her blouse where it and her brassiere cover one of her breasts.

She startles me further by two-fingering my hand away and holding it like a small, rabid animal. 'Don't, please.'

Feeling truly foolish now, I say, 'Don't *you* do *that*. I don't like that cute, inviolable crap.'

'It's my breast, JD.'

We're heading for thirty and we're carrying on like we're fifteen, except at fifteen I was still on my way to golfing immortality and all there was to write about my sex life could have been written on the head of my three

wood. Still, something in me erupts and I say, 'Now, I'm
going to give your knob here a turn, Sandra, and if you
pull any of that Miami Beach Jewish princess bullshit,
there's going to be trouble.'

'I'm not a Jewish princess!'

'You're the prototype!'

I remember that in anger tiny capillaries ignite just
beneath the surface of Sandra's skin like tracks of neon
run amok. Though I cannot see well enough to be sure,
I imagine her face ablaze.

'Propriety of self has nothing to do with being Jewish!'

'Don't construct pretentious sentences like that,
Sandra – you're really pissing me off!'

I crave . . .

I launch a hand toward the breast. She catches the
hand in both of hers.

'JD,' she says, 'it's been too long, and you may not!'

I dump her fall into her lap, scoop her into my arms,
carry her into the water up to my knees, and heave her
screaming into the sea.

. . . violence!

Feeling deliciously impenitent, I leave Sandra there
and go home.

My sister lies on my ancient paisley bedspread, reading my dissertation manuscript.

I drop onto the chair at my desk, a chair on which in high school and college I scrape a nick for each girl I feel up or finger, from Myrna Horovitz to Sandra Pollack — seven notches in all.

Where are they now?

Where is Candi Garfunkel? Rochelle Isser? Deanna Kugel?

Married, probably. Women, in all likelihood, who speak wistfully of Woodstock (having missed it, I imagine unkindly, due to hair appointments), who have given up oral sex, having tried it and liked it, and now spend a lot of time misquoting Buber and Tillich? Mothers now, full of practical intelligence, who have forgotten my hands on their breasts, which have begun to sag earthward from breast-feeding their babies.

How old would our child be in Leslie Ann's womb now? Hours? Days? Months?

'How was it, venturing back into your lurid past?' Susan asks with more interest than she'll allow her voice to convey.

'Little tricky,' I confess.

She riffles some pages of my manuscript and says, 'This is pretty radical stuff, you know.'

'Na,' I say. 'Believe me, it's just whacking off.'

'Using "adamantine" in the first sentence to describe a group of people we think of as resolutely free-spirited – got to be either radical or whacking off, I guess.'

'All free-spirited movements eventually make a religion out of their freedom. Once it's a religion, it becomes adamantine.'

'Nice words,' she says. 'Nice aphorism.'

'Mm.'

'Your shoes are wet.'

'You need to talk about anything?'

'What's that mean?'

'It means if you want to talk, we'll talk; otherwise, I want to get in bed and dwell on my own discontent.'

'Hey, I got along without your counsel for three years, know what I mean?'

'I think I know exactly what you mean, so I'm going to hit the sack.'

I'm disappointed. I feel the need to be needed, to be forced to convey some intelligent advice to her from which I might glean something for myself. I kiss the top of her head and disappear into the bathroom. 'G'night.'

'Hey, don't be mad.'

'I'm not.'

'Just that it's not the old days. I'm not hanging around waiting for you to solve my problems for me.'

'Sounds good,' I say through the door.

I've never thought about it in this way, but maybe one of the reasons I haven't come home for three years is because I knew if I was here, I would feel obligated to make right all the wrongs in the lives of the other three people who reside here.

And maybe they wouldn't cooperate.
Or worse, maybe I couldn't do it.

12

At the cabana the next day, I commit rape.

It happens this way: Sandra Pollack doesn't favor me with so much as a glance when she arrives just after one from her half day of work at her father's jewelry store. (The other half of the day, she told me at dinner, her father had invited her 'to improve herself.' 'How?' I had asked. 'Read,' she had said, 'think.') She disappears behind the doors to one of the two dressing rooms that stand on either side of the shower in each of the Fontainebleau's several hundred cabanas.

Since I have come expressly to see Sandra (for admittedly murky reasons), I'm offended.

So I cross the deck and silently enter the dressing room Sandra hasn't. Soundlessly I climb onto the dressing room bench and peer over the wall separating the two cubicles.

Sandra stands in pink lace bikini panties, shedding her blouse over her head.

I pull myself to the top of the wall, throw my legs over, and drop commando style to the cement floor.

Before the scream that comes instinctively to her lips can hit the airwaves, I trap the sound in her mouth with my hand. The impression of her rosebud lips is lipstick creamy against my palm.

'If you scream,' I promise her, 'somebody's going to come and you're going to be very embarrassed.'

Something in her eyes says she thinks I'm kidding, that the one thing this *isn't* is a legitimate rape.

I feel compelled to convince Sandra Pollack she's kidding herself if she thinks I'm kidding.

My hand fast against her mouth, her body wedged along my side, I take her brassiere by the lace coupler that binds its two cups and rip the device off her body – something I've dreamed of doing since puberty but has always seemed not only wrong but cost prohibitive.

Sandra's breasts are as proportionally small as the rest of her – what were referred to in the girlie magazines of my youth as 'pert' – and her nipples turn inward, as if in retreat, what I used to call unkindly her 'Nay-Nay Nipples,' as in 'Nay, nay, you must not touch me. See, I disappear. Zoop!'

I cup one of the breasts in my palm. There is a change in Sandra's eyes: she's beginning to take me seriously.

She squirms against me, tries to speak from behind my hand.

Curious to know what she has to say, I make her an offer: 'I'll take my hand away,' I tell her, 'but if you scream, it's Cronkite at six.'

Sandra gives me the benefit of one sharp nod of her head, and I remove my hand. 'JD, you idiot,' she whispers, 'my mother! Have you regressed from merely insensitive to Neanderthal since you were nineteen?'

Idiot! Neanderthal – whoa! I imprison her hands in one of mine and press her backward onto the dressing bench as she struggles to free herself. I drop to my knees, yanking her panties down and off one ankle with my free hand as I do so.

There is no question any longer in either of our minds that this is a no-nonsense violation of Sandra's rights and very person.

She liberates her right hand, squeezes it into a fist, and swings it with significant force into the side of my head, setting off a series of door buzzers in my left ear. She then cocks her right leg and explodes her pedicured right foot into my chest, sending me tumbling backward into the cabana door.

'Cut it out, Jacob, and I mean it!'

I know that if I counterattack now, I'll be compelled to seriously injure Sandra Pollack.

I get to my feet, the desire to ravish her almost as powerful as my respect for her resistance. I bob my head up and down at her as if she's deeply insulted me in some obscure fashion and turn to the door latch, flip it up, and throw the door open.

In the distance, half of Miami Beach is bathing, frolicking, spritzing and urinating in the commodious Fontainebleau pool.

I touch the ache on the side of my head where Sandra belted me. My fingers come away with just the hint of blood. She got me with the softball-size bloodstone she wears on her right pinkie finger – her birthstone, gift of her loving father when she was sixteen.

'Are you bleeding?'

'I believe I am.'

'Good.'

'I like it, too,' I said, and start out the door.

Behind me Sandra says, 'Wait.'

I stop. Turn to her.

'I didn't dismiss you, did I?'

She's on her feet, staring at me, hands at her sides, private parts exposed, lips pursed, compressing there some deep thought to which I'm not privy.

'Shut the door, little boy.'

Sensing distantly that I have badly misread this young

woman and that it may be I, not she, who's in danger here, I feel the battering ram between my legs engorging with blood and desire and therefore follow instructions.

'Don't quite have the grit to do something *really* criminal, do you, Jacob Daniel? I'm kind of disappointed, but at least you're not *totally* uncivilized, are you?'

She lifts one arm, baring her slick armpit and just the hint of some chalky antiperspirant. 'Lick,' she says.

Lick her *armpit*?

'Come on,' she says. 'You want to give me a thrill – isn't that what this is about? Huh? Thrilling me?'

I advance toward the offered armpit. Serenely she watches my approach.

I run my tongue across the just barely bristling flesh. The chalk tastes of lemons.

Air rushes from between Sandra Pollack's teeth.

I press her back down onto the little changing bench, return to my knees, slide her legs over my shoulders as I insinuate my tongue between her slick lips.

It's evidently not the part of me she was anticipating.

Her legs clamp like a vise around my ears.

'JD . . . no, don't . . . I don't do that.'

She doesn't do that? What's *she* doing? *I'm* doing the doing, she's getting done – and I ponder in passing how it was we never progressed at least to this in our half year of panting, collegiate, preRevolution, nonlovemaking.

'Damn you, stop that disgusting – '

I get a good grip on Sandra's warm buttocks and imprison her center against my mouth.

She tests the very ability of my scalp to retain hair and tries to free a foot to separate my mouth from her vagina.

I clamp my elbows over her knees, neutralize her legs.

And now Sandra Pollack suddenly whimpers, grasps my ears in her fingers, practically tearing them off my head, and fiercely mashes my entire face into her viscous center. 'Great, *Myron*,' she hisses (the derivation of that totally inexplicable), 'no wonder they call you "Doctor"!'

I have forgotten Sandra's propensity for somehow lightening many of the more enchanting moments in our life together. Don't just give a guy a hand job; no, be sure to make choo-choo sounds as the ole rhythm increases so that a guy can know the amusement of having an orgasm accompanied by the sound of the ten-twenty from Palm Beach.

Her fingers straining my hair at its roots, she goes silent now except for the air that spills out of her mouth, and I am about to rip my pants off and fulfill the last of the fantasy and end our long celibacy when the cubicle fills with sunlight and Sandra's mother, Nedra Pollack, stands behind us in her beach jacket, shades, and wedgies, a BLT on whole wheat on a paper plate in one hand.

Neddie's head recoils as if she's been struck in the face, the BLT flies, and her hand goes to her mouth and captures there the sound she's about to make, a sound no doubt loud enough to summon to the doorway of the cabana everyone in the southern United States.

I rise from between Sandra's legs and dab at my mouth with the back of my hand, wondering if Sandra's nippleless breasts are inherited from her mother or her father's side of the family.

'I hope,' says Neddie Pollack with admirable evenness, 'that you're planning an honorable arrangement with my daughter, JD, because if you're not, I'm going to hire someone of Latin descent to cut your balls off.'

'Actually,' I say, 'an honorable arrangement with your daughter is one of about eleven things I have on my master agenda to consider, Mrs P., so hold off on the Latin guy until I can get back to you. Okay?'

My heart crashing in joy and fear against my chest, I lift a piece of Bibb lettuce off Neddie Pollack's shoulder and edge past her in the cramped doorway, step over some bacon and tomato, and turn to wink at naked Sandra, popping the piece of lettuce into my mouth.

Then I go home to contemplate what I'm going to do with myself for the next couple of months until I can go to New Mexico and get on with the end of my life.

Out of some instinct I can't believe really wants resurrection, I set up my typewriter on my desk and begin to write a play about a young man who returns home from graduate school to a failed, confused love affair and ends up marrying his old college sweetheart.

In the course of several hours, I find that only one person is talking.

There is only one character.

Me.

And that he has traveled backward in time and is romping historically and maniacally through a boy's life growing up Jewish in Miami Beach, Florida.

In Pastrami Land.

13

I arrive at the Pollacks' a calculated fifteen minutes late that evening (it is Ernie Pollack himself who calls late afternoon to see if I would be kind enough to drop by at precisely seven P.M.).

Certain I'm in danger of no greater penalty than a dressing-down in the privacy of the Pollack's home, I arrive, unshaven, wearing jeans, my rough-outs, and a dashiki Leslie Ann made me in a costume design class. All in all I am confident I look thoroughly repellent and, more important, like someone from somewhere else. An alien.

A writer.

I fantasize becoming sufficiently famous that there will be a biography one day, this little episode a beauty in the midst of my young manhood.

I am met at the door by Sandra Pollack, who is wearing a shirtwaist dress and her own hair, short and close to her head. She looks like a novitiate. Yet there is an equanimity behind her eyes that reminds me to remember what I thought this morning: that I have badly misread this young woman.

But I am charged too high by the voltage of my presence here to permit that reminder to alter my behavior. And so I seek in her eyes to know only whether she's with me or against me here.

The answer to that question is not clear.

'Hi there, JD,' she says, and she lifts a wrist that

jangles with a charm bracelet commemorating her entire life, inviting me to enter the living room of her life-long home.

Where, seated in rococo splendor, are her parents. There is a gravity to Ernie and Neddie Pollack's demeanor that brings me into their austere presence humming Bach's B-minor Mass and smiling.

Ernie Pollack hurtles to his feet, rams a finger at me, and says, 'You take that smile off your face, mister, and stop that humming!'

The humming I kill, but I try and fail to get rid of the smile and the failure causes me to laugh.

'Think this is funny, do you?' asks Ernie Pollack, taking his seat again, a position from which he seems to feel on firmer ground.

And I am struck by this thought: *I must not make a shambles of this man's recourse against me. It is up to me, somehow, to redeem the efficacy of fatherhood in the world. Here. Tonight.*

'No, sir, I don't think it's funny,' I say supportively, urging Ernie Pollack to go on, wishing now I'd shaved.

'Just what in the hell,' says Ernie Pollack, 'do you think you were doing in that cabana this morning with my daughter?'

Full of denunciatory contempt for myself, I tell Ernie Pollack, 'I was doing something I definitely shouldn't have been doing at that time and in that particular location, sir.'

Except for my army physical, where it seemed a smart move, I have never in my life called anyone 'sir.'

'Yes, and what *was* that something, JD?'

What *was* that something? 'Uhm . . . what *was* it? I'm not sure I follow you, Mr P.'

'I mean,' he says, 'just exactly what were you doing that, admittedly, you should not have been doing?'

Is he looking to test my verbal descriptive skills? Does he want an anatomy lesson?

Comfortable in the role of penitent, I try to make the words as inoffensive as possible. 'I was performing cunnilingus on Sandra, sir,' I tell him.

Ernie Pollack leans forward on his maroon Hepplewhite sofa, cocks an ear at me. 'I beg your pardon,' he says.

Does he want another word? The vernacular? Is he shocked to hear what he demanded I tell him? 'Cunni*lingus*,' I say, the first hint of irritation seeping through a hairline fracture in my remorse.

Ernie and Neddie Pollack stare at each other, and off to my side I can see Sandra watching with placid interest – does she think that *she* somehow is controlling this situation? – and now in a flash my mission to redeem fatherhood in the world evaporates and blood fills my eyes. 'I was eating her twat,' I say, 'Is that better, Mr P.?'

Sandra leans forward.

She obviously didn't tell them she was not simply a victim of the event.

Fear?

Or calculation?

Ernie and Neddie Pollack don't appear to believe what they've just heard someone say in their living room, polluting the air above their Hepplewhite, and they lean forward, seeking clarification.

'*What* did you say?' Ernie Pollack wants to know.

My eyes flick at Sandra, wondering if somehow she *is* in control here.

Even as I say with a dollop of venom, 'I was lapping her *cunt*.'

not comfortable engaging in, so I would say that at least then I had the utmost respect for her rights.'

I glance at inscrutable Sandra. Nothing.

'But we're talking about now, you insufferable prick,' says Neddie Pollack, her restraint going into the toilet. 'What about her rights now?'

'Fuck 'em,' I say.

Armies of capillaries flood Neddie Pollack's cheeks and rush for the nether parts of her face.

Ernie Pollack presses his hand more aggressively into his wife's shoulder, reminding her that, though they've strayed a bit from the script, she must remember her role. He turns his eyes on the massive picture window that looks onto the manicured jungle of his front yard, and he asks me, 'Do you know what conclusion I'm coming to, JD?'

'Nope,' I say, 'sure don't,' and I step toward Ernie Pollack. I don't intend the movement to be threatening. It's spontaneous, yet Ernie Pollack stiffens just noticeably. 'And what's more,' I add, 'if I can be candid, Ernie, I honestly don't give a good goddamn what conclusion you're coming to. I wish to hell I did, but I don't.'

Ernie Pollack's face flushes bright pink. 'Well, that's just too damn bad for you, because you're going to listen to what I have to say anyway.'

I could walk out, but I don't (*efficacy of fatherhood*), and as I don't make an exit, Ernie Pollack is free to go on: 'I'm coming to the conclusion that things are getting a little out of hand in this country. Assassinations, riots, you kids with your lack of morals and physical slovenliness. This country's running amok! Don't you see how crucial it is that some of you help make it stop?'

In a burst of empathy, I like Ernie Pollack as a father, and for a moment I imagine my child not only born but facing the world ahead, and I hear myself say, ' "O generation of vipers, who hath warned you to flee the wrath to come?" '

But Ernie Pollack thinks I'm making fun of him. 'All right, JD, that's fine, thank you.'

And the Sphinx speaks: 'I think, Daddy,' says Sandra Pollack, 'that JD is agreeing with you.'

Cautiously Ernie Pollack looks at his child, unwilling to be duped or abused further.

'Aren't you, JD?' Sandra asks, those maddeningly impassive eyes on me, sending a hot flash through my chest.

'Yes.' But now, totally unexpectedly, I feel I'm about to cry and am impelled to speak quickly before that can happen, and so I say, 'Now, will there be anything else, Mr Pollack, Mrs Pollack, or can Sandra and I get going? I thought we'd catch an eight o'clock flick.'

The glances of Sandra Pollack and her mother and father come together at a midpoint in the triangle they form at the Hepplewhite and bounce off each other like balloons.

'I hope it won't surprise you, JD, if I tell you I don't expect you ever again to see my daughter or enter our home so long as you live.'

'You're only talking about this lifetime, though, right?' I don't know why I say that. At this moment, I like the hell out of Ernie Pollack but don't know how to get past my disdain for his disdain of me to communicate it. 'Welp,' I say, 'in that case, I'll be running along.'

I see myself to the door, turning for a last glimpse of the three of them arrayed at their exquisite couch like some whacko, regional version of *American Gothic*.

14

I hop in my Volkswagen and tool down the driveway, around the front hedge, assuming I'll go home and never see Sandra Pollack – devious, confounding Sandra – again in my life.

So it's with curiosity that I watch the car come to a stop, park itself, and eject me into the dusk.

I continue in the role of interested observer as I hunker my way through the Pollack coconut palms and shrubbery to the back of the house. There I crouch behind the filter system and heater for the marquise-shaped swimming pool that dominates the backyard.

A dock rises out of Biscayne Bay to which is moored a cabin cruiser that sleeps four. The word *Sandra* is stenciled on the tail of the boat.

I belly crawl across the Pollack backyard and beneath the dining room window, where I can hear Pollack dining room chairs scrape against terrazzo as they sit down to dinner. I crawl past the kitchen door, beyond which I glimpse the Pollacks' black housekeeper-cook carting food to the table, and on to the French doors leading from a small, covered patio into the house. One of the French doors opens to my hand. I slip through the master bedroom and down the hallway into Sandra's bedroom.

Where I face a wall of photographs of Sandra at various ages. There's a picture of Sandra as a junior high school cheerleader with a sicklelike nose; there are pictures of Sandra as a Miami Beach High School cheerleader with Natalie Wood's nose; a studied portrait of Sandra, resplendent in her Beach High cheerleading outfit complete with black-and-gold pom-poms, backed up by her brother, Michael, he holding his mallet-head putter and wearing his Beach High letter sweater with the somber black 'B' on one rib cage, the almost indiscernible crossed golf clubs stitched into the letter's center bar; and finally, set away in isolation and mounted onto an escutcheon of black beaver board, there's a series of pictures of Sandra and a boy I recognize as the president of student council the year after I graduated, one of the few guys from Miami Beach who had been dumb enough to let himself be drafted into the United States Army and who saw his stupidity compounded by being sent to Vietnam and killed.

There are no pictures of me. If one were to judge Sandra Pollack's life by this wall, I never existed. In a way, I like the idea of being able to create myself from scratch.

On Sandra's bedside table is one of Anaïs Nin's diaries.

In French.

Is she *kidding*?

In the little open area beneath the bedside table's single drawer is a collection of books – dog-eared, underlined, and annotated – that appears to be from a class in post-World War II American fiction (the back end of my field!): *The Catcher in the Rye, Invisible Man, Lie Down in Darkness, Seize the Day, Everything That Rises Must Converge, The Pawnbroker, Goodbye, Columbus, Rabbit, Run, Last Exit to Brooklyn, Stern, Cat's Cradle, Catch-22.*

Surely she wasn't anticipating my return and boning up on material for conversation.

I open the top drawer of her dresser and handle some of her underpants and brassieres and, in doing so, realize that one of the things I came to dislike about the Miami Beach girls I knew all my life was their underwear: From the time they are pubescent, it is always lacy, soft, sensual rather than sexy – aimed, in short, at driving a boy toward not rape but adoration. In some convoluted way I conclude that it was the demand that morning that I adore her underwear and her for so primly wearing it that drove me to rip off her panties and brassiere and force *her* to adore my *tongue* between her legs.

In Sandra's middle drawer, underneath a cluster of synthetic print shirts, I find what I didn't know I'm looking for: her diary covering the past four years.

On the first page, dated June 7, 1966, she has written: 'Ronny and I graduated from college tonight. For our present to each other, we made love for the first time. I dreamed it, I planned it, and I have known for months that when it was done I would feel only joy. Even here, in the privacy of this journal, it's hard to admit that it was, if not a MAJOR, at least a MINOR disappointment. R. assured me we'd improve. I wish I could say I can hardly wait.'

I know there are private things that should remain sacred, and I am sorely tempted to put Sandra's diary back where it belongs.

But I don't.

Because there are things about her – like the invitation to her armpit, the coolness of her gaze tonight, the excellence of her taste in books – I have to fathom.

I scan pages. Vaginitis to hide from her mother – antibiotic copped surreptitiously from Cuban doctor father of promiscuous friend. No-nonsense dismissal of R.'s 'obsessive obeisance to the vocal stylings of Connie Francis.' Sarcasm about her mother's 'premenopause schizophrenia and tranquilizer-itis.' The recurrent issue of breast enlargement – 'There's this stuff called silicon, and they shoot it into your boobs and they get bigger. If I did it very slowly, maybe no one would notice. I hate my boobs! I hate my boobs! I hate my boobs!!!!'

I come to this:

'July 3, 1966!! It's official. He will be drafted. It's only a question now of when. I'm sick. The bastard who tells them at the end of the physical whether they've passed or failed said he would be classified 1A. R. asked him what about his letter from his doctor saying he has (chronic!) asthma – I mean he only almost *died* of it as a child??? The guy, a man, a sergeant (very, very BIG DEAL), said they were getting pretty G-ddamn tired of the boys from Miami Bch. coming over with their doctors' letters full of b.s. about asthma and trick knees. "You're in, Moishe," the bastard said. I have made R. swear on the life of our first child (which I'm not going to get to have now for G-d knows how long) that NO MATTER WHAT – let them court-martial him!! – he won't go to Vietnam. I told him we'll change our name first and go to Canada, and Daddy backs me all the way. He told R. he'd open a branch of Pollack's in Toronto if it came to that.

'Merdemerdemerdemerdeshitfuck!!'

I had in fact achieved 4-F draft status thanks to a letter my father got from a gin rummy-playing doctor friend at the cabana who chronicled for me a lifetime of asthma I never had.

On February 2, 1967 (the day I assume she learned

of Ronny Rosenthal's death), Sandra stopped writing in her diary. She has not written again until last night.

'6/16/71. It's been a long time – and I don't even know why I feel like doing this – I'm sure I'll be just as embarrassed reading this a few years from now as I am reading what I wrote a few years ago now.

'But.

'I went out with Jacob Daniel tonight. It's been a long time since I wanted someone to touch me enough to deal with letting it happen. I resented the shit out of his presumption, though, that he could touch me because he wanted to. So when I wouldn't let him touch my breast, he threw me into the ocean and left me. Once it was done, though, I found I wasn't pissed like I thought I should be. Now I'm sitting here feeling guilty for not feeling guilty.

'I'm twenty-five years old!

'And I don't know what that means except some of my friends have two children already, have built elaborate homes, Phyllis and Larry have a Chrysler Imperial. Some of them are already divorced and remarried.

'Christ.'

I put the diary back into the drawer beneath the pile of synthetic print shirts and crawl under Sandra Pollack's bed to wait.

Under there, wedged up between the bedstead and the box spring, is a paperback book wrapped, literally, in a plain brown wrapper.

I slip the book free: *Valley of the Dolls*, by Jacqueline Susann.

I am suffused by a stunning warmth for Sandra Pollack.

15

Several hours later she enters her bedroom. I can see only her feet.

She sits at her desk and writes briefly, her feet rubbing against each other like a cricket's.

Then she takes her clothes off and gets into the shower.

I slip out from under the bed and slide open the middle drawer. I flip the diary open to the last entry: '6/17/71. JDL thought I was no match for him. That he would simply call the shots like when we were in college. Surprise! Though he certainly acquitted himself well in the Inquisition. I don't think the word 'cunt' has ever been spoken aloud in this house – though I wouldn't be surprised if Daddy or Mickey has uttered it silently a time or two. Loved Daddy defending my honor. Even Jacob Daniel I thought for a minute there found him kind of . . . what? Noble, maybe. I have to digest the happenings of the morning and evening somemore before I decide whether to rebel or retreat. I confuse myself – am furious and repelled and fascinated.'

I'm tempted to put a line between 'some' and 'more' to indicate to her that 'some more' is not one word, but instead I take my clothes off, walk into Sandra Pollack's bathroom, open her shower door, and get in with her.

When I tap her on the shoulder, she leaves the ground and levitates briefly. Earthbound, she digests my presence. Water pelts her small head, cascading off her nose, circling uniformly the edges of her round chin.

'Hi,' I say. 'Norman Bates.'

I twist the shower off and open the door. I lift Sandra up – there is no resistance this time – and I carry her soaking wet to her bed and lay her down on the spread, elbowing an ancient teddy bear and two angora cats out of the way.

'You can't, as they say, San, tell a book by its cover.'

'I'm not entirely obligated to be a cliché, am I, Jacob?'

'Not entirely. But don't jolt me too hard, okay?'

'We'll see,' she says, and reaches down between my legs, consumes an amazing amount of me very firmly in her small hand.

I run my mouth and tongue over her face, down her neck, around her breasts, try to suck the nipples out, but failing move down her belly and into her navel, around it and down the line of faint, airy hair between her navel and her center, and once there I kneel between her legs and pay homage with my tongue and lips and teeth until she whimpers into the hand she holds clamped across her mouth, until she drives herself so frantically into my face that I slide forward, lay over her, hook my mouth on hers and, slowly, carefully, ease myself into her while she sucks my tongue, nibbles my lips. Implanted inside her, I begin to move in and out, up and down, side to side, and when I am absolutely positive I've brought her to orgasm, I ejaculate into her a tracer of semen that feels as if it might have force enough to pierce her palate.

I lie beside Sandra Pollack, stroke her, hold her in the angle of my arm, grateful and guilty and wishing it wasn't over so we could still have the first time to look forward to.

16

Information for what city?'
'Los Angeles.'
'What part of Los Angeles, sir?'
'How many parts you got?'
'Quite a few.'
' "Quite a few." How 'bout Hollywood?'
'All righty.'
'A listing for a Leslie Ann Masterson?'
I wait.
'I'm sorry, checking Hollywood and North Hollywood, I have no listing for Leslie Ann Masterson.'
'How about L. Masterson.'
I wait.
'I have quite a number of those, sir. Do you have an address?'
'No. Can you give me all of them?'
'No, I'm sorry, sir, I cannot do that.'
'How about an L. A. Masterson.'
I wait.
'No, I'm sorry.'
'How about outside Hollywood, like an area where someone interested in getting into acting might rent an apartment if she were by herself and living frugally.'
'Sir, how familiar are you with Los Angeles?'
'Well, let me see. The Lincoln Memorial, right?'
If the operator is amused, her amusement is not

audible, 'Sir, Hollywood has nothing to do with *Hollywood*. Hollywood is just a junky area of the city. The Hollywood you're talking about where they make the movies and the TV shows is scattered all the hell over the place.'

'Please,' I say, 'her mother died about ten minutes ago, I'm a doctor and I've got to find her.'

'Sir, do you know how many times I've heard that one?'

'How about this, then: I *really* need to find this person.'

It takes twenty minutes, but she assures me finally that there is no Leslie Ann, L., or L. A. Masterson anywhere from the Valley – wherever that is – to Manhattan Beach – wherever that is.

In bed alone, on the edge of sleep, I pose myself this question: *What would I have told her if I found her? That I cheated on her? That I'm in the process of getting free of her? Why do I feel I want to continue to hurt her?*

I am asleep before I answer the question and assiduously avoid asking it again for a long time afterward.

17

Sandra and I spend most of the next afternoon copulating in the Atlantic Ocean, our swimming suits clutched in our hands like scepters of majesty, our bodies bolted together beneath the roiling sea. (This is Neddie's 'doctor day,' Sandra tells me, 'so we won't be interrupted.' I'm a little disappointed to have that particular element of danger reduced, but having sex with bathers swimming close around us isn't without its stimulation.)

When we aren't connected sexually, we try to connect otherwise.

'Why are you living at home?' I ask her.

'So I can't have guys like you ask to spend the night in my apartment.'

'Is that the real reason?'

'How did it sound?'

'Plausible.'

'I went through a difficult period after Ronny was killed.'

'I'm sure,' I say, trying to sound appropriately sympathetic concerning the death of someone about whom I feel a sort of generic jealousy. Improbable – to say nothing of unfair – as it is, I find myself a little angry at Sandra because, even though I dumped her, she didn't keep herself chaste for me, in the event I decided – out of this current confusion, for instance – to return for her.

'During that time – six, eight months, I had sex with about anybody who wanted me.'

What!

Trying not to sound illiberal or unenlightened, I managed an edgy little smile and say, 'No, you didn't.'

With the hand that isn't holding her bathing suit, Sandra Pollack pushes salt sea water with her fingers through the thick pale hair on my chest, keeping herself low enough in the water that her nakedness isn't apparent to the several bathers in our area. 'Okay, I didn't,' she says.

'Did you?'

'What do you want to hear?'

'The truth.'

'You sure?'

'No. Did you sleep with anybody who'd have you?'

'No.'

'I think you did.'

'You hope I didn't. I wish I had. In fact, I didn't.'

And in the face of her honesty, I tell her this lie: 'I've missed you so much all these years.'

The ocean is calm, the water barely moving past us. She glances around; no one seems to find us the least bit suspicious. She wraps her legs around my waist, puts her hand between my legs, and brings me with shocking rapidity to tensile erectness.

Slides me gently into her, and seeming only to be moving to the gentle rhythm of the water, she guides me to sweet completion.

18

It's too nice. Feels too good.

By the end of the afternoon, I'm looking for a hedge.

When we part and Sandra says we have to see each other secretly until she can ease me back into her family's good graces, I have it.

I arrive at the Pollacks' that evening to discover Ernie Pollack grilling dogs and burgers in his backyard for his wife, Neddie, his recently chastened daughter, Sandra, and their son, Michael, the gynecologist, Michael's mordant, horse-faced, cigarette-puffing wife, Carol, and their two mordant, horse-faced children, Scott, age three, and Stacy, age one and a half.

Adrenaline pumping, I enter boldly stage right around the oleander. 'Sorry, I'm late,' I call cheerfully, sticking my hand out to my old buddy Michael Pollack. 'Mickey, how you hitting 'em?'

Michael Pollack looks around at his family, his tone of voice and countenance suggesting trepidation that some wonderful surprise has been whipped up especially for him that he can't begin to deserve but will graciously accept. 'Who's that?'

I hit an imaginary nine iron into the sunset.

'Jesus H. Schwartz,' says Michael Pollack without a trace of warmth, 'Snake?'

'You ain't just awhistlin' "Hatikvah," kid.'

With poorly feigned excitement, Michael Pollack says,

'Mom didn't tell me you were coming.'

I am six feet and weigh one sixty-five. Michael Pollack is five ten and must now, at twenty-seven, weigh a good two ten. I have all my hair. Michael is losing his even as we stand here. I'm passing out of cadaverous back into lean; I have some color from my two days in the sun. Michael is pasty and has a gut that rides the top of his double-knit slacks and presses against the line of his synthetic print shirt like a tractor tire.

Michael Pollack slaps the tire around his waist. '–Doctor Snake,' he says.

Oh, I like that – 'Doctor Snake' – its evocation of status and power and wickedness. 'Micker Ticker,' say I.

It is all too apparent to me that Michael Pollack can be a stumbling block along the trail of my current, if muddy, plans for his sister, Sandra – who sits on a canvas director's chair with 'World's Greatest SalesPERSON' printed on its back and who, though she seems to be making some effort not to, smiles with unmistakable affection at me, stiffening not out of fear, but, like an audience at a fight, out of anticipation that someone might die.

Who is not smiling at me is Ernie Pollack.

'I wonder if I might ask just what you think you're doing here?'

I offer my hand. 'Mr Pollack, how are you this evening?' I turn my rejected hand toward Neddie Pollack. 'Mrs Pollack, what an evening, eh?'

Neddie Pollack stares at me from behind repugnance almost as large as her sunglasses. An overrevved outboard towing a skier roars past the Pollack dock, setting the *Sandra* to rocking gently. Pollack eyes turn there, hopeful they'll return their gazes to this spot and I'll be gone.

But when they look, I'm still here, the depth of my enjoyment of their rejection, the ease with which I stand here, both impressing the hell out of me and making me wonder at the direction in which my neuroses seem to be expanding.

Michael Pollack looks from parent to parent. His wife's cigarette smoke wafts between him and them, and he blows at it irascibly. 'What's going on here?' he wants to know.

'Oh, nothing much,' says Ernie Pollack, pointing his spatula. 'Your friend here merely raped your sister at the cabana yesterday – but that's all.'

The last thing Michael Pollack expects his father to introduce into what was no doubt billed as an ordinary cookout is rape. Consequently he has no ready response to the announcement. He looks at his sister – who seems to be smiling – and at his mother and father – who are carved in stone.

For a moment there is only the sound of insects electrocuting themselves against the mechanical bug crematorium swaying above the arena from a big cypress.

Michael Pollack is dubious, but for the sake of clarity he asks his old golf teammate, 'Is there any truth to that, Snaker?'

I wonder how I would take similar news about my own sister. An imperfect image of myself as redeemer bursts with a rocket's red glare in my head. 'Yes, there is, Mickey,' I confess to Michael Pollack, and then wait, a curious student, to see what course Michael will take.

Michael nods slowly. I nod slowly along with him, corroborating for Michael whatever it is he's nodding about. When Michael continues to nod slowly and to remain mute, Ernie Pollack says to his son's old golf teammate, who many times ate grilled dogs and burgers in the Pollack backyard during his adolescence, 'Now, you just tell me what the *fuck* you're doing here.'

The word *fuck* uttered by Ernie Pollack at a cookout, even a cookout complicated by accusations of rape, seems to take all of the adult Pollacks slightly aback – except Michael's wife, Carol, who explodes a puffball from her lungs and then makes every effort to muffle her gravel-throated laughter.

Her outburst draws notice only from her two children, however, and from me, as everyone else seems more interested in what response I'll make to Ernie Pollack's question.

I wonder myself what I'll come up with. 'I have come,' I hear myself say to Ernie Pollack, 'to ask for permission to officially court your daughter.'

The dogs and burgers sizzle on the grill, and above us, instrumental music beats bluntly against the humid air, piped magically out of the Pollack house through a speaker hung from an eighty-foot coconut palm. That palm has stood longer probably than the combined age of all of us gathered beneath it. I wonder if it has ever sheltered anything dumber than what's afoot here at this moment.

'I don't think I heard you correctly,' says Ernie Pollack.

I know very well that I can deny I said what I said, that I can escape, having merely committed acts so outlandish that guys all over the Beach will secretly envy me for decades. But instead of laughing off my pronouncement, I hear myself say, 'I made a mistake in college, terminating my relationship with Sandra. I would like, at this time, to begin restitution for that error.'

Ernie Pollack's response to that is this: 'I'm going to

give you fifteen seconds,' he says to me, 'to get off my property.'

'Why fifteen?' I ask him.

'Because,' he says, 'fifteen seems reasonable.'

'And then what?' I ask Ernie Pollack.

'And then,' says Ernie Pollack, 'there's going to be trouble.'

Out of the corner of my eye I glance at Sandra. She has not moved in her 'World's Greatest SalesPERSON' chair. There is not so much as a flicker of anxiety on her face.

'You mention trouble,' I say, passionately and utterly resisting a voice in me that tells me firmly to stop. 'How would you like everybody in this really rather small town to know that Ernie Pollack's daughter – he of Pollack's Jewelers – was fornicating in her bedroom last night with a person who is neither a doctor of medicine nor a lawyer while her parents were three doors away doing God knows what in their own bedroom, and that the same daughter spent most of this afternoon fornicating with that same nonmedical doctor in the Atlantic Ocean in plain sight of the Fontainebleau Hotel?'

One of the things I never told Michael Pollack that I liked about him was that he could always take a joke – many of which I played on him during our adolescence, some harmless, more than a few cruel. I will appreciate for the rest of my life the manner in which Michael takes this current joke, played not only on him, but on his entire family, present and long past.

Having read and assimilated the writing on the wall more quickly than either his mother or father, Michael looks at his sister, who smiles a small smile at him, and he rises from his seat and says to me, 'Would you like a hot dog, Snaker, or a hamburger?'

'Steak,' say I – then boom a laugh off the wall of Pollacks arrayed before me, adding, 'Only kidding. Let me start with a dog, see where that leads.'

Ernie Pollack has a can of lighter fluid in hand. It's aimed at my face.

But then Sandra is standing between her father and her lover. 'You've been asking me since Ronny died when I'm going to get interested in something besides books and melancholy, Daddy. Well, I'm interested in something. In some*one*.'

Out there somewhere in Miami Beach, barely audible here in the sequestered Pollack backyard, a police siren wails toward some living being's distress.

An hour later Sandra walks me to my car. My hand is within her slacks and underwear, stroking her coccyx.

I feel nauseated, and I know well that the nausea has only partially to do with the three Schlitzes, two dogs, and a burger I consumed with omnivorous excitement at the mess I'm making.

I am becoming my behavior!

Violently!

Sandra opens my door for me. I get in. She closes the door, leans in through the open window. Close, that faint aroma coming from her mouth.

'Seat belt,' she says.

I try to fasten the seat belt across my lap. I'm more than a little tipsy, and it takes several fumbles to get the job done. When the two ends snap together, Sandra turns my face to her.

'My life has been so unutterably boring. How long can you keep this kind of behavior up, you figure?'

'If I stop, you mean, you'll lose interest in me?'

'Possible. Of course, if you're just doing this to be perverse, that could get old, too.'

I don't know what I want to say or what she wants to hear. I endeavor to give her my coolest taciturn look – mouth closed, jaw tensed, hooded eyes.

'Just have to see, won't we?' I ask.

She looks at me with a light in her eyes, a twist to

her mouth that's just downright scarifyingly sensual. 'Surprise me,' she says, and steps back, permitting me my exit.

Information for what city?'

'Los Angeles,' I say, changing my voice from the last time, falling prey to the drunken, idiotic assumption that I might get the same information operator I got last time and that she might disapprove of my calling again.

'What part of Los Angeles, sir?'

I try not to sound like someone numbed by three cans of beer. 'The Valley to Manhattan Beach.'

'I beg your pardon?'

'Please.'

21

I'm not sure if 'Surprise me' was an admonition, a plea, or both.

Nor do I know whether what our relationship begins to become constitutes a surprise to her or not.

I know it surprises me. Because it becomes ever more comfortable. And pleasant.

And scary.

She's well read, she's interested in the world, she's interested in me.

She's the best salesperson in her father's store (the 'World's Greatest SalesPERSON' chair she was sitting on the night of the cookout was, in fact, her chair – she earned it in competition against the other six salespersons at her father's store).

She likes food, she likes movies, she likes sex.

She says she will even take golf lessons if I want to start to play again.

After three weeks I know I have to put an end to the relationship, pack up, and head for New Mexico six weeks early in a humanitarian effort to minimize the disaster I'm fomenting.

And so I get in my car to drive to Sandra's, tell her as honestly as I can that I love someone else, that I could never love her, then gas up, pack up, and hit the highway west.

Instead I end up on Lincoln Road, where I walk into Pollack's Jewelers and head for Ernie Pollack at the diamond counter.

Simulating the breezy tone of guys who work for their living in storefront businesses and take well-earned hours for energy-replenishing lunches, I say, 'Mr Pollack, I'll bet you could pack away the lunch special at Sy's about now, whudduya say?'

Ernie Pollack does not acknowledge me for a moment, his one eye closed, his other studying a rough-shape brown gem through a jeweler's glass. His free eye pops open; the sound of my voice has belatedly reached his brain and set off a red alert. The eye sends glancing blows off my face, then flicks toward my hand, looking to see, I suppose, if I'm armed.

Disgorging the jeweler's eye into his hand, Ernie Pollack says, 'For one thing, I don't eat lunch.'

'Better for your health,' I say agreeably.

'For another thing, it's three in the afternoon. If I was going to eat lunch, I'd have done it at lunchtime when Sy *serves* the lunch special.'

I glance at my wrist at the watch I don't wear.

Where have I been for the last three hours?

I remember getting into my car a little past twelve and heading for the Pollacks' house. I remember stopping for what I thought was a minute or two to make some notes about the monologue I'm not convinced I'm writing about the young man who returns home and marries his old college sweetheart. The minute or two must have been nearly three hours.

'Well,' I say to Ernie Pollack, 'how *are* you, Mr P.?'

Go out the door! Get in your car! Floor it for New Mexico!

Ernie Pollack dumps the strange-looking brown gem on a felt pad on the countertop and clamps a manicured thumb and index finger to the bridge of his crescent-shaped nose, as if trapping a sudden bolt of pain there and keeping it from extending down his nose and blowing the end off. 'What do you want, JD?'

I am as interested to find that out as he, and so I seat myself erectly on a leather stool at Ernie Pollack's counter, splaying my shadow across hundreds of thousands of dollars' worth of carbon crystals.

'I know,' I say, 'that Sandra and I have only been back together for a short time, but let's face it, sir, we were in love eight years ago and we're going to be in love until the day we die – or days, since you're probably thinking it's unlikely we'll die the same day – unless,' I add jovially, 'one of us kills the other and commits suicide.'

After three weeks of having me hanging around his house, Ernie Pollack is still not sure when I'm kidding and when I'm serious; he only knows for sure that I tire him – which makes the two of us similar in at least that way. 'I wasn't thinking that,' he said. 'Believe me, I wasn't thinking anything like that.'

'No, of course you weren't. But let me just say this right, okay, it's important to me: I love Sandra and *I'm* going to love her until the day *I* die.'

For years I've wanted to say that to some girl's father; the fact that I know it's a lie fails to blunt my pleasure in saying it to Ernie Pollack, who responds with a fervor that I find riveting. 'Jesus,' he says, squeezing the bridge of his nose until the tanned flesh under his fingers turns white, 'I *hope* so.'

Get on the highway! says the voice inside, as the one that speaks out loud through my mouth exceeds Ernie Pollack's zeal and says, 'I *know* so, sir, I *know* so!'

Ernie Pollack no longer seems the robust man whose life I reinvaded just twenty-one days ago, but someone

much older. 'Well,' he said, 'that's good, JD. That's . . .
that's . . . that's . . . good.'

'That *is* good,' I agree, glimpsing not only Ernie
Pollack, but my own father and then me, all of us
old, invalided, hopeless, and unattended – wifeless,
womanless, nurseless, relativeless. Alone. 'But what's
bad is that I haven't got a dime to my name, and my
relationship with my own father is such that I wouldn't
ask him to lend me a nickel. I mean, not that he wouldn't
if he had one – a nickel – to lend, in which case I might
ask him, but he doesn't, so I can't. Yet what's pertinent
here, sir, of course, is that I want to become engaged
to your daughter, and I want to do it after the proper
fashion, as I'm sure you would insist.'

Ernie Pollack's head bobs spasmodically like a ball
attached to a rubber band, and he meditates on the
brown gem on top of the diamond ring-packed display
case that separates him from this babbling degenerate
who's asking for the hand of his only daughter.

In the absence of any response, I tell this man, 'Now
I know and I know *you* know that you don't want me
to marry your daughter.'

Ernie Pollack clamps his fingers back on his nose a
third time and closes his eyes.

I take Ernie Pollack's other hand in mine – he doesn't
resist, seems in fact to welcome the sympathy (we both
feel so sorry for this aging man, this compromised
father). 'But,' I say, 'we both also know that you're
not going to stand in our way, because if you do,
you're pretty sure she'll marry me anyway. We'll elope
and exclude you completely from the marriage of your
only daughter, and Mrs P. – you'll pardon the expression
– will shit a tea service, and I think we're both pretty
well aware that, medication aside, she's one of the most

vindictive human beings either of us has ever known. But, relax, nobody wants elopement, nobody wants embarrassment or vindictiveness – least of all you. Tell me if I get off course anywhere along here.'

I am outside myself. For the first time I have a sense of what Leslie Ann must feel like when she's immersed in a 'character,' when she *becomes* someone else's creation. I am, in fact, the character about whom I stopped for what seemed like only a moment to make notes for the play I'm pretending not to write.

I'm someone I'm inventing out of my imagination.

There is no love inherent in the little putt-putt, kissing sounds Ernie Pollack is making with the air he's forcing through his tightly compressed lips. He retrieves his hand from mine and places it against his lips to stop the sounds.

We must not come to this, my character thinks. *We must never come to this.*

But the out-loud voice says, 'So I stand before you today and I ask you to make me an unbelievable – I'm talking close-out-sale kind of deal – on, say, a three-carat solitaire.'

Never to this, thinks my character.

'And the deal I would like you to make me – your decision, finally, of course – is I would like you to give me the ring gratis. I'm going to go down the street now and buy some sweat socks, I'll stop back in twenty minutes, you can give me your answer. No pressure, okay?'

Ernie Pollack doesn't answer. Why should he? No way he's going to take me seriously. Clearly I'm off my rocker.

No, no, Ernie, not off my rocker, see. A character in a play! Huh? What do you think?

Ernie Pollack picks up the strange little brown gem, hands it to me.

'Here, take it.'

'Oh, no, Mr P., really, the ring'll be more than sufficient – what is it?'

'A kidney stone. I pissed it outta my *schvontz* about an hour ago. You and it – you should both only burn and rot in eternal hell.'

l hold the little rock in my hand and I think:

This . . . this is way beyond my creative ability as a playwright.

22

The three-carat solitaire is secreted beneath a dollop of mint apple jelly on Sandra's plate at the lamb chop cookout attended by all the Pollacks and all the Landaus, and there are tears in more than one set of eyes when she discovers the rock and I slip it stickily over her ring finger.

I figure the votes are about even on whether my engagement to Sandra is a good thing or a bad thing. Among those I figure think it's good are Sandra, my mother, and, for all the wrong reasons, Michael Pollack's wife, Carol, who whispers to me with admiration that night, 'I don't *believe* what you're doing to these shitheads.'

Opposed: Ernie and Neddie Pollack, their son, Michael, and my sister, Susan (who thinks, simply enough, that I'm committing suicide by marriage).

Unreadable: My father.

For it *and* against it: My character and me.

But it's done.

Flying on the wings of my preposterous behavior and numerous glasses of champagne, Sandra and I sneak onto the yacht late that night when everyone else has gone to bed and excrete our juices all over each other in a frothy, drunken romp.

'I want you to know something,' Sandra says.

'Tell me,' I say.

'I didn't accept your ring because I have no other choices.'

'Who said you did?'

'I'm afraid that's what you're thinking.'

'That's not what I'm thinking,' I say.

'What *are* you thinking?'

Frankly, I don't know what I'm thinking. I'm *not* thinking.

'Well, I suppose if someone were to ask me why you became engaged to me – which you are, you are asking me that – I would say it was because you had loved me for a long time and I was good enough to select you again.'

She smiles.

'But not,' she says, 'because I'm twenty-five in a community where an unmarried woman of that age is an old maid.'

'No,' I say, 'not because of that.'

There is something steely about her eye – only one of which is visible in the light from the porthole above the facing bunk. Drunk, I am conscious only of the image, not its portent.

'I became engaged to you,' she says, 'because I've always seen in you what others didn't.'

What does *that* mean?

I don't ask.

23

Information for what city?'

I go through my routine. No listing. I hang up.

I turn my attention back to madly writing the monologue about the life I'm fabricating to live.

Twenty seconds later the phone rings. I snap it up so as not to wake anyone else. I know it'll be Sandra, telling me how happy she is, cuddled up in bed with her ring . . . *because that's what I just wrote.*

'Jacob?'

Incredibly, the first thing that pops into my mind to tell her is that I've begun another play.

'I just tried to call you,' I say.

'How did you get my number?'

'I mean I just tried to get your number. Aren't you in Los Angeles?'

'Yes.'

'You're not listed.'

'I'm listed.'

'Using a different name?'

'Yes.'

'So I can't find you.'

Obliquely she says, 'A stage name.'

'Ah.'

'Jacob.'

I am acutely aware now that she's disturbed and tune to her.

'Yes, Les.'

'I lost my rock.'

'What rock?'

'You remember that rock you gave me the night you came to see *Taming of the Shrew*?'

'You kept that rock?'

'I've unpacked everything and I can't find it. Do you have it?'

'No.'

'Oh, darn it!'

'Somebody gave me a kidney stone a coupla days ago, though. You want me to send you that?'

'I'm not kidding, Jacob, I know it's stupid, but I want that rock!' As quickly as she explodes, she says, 'I'm sorry, don't hang up on me okay?'

'I wouldn't hang up on you, Les.'

'Okay,' she says, 'I know.'

She exhales a deep, long breath.

Something's very wrong.

'Doing?' I ask her.

The phone line crackles, and for a moment I think she hasn't heard.

'Looking for an agent,' she says. 'Everybody says I need an agent. I can go to some of the off-street theater auditions, but the good theater auditions aren't for actors not in the union and who aren't – as they say – "represented." '

She says 'represented' with a British accent, trying to sound ironic and playful. Normal. It doesn't work. Her voice has a notable quaver in it. Is barely under her control.

'So how do you get an agent?'

Again the line crackles, and I wonder if she's heard me.

'I sent out twenty letters,' she says, 'asking if they'd

be interested in meeting me and considering representing me. You know what every single one wrote back? Let me know when you're doing something, I'll try to come see you. Now, here's the rub, this is great, you'll appreciate this kind of logic: You have to have something *to* do before they can come to see you, right?'

'Makes sense.'

'And you have to have an agent – or be in the union – to get into something they'd care to see you *in*.'

I whistle appreciatively.

She's silent again, and I sense that important as this agent business is, it's not what's making her voice quaver. Something else has happened, and she's wondering whether to address it with me or not.

'I quit my acting class today.'

And that's it.

'I didn't know you were in one.'

'I was.'

'I heard that.'

There's no bemusement from her end. 'The guy thinks he's running a group therapy session, not an acting class. I might as well go to a psychiatrist.'

The last sentence hangs between us a moment, seeming to invite a response – this one, maybe: 'Do you want to see a psychiatrist?'

'Me? No, I just meant I don't need to go to an acting class if I want a shrink.'

'And I'm asking you if you *do* want to see a psychiatrist, Les.'

And she says, 'D'know – wouldn't hurt, I guess.'

'How can I help you, Les?'

What if she says 'Come to me! Fix me! Solve me!'

My first response is I'd be on the next flight.

But a second response follows, and that one is far from certain.

'How are you, Jakey?'

'I got engaged tonight.'

I don't think I mean it to come out that way. Unencumbered by disclaimers and cushions. I think I intended to pursue the distress in her voice, to urge her to seek psychiatric help, to at least find out why she quit her acting class.

The phone line crackles. She breathes.

And what do I want from her now? Do I want her to weep, to beg me to extricate myself from the engagement and reclaim her?

And why did the second response to the invitation to come to her – which she didn't extend – give me pause, make me wonder if I'd really go?

Simply the old fear of being unequal to her needs?

When her silence continues I say, 'She's my old college sweetheart.' And then add: 'I never told you about her.'

'Only fair that you have some secrets of your own. Well, work hard at it, Jakey. Don't ever have to say you didn't try as hard as you could to make it work.' And then she says with a voice bereft of emotion, 'I hate you, Jacob. I don't want to know you anymore.'

The phone goes dead.

I wonder why I don't feel the wound of those words: *I hate you, Jacob. I don't want to know you anymore.*

Perhaps because I am too busy writing them down.

24

I know the question is inevitable. And it gets asked late one night when Sandra and I return from a movie and a late deli snack, which, in my case, I accompany with three bottles of Bass Ale, a liquid antidote to a thirst I know isn't physical.

Ernie Pollack, insomnious and aging rapidly, awaits us and begins dishing up orange sherbet.

'I'm sure,' he says to his future son-in-law, 'that you and Sanny have given a great deal of thought to your future.'

As a team – an engaged couple – we've given virtually no thought whatsoever to that subject, but I'm feeling very frisky on the strength of my three bottles of ale and assure Ernie Pollack, 'Mr P., we've given a lot of thought to our future, believe me. I mean, when you think about it, what else *is* there to give a lot of thought to? Except the past, and what are we – historians?'

Following our nightly – and progressively more pleasant and dexterous – bout in the lower bunk of the back cabin on the *Sandra* a few nights ago, we did name (if not actually discuss) my 'options,' as we called them.

It wasn't hard to do.

There were only two.

I could teach (and in twenty years be making something in the neighborhood of what Sandra's father makes in a month), or I could join Sandra in 'the retail business' (her phrase again; in English I read the phrase to mean the retail *jewelry* business, though Sandra has dropped some hints about wanting to go into the retail clothing business).

'You could go out there,' Sandra said, 'and see if you like teaching. If you do, we could be married during your Christmas or spring break and I could go back with you. If you don't like it, you could finish out the year, we could be married next summer, and you can rethink your options.'

Sandra is turning her three-carat solitaire round and round on her finger, her pretty hands less than at ease in her double-knit lap, her eyes focused with interest on me.

I dip into my sherbet and wonder if Sandra is not at least an itsy bit concerned about our future because she sees, as I do, the ultimate futility of it, whatever we decide to do.

I became engaged to you because I've always seen in you what others didn't.

'I just wonder,' Ernie Pollack says tactfully, 'if maybe it's not time for all of us – or at least the three of us' – is he offering to forge an alliance with us against his wife? – 'to discuss just what your plan *is*.'

'What we're planning to do with our future,' I say, flinging myself with tipsy abandon into the moment, speaking to the future of my only life, 'is we intend . . . that is, our plan is we're planning to go out to . . . to go toward . . . into . . . we're planning for *me* to go *into* . . . the retail jewelry business with Sandra and you, sir . . . Dad.'

A tidal wave sweeps across the Pollack kitchen; it inundates the three of us beneath its force. The wave bears at its peak a froth of effervescing curiosity; the main body of the wave, however, its very essence and spirit, is composed of a horror I know no one feels any more acutely than I do.

When it comes right down to it, I did not expect to say what I just said – ale or no ale, out of control or in.

The wave washes back over us, leaving me limp amid a residue of nausea and sherbet.

Although now that the words are out, I suspect they are the very words I wouldn't admit I knew I planned to speak eventually since the day I had my way with Sandra in her cabana.

The day, come to think of it, I also stopped working on my course syllabi and stopped worrying about where I was going to live in Albuquerque, New Mexico.

Nowhere. I'm not going to live anywhere in Albuquerque, New Mexico, because I'm not going there, and I certainly won't need syllabi if I'm not going there because I'm not going to be teaching.

My respect for Sandra abounds. She is, I realize, much smarter than I will ever let her know I think she is. This is what she's wanted all along. And she knew the only way to achieve it was to let me assume she would follow me anywhere, no matter how far away – as far away, even, as the place she never wanted to leave in the first place: Miami Beach, Lincoln Road, Pollack's Jewelers.

Here.

Home.

Yet why isn't she exhibiting her relief?

Because she's much, *much* smarter than I will ever give her credit for!

'I cannot tell you,' Ernie Pollack says tremulously and without pleasure, 'how pleased I am . . . and Neddie will be when I tell her your decision.'

With quaking ambivalence, Ernie Pollack rises in slow motion, steps around the table, and drags me to my feet,

embraces me with his spongy arms, and kisses my cheek
with his chilly, sherbety lips; then he reaches out for his
daughter, inviting her into the embrace.

'Oh, Sanny,' says Ernie Pollack, 'huh, baby, what do
you say?'

Crushed to Ernie Pollack's shoulder, I cannot see
Sandra's face, only feel her clutch a handful of my
waist as she says, 'That's so great, Daddy. I was so
afraid I was going to have to go away.'

25

In her old bentwood rocker, my sister has her fingers around her own throat and is choking herself. On her belly a world atlas lies open.

'Stop that, for chrissake!' I tell her. 'Do you know how ridiculous you look? Just tell me what you honestly think – if you can possibly put away your biases and preconceptions and *be* honest.'

She flings her fingers away from her throat. She has left finger marks there. Blood rushes to fill the marks. 'I think you're kidding me!'

'Let's say I'm not kidding you. What do you think – honestly – in that event?'

'I think you're out of your mind.'

'But no worse than that, right?'

'A moron.'

'So crazy *and* stupid, you're saying.'

She whirls and fires the world atlas at me, one of its corners striking me in the chest and leaving an indentation in my shirt.

'Ever hear the phrase "financial security" – '

'Oh, shut up!'

I do, and so does she. The silence is stultifying.

'Why are you reading the world atlas?' I ask her.

'Because I'm looking for a place to go where I don't have to be around crazy fucking morons like you anymore!'

In the next bedroom down the hall, I hear sheets

rustling, sleep disturbed. Cicadas rattle the trees outside my sister's open window. Next door the Marmelsteins are listening to the Carson show.

'They gonna buy you a house, you psychotic moron?'

'They're going to, well, you know, they may help us with the down payment or – '

'Where?'

I laugh. 'Where? Jesus, give us a chance to look a – '

'Don't try to con me, asshole. Sandra's already got the house picked out.'

'She doesn't have it picked out!'

'Then her mother does!'

I've never liked entering my sister's room; it has seemed throughout our lives, at whatever age and after whatever fashion, to be a room without humor.

I engross myself in the shapes on the bedspread that has been on her bed since she was fourteen. I wait for her to go on, eerily cozy in the cocoon of well-being her fury is spinning around me.

'Her father, actually,' I say after a moment, indicating who suggested to us where we might live as we begin our life together in the jewelry business.

'Where?' Susan demands.

'Bay Drive,' I tell her.

'How much?'

'Sixty-six.'

'Sixty-six thousand? Do you know how astronomical the monthly payments on sixty-six thousand dollars are?'

'Doesn't matter.'

'Why not?'

'Because Ernie's starting me off at a base salary of twenty-five thou, a mere thirteen more than I'd be making at Wells Fargo U. And that doesn't include commish or bonuses. With what Sandra's making working half-time, we'll be bringing home – '

'*Sandra's* working? *She's* working? *San*dra!'

'Matter of fact, she's the top sales – '

'For how long, till she starts taking fertility drugs – twins, triplets, fucking septuplets!'

Susan throws herself into the bathroom, slamming the door. I walk to the door, try to determine what to deal with here: my lunacy or Susan's jealousy.

I could cover both if I told her I'm only kidding, it's all a practical joke – there's no engagement, no marriage, no house, no jewelry business, that we'll arbitrarily select a page out of the atlas and go there together.

But it's not a practical joke.

So I go to my room and get into bed, and as I'm about to turn off my light, my mother stands in my doorway.

She wears a glossy black kimono but no makeup, somehow making her hair, once as black as licorice, look all too obviously black from a bottle.

And rollers. I don't remember ever seeing my mother at bedtime without rollers in her hair, preparing to look stunning for the customers in the shoe store the next day.

'Hi, Ma.'

'Why do you fight with your sister?'

'She's the only one in the house in my weight class, kid.'

My mother smiles thinly. There was a time when she would laugh at anything I said, as long as she thought I intended to entertain *her*. Now, I think, it would take more energy than she has available to get laughter from her belly up her throat and out over her lips.

Unless something was really funny.

Which that wasn't.

I want to say something tender and reassuring to her about her still being my best girl, but I say, 'Hey, I'm sorry we woke you.'

'You didn't wake me,' she says.

'Watching television?'

She shakes her head in one of those simple demonstrations of boredom that invites the interrogator to continue. 'Doing the ole in-out with Pop?'

The eyes that land on me are those of a stranger whose privacy has been wrongfully invaded.

'Is that supposed to be amusing, Jacob?'

'Well, yeah, I kind of intended it to have an element of humor.'

'You think it's a joke to talk about the sex lives of people our age?'

'Evidently not.'

'*Definitely* not.'

'I'm sorry, I don't mean to make jokes that aren't funny.'

Why *would* I say something like that?

Because I'd like to know they still make love?

Florence Landau stares at me, unutterable needs stitched into her face.

I don't know what to say to this woman, my mother, to make her okay. 'I love you'? Is that good? Maybe that would be good to say; unfortunately I've never been able simply to say to my parents, to sign my letters from a distance, even: 'I love you.' Everything has always been couched: 'Love Ya!' 'With love.' 'Lotsa love.' But never just 'I love you.'

I could cross the six feet between my mother and me in two steps right now and take her in my arms, hold her, give her at least that comfort; kiss her sixty-three-year-old cheek and say 'I love you, Ma.'

I could easily do that.

But I don't.

'We never talk anymore,' my mother says.

And I cannot remember, of course, when we did, and I would like her to remind me, but I'm sure she couldn't and I say, 'Oh Jesus, Mom, I know it. We have to start doing that again. Talking.'

Yet we're here now. What's wrong with now? Why doesn't real talking commence immediately?

Now!

My mother's eyes mist over. I feel my quadriceps contract, and I think I am readying myself to get off my bed and head for her – *Iloveyou* – when she comes apart in pieces here, but instead of coming apart, she inhales abruptly, lifting her small bosom, and says, 'Well, goodnight, Jacob. Maybe when you have a minute, you'll come by the store and we'll have a coffee.'

'I will, Mom, that's a great idea. I'll come by the store and we'll have a coffee and a good *talk*. Very soon. Believe me.'

Leslie Ann maintained her mother was perfect. Is this woman any less perfect? Are her things-to-do lists any shorter? Has she suffered any less than Leslie Ann's mother could have? Why has no one – me, for instance – built a monument to Flossie Landau like Leslie Ann has to her mother? Because Flossie hasn't killed herself? Because she has endured her life with Morris, Susan, and me up to, and including, this moment?

'And Jacob.'

'Yes, Ma.'

'Someday, before he dies or has a paralysis, you and your father, you really ought to talk about what happened back then.'

What does she mean by 'back then'? What happened to my father as a boy in Warsaw before the war . . . or on that eighteenth hole that day twelve years ago . . . or when I declined my father's legacy to me and left the shoe business?

She's here now, I could ask her.

But don't.

'Just a suggestion,' she says. 'Goodnight, son.'

And she's gone.

Her scent remains in the air – ma griffe infiltrated by Lifebuoy – and carries me backward to a time in my life when that smell represented sanctuary, though from what or whom or how she provided it I can't remember.

I miss my mommy!

And I miss my putter!

And I miss my daddy!

And I miss Leslie Ann Masterson.

All of whom I did not help, care for, or understand sufficiently.

And of course I did not say anything to my mother about becoming a jeweler.

Why not?

D'know.

nformation for what city?'

'The Valley to Manhattan Beach – a Leslie Ann Masters or Leslie Masters or an Ann Leslie or an Annie Masters –'

'Sir, sir, please, sir, slow down!'

'Skip it. Never mind.'

27

We're in the game room at the Pollacks' the next night, playing eight ball, Sandra and me against Ernie and Neddie (though Neddie is never good for more than one focused shot before she slips back to the meprobamate limbo in which she lives).

It's I who raise the question of a wedding date (and get Neddie's attention through the fog).

Following the decision to stay here and go into the jewelry business, Sandra suggested we be married on the day in October we first went on an official date eight years ago.

Now that her dosage has been raised, Neddie is sometimes almost inaudible; Ernie has to stop cracking the balls against each other in order for us to hear her say she wants us to wait until we've been engaged at least a year (implicit here, I'm sure, the hope that I'll make a run for it before next summer or her daughter will come to her senses).

Ernie doesn't care how long we wait, but he does feel I should get settled into my position at Pollacks' Jewelers first and be sure it's what I want to do with my life (the implication being that if I don't like the business, somehow I lose the daughter).

As for me, I want to get it over with, so I tell the three of them that I've become pretty fanatically numerological as I grow older, and I hope they won't think I'm nuts (fat chance!), but they've got to trust me, it's gotta be August 16.

This August 16.

Speaking for the group, Sandra asks, 'Why, Jay? Why August sixteen?'

'What's my lucky number?' I ask her.

'God,' she says, 'let me think.'

How would she know my lucky number? I don't have one.

'Seven?' she proffers gamely.

'*Seven?*' I ask her. Hurt is writ large on my furrowed face.

'Isn't it seven? I thought it – '

'Four,' I tell her.

'Oh,' she says, 'oh, yeah – four.'

'Remember now?'

'Yeah.'

'No, you don't.'

'I do, sweetheart.'

'Are you sure?'

'I think,' says Sandra.

'She *does*,' says Neddie, almost raising her voice. 'Get to the point.'

'Okay – listen to this, this is amazing. Are you ready for amazement? Sixteen is how many fours?'

The Pollacks look at each other, and Sandra says with mock stupidity, 'Duh – four.'

'Four fours – correct. August is the which month?'

'The eighth,' she says.

'The eighth month – so that's two fours; and nineteen seventy-one – one, nine, seven, one, right?'

Sandra nods, Ernie and Neddie spectate, content to let their college-educated daughter do the work.

'One from nine equals eight – two fours again; seven

plus one equals eight – two fours *again*. We can't lose. The sixteenth of August, nineteen hundred and seventy-one, is sanctified.'

I'm sure that Ernie and Neddie Pollack are thinking cruel things about hippies and Eastern mystical googaw, but it doesn't matter because the fact is I sound convinced that I believe what I'm saying, even if I'm not convincing them they should buy in.

Because it doesn't really matter if I'm convincing them . . . as the key to this, Sandra, says that if I feel that strongly about it, she's with me.

Neddie says that doesn't give her enough time to prepare.

I suggest that perhaps we should just elope, then – save them a lot of money and aggravation.

Ernie says if Sandra's committed to August, he thinks that's fine, and he'll hire Neddie all the help she needs to be ready then.

Neddie almost raises her voice again; she says she doesn't need any goddamn help. If she has to be ready, she'll be ready.

At breakfast the next morning I tell my parents I'm going to be married on August 16.

They think that's fine; that way I won't have to go to New Mexico alone.

I tell them I'm not going to New Mexico. I tell them I'm going into the retail jewelry business.

They look at me. They look at each other, their respective looks asking the other if what he/she heard is what the *other* heard?

My father doesn't speak.

'You're not going to teach?' my mother asks.

'Na,' I say.

'Then why did you spend three years on the other side

of the country getting a Ph.D.?' she wants to know.

'How else was I going to find out I didn't want to teach?'

My mother looks at my father. My father doesn't speak.

'You want to sell jewelry, Jacob,' says my mother, 'you could come sell shoes and carry on the Landau tradition.'

'I'm not going to *sell* jewelry, Mom. I'm going to become a *jeweler*. I'm going to become an expert in *gem*ology and *chron*ology and I'm going to make a veritable shitload of greenbacks. I'll be able to afford all the finer things in life, take care of you and Pop when – '

'You're a highly educated man, Jacob,' says my mother. 'You possess information that needs to be passed on.'

'Mom, Mom, the Revolution's over. We lost. Most of my generation's going to become Republicans – I'm just going to get a head start.'

My mother looks at my father.

'Jacob,' he says.

Uh-oh.

'Yeah, Pop?'

But my father shakes his head. He shrugs. He takes two walnuts from the bowl on the kitchen table and crushes them in his fist.

28

L ate that night I stand against the underpinnings of the First Street Pier, that haven of my childhood where my father and I fished for snapper and grunt and I dreamed of immortality.

Everything out there before me. Everything imaginable possible.

Jake the (Good) Snake.

'Shit!' I cry against the crusty underside of the pier, now twenty-seven years old and nowhere.

That evening at dinner at the Pollacks', Neddie told me to let her have the list of my groomsmen by Monday. Sandra, she informed me, has a list of eleven possible bridesmaids, and she can enlarge or compress her list a little depending on how many groomsmen I need.

In other words, she was asking me how many friends from high school and college and graduate school I wanted to stand up for me at my wedding.

'Oh,' I said to Neddie as offhandedly as possible, 'just the Micker, I guess.'

'Just the Micker what?' Neddie wanted to know.

'Michael will be my best man, and I don't need any groomsmen.'

Neddie was perplexed. I had just said something in the only language spoken on the planet in which she wasn't fluent. She tried to glean a translation from just above my head and almost drove a wedge of sarcasm through the meprobamate when she asked me, 'Then what's Sandra supposed to do about brides-maids?'

'Whatever people do,' I told Neddie, 'when their future husbands have no friends, I guess.'

I walk toward the pier, and I remember a time with my father, leaning against the rail, tickling our hand lines, my father sternly remonstrating with me.

Rusty, Rusty, to dream of fame, boychik, is to dream only of yourself. How long can such a dream last? A person can be famous in a minute, by one act, or can pursue such a selfish dream all his life and never achieve it for one second even and therefore never share his life with another human person, with other living people.

I remember he looks east and the little boy I am wonders what my poppy is thinking.

Didn't you dream of being famous, Poppy?

Of course, certainly, for a little while, a short time.

What did you dream?

To be the greatest surgeon of all time.

Oh.

East east east. Lyons. Warsaw. The place called Auschwitz.

What do you dream now, Poppy?

Ah, Jakey, now I dream only the dreams that last.

What dreams are those, Poppy, the ones that last?

Dreams of redemption, Jakey, last long. Dreams of love last longest. If I didn't have those dreams, I would have to go and get a gun and blow my brains out.

And he takes my cheeks in his fists and shakes my head gently, staring into my eyes as through the wide end of a telescope.

And then seeing what he sees on my face, he says, *I'm kidding – about the blowing my brains out part. Don't worry, okay? That was just a kidding part. You would*

*be right to never forgive me for such an act. And so I
would never do that to you.*

I nod, and he clutches me to him.

Crushed against the rough texture of his flannel 'fishing shirt' I ask him, *What's redemption mean, Poppy?*

To make up for all that you did wrong, Jakey.

What did you do wrong, Poppy?

Me, says my poppy. *What could I have done wrong?
I helped make you.*

When was that? When did that conversation take
place?

Did that conversation take place?

It's almost one A.M. I walk out on the pier with a
kosher frankfurter for bait and a hand line I dug out
of our so-called junk closet, a repository of our athletic
history. Roller skates and bats and tennis rackets; a hula
hoop, a pogo stick, a slalom ski; my old catcher's mitt,
two basketballs, four sets of golf clubs; three deep-sea
rods, a fly rod I got for my bar mitzvah, a half dozen
hand lines.

The only other person fishing the pier at this hour is a
big black woman in pedal pushers and a Florida A&M
T-shirt, tending three battered deep-sea rods and a pair
of hand lines tied to a light post on which is bolted a
sign that says 'No multiple-line fishing allowed.'

The memory of the real or imagined conversation
with my father combines with the sight of this woman
to make me regretful that I was not more committed to
the Civil Rights Movement, did not do more.

And makes me wish that I had put my lips on those
of Amy Polynice.

Jesus – Amy Polynice!

How did I bury *her* so deep so long?

Demons past and present convoking in the night.

I feed my line into the water a few yards down from the black woman and begin to sing Screamin' Jay Hawkins.

She glances my way. Buckteeth behind the tightly judgmental lips of her prominent, convex mouth. Amy Polynice had snaggled eyeteeth and a row of chaotic lowers. Morris Landau paid for her to get braces when she was thirty-nine.

How come, Poppa, you did that?

So maybe she could find a mate for her middle age. How much fun is she going to have when her children are all gone with those teeth?

'You got the whole other side a this pier to fish, white boy. Whu'chu crowdin' me?'

'Better side,' I say. 'Anybody's ever fished First Street knows that. South side eats doodey.'

The big black woman stares at me disdainfully. 'Used to work for white folks said doodey.'

'Hmph.'

'And poopie. Sissy. Tinkle. They thought it was just real cute. You know the Cohens?'

'Oh, sure,' I say. (There are probably only five thousand Cohens on the Beach.)

'Like 'em?'

'I could live without 'em.'

'You ain't the only one,' she says.

'Fire your black ass, huh?'

She fires a howitzer my way with her rheumy, dark eyes. 'They said I was stealin' from 'em.'

'You probably were. You look like a thief to me.'

Her mouth gapes, the big upper, front teeth hang like an awning over her chin. 'Whu'chu say?'

'You heard me.'

She pulls out a Saturday Night Special, puts six bullets into my gut, and I'm out of it.

*This fo' Amy Polynice, white slug, and fo' all yo'
black brothers out to that school you dint support worth
doodey!*

But the big black woman thrusts her tumid face at me
and says with a defiance that rattles the ages, 'You bet
yo' white *ass* I was stealin' from 'em. They gots mo'n they
need. A *lots* mo'.'

She tickles two of the deep-sea lines.

I pick up where I left off with Screamin' Jay.

She asks me, 'How come you ain't home in yo' cozy
big ole white-boy bed this time a night?'

'Gotta fish,' I tell her.

'Boo-shit,' she says.

'Born to fish. It's in my genes – fishin'.'

'But you don't gotta do it fo' *food*. Do ya now?'

'Nope, sure don't. Wish I did.'

The awning's out over her chin again. 'Wha'fo'?'

'Hell if I know. Seems like it'd be kinda nice to be
black and poor and despised and have something really
legitimate to rebel about. Make a lot of demands, maybe
go berserk one day, kill a lot of white folks.'

'Whu'chu talkin'?'

'Or be Martin Luther King – wield the language the
way he did. The Bible, all that poetic rhetoric to weave
into my speeches.'

She tickles one of the hand lines, studies me, head
canted, mouth stretched across all those teeth. She
indicates the heavens. 'Things be a lot different up *there*,'
she says.

'I bet they will. Why do you think I came down here
tonight? Taking out insurance for that day we find out
God's a big-assed black lady like yourself.'

She laughs deeply and shakes her head at this crazy
white boy.

'How many mouths you got to feed, chitlin cheeks?'

She thrusts her face at me. 'Seven,' she says, challenging me to attack her for her profligacy.

'Got a husband?'

'What's that 'sposed to mean?'

'He split on you?'

'You watch yo' mouf! You think I don't got me no ole man?'

'I'd bet the ranch on it.'

She shakes the line in her hand ever so gently; her anger at me cannot affect her pursuit of the fish. 'Up there,' she says, 'things gone be *real* different.'

We are both fixed on the full moon.

'Guy walked on that thing couple of years ago.'

'You think I don't know that?'

'Just checking.'

'July twenty, nineteen and sixty-nine,' she says.

In my apartment complex in Palo Alto, someone brought a television outside that afternoon and we sat and watched as a guy got out of a studio apartment several hundred thousand miles away and made the first sneaker track up there, and said as we knew he would that we've come a long way since the wheel, and all of us cocky and angry young people sat there and hooted as each of us secretly revered the moment and envied the man.

The big black woman and I try to spot those footsteps from here. 'I played golf with him once,' I hear my voice say.

'With who, golf? Neil Armstrong?'

'Kennedy.'

'What trash you talkin' now?'

'Nineteen and fifty-seven. He was testing the waters, courting the local Hebrew vote.'

'John Kennedy didn't play no golf. He play touch foo'ball.'

'I was fourteen. I shot a sixty-eight.'

'*White* boys killed him.'

'He said, "You're the best I've ever seen at your age, JD." '

'You just 'member that: *white* boys killed him *and* Martin *and* Bobby.'

And you, Rusty Landau, you killed Amy Polynice.

'I had a picture. JFK and me and What's-his-name – the comedian.'

'Flip Wilson.'

'Gleason.'

'Paw,' says the black woman, dismissing Gleason and commenting in passing on a hundred years of unmet promises.

'Wanna know something?' I ask her.

'Depends.'

'I hated JFK as much as I loved him.'

'How come?'

'I guess because he was him and I wasn't.'

'Whu'chu wanna be him fo' if he told *you* you the best he ever seen at golfin'?'

'You got a choice between being a golfer and boffing Marilyn Monroe, which would you choose?'

'Golf,' she says.

'Me too,' I say.

'You a famous golfer now or some booshit like that?'

'No.'

'What are you – whu'chu do for a livin'?'

'I'm a jeweler.'

Jesus, that sounds . . .

'Now I *knows* you booshittin' me.'

'How do you figure?'

It sounded . . .

'You don't look like no *jeweler*.'

'What do I look like?'

There's no word powerful enough in the English language to connote how *ridiculous* that sounded to me.

She studies me a moment. Shrugs. 'D'know,' she says. She averts her eyes, concentrating on the fishing tackle in her hands. She laughs. At me.

She doesn't know *what* I am – she knows only what I know, really: that I'm a fool and not a jeweler.

'You mind if I fish here?'

'You gonna gimme whu'chu catch?'

'Sure.'

'Then fish ahead.'

I put some frankfurter on my hook and feed my line into the water beating against the pilings of the pier.

The black woman stares at the moon. I stare at her. And see Amy Polynice.

Amy Polynice worked for my father in the store when I was a boy and no one on Washington Avenue on Miami Beach hired colored folks to work for them in any capacity other than maid or custodian.

Amy Polynice was a caring, big-voiced, big laughing black woman, and my father hired her as a salesperson.

My sister and I thought this hiring as strange as my mother and most of my father's patrons did. We inquired why he had this colored lady working side by side with him.

'Not out of goodness,' he said, 'I promise you that.'

'Then how come?' my sister asked.

'Maybe,' he said, 'because I am afraid.'

Morris the Bear afraid? Get serious. ''Of what, Poppy?'

'Of my feelings against the coloreds. I am afraid to sometimes think I know what the Nazis felt toward us.'

Dark visions filled my head. The store failing, closing. My father broke. The family on the street because his patrons would not allow a colored person to touch their smelly feet.

Though my father lost some regulars, most stayed and became accustomed to Amy Polynice, and soon colored people who worked on the South Beach (many more customers than he lost) began to buy their shoes from Amy and therefore from my father.

It was the summer the kid from Birmingham let me know what a chickenshit I was. Susan and I had just come home from camp. I was the stock boy in the store until school started. I spent a lot of time in the back, alone, stacking shoes in anal compulsive symmetry and imagining gory acts of revenge against all who knew me for what I was.

On the day Amy Polynice died, the other salesman, Irwin, had gone for coffee, my mother was home sick, and because it was ten forty-five in the morning, my father had to move his bowels, an activity that knew no variance.

At the moment of Amy Polynice's cry for help, I was in the stockroom trying on a pair of women's capped-toed pumps, wondering if life would be easier for me if I were a girl.

The first thing I did was hide behind the nearest wall of boxed footwear – ladies' opened-toed, low heels. Then I heard a man's voice yell, 'Call an ambulance, call an ambulance!' and so I peeked into the store, where Amy Polynice lay on the floor, face up, trying to get air through an apparatus – her esophagus – which wasn't cooperating. She was diluting from her normal, deep chocolate brown to a chalky gray. A customer, an old man in a terrible plaid jacket and straw fedora, stood twitching in horror over her.

'The *shvartzeh* just fell over. She just ga-bumped.'

From the toilet my father called, 'What is it, what's happening out there, Mrs Polynice?'

Always Mrs Polynice.

'I'm thinking maybe a heart attack!' cried the old man toward the toilet. 'Somebody should be giving her artificial respiration.'

And he's looking at me.

What's wrong with *him*? He's the grown-up. I'm a little kid.

In school we had been taught the new kind of artificial respiration where you breathe directly into the mouth of the victim.

'In case,' the very sensitive school nurse told us, 'one of your parents has a heart attack or drowns.'

Without knowing how I got there, I was on my knees, prostrate over the mouth of Amy Polynice. She had five young children, my father had told us. She was their sole support, he had said. Thank God they had her, said my mother, and that she had a good job.

She had to be saved.

And yet I could not bring myself to put my mouth to hers.

What's the *old*-style artificial respiration?

You put the person on their stomach and you push down on their back and pull up on their arms.

Or something.

I didn't know that way. We learned the new way. Mouth-to-mouth resuscitation, it was called.

Mouth *to* mouth.

How long had I been hovering over her mouth?

'Turn her over,' I cry. 'Turn her over!'

'What? Why?' the old man demanded. He was unequivocally not in favor of turning her over.

'So we can . . . so I can . . .'

And now Amy Polynice opened her eyes. They practically ejected from their sockets onto her cheeks.

And they implored me to do something.

And yet I couldn't – or wouldn't – in any case, *didn't*, and when I continued to hover over her mouth, those eyes accused me.

Those eyes, acting for her dying person, accused me of not saving her life because I didn't want to put my white mouth on her black one.

And then my father was there. And I watched him hunker to Amy Polynice's mouth without a moment's hesitation and breathe oxygen into her lungs, turn away and inhale, breathe into her lungs, turn away and inhale . . .

He did this until the ambulance the old man called arrived and put a sheet over Amy Polynice, put her on a stretcher, and took her away to where dead bodies of poor black persons with five children were taken.

Nothing was ever said to me. My father didn't seem to suspect that I hadn't acted. It did not seem to occur to anyone that I could have done anything to help.

Jesus, I buried that real deep.

The big black woman continues to stare at the moon. 'Things gone be real diff'rent when we all gets up there,' she says. 'My last boy born the next week after they beat they feet up there. Named him Rhadamanthys.'

'You folks got a knack for naming, I'll tell you that.'

'You know where that name come from?'

Uh-oh – quiz.

'You a college boy, right?'

Rhadamanthys, Rhadamanthys.

'I took a couple of courses – you know.'

Rhadamanthys.

'Mythology.'

Mythology!

'Big field,' I say.

Rhadamanthys.

'He was real *just* when he was on earth. And for that, he was rewarded in the hereafter. My boy Rhad, though, you know what I'm gone tell him 'bout justice down here when he old enough to understand?'

'What?'

'That it's one great big, extra-special crock a *doodey*.'

She nods her head my way and hurls her big black-lady laugh into the night.

29

At three A.M. I sit parked outside the Bi-Rite shoe store on Washington Avenue and Thirteenth Street.

When he left upscale A. S. Beck's on Lincoln Road seventeen years ago and opened his own shop next to the kosher deli in the heart of the South Beach, the so-called Yenta Centa, to sell 'decent shoes that everyone can afford' ('Who shouldn't be able to afford a decent shoe for a foot?'), I asked him why he called the store Bi-Rite and not Landau's.

Morrie the Bear shrugged.

Later my mother told us, 'To him, it would be boastful to name a business after yourself. To him,' she said, 'Bi-Rite has a ring.'

Thirty years in all. People's feet in your hands, beneath your nose, before your eyes. Toenails of all shapes and lengths, manicured and torn and, 'Oh, yes,' said my father one night to my sister's inquiry, 'bitten.' Feet with toes of the prescribed number and feet with more or less than the prescribed number.

'Feet,' my mother once said in defending an attack by my sister and me on this former surgeon's vocation, 'are the most important appendage on the body. Without good feet you can't even *get* to a doctor to take care of your other appendages. So without good shoes . . .'

Well, the specieswide implications were obvious. Selling shoes, we were asked to believe, was easily as respectable a vocation as being a surgeon.

And when I graduated college and had no aspirations or plans for the final sixty, seventy years of my only life, I went to work beside my father.

It had been, no doubt, an at least unconscious effort to make my peace with him for my share of the silence that had become our relationship.

I was a terrible shoe salesman. I despised kneeling at people's feet.

'You can't sell shoes from a crouch,' my father said. 'You sit on a stool or you kneel.'

I had to maintain a 'reasonable' haircut. I had to wear *our* shoes instead of the Florsheim's I preferred. Socks that didn't 'shlump.' Ties with *short*-sleeve shirts.

'Why wear a long sleeve?' my father asked. 'It looks hot. If the salesman looks hot, people hurry. If they hurry, they don't get a good fit. You want people to develop carbuncles because you wanted to wear a long-sleeve shirt?'

For the first year or so there was a grotesque satisfaction in dedicating my waking hours to the pursuit of a life I found abhorrent. I sized and fit shoes on hundreds of pairs of feet with the same compulsive thoroughness I used to practice hitting five irons from the rough or plugged sand shots or with which I researched a paper for a lit class. I dated hardly at all. I read books and bought this week the ones I would read next week, and my sister and I went to three or four movies a week, before and afterward parading our dissatisfaction with our lives past each other, plotting mutinies we never carried out.

But into the second year I began to stew and to mope and to insult the customers with my truculence, and my father asked me one night at dinner over his pot roast and boiled potatoes this simple question: 'Why do you do this if you hate it?'

Having long ago devised an answer to this question that absolved me of any blame for my predicament, I said instantly, 'I owe it to you.'

'You owe it to me for what? What have I done for you that you owe me?'

'You want me to take over the business.'

'I never said that. I wanted you to become something you didn't want to become.'

'A lawyer.'

'A lawyer, I could care less. That was only a suggestion. I wanted you to become something that would stimulate the best that is in you, that's all. I thought when you came to me in the business it was because you saw the potential for yourself to take this from what I've made it to heights beyond my imagination.'

That particular sentence, though I hadn't known it beforehand, was the one I'd been waiting months for.

'Heights beyond your imagination, Pop?' My voice fairly frothed with indignation and sarcasm. 'We're not talking about a monument here, Pop. We're not talking about General Motors! We're talking about a shoe store!'

My father barely glanced up from mashing a boiled potato.

So I turned the insult up a notch. 'We're not talking about protecting human rights here or an end to the Cold War! We're talking about selling frigging *shoes*!'

I wanted to say selling *fucking* shoes but couldn't make the leap.

My sister put her utensils aside, leaned back to spectate.

'Pass me the gravy,' said my father to my mother,

who passed him the gravy. Which he dribbled with a teaspoon over his potato. 'You think you're hurting me by becoming the least you can become, Jacob?'

When I didn't respond to that, he said, 'If you stay in my employ, you owe it to me not to ruin the business atmosphere I've been fourteen years developing.'

'Whoa, whoa, hey, wait a minute. Are you threatening to fire me?'

'I am telling you how things must be if you stay. But I am also giving you permission to leave.'

I laughed – what a gift! 'Great!' I said. I looked at my sister. She wasn't laughing. Only watching. 'And do what?' I asked my father.

'I don't think that, too, should be my problem. Horseradish, please.'

Susan bounced forward, passed my father the horse-radish, bounced back into her spectating position.

'You like to read books,' my mother said.

As if I were speaking to someone with hugely limited intelligence, I inquired of my mother, '*And?*'

'Don't use that tone with your mother, Jacob. We've talked, the two of us. So you don't want to be a lawyer or a dentist, fine; you studied all this Literature, there must have been a reason. So go to graduate school, become a doctor of philosophy, become a teacher or a writer.'

'Sure, great, but what if I don't like *that?*'

And suddenly, for the first time since my father exploded over Allan Adelman years before, he erupted over his pot roast and boiled potato. '*Then, if life is so tough for you, Jacob, if you cannot bear it, you will kill yourself!*'

'Morris,' said my mother.

'*Do you think I don't already have marked into my debit column that I was not able to instill in you the will*

*to succeed in your aspirations? If you find you cannot
stand this life, then leave it. I have an endless capacity
for regret.'*

My father pronged a wedge of pot roast, shoved it into
his pile of gravied potato, the muddy brown vegetable
adhering to the roast, and he filled his mouth. Chewed.
Took a sip of tea. Masticated some more. Swallowed.

'Is the pot roast dry?' asked my mother.

'It's fine,' said my father.

'Pass the kasha to your father, Jacob. Take some
first.'

I took some kasha.

'You can always,' my father said, 'come back to the
business.'

The offer of safe harbor did nothing to abate my guilt
and therefore intensified my anger. 'A Ph.D. in Literature
running a shoe store, Pop? Get serious.'

'What – does everyone in a business that's not romantic have to be an imbecile?'

As I had many times in my life, I pictured my father
entering St Francis or Mt Sinai Hospital, moving briskly
down a hallway, entering an operating theater . . . and
saving a life. 'I didn't mean that, Pop.'

'Your problem is you don't *know* what you mean.'

My mother briskly brushed crumbs that didn't exist
from the perfectly centered Irish linen tablecloth on
which we ate each evening. My father's eyes pounced
on her brushing fingers; she stopped.

'But why should you know *any*thing?' my father
inquired of no one in particular. 'You're a child who
thinks because he finished college he's a man. All you
really know, the important point, is you don't want to
grow up to be your father. And who could blame you?
Me? No.'

My father took the bowl of kasha from between us and took a mountainous serving, spilling several grains over onto the linen. He two-fingered the grains into his mouth.

Having made him feel terrible, I now set out to make amends. 'But I am you in a way, Pop. Who made me love books?'

'Yes, yes.' And my father smiled, alerting me that he was about to say something that would allow this to proceed no further into unpleasantness. 'But how can you be Jake the Good Snake from a shoe store, huh? Who is there in a shoe store to rescue, right?'

And then I heard myself say, 'You could have had so much more prestige, Pop, could have been so highly respected.'

My mother found one extremely stubborn nonexistent crumb on the linen at which she dug and flicked.

'What – people don't respect me?' my father wanted to know. 'What I do, I do the best I can – what's the difference if it's surgery or selling shoes? When you say prestige, you're really talking money, right?'

When I didn't respond my father demanded, 'Right – money?'

'I think I'm talking . . .' I couldn't say the word. I shook my head. 'Pass the gravy, please.'

'What? You think you're talking *what*?'

'Nothing, I don't know.'

'Say it.'

'He said he doesn't know, Morris,' said my mother. 'He's waiting for the gravy.'

'He knows the word, believe me. Say it, Jacob. If we're not talking money, we're talking what?'

'We're talking courage, Pop. We're talking guts.'

My father shoved away from the table, stood, his

napkin tucked into the top of his short-sleeve shirt to protect one of his two ties. 'Guts?' he said. 'Courage? Twenty-two – you know so much. What do you need a degree for that says you are a doctor of ideas – you already know everything. Put out a shingle, Jacob – teach, heal.'

And my father lumbered through the kitchen and out the back door, into the yard and to the fence where he had just planted his tomatoes for the summer. He bent over and stroked the latticework, against which low vines had begun to climb.

My mother exhaled sharply and said, 'And you, Jacob, I can only assume you learned your own lack of courage, then, from that man out there.' She leaned toward my father's place and passed me the gravy.

The next day I sent for applications to the best schools I could think of that were geographically as far away as I could go and still be in an area where English was the first language.

30

I am to 'enjoy my last days of freedom' ('Dad' Pollack's words) and come into the business after the honeymoon.

September 1.

The same day classes start in Albuquerque, New Mexico.

I 'enjoy my last days of freedom' by spending most of them accompanying my affianced, Sandra Pollack, and her mother, Neddie, around Miami Beach while they make frantic arrangements for her wedding (in which I am scheduled to be a supporting player). The role they assign me in the making of the arrangements is that of Unobtrusive Listener.

The problem, as I learn abruptly, is that though I often appear to be listening unobtrusively, in truth I hardly ever am. Instead I am helplessly listening to conversations in my head and watching the actions and reactions of fictitious people who refuse to be banished from my imagination (the newest being a black woman and white young man on a fishing pier).

Had I indulged my imagination less and listened more, I would have known much sooner about the cloud machine.

'What cloud machine?' I ask Sandra and her mother the morning we arrive at the theatrical supply house and Sandra insists I come in with them to look at 'it.'

Sandra and her mother contemplate me, wondering,

no doubt, where I've been these last ten days they've been slaving to set this thing up for me.

'*The* cloud machine, Jay,' says Sandra with a glance that warns me not to kid around on this.

'Ah,' I say, '*the* cloud machine,' and I join Sandra and her mother in poking and kicking at the air conditioner-size contraption as if it were a tire on a used car.

'It looks good,' says Neddie Pollack to the man in charge of the machine.

'It's look *very* good,' I say to the same man. 'You don't find a lot of these in shape this good.'

'No,' says the man, 'you don't. Not this good.'

'No,' I say, 'this is inarguably a good one.'

The cloud machine man nods as if, more than merely the rental agent for the machine, he is its progenitor.

'Just one question,' I say to everyone in general.

Assuming the role of spokesperson for the group, Sandra asks. 'What's that, darling?'

'What's it for?'

Neddie Pollack looks at Sandra. Sandra looks at her mother. Both women look at the cloud machine man. The three of them look at me.

More than a touch of unease in her voice (is it possible I *haven't* been paying attention?), Sandra says, 'I'm going to come out of clouds, Jay.'

I repeat each word I've just heard her say – one simply makes no sense whatever when combined with any or all of the others in their present syntactical arrangement: 'You're ... going ... to ... come ... out ... of ... clouds.'

'Down the stairs,' Neddie Pollack says aridly to the ceiling. (Sandra told me her mother's doctor upped her dose again – just until after the wedding.)

'Down *what* stairs?'

'The stairs,' Neddie Pollack tells the ceiling, 'at the rear of the grand ballroom of the Fontainebleau Hotel.'

Like a retarded individual suffering from echolalia, I now repeat those words, as follows: 'Sandra ... is ... going ... to ... come ... out ... of ... clouds ... down ... the ... stairs ... at ... the ... rear ... of ... the ... grand ... ballroom ... of ... the ... Fontainebleau ... Hotel.'

Sandra couches her remonstrance in immediate forgiveness. 'You've been wonderful about driving us everywhere, darling, and I know you must get bored on occasion, but – '

'But,' snaps Neddie Pollack, rising wrathfully above her tranquillity, 'we've only been talking about this incessantly for ten days.'

'Of course you have,' I say.

'Are you implying,' Neddie Pollack wants to know, 'that we excluded you from the plans?'

'No,' I say, 'no, I'm not. I'm implying, I think – though I'm not absolutely sure – that I probably should, starting right now, today, pay more attention to the decisions others make which directly affect my life.'

'Well,' says Neddie Pollack, slightly askew of the subject, 'that's just your hard luck now, isn't it?'

'Yes,' I say, 'yes, it is.'

'Don't you like the idea, Jay?'

'Frankly,' says Neddie Pollack to her daughter, 'I don't give a good goddamn whether he likes it or not. I like it and you like it and it's our goddamn wedding.'

'Mommy,' says Sandra, 'please.'

Neddie Pollack excises herself from the group and takes up a vigil at the storeroom's only window, heavily barred against the world outside, smudged opaque with years of coruscating gunk.

She's making a quiet sound that is neither mantra nor music.

'Nobody's ever done it before, darling,' Sandra says to me. 'I mean, it's very, very theatrical, to be sure, but what, after all, is more theatrical than our wedding?' And then she whispers quickly, smoothly, 'It's very important to my mother, Jay.'

Neddie Pollack studies the window, its bars, what lies blurred beyond, outside, where there are hundreds of thousands of people who are not trapped inside with me; I turn my own eyes to the ceiling and try to read my future in the palmate lines of the acoustic tile up there.

Sandra takes my silence for acquiescence. 'Thank you,' she says. She kisses my cheek and turns with a smile as big as all outdoors to her mother.

31

From the time it opened when I was in elementary school until I went away to college, few Sundays passed that our family didn't have dinner at Fun Fair.

Fun Fair! The very words conjure a profusion of memories spinning around cement picnic tables, the 'world famous' Fun Fair hot dogs, the nine-ingredient relish pit, the pinball machines and mind-boggling array of other electronic games that could occupy a boy and his dad for hours. And, of course, there is the miniature golf course with its oscillating, carpeted putting surfaces on which, once, when I was fourteen, I shot a nineteen for eighteen holes.

Fun Fair! I bring Sandra Elaine Pollack here for dinner to inform her that she is to become the former future Mrs Jacob Daniel Landau.

We load a tray with hot dogs and French fries, with corn on the cob and kosher pickle slices, with minced onions and diced tomatoes and blops of hot mustard, with Dr Peppers plumbed with two straws each, and with plenty of extra napkins. We unload on one of the cement picnic tables facing the Seventy-first Street Causeway that rises out of Biscayne Bay like a colorless rainbow. We sit facing each other, and Sandra purses her rosebud lips and smacks a kiss through the torpid air at me.

I smile at her benignly and realize that since we decided to get married ten days ago, we haven't really had a conversation. We travel in the Lincoln together and she talks to her mother; we watch movies in crowded theaters in silence and television en famille in virtual silence, emitting only occasional sentence fragments ordering food from the kitchen; we accompany our lovemaking with monosyllabic, polymorphous noises.

Consequently it seems whimsically anomalous to use the English language to do what I'm about to do. The thought must cause me to smile because Sandra asks me, 'What's so funny, darling?'

'Nothing,' I say. 'Nothing's funny.'

'Then why are you smiling?' she wants to know, smiling at me smiling.

'Because,' I say, 'nothing's funny.' And because it isn't, I laugh and chomp into my world-famous Fun Fair hot dog.

Sandra also laughs. 'Do you know what's funny, Jay?'

'No,' I said, 'what? What's funny?'

'The way you look with mustard on your chin.'

I whip my napkin from my lap and swipe at my chin, wanting to appear just now, at least on the surface, at my least preposterous.

'All gone,' she says. She wrinkles her nose at me in this very sweet way that, hard as I try, I can't help find appealing.

She takes a dainty bite of her hot dog and goes for a French fry, which she dabs in the pond of ketchup on her plate and holds out to me like a lean, drooping wang.

I shake my head.

She folds the French fry into her mouth, masticates several times, then sucks up some Dr Pepper for lubrication. 'Dr Pepper,' she says with respect. 'I forget how good it is.'

'Slurp,' I say, taking a belt of my own.

'I've gotten so used to Coke.'

I nod. I purse my lips. She really nailed something there. 'I know,' I say.

She shakes her head disparagingly, purses *her* lips. 'Habits,' she says.

'Mmph,' say I.

I asked Leslie Ann once why she drank RC. She said because it was so 'peaceful.' Why peaceful?

D'know, said she.

Sandra looks out onto Biscayne Bay and she sighs. It is a sign, I understand, of Sandra Pollack's contentment. She is engaged to me, assumes that she's going to come out of a cloud machine and marry me. And she's happy.

Why?

Can anyone, even a young woman who thinks she should be married already and who, even unconsciously, is starting to panic a bit, can she really want to marry someone who's going to become a jeweler? Does the prospect of replicating her parents really bode satisfaction, if not of her girlhood dreams, even of her young-adulthood compromises?

For a moment it saddens me that I'll never again make with her what Sandra calls 'Uh-uh' on the lower bunk in the back cabin of the *Sandra*.

She has stopped making choo-choo sounds and other self-conscious jokes. She has stopped tensing either when my tongue strays toward her middle or her mouth finds itself in the vicinity of mine.

Touching her, being touched by her, is really very nice.

Gotta get out!

'You don't know any better,' I hear myself say to her,

deciding in an instant, though, that I can't tell this young woman that the reason I'm not going to marry her is because she's planning to come out of clouds.

Because that isn't it.

I can't marry her because we are living our only lives and we have no right to bind ourselves to each other when I know I don't love her and when I know she can't possibly – or, if she does, shouldn't – love me.

'I beg your pardon, darling?'

'Marrying me.'

'Marrying you what?'

'You don't know any better than to do it.'

'Why should I know better than to –'

'San? . . .'

The look on Sandra Pollack's face is one determined to wait until the very last moment to admit that catastrophe is on its way, is mere words and seconds away, is about to descend like an insuperable blow from her blind side.

For the second time in eight years.

'Yes, Jay . . . ?'

'I can't . . .'

Sandra Pollack's tongue wets her lips and her eyes flit left and right to see who is near enough to bear witness to her impending disgrace.

'. . . become a jeweler,' I hear myself say, finishing the sentence intended to end our engagement, our relationship, our future together.

'What?' asks Sandra. 'What . . . what . . . what did you say, darling?'

'A jeweler,' I hear my voice repeat. 'I can't be*come* one.'

'Then . . . then . . . then don't,' says Sandra Pollack,

her breath coming across the table on currents of suddenly sour air. '*Don't* become a jeweler. Don't be*come* one. Don't become a *jeweler*.'

I lean away from Sandra's graveside breath. '*Don't* become a jeweler,' my voice says.

A revolutionary idea!

'Don't become a jeweler,' she says. 'Who said you *had* to become a jeweler?'

'No one,' I proclaim emphatically, defending to the death all those innocent Pollacks who haven't said I have to become a jeweler.

'What . . . what do you want to do, darling?'

Sandra wants to know this, I assume, so she can tell her parents what the man she's about to marry, with whom she plans to live the rest of her life, is going to do five days a week during those hours he isn't home.

'What I want to do,' I say, straining to see into my mind so that I might know what my lips are going to say before they say it. Seeing nothing, though, I am left to listen to my voice say, 'What I want to do is I want to go to Albuquerque and teach English at the University of New Mexico.'

I am not really surprised by this announcement. How many other choices were there? If I'm going to marry someone I don't love, why not dedicate my life's work to the very vocation I suspect I least want to enter in the least palatable place I can think of?

'Didn't you tell them already you weren't coming?'

As a matter of fact, I hadn't. I kept intending to . . .

'No,' I say, 'I haven't told them. They still assume I *am* coming.'

'I . . .' says Sandra. 'Darling . . .' she says.

'Yes, Sandra?'

Sandra is looking at me queerly, her jaw slack, her big hazel eyes dancing about my face, and I realize that it is not too late for my urge to self-destruct to be aborted by an unexpected source.

Is it possible that I am about to become the dumpee, that I have jolted her to her senses?

Smart girl!

'Do you have something to say to me, San?' I prompt gently.

Sandra Pollack definitely has something to say. Her eyes fill with tears, she reaches across the cement table at which both of us sat separately a hundred times as children when it had never occurred to either of us that our futures might entwine, and she takes my hand in hers, in one of which I still hold most of my world-famous Fun Fair hot dog, and what she says to me is this: 'I am so proud to know you.'

'Well, that's . . . that's very generous of you, Sandra. Very generous. But why?'

'Because I've felt all along,' says Sandra Pollack, the tears spilling over her eyelids, 'that's what you – what we should do; but I didn't want to push you because I know how confused you've been.'

I have stopped breathing, an act I understand distantly will bring death if sustained long enough. Against my better judgment, I gasp for air, creating a sound very much like astonishment. It resonates around my ears, pierces the top of my head like a bolo punch, and makes my temples quaver. I crush the hot dog and bun and relish that I hold in my hand that Sandra squeezes, and the stuff rushes up out of the volcano of our fingers like some primordial ooze. I watch the stuff metamorphose into a brute beast that consumes me in one awesome, flesh-rending bite.

Trick of vision. I'm still here!

'Thank you, darling,' I say to Sandra Pollack, to this stranger, 'I was so afraid that you wouldn't understand and I would lose you.'

32

Sandra thinks it will be less incendiary – her word – if she tells her parents alone.

I'm tired of watching me make them miserable, so I readily agree.

When I get home I find my father in the kitchen in his pajamas, disheveled from interrupted sleep, hunkered at the counter, eating saltines in skim milk with a spoon. The metal stool beneath him seems incapable of accommodating his mass.

'Can't sleep, Pop?'

My father shrugs. His shoulders swallow his neck. 'I sleep,' he says, 'don't worry.'

I want to ask him: What's the nightmare, Pop?

I open the refrigerator. 'What do you feel like?' he wants to know.

He hated it when Susan and I were kids and stood in front of the refrigerator, surveying the choices. *Why do you look so long? You think what's in there's going to change while you're standing there wasting electricity that who-do-you-think pays for?*

'How about some tuna-fish salad?' he asks.

'That's salad that she makes from a tuna fish, right?'

My father smiles, he gives me a little nod that indicates he remembers.

Long ago we had a little routine we would do for my mother's entertainment. *How about some egg salad, Morris?*

Egg salad – that's salad from eggs, right?
How 'bout some tossed salad, Rusty?
That's salad she makes from tosses, right, Poppy?

'Maybe I'll have a beer,' I say, gazing into the packed but impeccable storage space that is the refrigerator of Flossie Landau.

'Better for you would be this – here, you want some? There's plenty – the crackers get in the milk, they expand.'

I hate this wooden concoction of crackers and milk, but I say, 'You bet,' and grab a long teaspoon out of the silver drawer and take a position across the counter from my father.

He pushes the glass between us, and I dig in.

He fixes his gaze on me. Because of the great spread of his trapezoidal nose, his eyes appear closer together than they are, making his head seem more simian than it is. His chest rises and falls. He wants to tell me something, to reassume at least for the moment the mantle of mentor, of guide.

Friend.

Father.

'What, Pop?'

'Na,' he says, 'it's nothing.'

'Please,' I say, 'tell me.'

And quickly, without preamble or further precaution, he lets go of the spoon, stands free of the counter, says, 'Don't waste your mind, your talent, your life.'

'Waste it how, Pop?'

'In a store. Never mind, shoe store, jewelry store. You were right to leave the store after college like you did. At the time I was hurt, but you were right to go. To have that courage. So now, okay, get married, fine. I always liked Sandi – she's all right; a woman is there to

support you; you got that, then one is not so different
from another. But go to New Mexico, write books or
plays and teach children.'

'I'm going to, Pop.'

'Since?'

'Today. Tonight.'

'Yes?'

'Yeah.'

He nods his approval, yet I sense there's more. He
digs at the white stuff in the tall glass, excavating but
not eating.

'What, Pop? Go on.'

'You're sure?'

'Oh, yeah – please.'

Some impulse attacks the muscles that control my
eyes, demanding I deflect my gaze, but I manage not
to. I manage to stay right in my father's face.

'I was exposed,' he says, 'to many of the lessons
of my life, Jacob, in a ghetto prison conceived by
some pretty smart guys. Thinkers, each of them. No
question, herding us together, they made a place of
science, that ghetto, as instructive as any laboratory of
rats in any university in the world. My father, he died
in a laboratory imagined by philosophers and physi-
cists and biologists where his education was expanded
and enhanced by viewing in person tiny babies being
butchered by surgeons and physicians who took the
same oath he and I took to make the sick well; where
furious and hateful acts of what I had been taught was
to be love were committed on women and children by
young college men charged with protecting their country
from barbarians. Such a time did I grow up in and my
father die, Jacob, that men of the cloth educated to the
word of God sat in malevolent silence in the face of

these and other atrocities and imbecilities too numerous to name. And so I have come to be distrustful of people with "Doctor" or "Professor" in front of their names and the letters of academic degrees behind them. If you are going to teach children, Jacob, if you are going to be a doctor, a professor, teach your students to be more than we have become. If you are going to write, Jacob, write to change the world, to make a better place for your babies.'

In the space of thirty seconds, my father has said more to me than he has in a decade.

Dreams of redemption last long. Dreams of love last longest.

'Thank you, Pop.'

'Don't say that.'

'Why not?'

'I don't know – just don't. You don't know me. Anyone with some words at his command can make pretty talk. That doesn't mean ...' The massive shoulders shrug, storm clouds fill his eyes.

'Doesn't mean what, Pop?'

The big head turns side to side, indicating much more than simply the negative.

We want to tear this counter out from between us, want to reach across this island and clutch each other.

But we don't!

'Let me get some more crackers,' he says. 'You didn't used to like this. It's a sign of your maturity that you're finally learning what's delicious for a midnight snack.'

The phone rings once. I snap it up. I assume it's Sandra, hope it's Leslie Ann. Find myself relieved to hear not Leslie Ann's voice, but Sandra's.

'They're not happy,' she says, 'but they're fine. Or Daddy's fine, even though he's the most hurt. Mother's angry, but that's Mother. I think she's glad we won't be here. That way she can be angry *and* glad.'

'Good job,' I tell her.

'Actually,' she says, 'I was very proud of the way I handled it. We've made a good decision, Jay. What's more, we've made the right decision.'

Some force in her voice I've never heard – or noticed – makes her words sound unimpeachable. If I didn't know she was absolutely wrong, I'd think she was right.

33

I arrive at the Pollacks' early to pick up Sandra to go for the final fitting of the seven-hundred-dollar 'Hand-stitched by Max of Arthur Godfrey Road' tuxedo Ernie Pollack insists I have made.

(ME: 'Why not just rent?'

NEDDIE: ''Who knows who else has worn a rental?'

ME: 'You mean like maybe someone with poison skin? Or maybe a Neeeegro?'

SANDRA: :'Darling. You'll be able to wear it for years.'

ME: 'You don't think the fact that I've worn one exactly once in my first twenty-seven years doesn't vitiate against that prospect?'

SANDRA: 'No.')

In the kitchen I find Neddie Pollack alone, sitting stuporously at the breakfast nook, writing on a piece of her pale blue monogrammed stationery. The place is embalmed with the aroma of smoked salmon.

Neddie is wearing her face, her mules, a nightgown and matching peignoir. I have, in fact, never seen her without her face – even at the cabana at the Fontainebleau where she has perfected the art of swimming with every part of her anatomy submerged but that forefrontal area between her neck and hairline.

'Sandra's getting dressed.'

Neddie crumples the piece of stationery into a geodesic ball and pours herself a cup of the dark Colombian decaf she has ground at the gourmet store on Alton Road.

'Help yourself,' she says.

I butter a pumpernickel bagel, stare at the ravaged carcass of the reason the room stinks of smoked salmon. The dead fish lies before me on the counter, replete with head and single thoughtful eye contemplating me. Great hunks have been gouged from its orange flesh like some disorganized archaeological dig.

Behind me, Neddie Pollack says, 'I want to talk to you.' This is not a request but a demand, yet delivered by someone who knows she has no power to make such a demand stick unless I choose to cooperate.

I bite into my bagel. I know instinctively I should excuse myself and leave the kitchen.

But when I turn around to say so, the sight of Neddie Pollack makes me stay still. Because more than wanting to leave the room, I want to stay and see where we're going.

Neddie Pollack sips her coffee, replaces the cup in its saucer. She steeples her fingers on the table and says, 'I have been in psychoanalysis for seven years.'

'I'm surprised,' I tell her.

Warm fronts are addressing cold fronts. A shitstorm's abrewin'.

Neddie blinks her eyes several times at me, causing tiny crow's-feet to trod the confluence where her eyebrows meet her temples. 'Needless to say, for the past several months I have told Arthur – my doctor – off and on, things about you.'

I know where this is going. 'Yes,' I say. 'And?'

'Have you ever contemplated going into therapy?'

'No,' I say.

'I don't believe you. But never mind that.'

I think: *I wish I were about to enter a marriage with someone whose mother I might turn to for advice.*

Because I need advice.

I need an adult to turn to for guidance.

Before me, this woman, this mother, is talking about something that matters to her – her child. 'My daughter doesn't have the good sense to get out of this thing with you while she's young enough to marry someone better suited to her. So we both – I'm talking about Arthur and I now – feel it's very important that you seek and receive help.'

Yes, I think, *you're right. Okay, good, please, I accept. Someone to talk to. To put me on the right path before I've gone hopelessly down the wrong one.*

'I am prepared to pay for you to begin treatment when you get to Albuquerque. The fact that you are seeking and receiving treatment will be, if you wish, our secret – yours and mine.'

Albuquerque will be too late. I need help now – today. This morning.

Neddie Pollack is through. She has said what she has to say, and she sits now in seeming tranquillity waiting for me to respond. The cannibalized salmon gazes at me with its dark, dead eye.

'Arthur and me,' I say.

'What?'

I don't intend to fall back under the cover of language. But do.

'You said, "I'm talking about Arthur and I." It's Arthur and me.'

Behind me I'm sure she's wondering if I am truly as insufferable a prick as her experiences with me seem to suggest.

I hear myself say, 'I don't need a psychiatrist,' and feel

myself moving away from the salmon, bagel in hand, toward my almost mother-in-law.

'Oh, JD, you do, sweetie.'

'No,' I say, 'I have something better.'

'Oh – what?'

I point at the pen with which Neddie was writing when I arrived. 'That,' I say.

'That what?'

'Pen.'

She looks at her pen. She gets it. 'Oh, Jesus.'

'Don't "Oh, Jesus" me!' The vehemence of this command moves Neddie Pollack backward just noticeably on her chair. 'I can exorcise my demons from within. Alone. Without help or subversion of my creative instincts.'

Christ! Subversion of my creative –

'Oh, my my my,' says Neddie Pollack, her voice fairly spuming with sarcastic relish. 'Subversion of your – '

'Don't,' I say quietly.

'Don't what?'

'Don't make fun of what I just said.'

'But it's funny. You're so un*bear*ably pretentious. Are you saying that suddenly you're an artiste, so we're all supposed to put up with your idiotic indulgences? Ha!'

Her use of the French – artiste – sends me over the edge, and I coin-flip my bagel over my shoulder and devour the remaining distance between us in one loping step.

As I hover over her, Neddie Pollack begins to experience a tonic muscle spasm in her face.

'Don't you stand threateningly over me like that,' she says with the authority of a parent to a child; yet she grips the edge of the table before her.

'You're not,' I say, 'a nice person, Neddie.'

Those words startle Neddie Pollack, and something goes out of her eyes, some anger, some secret.

'But you *are*,' she says, the equation lacking the malignity I am perfectly willing to grant it.

'No,' I say, 'I'm not.' And a strange coefficient nudges me, and before I can decide not to speak it, I say, 'But I think maybe I'm trying harder than you are to change.'

Neddie reflects on that, and almost docilely she puts her lips to her coffee cup, waits to catch in the black surface within, perhaps, a glimpse of whatever terrible punishment her future son-in-law is about to exact on her.

What am I going to do to her, now that I'm here?

Nothing.

Because in bringing her coffee to her lips, Neddie Pollack has curled forward just slightly, and her peignoir and nightgown fall away from her sternum several inches, and from above I catch a glimpse into her collapsed brassiere, and inside the brassiere, where I anticipate seeing two small, flaccid, nippleless breasts, I see instead *one* small, flaccid, nippleless breast and *one* narrow ridge of wailing scar tissue.

My hand leaves my side, lifts, and descends from above toward Neddie Pollack's head. She shrinks only minutely from the descending blow.

My hand pats Neddie's hairspray-tempered hair, its roots deep within divulging the gray truth. Under my fingers, the hair bends and rebounds.

I lean close to Neddie Pollack's cheek. The muscle spasm pulses like a heart in her face. 'Don't be afraid,' I whisper to her, unsure what I'm instructing her not to be afraid *of*.

'Good morning, darling.'

Sandra stands in the doorway, looking curiously

at this tableau. She glides forward, kisses me, that styptic smell battling the fresh taste of toothpaste in her mouth.

I retrieve my bagel from under the table as Sandra kisses her mother.

'Good morning, Mommy.'

Upright, bagel in hand, I find Neddie squeezing her daughter tightly. Tears well in her eyes and she presses her lips together to keep from sobbing in such a way that I see what she'll look like in very old age, her mouth lined like graph paper, cheeks overlapping jaw, a period of her life in which I know we will no longer be acquainted because surely her daughter and I will be divorced.

I wonder if, in Neddie Pollack's old age, I'll even be alive.

'All right, we're off to Max for the final fitting and to pick out a *white* tuxedo shirt,' she says, as if that, at least, is one thing amid all the questions facing all of us millions on this planet that has been irrevocably settled, no matter what eccentric notions I might have.

A *white* tuxedo shirt.

For my first wedding.

34

L ying in bed that night, it hits me.
    Na.

'Information for what city, please?'

'A Leslie Ann Landau, please.' I've talked to enough Information operators to have decided she wasn't living in the Valley, so I say, 'Try starting at Manhattan Beach and working north and east toward Crescent Heights and – '

'I have an L. A. Landau in North Hollywood, sir. Might that be her?'

I dial the number. It rings twice before she answers.

'Hello.'

I don't know why, but hearing her voice, I think about her feet. Leslie Ann can't point her toes without them spreading apart.

'Hello,' she says again.

'Doing?' I ask in the old, familiar manner, as if we hadn't spoken, perhaps, since this morning.

And then, as if it had only been a matter of hours since we spoke, she says, 'You won't believe this, but I just finished making a salad and a shake and I was going to call you.'

'Really?'

'Jacob, I got a part. I got a role in a play, a new play. One of the major theaters here is doing this whole festival of new plays on their second stage. I went to this once-a-month open call they do. I got a callback.

The playwright and the director were there. They had me read for almost two hours. The director just called me ten minutes ago. Jacob, I'm going to get my Equity card. All the papers and agencies and a lot of producers and studio people will come.'

And so she made a salad and was going to call me.

'Jacob?'

'Yeah, Les?'

'I'm afraid to think that maybe you're right about me. Maybe I have something.'

'A lot more than "something," Les. Is it a nice size role?'

'It's the lead, Jacob.'

She laughs a small laugh, then tries to stifle it as if it isn't appropriate to feel glee concerning this event in her life.

'Wow,' she says quietly.

I feel my face crack wide in a smile.

'I wondered how long it would take you to figure out how to get my number, and once you did if you'd call. But it took you this long and you did call.'

'Why are you hiding from me, Leslie Ann?'

'Because I wanted you to find me, Jacob.'

'I don't want to play games, Les.'

'I don't think of it as a game, Jacob. I think of it as a dream. I dream ten, fifteen, twenty times a day that you'll find me and . . .'

In several heartbeats I sense she wants to tell me that what she dreams is that I will come and get her. But she won't permit herself to say those words. She doesn't want to plead, she wants to be chosen.

'I have dreamed so many times,' she says, 'of getting the call I got ten minutes ago, Jacob, and of you coming to see me in something that would allow you to convince me I'm what you've said I am.'

And then she makes as strong a plea as she's willing to make. 'Will you come see me?' she asks.

When I don't respond immediately, she adds this qualifier: 'In this play?'

And I say very quietly, 'I'm getting married tomorrow.'

Maybe, I think, I speak so quietly because neither of us will hear the words and therefore it will be the same as if they weren't said and what they connote isn't true.

There is silence on her end — perhaps she didn't hear the words I spoke, is waiting for me to answer her question.

'What do you want me to say?' she asks finally.

'What are my choices?'

'If I said don't do it, would you not do it?'

'What if I said I was coming for you, that I'm going to be with you or you're going to be with me, but that in either case, we're going to be together.'

'Are you saying that, Jacob, or are you saying what if you said that?'

Seems strange, now that the moment has arrived, that I actually won't give up what I'm about to acquire to have what I assume I want.

'I guess I'm saying what if.'

'To quote someone I know, Jacob: "Don't guess. This isn't the time for uncertainty." '

I don't speak.

She does. Says: 'I remember sweet Howard telling me on the way to rehearsal one night that I was kidding myself if I thought you'd ever commit your life to our life together. "Jews fuck gentile women, but even the reprobates like Landau and me, we settle down with Jewish princesses because, with them, we know satisfaction is impossible." I learned a long time ago not to bother arguing with Howard, and it didn't matter, really, what he thought. The truth is, I knew that night he was wrong. But he wasn't. I'm questioning everything I thought was true about you and about us. For someone so smart, you're really stupid.'

'Why is it all on me, Les? Why couldn't you have made me go with you or let me or whatever was required the day you left? Or days or weeks or months before, why couldn't you have said what needed to be said so we wouldn't be here today?'

And simply and without the sound of whimsy or rancor, she says, 'Because I needed you to make me know it was all right to believe what I dreamed was possible.' And then, on the edge of tears, she says, 'I really loved being loved by you, Jacob. And I really, really hate and love you, Jacob.' And finally, from deep in her throat, these words rasped in sorrow, 'Oh, Jacob, how can I blame you? You know me for who I am.'

She's gone.

And though every impulse in me tells me to pick up the phone and call back, I don't.

35

On the morning of the wedding, I determine to cause the Pollacks no more grief. Therefore, it comes as something of a surprise to me that it is I who literally cause a monkey wrench to be thrown into this momentous event.

An hour beforehand, I am closeted safely enough with Michael Pollack, my best man, in a suite at the Fontainebleau the Pollacks have rented so that Michael and I can change into our tuxes and await curtain time in comfort.

If there were even a hint of trouble on the horizon, it would be incipient in the fact that Sandra makes a 'mystery' call to me midday, hand muffling the phone, voice a ghostly basso profundo, to whisper, 'She believed in you even when you stopped. She sees in you even what you don't,' following which I lead Michael in tossing down a couple of quick bourbon and gingers – four each, to be exact.

We begin levitating pretty good.

We are watching a Three Stooges movie on the TV in our room and begin to converse in our native language.

'Micker Ticker Nicker Wicker,' I say, toasting my almost brother-in-law with my highball glass.

'Doctor Snake,' says Michael Pollack, doffing his own glass my way.

On the TV the Stooges belt and bong and boink each other.

'Hey, Micker, you're a doctor, too, right?'

'That's right.'

'Okay, so answer me this,' I say. 'Aside from you, my best man, my best pal, *mi amigo* who's always hated my puking guts, how come I never had any friends, Zick?'

'How come?' asks Michael Pollack, nibbling on his lower lip, smiling imbecilically at Curly's imbecility. *Bong! Doink!*

'Yeah,' I say, 'yeah, how come?'

Michael ponders this for a moment, and then he shrugs his gummy shoulders and fills his jowls with air. 'Cuz,' he says, popping the vacuum – *phoit!* – 'nobody likes people who are too good at things.'

'So there you have it.'

'That's it,' Michael Pollack says conclusively.

'Problem is I wasn't that good.'

'You were *too* goddamn good, Snakey. You just didn't have the guts to face it. Me, I had the guts, but I didn't have the mechanics.'

'The mechanics?'

'Yeah.'

'You had the guts, I had the mechanics.'

I'm not sure I like hearing this from Michael Pollack. On the off chance I don't, I say, 'Hey, but listen – seriously . . .'

Seriously? Seriously what?

Moe's pissed. He belts Curly – *bwong!* – he belts Larry – *poing!* 'What I really wanna say to you is that . . . is this gonna be the biggest wedding in the history of Miami Beach or what?'

'Seventeen thousand dollars,' says Michael Pollack.

'Seventeen thousand dollars.' Something flashes in my inebriated brain: a scene on the pier between the

Me character and the Black Woman: *Seventeen thousand dollars!* she says in absolute, stupefied, cataleptic wonder. *You mean seventeen dollars!* . . . To Michael Pollack I say, 'Now I call *that* a big wedding – seventeen *thousand* dollars. You?'

'Big frigging wedding!'

'Big frigging wedding!'

Seventeen thousand dollars, she says. She can't begin to translate what she could do with that money for her children. For a year. Two years!

Moe jabs his fingers in Larry's eyes – *spoing!* Winds up to give Curly a dose of the same. Curly puts up a hand parallel to his face to block his eyes. So Moe whacks him in the face – *thwap!* – bolos him on the head – *thrang!*

The Black Woman's eyes fill with tears. *Seventeen thousand dollars?*

Yes'm.

American money?

Mostly.

I feel nauseated. As recently as fifteen minutes ago I called the store to try one last time to get my sister to speak to me, to reconsider coming to my wedding, to reconsider, at least, giving me her blessing. But the Cuban woman who helps out on Saturdays says Susan's busy and can't speak to me. (At home this morning she locked her door and refused to open it to me, even when our mother stood with me and tried to reason with her that she shouldn't make mishmosh of this mitzvah for all of us.)

Moe chases Curly and Larry with a butcher knife. *yiyiyiyiyiyi!*

Suddenly I wrap my arms around the rotund Dr Michael Pollack, crushing him to me, and whisper this in his ear so that no one but he and I will ever know these

words were spoken, despite the fact that we are absolutely alone in this room: 'How embarrassing would it
be,' I ask Michael Pollack, 'to spend seventeen thousand
dollars on a wedding for your only daughter, to which
five hundred guests are invited, if the groom . . .'

I take a dramatic pause. I smell Michael's Pollack's
breath – maybe it's an inherited Pollack family smell
– and I put one hand over Michael's mouth to block
it, and I say, 'If the groom *what*? Whisper back to
me.'

He looks at my hand, wondering what it's there for.
He looks at my eyes, wondering if the rest of the sentence
is what he thinks it might be.

'If the groom,' Michael Pollack barbles hotly against
my palm, 'didn't show up.'

I squeeze Michael Pollack, indicating to him he has
answered my question correctly.

'That,' says Michael, 'would be very embarrassing.'

I press my cheek to Michael Pollack's and whisper,
'That would constitute distress beyond the wildest sce-
narios anyone in your family has ever entertained.'

'Way beyond,' Michael Pollack agrees.

'You know what I want, Micker?' I whisper into
Michael's elfin ear, the same ear his sister has hidden
under her hair and which I would be loath to see on
my children. 'I only want one small thing.'

'One small,' belches Michael Pollack, 'thing.'

'The cloud machine,' I tell him.

'What about it?' Michael wants to know.

'I don't want it to work.' Curly, Moe, and Larry are
into their curtain call. They all try to kiss the Girl. *Bong!
Wong! Doink! Boink! Pwong!* 'In fact,' I tell Michael
Pollack, 'it *mustn't* work.'

Michael tries to turn his head to catch a glimpse of the

wrap-up of the film even as he says, 'That cloud machine is very important to my mother, Snakey.'

I catch his chin in my hand, hold his head in place, nose to nose with me. 'More important than her rep, Tick-Tock?'

Michael Pollack's eyes look deeply into mine. I wonder if I look as insensible as he does.

Moe chases Curly and Larry off behind '*The End.*' An MC in an oversize bow tie and a fright wig comes onscreen to tell us in Daffy Duck's voice what fun we've had watching these three imbeciles beat the crap out of each other for an hour.

I take Michael Pollack's highball glass from him and aim him toward the door. 'Break it,' I tell him. 'Break it good.'

With the black bow tie of his tuxedo pointing stupidly northwest and southeast, Michael Pollack stands before his former nemesis, his almost brother-in-law, and he nods and grunts and says after the fashion of many Hollywood Indians, 'Break.'

'Or else,' I caution.

'Or else,' says Michael Pollack.

'If I see clouds, don't ask me what's going to happen to that seventeen grand.'

'I don't want to know,' Michael assures me.

I reach out to straighten Michael Pollack's bow tie, but he flinches. 'Bow tie,' I tell him, and straighten it, give him a *potch* on the cheek, and shove him into the hallway of the sixth floor of the Fontainebleau. I close the door and mix myself another bourbon and ginger. 'The Baseball Game of the Week' is revving up.

It seems so long since I watched baseball. I used to know the averages and ERAs of all the Dodgers, even into my twenties somewhere. In three years at Stanford

I never once got around to driving twenty minutes up the road to Candlestick to watch the Jewish kid Koufax pitch.

I slump onto the couch for a little baseball, and the phone rings. Thinking it will be my sister, I snap it up. 'Yeeeesssss?' I say coyly. 'Can't resist coming, riiiiigghht?'

'Darling,' my mother says, 'I'm dressed. I thought maybe I would come up and be with you until it's time.'

'Aw, Mom, Jesus, that would be . . . wouldn't that be great! But you can't believe how late I'm running. I gotta be downstairs in twenty minutes and I got hair that went into revolt about twenty minutes ago and a guy here trying to make sense of it and Michael's running around naked.' Whispering, I tell her, 'For a gynecologist, this guy knows zilch about getting into a tux, I'm telling you.' I yell irascibly at the absent Michael Pollack, 'No, it's right there, Michael – look, behind you, nitwit!'

I laugh – that silly Michael!

Behind my mother, I hear the sounds of the Fontaine-bleau lobby. I can see her down there done up meticulously, but I'm getting pissed that, no matter what, she'll look much less *done* than Neddie Pollack and am happy to add validation to the mission I sent Michael on.

'Well, all right, darling, of course. I'll . . . I guess I'll just see you after you're married, then.'

My mother.

I replace the receiver and take my drink with me onto the balcony. Below, on a distant patio, another wedding is in progress. There are eight bridesmaids and eight groomsmen. Sandra could have had eleven bridesmaids and is settling for only a matron of honor (her sister-in-law, Carol Pollack) since I have no groomsmen –

only Michael, who never liked me. Neddie has hired three waiters from the hotel to usher and, I suppose, to the unknowing, to masquerade for the afternoon as my close friends.

Moe, Larry, Curly.

Pals to Dr Snake.

Sixth floor. I lean far out over the railing, picture myself airborne, reverse piking into the botanical gardens far below.

Splonk!

36

I'm drunk as a skunk. Have no peripheral vision. Am totally convinced I am not responsible for my actions.

'Rusty, Rusty, my friend,' says Rabbi Oscar Lerner as groom and holy man convene in the wings. 'Mazel tov, my friend, mazel tov.'

'Mazel tov to you, too, Rabbee.'

'You're the one getting married, my boy,' Rabbi Oscar Lerner reminds me jovially. He's making an easy five hundred for twenty minutes' work – why shouldn't he be jovial? (Two, three hundred is the standard, but Neddie confides to Sandra in my presence in the Lincoln one day that she wants to set benchmarks in all areas for a long time to come.)

'I just feel like tossin' a few mazel tovs around, Brer Rabbee.'

Rabbi Oscar Lerner chuckles indulgently.

'Listen, Brer Rabbee, just one thing, pal.'

'Anything for you, Rusty.'

I pat Rabbi Oscar Lerner's yarmulke on his head. 'I would really appreciate it if you'd keep the religious shit – pardon me, the religious doodey – as thin as possible.'

Rabbi Oscar Lerner gives me a look: I remember you from Hebrew School, Rusty, says the look; you were a *tummler* then, you're a *tummler* now.

I am tempted to inquire whether Rabbi Oscar Lerner

is aware that it was I, Rusty Landau, who composed
and first sang with Buddy Rapchik and Scooter Katz
the little hot dog jingle from which Rabbi Oscar Lerner
has become inseparable over the years: *If I could be
an Oscar Lerner rabbi, I'd read the Torah just from
downright fright, cuz the Lord of Hosts would know
I'm not a mensh, cuz I pull my wire every single, lonely,
Jewish night.*

'I ain't kiddin', Rabbee,' I assure him. 'You invoke
Yahoo's name on me more than a brace of times here
and I won't be responsible for the consequences.'

'Rusty, where's your yarmulke?'

'I ain't wearing one.'

'Rusty, this is a Conservative ceremony, you have to
wear a yarmulke.'

I raise my eyebrows, inviting Rabbi Oscar Lerner to
combat. 'Have to?'

'You should, Rusty.'

'*Should?*' I inquire. 'Or *have* to?'

'People will feel uncomfortable if you don't, Rusty.'

'Little discomfort'll keep 'em sharp, keep 'em tuned
in.'

Beside me cloud machine mechanic Michael Pollack,
slightly more sober than his almost brother-in-law,
cackles like a goose.

I belch and almost throw up. Rabbi Oscar Lerner pats
me on the back.

'Are you all right, Rusty?'

'Never better, Rabbee.' I pinch the cheek of this man
who taught me as much as anybody about Judaism, the
deity, the ethics and ethos of my legacy, and who is,
consequently, I figure, as responsible as anyone for my
current despicable behavior.

The music begins.

'Where's your yarmulke?' Michael Pollack wants to know.

'Toilet.'

Michael rips his yarmulke off his head, stuffs it in his tux pocket, mashes at his remaining hair.

'I am very displeased by this, Michael.'

Michael looks at me. He looks alive. He looks up.

'Good!' says Michael Pollack.

'Is this proper behavior for two doctors – one of medicine, the other, yet, of philosophy?'

Michael and I nod like two crazed jackhammers.

Rabbi Oscar Lerner exhales Mogen David at us and steps into position for our entrance with massive rabbinical displeasure.

And I find myself chilled and shaking.

I seize the rabbi's incredibly soft hand, softer than a woman's, than a baby's. 'Wait a minute, Rabbee, not yet, pal, wait a second.'

Rabbi Oscar Lerner waits.

'Okay, say you're at a wedding – I mean, you *are* at a wedding, you're here at *my* wedding – but say you're at *another* wedding, a hypothetical wedding, and let's complicate matters a little, a *bissel*, and say you're the intended groom – okay, you with me? Say you're him and everyone's here – there – at that hypothetical wedding – the food's prepared, the bride's dressed, her mother, an odious individual, sure, she's there and she's decked out in about two thousand pounds of precious stones and metals and she's put in a lot of effort to make this an event for the ages okay – you got the picture? Okay, now the music starts, right? The music starts, the participants line up, and the groom makes an enlightened decision not to participate. How bad, you figure, that is – give me a no-holds-barred rabbinical opinion.'

Mouth agape, Michael Pollack peers through his inebriation at me. In his eyes I can see that part of him would love to record for posterity the exit I have just described.

'Do you really want me to answer that, Rusty?'

The music has arrived at our cue. The rabbi is holding the curtains in his two hands, ready to part them, and lead me through the Red Sea of guests to the *huppah*, to the other side – to *marriage*. Through a little slit where the two halves of the curtain come together, I can see my mother and father. My father has one of his tree-stump arms around my mother and is patting her shoulder.

My mother looks . . . radiant. And proud.

'Are you serious?' I say. 'Are you kidding? Don't you know yet when a guy's joking? Hey, where's my yarmulke?' I dig it out of my jacket pocket, slap it on my head. 'Micker, put on your yarmulke, for chrissake!'

Michael is a little confused, but he's a lot drunk, and he does as he's told.

'Rusty, Rusty, Rusty,' says Rabbi Oscar Lerner, the repetition of my name meaning more than I can know, more than he can say, and, really, absolutely nothing when you come right down to it, as I am only a prop here, he is saying, and if I don't know it, I should and get on with the business of supporting people who know what they *really* want from their lives.

Like Sandra Pollack and her mother.

Rabbi Oscar Lerner leads Michael and me to our positions under the *huppah*. As we make our entrance, the eyes of five hundred spectators on us, I begin quietly singing the Oscar Lerner hot dog jingle under the organ music in an effort to control my rampaging, cockeyed brain. And when the rabbi folds his hands across his belly in repose, Michael and I turn, just as we rehearsed, to witness with the five hundred the spectacle of the star of my wedding, Sandra Elaine Pollack, descend to me through clouds.

'Here,' whispers Michael Pollack, and, unknown to anyone in the hall save perhaps Rabbi Oscar Lerner, he slips to me a handful of nuts and bolts.

For a moment I have forgotten the mission on which I sent Michael Pollack, and I am tempted to cry out, 'Wait, no!' and send Michael back to the machine, to render it whole again.

But it's too late, for there at the top of the stairs strung in rosebuds and Boston Fern stands Miss Sandra amid nary a cloud – nay, not even a wisp of smoke that a malfunctioning machine might belch forth as it gives up the ghost.

For just a moment, the organist's fingers freeze at the keyboard and the only sounds in the immense hall are the barely audible strains of someone singing the Oscar Meyer hot dog jingle with the wrong lyrics.

Mere minutes later I lift Sandra Pollack's veil and kiss Sandra Landau. At that moment I feel a sense of deliverance.

I'm married.

For life.

To someone I don't love.

To someone I don't even like.

I feel good!

GERTRUDE STEIN'S
UNDERWEAR

1

Because it was the fulfillment of a little girl's fantasy, Ernie Pollack – who could make fantasies that require cash come true – sent his daughter to Paris, France.

Since it was his daughter's honeymoon, he sent her husband along.

In my own shallowness I assumed my wife would spend our week in one of the cultural capitals of the world buying clothing for herself, and I was prepared to revel in disdain for her shallowness.

Were it firmly wedged into my head that she was a well-educated woman who actually did read Anaïs Nin in French, I wouldn't have still been surprised to find myself in the company of someone fluent in the language of the natives, who knew a great deal about antiques and French art, and who had memorized somewhere in that childhood fantasy of hers a glossary and map of most of the historic and architectural wonders of the City of Light.

'I majored in Art History, darling,' she reminded me.

I didn't recall knowing that, though I'm certain that when we were together in college, I must have heard her tell me at some point what her major was.

In Paris, far from Miami Beach and contrary to the scenario I imagined, I found myself in the trust of this ravenous, inexhaustible, well-informed woman – my wife.

I found myself engaged and sexually stimulated by this person's appetite as if I'd just met her and didn't know I didn't like her, so I refrained from explaining to her things with which I *was* fluent so that she could explain them to me as she gleaned the facts about them from her memory and, presumably, largely unused education.

Finally, though, when she got around to escorting me to the Rue de Fleurs apartment of Stein and Toklas, I could no longer stand my humility, which I began to fear smacked of ignorance.

There in Stein's living room, Sandra Pollack Landau said to me, 'Okay, darling, here some of the greatest turn-of-the-century artists and, later, some of the greatest writers of the first half of the century sat around and chewed the fat, or shot the *merde*, as they liked to say.'

I forced myself not to laugh at that – though in fact I thought it was very clever – and I told Sandra that Stein and her circle were the subject of my dissertation.

'Your dissertation is about Gertrude *Stein*?'

As if my dissertation topic were common knowledge throughout the Americas and abroad, I inquired smugly of my wife, 'What did you think it was about, darling?'

'I have no idea. You've never said boo to me about your dissertation. I just assumed it was one of those arcane scholarly treatises about vegetation metaphors in Shakespeare or – '

'The Lost Generation,' I said, 'all of it, all of them,' and with proprietary spleen added, 'I own them.'

She seemed impervious to both my spleen and my arrogance. She grasped my hands in hers and said, 'I love Stein! All of them! Have you read Ford Madox Ford's *The Good Soldier*? Of course you have – what a question. And the Impressionists who used to hang out with her – I mean, those are some of my favorite artists! I can't believe this.'

We really know zilch about each other.

And now I got really pissed.

At myself.

And therefore took it out on her.

'Hart Crane,' I said. 'Dos Passos, e.e. cummings, Archibald MacLeish – you've read them?'

'Oh sure,' she said. 'Well, I mean a little of each. My professor said *Tender Is the Night* and Dos Passos's *The Big Money* were the last works of the group. Do you agree?'

I made one of those positively scornful sounds with my tongue and air against the back of my front teeth. 'Fitzgerald and Dos Passos? What about Logan Stanwyck – *The Bookbinder*? What about Jacques Dahlric – *Au Revoir Mon Terrible*?'

'I'm not familiar with those works,' Sandra said. 'Or those writers.'

'Mason Potts.'

She shook her head and actually took out a little notebook, in which she scribbled.

'Well then, you're not quite an expert on the period, are you?'

She stopped writing. She looked at me; her eyes said she didn't understand my malevolence. 'I never said I was, Jay.'

'I'm kidding,' I said.

'Are you?'

'Are *you* kidding? Of course I'm kidding. I'm joshing.'

'I don't think you are.'

'I am! I'm fucking *kidding*, Sandra. Learn to take a joke!'

She managed what passed for a smile.

I embraced Sandra Pollack Landau. My wife.

So: Stuck in Paris with an adversary – or worse, an equal.

While the security guard in Stein and Toklas's bedroom discussed with Sandra the intricacies of a Picasso pen-and-ink drawing of Stein, impulsively I opened with silent hands the middle drawer of a tall chiffonier, even though we had been instructed not to touch anything.

In the drawer I found girdles and underwear. Even more impulsively, I grabbed a pair of cotton panties, stuck them in my jeans, and slid the drawer shut without detection.

Sandra wanted to go looking for Jean Paul Sartre and Simone de Beauvoir at the cafe they were reputed to frequent in the late afternoon. I declined. That was all I needed – for her to begin conversing with Sartre and de Beauvoir in their native tongue, grilling them on existentialist dogma and feminist propaganda.

Back in our room in our hotel on the Boulevard San Michel, I went into the bathroom and took the underwear from my pants.

They were large – therefore Stein's.

And they had a faint stain in the crotch. What I assumed was a faint menstrual stain. Of Gertrude Stein's.

I wore them to dinner.

We shared an appetizer of *coquelles* set between us, savored from a shared fork. I had never really noted the way Sandra looked at me. Leslie Ann Masterson listened with her eyes, and because of their incandescence, she made me feel inspected. Sandra Pollack Landau's eyes were a very soft, dense golden brown; they seemed to stroke. To permit.

2

We lived in Sandra's room in her father's house for the several days before we were to leave for Albuquerque, New Mexico.

One morning she woke up early to find me writing at her desk.

The truth in this instance came easily, and I invited her to read *Who Stalk the Tiger* and the monologue I was writing, intended to be the curtain raiser for the play about the young man and the black woman on the pier.

'Am I supposed to really tell you how I feel,' she asked when she'd finished, 'or would I be smarter to lie?'

'Try the truth once,' I suggested. 'If I go nuts, don't do it again.'

And with infuriating accuracy, she told me in one sentence what I'd come to know about *Who Stalk the Tiger*. 'It's an exciting idea with interesting people,' she said, 'but it's all just too glib and superficial and unexplored and safe.'

She waited for me to go nuts. I, too, waited.

When I didn't explode, she continued.

Concerning the monologue, she said: 'This is going to be about Miami Beach and my parents, isn't it? And you. And me.'

'Yes.'

'Is this the way you see us?'

'I think so.'

'It's very mean, Jay.'

'I know.'

'It's also about the funniest damn thing I've ever read in my life.'

'It is?'

She nodded. 'Will somebody put it on?'

'I don't know if I want anybody to.'

'Why not?'

'I don't know if I want to be a playwright.'

'How can you *not* pursue something you could clearly be very good at?'

Her eyes stroked. I recoiled.

'Look, we'll see, okay? What else? Anything else?'

'Well, I have a lot of specific thoughts, if you want to hear them.'

'Of course, yes, of course I want to hear them. What good are generalizations? They're not. No good. None.'

I stared at her. Waited. Wondered if it was possible this person could say anything to me that would make either of these plays better, might catapult me from where I am to somewhere else. Somewhere better.

'Jay.'

'That's me.'

'If you want to try to become a writer, I want you to know I'll help you any way I can.'

'Well, that's very nice, San, thank you. If I decide that's what I want to do, you'll be one of the first people I contact.'

'I'm grateful.'

'And I appreciate your gratitude.'

Her eyes gave me room – to approach and retreat.

3

On the morning we pulled out of the Pollack driveway, with both sets of parents in attendance, I looked at my wife, decked out in a pair of Wrangler's (her first since she was eight), a Big Mac workshirt, a red bandanna that bound her lengthening hair, and the one concession to her roots, the Pappagallo kidskin boots, and I had the impulse to urge her one more time to stay here.

But as I watched her say her tearless good-byes to her mother and father, her brother and sister-in-law, her in-laws, I was startled to realize that as much as she felt for her family, as strong as the bonds holding her to them and this place were, she was not leaving with me simply because she was my wife, but because she was glad, perhaps even invigorated, to be going.

It was she who had argued that we didn't need the Corvette her father presented us to drive west; it was she who felt it would be exciting to see what we could do 'out there' for ourselves on my salary (and hers once she got a job); and it was she who felt it would be excessive of us to buy a house as soon as we got to Albuquerque.

I couldn't agree with her more, and because I couldn't, it was I who insisted we accept the Corvette, the four hundred dollars a month from Ernie Pollack in supplemental income, and the ten thousand big ones for the down payment on the house Neddie believed absolutely necessary if we were to get started properly 'out there.'

The car, the monthly stipend from home, the down payment, were all proffered at a 'welcome home' dinner the night we got back from our honeymoon.

Nicely boiled afterward, in the privacy of my wife's childhood bedroom, I asked her, hoping to sound sensible and not cruel, 'Do you know how long you'll last "out there" without the creature comforts you're used to? Do you know what I'm afraid will happen? I'm afraid it will put a terrible strain on our marriage and the beginning of my teaching career if I'm constantly worried about whether you have everything you – '

She clutched my index finger in her fist. 'Jacob,' she said with a passion I have perhaps never exhibited in my life, 'I want to grow not simply older but *up*.'

What do you say to that? I wondered.

'What can I say to that?' I asked her.

'Say you'll support me when we get out there if I want to . . . if I should, say, decide to start a business or go to graduate school.'

'Start a business, or go to graduate school? Sandra . . . San . . . little kosher-face, find a manicurist, learn to wax linoleum, discover the proper moisturizer for the climate.'

And then she laughed and hurled her arms around me because she thought I was kidding, she thought I was being ironic, and I was *for* her, that I was on her side.

And so we gave back the 'Vette, the allowance, the down payment. And two pioneers, we headed west in my ancient Volkswagen.

Ernie Pollack shook my hand and nodded in a simple affirmation of resignation, Neddie Pollack offered me her cheek, which was gone before I could make contact with it.

I hugged my mother, kissed her meticulously painted lips, whispered in her ear, 'Listen,' I said, 'I know we never got to have our talk – '

'And we never will,' she said. 'But don't worry about it. I'll grow up without you.'

Tears sprang to my eyes, as they did to my mother's. My voice caught on itself. 'Oh, Jesus, Mom – '

'Sshh,' said my mother. 'Go. Work hard. Everything takes hard work.'

In her voice I heard her autobiography in that sentence; her life as wife and mother: *Everything takes hard work.*

'Listen,' I told her, 'tell my sister, tell Susan, tell her I said, that I said . . . *good-bye.*'

My mother nodded and winked at me as if I had just composed the quintessential message a brother might send to a sister from whom he was estranged. 'I will,' she said, 'I'll tell her.'

'Tell her I said, that I said . . . *so long.*'

Even better! The cutting edge of genius, words like those.

My mother squeezed her lips together until they were maroon through her pink lipstick.

And then there was no one left but my father. He offered his big, stiff right paw, and I shook it stiffly.

'You're a lucky boy,' he said. And then he gave me this piece of advice: 'Women,' my father whispered to me so that no one else could hear, 'like a little tenderness.' He gave me a short, uncoordinated jab in the gut to punctuate this counsel.

I wanted to embrace him, not because what he told me was so stunning, but because he was able to say it.

But as I was sending a message to my arms to engulf him, I found myself looking down into the face of my mother, pressing forward, slipping between us as if she were being pushed from behind, though in fact she was just trying to help her two emotionally retarded men negotiate these treacherous shoals.

She pressed me toward Sandra and the car and, distantly, New Mexico. 'Go,' she said, 'please.'

'And do me a favor,' my father said, 'drive with both hands on the wheel on those turnpikes.'

'I will, Pop.'

'And if there are any anti-Semitic shenanigans out there, you call the ACLU in five seconds, you understand? I send them enough money, it wouldn't hurt them to send a guy.'

'I understand, Pop.'

'All right,' said my father.

And then Morris the Bear, Flossie, Ernie and Neddie, Michael and Carol – all of them waved, and I rammed my eyes shut and for just a moment *knew* that by some ultimately explicable trick of magic I had truly become disembodied and that everything that had happened the last two and a half months had happened to someone other than me. It struck me as a good joke on the poor, stupid schmuck who was that other me.

But when I opened my eyes I saw myself slipping into the V-dub, shooting down the Pollack driveway, and turning for New Mexico, spurred on by the young woman seated next to me, who screamed in exultation:

'Free at last, free at last, thank Jacob Landau, I'm free at last!'

4

D r Joel D'Amico lived with his wife and two beavers in an old adobe house beyond the eastern limits of Albuquerque.

The two beavers splashed happily in a cattle trough set like a centerpiece in the middle of the circular crushed-gravel driveway amid what looked like some wonderfully randomly located desert landscaping that we realized was merely desert surrounding a house that at some point was intruded into it.

Dr Joel D'Amico was awaiting us at the trough, speaking to the beavers in a language I could only assume was Beaver itself and feeding them the remains of a Caesar salad. He was wearing old jeans, a workshirt, and battered cowboy boots, and he looked more than ever like Andy Devine as Jingles.

Though we had called for instructions, we were a half hour late as we arrived by way of Canada, and Dr Joel D'Amico said to us with pride, 'You got lost, Dr Landau.' Clearly he didn't want some greenhorn from Miami Beach out of Stanford University to just move out west and find his house first crack out of the box.

'Lost?' I said with a Guy Madison-esque crinkle to the corner of my mouth. 'Oh, no. No, we stopped en route at several interesting vistas.'

Dr Joel D'Amico was disappointed to hear that, but he gave us each a comradely smack on the back anyway and led us into a beautiful atrium filled with foliage. There

we met Mrs Rita D'Amico, whom if one were trying to
be polite one would call 'robust' rather than 'real big
and fat.' She wasn't wearing cowboy clothes, as was her
husband. To the contrary, she was wearing what looked
like a circus tent from somewhere out the Persian Gulf
way. 'Well, Dr and Mrs Landau,' she wanted to know
right off the bat, 'how do you like the desert?'

'Ah,' I said, 'the desert,' nodding and doing things
with my eyebrows to suggest it was quite spectacular.
In fact, I had never been anywhere in my life I liked less.
Albuquerque was a ferociously ugly city, festooning with
trailer parks and monotonic architecture from border to
border, pervaded from city limit to city limit with the
effluvium of cowshit; and whereas I had pictured the
southwestern desert as miles and miles of gently rolling
sand dunes, this parcel, at least, was miles and miles of
scrub vegetation and *dirt*.

Sandra, on the other hand, loved the place and said so,
'Oh, Mrs D'Amico,' she said, 'I've never been happier in
my life.'

Dr Joel D'Amico smiled his blessing on Sandra and
observed amiably to me, 'It just takes a little getting used
to. The dryness, the barrenness.'

'To say nothing,' noted Mrs Rita D'Amico, 'of the
mythic force of the region.'

The spouses of academics, I'd noticed, had the almost
unvarying habit in the presence of guests of endeavoring
to raise all conversation to the level of their spouses'
education.

Dr Joel dribbled some spit on a hanky and began
cleaning the leaf of a giant rubber plant beside his chair,
an act that Mrs D'Amico definitely didn't appreciate.

Abruptly she excused herself and left the atrium. It
crossed my mind that she was going to get a gun, that

she would return and, backed by the mythic force of the region, blow Dr Joel's brains out for fucking with her ficus.

But when Mrs D. waddled back in, she carried only a tray of coffee and some deep-dish confection.

'I've prepared some of my peach cobbler,' announced Mrs D'Amico. 'I don't think you've ever tasted a peach cobbler quite like it. Do you know cobbler?' she asked us.

'Oh, well, you know,' I said modestly, 'I've dabbled.'

Rita D'Amico smiled indulgently; she'd suffered through many a droll line by many a droll colleague of her husband.

Sandra said, 'My grandmother used to make a wonderful deep-dish apple *kugel*, but I've never had peach cobbler, I don't think.'

'*Kugel?*' asked Mrs Rita D'Amico, her eyes leaking just beyond the perimeter of Sandra's face but not quite reaching her husband.

'Noodles and cinnamon and raisins. It's quite delicious – hot or cold,' said Sandra. 'It's a Jewish dish.'

'Ah,' said Mrs Rita D'Amico, confirmed in the fact that, indeed, Jews bearing alien recipes had invaded this particular part of the southwestern region of the United States.

After we had each eaten two servings of the globular, lavalike cobbler and complimented Mrs D'Amico profusely, she said, 'I must give you the recipe,' including both Sandra *and* me in this generous offer. 'You must make a batch,' she said, 'and let me taste it.'

'Rita measures everyone,' said Dr Joel, 'by how well they replicate her cobbler. Of course, I must warn you, she's won ribbons at the State Fair.'

I envisioned Sandra and me in a few months, settled

in Albuquerque, protégés-in-cobbler to two-ton Mrs Rita D'Amico, the three of us in sunbonnets, picking and canning, hitting state fairs all over the West, me fornicating secretly with Rita in dingy little motels in places like Fargo and Dead Rock, wherever they were, defusing her antiSemitism with my circumcised banana, while Sandra went out to set up our booth and surreptitiously peddle some apple *kugel* on the side.

5

The next day, our first Sunday in New Mexico, we drove up to Santa Fe. We spent several hours on the Plaza, strolling in and out of galleries crammed with western art and sculpture, wandering past moribund Indians, seated on blankets, selling pottery and silver-and-turquoise jewelry.

Sandra was depressed by the Indians, wanted to talk racial inequity. I half listened, agreed with everything.

But my interest was elsewhere. I was waiting to see something like I'd seen in Leslie Ann's drawer, though her father the road-racing sculptor who put his fingers into his child had been dead more than a decade.

In a gallery off the Plaza where the woman who greeted us was especially warm, I waited for Sandra to wander off and then asked the woman if she knew of a Cherokee sculptor named Masterson, first initials W.B. She said she didn't, but if he had achieved any recognition, there would probably be an article about him in one of the numerous art magazines, so why didn't I try the periodical guide at the library.

Certainly a simple solution, one someone with a Ph.D. in English might have thought of himself.

I steered Sandra into a gallery next door to the downtown library, told her I was going to find a bathroom in the library, and headed for the periodical guide.

Where I found a lot of Mastersons, but no W.B.

Out of Mastersons and about to close the big guide-book, my eye flitted past Mawbry and caught on Mayes, W.B. The article was in the October 1954 issue of *Southwestern Art* entitled 'One Man's Trail of Tears.' From some history lesson somewhere, I remembered that the Trail of Tears had to do with the forced relocation of the Cherokee Indians.

Five minutes later I stood in the stacks and opened a volume containing the fourth quarterly issue of *Southwestern Art* from 1954. It took me another thirty seconds to find the article and open it to a picture of the sculpture I'd seen in Leslie Ann's drawer and an article about her father, Wilson Bushyhead Mayes.

The article discussed Wilson Bushyhead Mayes's debt to the Mexican/Indian Santo tradition and his particular divergence from the traditional and current Mexican and Pueblo stylings. All of his paint was natural, the article said, made from berries and herbs. The wood was all from an area near Chimayo the Indians considered sacred.

The author noted he made about two dozen of the particular Santo pictured opposite, called *Christa Margarite*, after his daughter, whom the artist main-tained was Christ come back in female form: 'In her eyes from birth,' said Wilson Bushyhead, 'was the antidote to human struggle and madness.' When the author asked what that antidote was, Wilson Bushyhead Mayes had answered: 'That love which passes all human comprehension.'

The author of the article (a woman) seemed to find Wilson Bushyhead Mayes's assertion of his daughter's divinity not the least eccentric. The writer, however, then went on to say that the bishop in Santa Fe and the local Catholic community, Anglo, Chicano, *and*

Indian, was expressing its unified rancor concerning the irreligious carvings and pronouncements of Wilson Bushyhead Mayes.

'At the same time,' the author wrote, 'there seems to be more to the rancor, in certain quarters, than art.'

She didn't say what the 'more' was, though. Had she been in my Freshman Comp class at Stanford, I would have left her a riot of red ink demanding she expand and support a titillating implication like that.

When I turned the page, however, I saw a picture of Wilson Bushyhead Mayes with his family and I sensed a reason.

He was too good-looking, too imposing. A tall, sleekly muscled man with pitch black hair tied with a leather thong behind his head, he seemed to encase the three people seated below him on a small wooden bench — two children and his wife — his arms tight around the children's shoulders, his huge, used-looking hands flat against the children's sternums, squeezing their bodies inward toward their mother, making her appear slightly abbreviated between them.

He had Leslie Ann's just barely imperfect nose and two fierce, piercing black eyes; those eyes stared with awesome defiance at the aperture of the camera that took this picture; his eyes said, *I am not manageable.* His son and his wife also were staring straight ahead, though their eyes were fixed on a locus just left of the camera's eye. As for Leslie Ann, she looked directly up, into her father's face.

Leslie Ann had inherited her eyes from her mother.

And her mother and brother must have inherited their coloring from the Swedish part of the family. Evan Mayes and his mother were blonds.

Below the family photo there were two other pictures.

The cutline beside the first noted the artist did only variations on three pieces: the *Christa Margarite* and the two pictured below. One was a pietà – mother and daughter. The author explained this was 'the *Christa* after she'd been crucified, being held by her mother, the Mary figure – this a likeness of Anna Leslie Mayes, the artist's wife.'

The third piece was father and daughter. He was dressed in Indian headdress, war paint, and high top black Keds. His palms were flat against her belly. The eyes of both figures were distant. A single tear was painted against the girl's cheek.

The author of the article noted that Wilson Bushyhead Mayes had done only one of these. It was titled *Sun and Master*.

Leslie Ann Masterson.

The writer said the artist would not comment on this piece except to say that it was, indeed, father and daughter. The writer assumed that father and daughter are worshiping the sun, the master, going on to explain the importance of the sun to the Cherokee.

But I knew in an instant that wasn't the case.

I knew Margaret was the Sun of God, and he was her master.

The writer of the article went on to reflect on Wilson Bushyhead Mayes's reputation in Santa Fe as a man who enjoyed a drink and a fight, chronicling two punch-outs involving Wilson and two detractors, one on 'religious grounds,' the other (and this again by implication) having to do with Wilson's evident attractiveness to the man's wife.

'Where have you been?' Sandra asked when I returned to the gallery where I'd abandoned her and found her standing in front of a women's clothing store.

I whistled, touched my stomach. 'You want to talk about those huevos rancheros we had for breakfast?'

Sandra clucked her tongue sympathetically and squeezed my arm to her side. 'Will you look at this crap,' she said.

I looked into the window. Saw nothing but reflections of Wilson Bushyhead Mayes, his wife and children.

6

In fibrillating half sleep through the next weeks, I heard my father tell me what he told me when I was twelve: *Women are not in fact born of Adam, not from his rib.*

I remember asking him where they come from, and him saying, *Beats the hell outta me, Jakey, beats the unholy hell outta me, boychik.*

Night after night these words echoed in my half-conscious mind like a litany.

Did women wonder where men came from? Or did most women assume Adam was a screwed-up, callous son of a bitch born of a screwed-up, callous God and that, at God's urging, he manipulated Eve into seducing him to eat the apple so he could righteously dump on her throughout human history?

Night after night, her back against my belly, I listened to Sandra Pollack Landau breathe; there was an almost silent clack on her exhales, like a tiny gate striking bone far up in her septum somewhere.

I smelled her skin – faint scent of Shalimar, the perfume she'd worn as long as I'd been conscious of her smell.

Living being. In my bed.

Our bed.

Community property state. Half of each other's everything belongs to the other.

We have nothing. An old car, some clothes. Wedding gifts.

Each other – at least by law.

Even in sleep, she held my index finger tightly.

I used to hold Daddy's finger like this when I was a little girl, she told me when I asked her why she liked to hold just that finger.

Children.

Parents.

Yet, in lying beside her, it was impossible for me not, also, each and every time I thought consciously of Sandra, to think of . . .

Leslie. Ann. Master. Sun.

No limbs over the edge. There could be wolves that would eat your arms.

Or parents who defy you not to drown in a sea of self-loathing and recrimination.

Sandra had announced to me on the way home from Santa Fe that first Sunday, my head fairly bursting now with Leslie Ann, that she was going to open a clothing store in Albuquerque.

'A clothing store?' I asked. 'Why?'

'Why not?'

'You can't announce something like that and then ask *me* to explain it to *you.*'

'Would you say the area could use a decent women's store?'

'Sure, I guess.'

'You guess?'

She smiled benignly on my ignorance of women's needs.

'And I'm going to hire at least one Indian and one Hispanic salesperson. If people want to accuse me of tokenism, they can just go screw themselves. What do you think?'

I had other things on my mind and figured we were talking about something half a year, a year, down the road, so I said, 'Great. Good. Go to it.'

Now, a month later, she had found the perfect space for Felicity, the store she would open in January with a loan *she* negotiated the Monday after that Sunday on *my* salary, and which would become, my gut told me, the most successful clothing store in the history of Albuquerque.

I tried to project myself into Sandra's and Leslie Ann's futures – a decade from now. Mid-thirties. Leslie Ann, a national celebrity, an icon even. Sandra, a clothing store mogul, owner of Albuquerque's first class A department store. Owner of shopping malls. Beloved employer of minorities.

And me. Where would I be?

Certainly not here.

Not with Sandra.

Might I be Mr Leslie Ann Masterson?

The phone rang.

I looked at the clock. It was two twenty-four A.M.

I knew it would be Leslie Ann. I snapped it up before the first ring finished, hoping to leave Sandra unconscious, conjuring nevertheless a reason why I was switching phones, who I was talking to at this hour of the night.

Sshh, sleep, it's my sister, she's –

'Fuckface,' said a voice I recognized immediately.

'Howard, how are you?'

'Who'zit?' asked Sandra.

Covering the mouthpiece, I whispered, 'Guy from graduate school – it's all right, go back to sleep.'

She curled close for warmth. The evaporative cooler in the old adobe house blew directly down on us.

'Wake you up?' Howard wanted to know.

'No, I was just lying here crocheting a sailboat, Howard. What's up?'

'You know that piece a shit of a play you wrote?'

'Has a familiar ring.'

'How do you feel about resurrecting it in Austin?'

When I was slow to respond, he asked, 'You there, *putzo?*'

'Yeah, I'm here.'

'The question on the floor is, you want the play done or you don't want it done?'

When I failed to respond: 'Landau, I'm in Austin, *Texas*, this is costing me a buck ten for three minutes.' He said 'Texas' as if it were at some colossal distance from New Mexico. Of course, it was plausible he didn't know it was right next door; like me, he may have thought it was where Utah was. 'You want that piece a shit of a play produced again or not? Simple question. Decide.'

'It's not good enough.'

'It's not good enough *now*. But that's why life gives us clean sheets of paper, Landau, and rehearsal periods.'

'With Leslie Ann?' I asked casually – or what sounded like casually to me.

'Who?' asked Howard.

I enunciated each word with care. 'With . . . Leslie . . . Ann?'

'Never heard of her.'

Beside me my wife whispered, 'We know yet why's calling two the morning?'

'He's in a different time zone.'

'Where?'

'Neptune. He wants to do *Who Stalk the Tiger.*'

Instantly alert, Sandra sat bolt upright, said, 'Tell him yes.'

I was wasting Howard's time. 'Fuckface, come on, who you talking to? Some beastie?'

'My wife.'

'Your what?'

'Wife.'

'Your *wife*?'

'Yes. Sandra.'

'*Sandra*?'

'Right.'

'You're *married*?'

'Most people who have a wife are married, Howard, yes.'

'To someone named *Sandra*?'

'You got it.'

'Oh, Jesus. Sandra what? Don't tell me! Sandra Katz. No, no – Sandy *Rabinowitz*. Am I close?'

I was startled to discover that after just a month and a half of marriage and three weeks of college teaching, doing this with Howard seemed wasteful.

I told him, 'I've got to teach a class at eight-thirty, Howard, I'm going to hang up now.'

'The hell you are!'

'It's the middle of the night, and you're – '

'What'd you expect me to do – call your secretary and make an appointment?'

'– playing games that were fun last year, but – '

'Okay, Leslie Ann, yeah, I think I've heard of her. Nice-looking chick, historic nipples. No, not with her. I'm involved with a new resident company here in Austin – did I tell you I'm calling from Austin?'

'Right – buck ten, three minutes.'

'We were going to do this piece-of-shit Broadway hit,

producers decide they may tour the piece of crap, so they yank it. We go into rehearsal next Monday, we need something fast. You're *teaching*?'

'Trying.'

'Oh, Jesus, not humility, please. Students love you, right? Gonna publish in all the anatomically correct scholarly journals. Forget it, I don't want to hear it. Can you get free for a couple of weeks in October, or do you already have your head stuck permanently up your ass looking for microscopic organisms in Melville?'

'The fall semester runs until mid-December. I could be free over Christmas, I guess, but otherwise – '

'You kill me, Landau.'

'I'd like to, Howard.'

'You wouldn't have the guts! Listen to me, Fuckface. You tell your department chairman that if you could discover some guts, you could be famous by next Wednesday, so the son of a bitch should cover your classes for you for two goddamn weeks.'

'Howard, the play was savaged out there. You can't do it again just because you need something to fill a slot.'

'Am I the kind of person to do a play because it'll fill a *slot*? Are you fucking deranged? This is my *life* we're talking about, Landau! I do not take defeat easily. Your failure was mine – you get what I'm saying? Now I'm telling you there's something in the piece of shit to build on. Retribution if not revenge is possible. You want to give it a shot, copy this number down, call me before noon – the artistic director goes before the Board at one.'

He gave me the number, which I didn't write down.

Call before noon. Fine. So I wouldn't, and he'd assume I couldn't arrange the leave of absence. Decision made by cowardice.

I slammed the phone down.

'What's the matter?'

'It's two-thirty in the morning and some lunatic's trying to shake my equanimity by dangling fame in front of me.'

'You should do it,' Sandra said.

Evasive response number one: 'I'd have to go to Austin for two weeks next month.'

'You should do it.'

Evasive response number two: 'What about you? You're getting ready to open a business.'

'Do it.'

Evasive response number three: 'I'm teaching my first semester. I have preparation.'

'You're prepared.'

Evasive response number four: 'I can't miss two weeks of class, though. The kids are already used to me.'

'Somebody can cover your class for two weeks, for Godsake, without doing permanent damage to their young minds.'

Evasive response number five: 'I didn't write the number down.'

'Oh, Jay.'

And, finally, evasive response number six: 'I don't want to be a writer!'

'You're a stinking liar.'

7

I went to get a drink of water.

On a whim, I took Stein's underwear from their hiding place under the towels beneath the sink in the bathroom and put them on.

They were cavernous, and I longed to fill them, if not physically, at least spiritually. What was that line of Stein's? 'What is the use of being a little boy if you are to grow up to be a man?'

What was the other thing my father had said to me that night over saltines and milk? *If you are going to write, Jacob, write to change the world, to make a better place for your babies.*

We must, my generation, change the quality of men.

Well, maybe that was overreaching a bit, if I'm an example of the quality of available men. How about if the world just didn't *end* during our tenure?

I wished I could speak to Leslie Ann, ask her if I should do the play again, if I had the ability to accomplish what I would have to in order to make it better.

Make it good enough.

She would know.

She wasn't available.

I went to Dr Joel after my first class and told him the offer.

Dr Joel was suitably dour throughout, and I was certain he wouldn't permit me, as a new faculty member, to arrive on campus and immediately go off to pursue selfish ends. He was going to save me from the challenge of improving my play and even the remote possibility of a life as a writer. And as a bonus, I could blame him ever after for the decades of bitterness that would ensue.

When I finished my unenthusiastic narrative of Howard's call, Dr Joel took a Jingles-size sip of coffee and said, 'Well, I'm afraid I must say this to you, Jake.'

I worked up a look of massive disappointment.

'I must place on you the burden of putting us on the theatrical map.' He reached across his desk and consumed one of my hands in one of his. 'Catapult us,' he said, 'into history.'

On the way back to my office, the number Howard gave me that I didn't write down came up with savage clarity behind my eyeballs.

I had him on the phone with minutes to spare.

8

S andra and I had decided that cocktails and wine or
beer with dinner made us feel married and adult.

On what she called 'the first seminal night of our
marriage,' we had cocktails and two bottles of wine.

By the time we arrived home, both of us were in a state
to which we were becoming accustomed: middle-level
inebriation.

Leslie Ann would have a glass of wine, which often she
didn't finish by a meal's end. Thinking back, I recalled
that anything remotely resembling overindulgence in
alcohol seemed to bother her, and I wondered now
(tipsily) if, on top of everything else, her father had
been an alcoholic.

I undressed to take my shower.

Sandra took a bath every night, and I took a shower:
there were no unclean organs in our bed at night, should
we be moved to engage in any of the various sexual
activities available to married couples in the privacy of
their homes.

I had forgotten through the evening that I was wearing
Stein's underpants.

'Jay,' she asked me as she stepped out of her own silk,
filigreed bikini briefs, 'what on earth are those?'

'Those what?' I asked, knowing instantly and too late
exactly what she was referring to.

She pointed.

Touching the underpants to be certain there was

absolutely no mistake as to the subject of this conversation, I asked, 'These?'

'Yes,' she confirmed, 'those.'

'These, believe it or not, are not my underwear.'

'I can see that. They look like Dr Joel's underpants.'

'They *are* Dr Joel's underpants,' I told her, laughing
a laugh that said, 'You're not gonna believe how I
got these.'

'Except,' she said, 'they don't have a pee hole.'

'That's right,' I said.

'How can they be Dr Joel's? Don't men's underwear
always have a pee hole?'

'Yes, they do. And do you know why these don't?'

'Because they're not men's underwear.'

'That's *right*!'

'They look like they have a menstrual stain on them.'

'They *do* have a menstrual stain on them,' I confirmed.
'You know why?'

'Why?'

'Because these are *Rita's* underpants.'

Sandra found this curious. 'What are you doing with
Rita's underpants?' she wanted to know.

'Borrowed 'em,' I told her.

'When?'

'That afternoon last month.'

'Why?'

'You're not gonna believe this.'

'Why not?'

'Actually, you *will* believe it.'

'Why shouldn't I?'

'Because I lie to you all the time.'

Where did that come from?

'You do?'

I stepped outside myself to watch as whoever remained

inside greased into a little purgation.

'You really don't know that I lie to you all the time?'

'No.'

'You should give me a polygraph every time I open my mouth unless I'm putting food in it.'

'Why do you lie all the time?'

'Why? Because I have no ethics, principles, or integrity.'

'Oh, Jay.'

'I'm a pathological liar.'

'Oh, Jay.'

'Don't "oh, Jay" me. I am a four-star dissembler.'

'For instance.'

'For instance? For instance, these underpants. You catch me in them, and instead of telling you the truth, I tell you they're Rita D'Amico's because you'll accept that.'

'Sometimes I don't know when you're kidding or not, and when I figure you're not kidding, I accept what you tell me because I assume you're telling me the truth.'

'Why would you assume something like that? Who invested you with the right to hear the truth?'

We stood naked on opposite sides of our bed. Her pubic hair, from a day in her silk, filigreed panties, was flat against her mons veneris as if it had just recently been mown. Unconsciously she ran her fingers down through it, fluffing it up. 'Why *don't* you tell me the truth?'

'Why? Because I suppose the truth is a thing that often embarrasses me, a thing capable of unmasking me and showing me to be what I really am.'

'Why shouldn't I see you as what you really are?'

'Because what I really am is not someone you could admire!'

'What on earth are you talking about, Jay? If doing

this play is going to make you crazy, maybe you shouldn't do it. I won't mind being married to an English professor – unless he's an English professor who hates himself for not trying to be more.'

Tired and angry at my inebriated self, I just wanted to sleep. I said to Sandra, 'I'm just having a small, pre-turning-thirty crisis or something. Look – forget it, okay?'

'Okay – except I didn't mean what I just said.'

'What'd you just say?'

'That maybe you shouldn't do the play. You should absolutely, definitely do the play – even if it makes both of us a little crazy for a while.'

This woman was *supporting* me.

'I have to quit drinking,' I said, and headed for the door to go down the hall to the three-quarter bath with the shower.

'Jay,' said Sandra.

'Mm.'

'Whose underwear *are* those?'

'Gertrude Stein's.'

Sandra blinked at me several times and smiled a tight-lipped little smile that let me know that starting now she was not going to believe everything I told her.

'Where did you get those underpants, Jay, seriously?'

'Seriously, I found them in one of my drawers when we moved in. Whoever lived here before left them, I guess. I thought they were interesting.'

She said, 'Oh,' and walked not quite steadily into the bathroom off our bedroom, where the tub was located.

I heard the bathtub running and heard Sandra singing the 'Lobo Fight Song.'

When we arrived, Sandra had immediately joined the faculty wives' club, gone to their 'new spouses orientation,' bought football and basketball tickets, and learned the fight song.

I tried to head for the shower, but I was rooted to the spot. I couldn't go downstairs to the shower, but I found I could go into the bathroom where my wife was.

And confess this: 'Stanwyck, Dahlric, Potts.'

She was pinning her hair up. She nodded.

'No such writers. Made them up to make me look smart, you look dumb.'

She said nothing.

'Just wanted you to know that,' I said.

'They sounded real to me,' she said.

'Yeah,' I said, 'good names. Good lie. Good liar.'

Now, I headed for the shower.

9

I had expected when I walked into my first class to feel only what I felt when I was at Stanford: the need to intimidate my students into assuming I knew more than they and that they should, therefore, never challenge me for fear they'd find out I was unjustly standing in front of them.

But that first day, walking across campus wearing a coat and tie, I had realized I not only looked different from the students, but I was expected to *be* different.

I'm an adult now.

Like it or not.

And I didn't.

Or I didn't think I did.

Until I walked into that first class, a graduate seminar in Southern Lit (Civil War to the Present).

Six MA and Ph.D. candidates, *my* six MA and Ph.D. candidates, looked at me with daunting expectations.

They were counting on me to prepare them to become what they assumed I was.

A scholar.

A grown-up scholar.

I was irrigating the jacket of one of the two new suits I'd bought before we left Miami Beach with flop sweat.

I never broke a sweat in a class at Stanford, either as student or teacher.

As I unloaded my books and lecture notes, I thought:

Well, I'm sweating from the fierce September New Mexico heat. But the heat in New Mexico was dry; I'd found when Sandra and I went hiking in the Sandia Mountains the weekend we arrived that I didn't sweat particularly even when I was exerting myself.

This sweat was not just from nerves, though. This sweat, quite simply, was from the exhilaration of walking into the classroom, officially, as Dr Jacob Landau, Assistant Professor of English.

Because, incredibly, I knew I could, should, and wanted to meet the expectations in my students' eyes.

Within days, however, I faced an acid test. I was discussing scansion through the twentieth century in my undergraduate Survey of Modern Lit course and placing it in historical perspective, connecting the political climate of the times with the emotional connotations of the meter used by various poetic movements throughout history. A student raised his hand. He wanted to know if we were only going to talk about the mechanics of poetry and about history. Would we ever just talk about passion and intuition? Would we ever just read and respond?

My first impulse was that I should so shame this kid that the word would go out throughout the Southwest that I was not to be challenged in class. Therefore, I knew, complacency could set in now, here, this day, and I could coast to retirement thirty-seven years from now.

But then I flashed on something else: This kid was me when I was an undergraduate. A pompous quasi-intellectual trying to impress girls. And a kid who just might really enjoy reading.

Should I try to kill that pleasure and humiliate him so *I* could keep the girls?

I thought of Leslie Ann, the way she taught.

And I found myself wondering what the Hippocratic

Oath might be for a teacher. Thou shalt heal with ideas and never willfully inflict death with them?

'Shit, yeah,' I heard myself say, 'let's talk passion, let's talk intuition.'

I closed my notes, dropped on the edge of the desk at the front of the class. 'You start. You respond.'

Soon after, I thought I understood this simple truth about teaching: The best classroom situation was one in which the teacher taught the students and the students taught the teacher. And that could only be accomplished in an atmosphere where no one was simply intimidating anyone else.

The Hippocratic Oath for teachers, perhaps, was: *I will strive to grow not simply older, but up.*

Amazing.

It was with real reluctance at the end of September that I told my classes I would not see them for the next two weeks while I went off to Make Art and try to become immortal.

10

I deplaned in Austin and was met at baggage claim by D.W. Cashbaugh, the stage manager, a hard-muscled Asian woman about an inch taller than I in a Greek sailor's cap and carrying a piece of cardboard with 'Landau' crayoned on it.

It didn't occur to me that as the playwright and the nominal reason we were all gathered here to make theater, I should be treated with respect, until she offered me none.

'Luggage?'

'One piece,' I said.

'Grab it,' she said. 'Car's out there.'

She pointed vaguely beyond the terminal, tensing the finely defined, almost masculine musculature in her arms and shoulders, and then she headed 'out there.'

I waited for my bag, walked outside, and found D.W. Cashbaugh leaning against an Olds Cutlass.

'How are rehearsals going?' I asked her in the car when she offered no information on her own.

'If you happen to like theater,' she said with a slight Texas accent, 'I guess pretty good.'

Though her face had the features of an Asian, her eyes were blue and more walnut- than almond-shaped. The nose was classically Asian, seeming to have been sent out into the world to do nose business before it had been supplied the requisite amount of cartilage.

Amid an acidic silence, she whisked me to the theater in the Olds with its open sun roof.

Where the first person we came upon was a young woman crouched inside the stage door, weeping.

Without sympathy D.W. asked, 'You all right, Diane?'

The weeping young woman looked up, looked at me, scrambled to her feet, nodded.

Her name was Diane Newbury, and, as she put it through her stifled tears, 'I'm your Daphne.'

Like D.W. Cashbaugh's nose, Diane Newbury's body seemed just amiss; it was as if skeletally she grew longer than the flesh allotted could adequately cover; consequently there was an opacity to her face, onionskin over bone, and just behind that skin there was the hint of the intricate system of vessels that carried blood to and from her cheeks and nose, while the gauntness of her chest and hips was in the current vogue among high-fashion models but, for my taste, bordered right on the grotesque.

Her eyes were a very pale gray, the aperture of the irises open wide, as if trying to see in the dark, and in there I saw someone in flight, like a fawn turned loose in a forest of predators.

And like a fawn in flight, the eyes bulged slightly from their sockets.

Yet she had a sweet, lopsided smile and the most correct posture I'd seen on anyone since our scoliosis test in sixth grade.

I felt activity in my underwear.

How could I?

D'know.

So as neutrally as I imagined the word could be articulated, I said, 'Hello,' and didn't offer to shake hands, hoping to suggest no willingness whatsoever to make physical contact with her, let alone protect her.

Her doe eyes searched the landscape of my face for hunters. Evidently feeling safe, she held up my manuscript. 'Thank you,' she said, 'for this,' and she pressed my play to her chest, and with that bit of armor between us, she kissed my cheek about as graciously as it could be done.

The brain in my underwear thought: *Someone has to protect this woman or she's going to get badly hurt.*

D.W. Cashbaugh gestured me irascibly onward, down a narrow corridor toward the rehearsal space.

I had overhauled the play during the few days after Howard called; he had sent notes, and I had rewritten it again during their first days of rehearsal. I had received a copy of it back at the end of their first week with annotations on one hundred four of the one hundred fifteen pages and had returned it again just this past week.

When I first reread it, I understood why it had been savaged — it wasn't foolish or pointless or without intelligence or wit; but, as a whole, it was just overwhelmingly facile (like its author).

But it also felt like something someone else had written and about which I had sensible, useful critical comments to make. The feeling of relief that I knew how to make it better was extraordinary.

Today, at this moment, I believed it could actually be pretty good.

Yet as I entered the rehearsal room, Howard said, 'Jesus, about time. This piece of shit of a play is fucking hopeless.'

My heart sank. But my mouth said, 'No, it isn't.'

'Okay,' he said, 'actually it's almost not half-bad. But

if it doesn't get a hell of a lot better, we're still going to get crucified again.'

11

Late that night Howard told me some of the things about Leslie Ann Masterson I had known better than to find out.

'What was her name?' he asked across the carved wooden table in Spaniel's Grill where we had just consumed a side of barely cooked cow flesh and imbibed two frozen margaritas and three cans of Tecaté each.

'Who?'

'Nips – the chick out at that school we went to.'

'Masterson. Leslie Ann.'

He pointed at me, indicating I had identified the person he was thinking of. 'Her.'

'What about her?'

'Pathological liar – didn't know if you knew that or not.'

In my drunkenness my mind corkscrewed and I wasn't sure if he was referring to her or if he knew me better than I thought he did.

'Who's a pathological liar?'

'Who were we talking about, *putzig*? Jesus, if you can't drink and think, either quit drinking or learn to shut the hell up and just listen to them that can!'

'What'd she lie about?'

'Who?'

I indicated to him with a hefty exhalation of breath that I was becoming exasperated.

He laughed and pinched my cheek hard. 'You're so

cute, Landau, you're a cute person! But you don't know your ass from your elbow.'

'What'd she lie about?'

'Name it. She was an actor – not a very good one – but an actor. All the time she was living with you, performing all that docile domesticity shit . . .'

'Yeah?'

'She was porking me and some other guy.'

'Uh-uh,' I told Howard.

' "Uh-uh," what does that mean, ' "uh-uh" '? Uh-huh!'

'No.'

'Oh, yes!'

'She never slept with you.'

'What?'

'You heard me.'

'She never slept with me? Who told you that?'

'She did.'

'She told you she never slept with me.'

'That's right.'

'And you believed her?'

'Yeah. You like to play mind games, Howard.'

'I *love* to play mind games. Only thing I like better is forcing a woman to her knees and having anal intercourse with her without benefit of a lubricant. And maybe the tacos at that place in whatchacallit – what's that little wetback town out in the wine country around Mendocino, you've been there.'

'Forget tacos – what other guy you think she was – '

'Hold it – this'll drive me crazy, I can't stand it when I can't . . . Rico's!'

'Good! So what other guy was – '

'No, no, hold it – Tico's! That's it – Tico's! Not tacos, though, that's what confused me. Tico's tacos. No. Burritos. Tico's burritos.'

'How'd you know about the place in Mendocino?'

'How'd I know? Gee, let me think. Nitwit, Nitwit, Nitwit! She took you there, she took me there, she took the other guy there, for all I know she took the Palo Alto Naval Reserve there.'

'You're lying.'

'Whatever you say, cutey.'

He raised his empty Tecaté can toward the bar, indicated we needed another pair.

'What other guy, Howard?'

'You obviously don't want to know.'

'Tell me who the other guy was, Howard, or I'm going to take the back of your head in the palm of this hand and I'm going to smash your face with all of my might, standing up – like this, look' – I got unsteadily to my feet, floated over him, and demonstrated – 'smash your face down into the table.'

'Sounds good. Do I bleed a lot and then get a new nose?'

'What other guy, Howard?'

'Beats me – never asked. Just knew some days she came next door in her sleepwear after you left for school and porked me and other days she went to pork the other guy. Some businessman.'

'Businessman?'

'Man in business.'

'What kind of business?'

'What am I – a private eye? Suit-and-tie guy.'

'I don't believe you.'

'I think there's wisdom in that, Jake. Shall I merely continue onward to the next item?'

'When was this?'

'Oh, round about after the play went into the shithouse and she was getting ready to send you packing.'

I was trying desperately to retrieve my sobriety so I could measure whether Howard could possibly be doing what I was adamantly insisting he wasn't: telling me the truth.

'What else?' I asked.

'Eh?'

'Continue to the next item.'

'I'd think about that, Jaker.'

'Please go on, Howard.'

The new beer arrived. We squeezed lime into the top of our cans, salted our rims.

We took a belt.

'That Christmas?'

'What Christmas?'

'How many Christmases you and Nips together?'

'One.'

He flicked an index finger at me, confirming it was, then, *that* Christmas.

'Go on,' I said.

'That trip to Hawaii to see her stepmother or whoever the hell that was supposed to be?'

'Yeah.'

He shook his head.

'Where'd she go, Howard?'

Howard winked, clucked his tongue, performed a reprise of the flicking index finger. 'Where do you think she went?'

'To visit her stepmother in Hawaii. Where do *you* think she went?'

'Skiing in the Sierras.'

'How do you know?'

'Take a guess.'

'You were with her.'

'With her? We drove my car and I paid for the gas.'

I was dimly conscious of D.W. Cashbaugh and the two actors playing the two men in my play sitting at the bar over Howard's shoulder drinking tequila, and I was vaguely conscious that I'd been aware of their eyes on us for some time.

'Didn't you feel guilty doing that behind my back?' I asked Howard.

'You feel guilty poking other guy's girls?'

'I'm not poking anyone else's girl.'

'You were poking Nips – she was my girl, the business guy's girl . . .'

Howard smiled at me. It was his crooked smile, the one that operated only on one side of his mouth, opening a teardrop-shaped aperture through which he shot air with unmistakable disdain. 'Now I've hurt your feelings; I've intruded reality into your little dream world. Starting to understand my character in the play a little better, Jaker?'

When I didn't answer that question, he said. 'Want to know what my ole man used to tell me, Jaker? This is optional.'

'Sure,' I said. 'What'd your ole man used to tell you?'

My eyes found D.W. Cashbaugh behind Howard; her eyes turned lazily away as mine landed on hers.

' "A hard cock," ' Howard said, ' "ain't got no conscience." And I swear to you, seems to me my Johnson is *always* hard.'

12

I hadn't tried to call Leslie Ann since the night before Sandra and I got married in August.

Though she had called me the first week of school.

I was in my office grading Freshman Comp themes on 'sensory experience' and was reading a piece by one of my kids on his rancid sneakers. Kid named Montoya, who burst one bubble of my racist preconceptions concerning the local Latino intelligence level by describing his tennies' smell as 'sending airward the effluvium of sea rot.'

'This is Jacob Landau,' I said, 'may I help you?' (Dr Joel had asked that we identify ourselves on the phone and solicit the student's ease. I still hadn't decided what to call myself. Though I liked it best, I wasn't comfortable yet with 'Dr' Landau. Since I *was* a doctor, 'Mr' Landau seemed coy. 'Professor' seemed ridiculous for someone in his twenties. So I settled on my name without any prefix, putting the burden on the caller to decide what to call me.)

Deep in the instrument against my ear, I heard her say, 'Jacob.'

I was instantly enveloped by a sensory experience without a tangible name that made me, to my surprise, almost sob her name.

'Les.'

'You said I could call any time.'

'Of course.'

I found my eyes on the calendar across my desk, and I knew why she might be calling today.

'Happy birthday,' I said.

Through the filaments going from my office across the land, through space, time zones, to wherever she was, I could sense in the silence that she wanted to weep, and I knew something terrible was coming.

'My little brother called to wish me happy birthday. He's in Vietnam. They sent him there. He's there.'

(In March her brother had been drafted, much as she said he would be if her stepmother didn't take care of his tuition and keep him in school.)

'I'm sorry,' I said.

'I've been sitting here for the last hour trying to feel only concern for my brother's safety, to remember only the good times; but you know how I keep remembering him?'

'Watching you with your father on the couch and doing nothing.'

'That, and that on the night my father said he was going to marry Magda, whom Evan despised above all human beings in the world, he didn't know what to do and so he said, "Congratulations, Dad, that's keen." ' She whistled long and low through the mouthpiece of her receiver into the earpiece of mine. 'Keen? That's *keen*?'

She laughed a very small, totally unamused laugh.

'I answered the phone and it was the operator; she wanted to know if I'd accept a collect call from Ft. Hood, Texas. I knew it was Evan and that he was dead. And I thought, Gee, shouldn't they pay to tell me my brother's dead? But I said, "Yes, of course I'll accept the charges," and then some military person got on and said my brother was calling from a foxhole in Vietnam and he would speak first and when he was through, he would say "Over" and then I would speak and when I was through I had to remember to say "Over." And then I was speaking to Evan. But I kept forgetting to say "Over." '

She was weeping now and trying not to. 'I'm sorry, just a minute.'

And for several seconds there was only the hum of the long-distance line.

'Are you okay for time?'

'Sure,' I said.

'Is this infidelity?' she wanted to know.

'I don't think so. Go on – I'm here.'

'Okay. So there we were, talking via radio waves that were bouncing off the stratosphere. For a second, the distance between us seemed really small. Then I heard noise in the background and he told me what I heard were rockets, that he was on a patrol and there was an air strike going on just ahead of them, and I started crying.'

As she did again then. But for only the barest second.

The line crackled.

'And then just when it seemed we'd gotten this "Over" business straight and were sailing along, he said he had to go, that his squad was moving, and I all the sudden blurted out that we really needed to talk about what happened when we were kids. And he said he didn't know what I meant, but sure, we'd talk when he got back and he said he loved me and I said I loved him, even though I don't know if I do. Over and out. Over and out.'

She sniffled. Her nose was running. I wanted to reach through the filaments, hold a tissue to her nose, tell her to blow. Wipe her nose.

'What if he dies before I have the chance to speak to him, Jacob? Twenty-six years old and I'll have no mommy, no daddy, no brother, and no you. Unfinished person with nothing but unfinished business.'

And then, as I was about to apologize in some way for my unavailability, she exploded: 'Me me me! My brother's life is in danger and I'm thinking about myself! God, I get so sick of being with myself all the time, Jacob. It's no goddamn wonder I'm an actor.'

I laughed. Couldn't help it.

So did she.

'And how are you, Jakey?'

'I'm good, Les. I like teaching.'

'You're lucky – you can make a difference.'

'You will too.'

'As an actor?'

'How'd the new play festival go?'

It took her a moment to hear the question, generate the enthusiasm to answer it.

'Really well. I was proud of my work.' Then, almost an afterthought, she said, 'Got offered a role on a TV pilot.'

'Really? That's terrific, Leslie Ann!'

'I guess.'

'Why isn't it?'

'It's pretty frigging stupid stuff, Jacob.'

'But if it's successful, it could allow you to make choices for yourself.'

From far down a tunnel, she said, 'I have choices, Jacob.'

'Any other theater roles in the offing?'

'Well, actually the man who runs the theater – have you heard of Gregory Davidoff? – he asked me to play Lady Macbeth in their October production.

Mr Davidoff is directing himself. I have to tell him tomorrow.'

I felt like a proud parent. 'Les — Jesus, you're on the brink.'

'I suppose.'

She supposed? 'Leslie Ann, remember what you're in Los Angeles to achieve.'

'Mm,' she said. 'But Lady Macbeth . . .'

'What's wrong with her?'

'She's an awful person.'

'The Professor in *The Lesson* wasn't exactly a charmer, Les.'

'I just don't know if I want to spend four weeks of rehearsal looking into all the sewage in my soul.'

'Look at it this way: a successful Lady Macbeth and you're a step closer to your dream of a *Lear* with Lorne Greene.'

She laughed a small, hollow laugh.

'Leslie Ann, I can't believe you're treating this like a trip to the grocery store — with less enthusiasm, actually, than you have for going to the grocery store.'

'Going to the grocery store is a gratifying experience.'

'Leslie Ann, listen to me. You're being recognized for the singular talent you are. So, humanize Mrs Macbeth, do to her what you do to everybody you play.'

Her voice was like a child's hand, reaching out through the wires to be held. 'I should, huh?' she asked.

'Absolutely.'

I listened to her breathe and then listened to someone very adult say: 'It's finally started to seem like our time together was a long time ago, Jacob. I think what happens is we don't forget people we love, but maybe to protect ourselves or to protect other people we love, at some point we forget to remember. You know what I mean?'

'Sounds good.'

'Thanks. I wrote it down and memorized it.'

I knew wherever she was calling from, she was smiling.

'Well, gotta go, get on with becoming famous,' she said.

'Your brother won't die, Leslie Ann. He'll come back and you'll clear things up with each other.'

'Promise?'

'Yeah.'

'Thanks, pal.'

And, of course, with that, she was gone. Leaving me feeling lonely and worried for her, but feeling validated for knowing she was, in fact, singular.

Tonight, from my musky room in the pervasively musky Travis Hotel in Austin, Texas, I called the last number I had for her, the one listed under L. A. Landau.

Why did I have to know who was lying? And who, really, did I hope was lying?

The trip to Honolulu.

Jesus, that trip at Christmas was to deal with her stepmother about the very issue of her brother's tuition. What if, in fact, she didn't go, didn't address that issue, didn't get the money from her stepmother she wanted to keep her brother out of the draft. What if she did, indeed, go with Howard Bellman skiing in the Sierras and her brother got drafted and sent to Vietnam where young men like Evan Mayes were dying every day?

After several rings, someone with a heavy Japanese

accent answered; he had no knowledge of someone named 'Resrie Randau' at that number.

Information, likewise, had no Leslie Ann Masterson or Landau or any clever variation of either in the Greater Los Angeles area.

13

Still drunk, I took the contact sheet D.W. Cashbaugh had given me down to the gay man at the desk and asked him to direct me to the address listed for Howard Bellman, which I noticed was the same address listed for Diane Newbury.

I followed the desk clerk's directions to an old apartment house several blocks away, and when Howard opened the door in his just slightly malodorous looking boxer shorts, I slammed him up against the wall and told him I was going to ask him one question and if he wanted to keep his eyeballs in his head, he'd answer the question with alacrity and clarity.

'Sure, Jaker,' he said, 'happy to. Shoot.'

'Do you,' I asked him, 'know where Leslie Ann is at this time?'

He looked at me blankly.

'Masterson,' I told him. 'The girl from Stanford. The one who didn't go to Hawaii. Another guy plus you. Pathological liar.' Very deliberately, letting him know this was the last time I was asking, I said, 'Do . . . you . . . know . . . where . . . she . . . is?' and I pressed my fingers into the upper orbital wall of his eye sockets, my fingertips pressing lightly down on the tops of his eyeballs. The look in Howard's eyes was new and confirmed that I'd never really had his undivided attention before this moment, prior indications to the contrary.

'No,' he said, and through the alcohol I think I read that this was the truth.

Diane Newbury, in a shapeless-looking cotton nightgown, came into the doorway. She was holding a Swiss Army knife, but it wasn't open to one of the blades; it was open to the tiny scissors. 'What are you doing, Jake?'

'I'm doing this,' I said. I flicked my fingers lightly downward on Howard's eyelids, closing his eyes. I opened them. Closed them. Opened. I was transfixed to discover his pupils dilated and his eyes fixed on my own each time the curtains rose. 'What are you doing with those little, teeny, tiny, eeny-weeny scissors, Diane?'

'I use them,' said Diane.

'Got it,' said I.

She looked touchingly exposed – no makeup, the translucent skin, the skeletal remains shoved into her meager skin.

'C'mere, Di.'

'How come?'

'C'mere.'

'Uh-uh.'

'I said c'mere!'

Tentatively, with a little nod from Howard, she advanced close enough for me to put a palm gently to her cheek. The cheek flushed instantly, a brigade of capillaries mobilizing into defensive position. I glanced at the Swiss Army knife; it was still clutched unthreateningly in her hand.

'Don't you know,' I asked her, 'what a pair of scumbags you're dealing with in Bellman and Landau?'

I thought I was going to say 'scumbag you're dealing with in Bellman.' I was surprised to hear my name associated on the end of the question with his.

Until this moment, I thought I had undergone via marriage and three weeks as an educator some noble alteration of character.

Drunks – and in all likelihood, especially drunken men – frightened Diane Newbury, and she didn't answer me.

I wanted to ease her concern (and dissociate myself from Howard). I wanted to assure her I was not an abusive drunk. But I was feeling so abusive I knew I'd never convince her.

'Tell you what,' I said, 'here's an idea: See you tomorrow.'

14

In my room I took two aspirins, got in the badly warped bed, turned out the light.

Turned *on* the light.

Stared at the phone.

Thought about calling Sandra, waking her up to say. . . what?

Okay so far. No threats to our marriage yet. Check in with you tomorrow, same time.

Why? Let her worry.

Why?

No answer forthcoming.

I picked up the phone and, uncertain whom I was calling until I gave the gay desk clerk downstairs the number, I called Motke Londovnik.

'What's the *matter*?' he asked.

'Nothing, Pop, I'm fine.'

I turned out the light and balanced myself precariously among the dunes on the bed.

'You know what time it is here, Jacob?'

'Time? Let me see – big hand on the . . . Jesus, three in the morning. I'm sorry, Pop.'

'Forget it, I was awake.'

'What were you doing, Pop?'

'Nothing.'

'Thinking, Pop?'

'I don't know – having crackers and milk, thinking, maybe, sure.'

'I mean, when you're awake in the middle of the night, what else is there to do, right?'

I laughed, as if for either of us not to understand that was what people did in the dead of night when they awakened in torment was just plain silly and what we should do was just have a good yack over my naiveté.

My father produced a little snort that passed for a laugh.

'What were you thinking about, Pop?'

'You've been drinking, Jacob.'

I made an overly wet sound of dismissal with my lips, spitting all over the hand holding the receiver. 'You're smelling my breath from two, three hours ago, Pop.'

The snort again. I tried to imagine him with a wry little smile on his simian face. 'What can I do for you, my boy?'

No, what can I do for you, Pop?

'Nothing. I just . . . Listen, I've been drinking, Pop, you're right. I should let you – '

'Wait, wait, what's the hurry? You're here, I'm here, I'll reimburse you the expense, tell me something – how's the teaching going?'

'It's good, Pop, it's really nice. I thought the kids would be morons and they're not. I thought I'd hate it and I don't. But, hey, I'm in Austin, they're doing my play here, the one I wrote at Stanford, in this new regional theater here. I'm here for the last two weeks of rehearsal.'

'Jacob, that's terrific! How's it going? You have good actors taking the leads – what, tell me!'

In an instant I understood that if I became a writer, a good one, my father could be proud of me again.

'I don't know, I just came in, but I've worked hard on it, it feels okay, feels like things are going okay.'

'Good, good, that's *good*, I'm glad to *hear* that.'

And now I sensed my father felt it was frivolous, irresponsible even, to display the sort of enthusiasm he'd just displayed, and so . . . 'So tell me – this Nixon, this nudnick, this *schnorrer*, do you believe he wants to cut the school lunch program?'

I didn't answer my father's question; rather, in one of those moments where my brain lagged behind my mouth, I heard myself say this to him instead:

'Pop, I want to write a play about you.'

Whereas my father's mouth lagged well behind his brain. After what seemed a very long time, almost inaudibly, he said, 'What do you mean?'

What *did* I mean? It didn't seem to me that I was acting on this still febrile notion of using the questionable ability I had to win my father's respect; it seemed more than that.

'I want to write about the pogroms, the ghetto, the camps, about you, your family, about what happened to all of you.'

'No.'

The word had always fascinated me, ever since I discovered in a speech class how the tongue worked to produce it, attacking the back of the teeth to achieve the *n* and then the expulsion of air and emotion that formed the *o*.

No!

You could say it like you meant it or like you didn't, with anger or irony, but you couldn't form it any way but decisively.

'Why not?' I asked my father.

'Because.'

'Because why, Pop?'

'Because you don't want to live all that – that's why.'

'But I do, Pop.'

'Then maybe I'm incorrect. Then maybe what I mean is *I* don't want to *relive* it so you can write about it.'

I want to know you, Pop!

'I want to know you, Pop.'

'What did you say?'

'I said, I want to know you.'

I heard what I thought was an inarticulate cry, yet after a moment my brain decoded the sound as these words blurted together, as one: 'Noyoudon't.'

'Why don't I want to know you, Pop?'

My life on the telephone, it struck me, was about other people's breathing. The sound of my father breathing echoed in my ear like oral history. I could picture his huge frame atop one of the bar stools at the kitchen counter. Glass of skim milk, saltines.

Now I could feel his rough cheek against my child's lips.

Long time ago.

I heard myself ask my father, 'Did you do something you're ashamed of, Pop?'

Fifteen hundred miles and many years away, my father gasped and his breath came back at me several seconds later in a gush: 'Good luck with the play, Jacob.'

My life on the telephone was also about other people hanging up on me, having tantalized me to mental erection, only to leave me cogitus interruptus.

You!

And what was that about?

You!

Schnorrer. Barely consciously, the word had been resonating in my head since he used it.

This Nixon, this nudnick, this schnorrer . . .

Not Nixon.

Schnorrer.

Now an image accompanied the word.

An old man. Diminutive. No, more than diminutive. Shrunken. Reduced. That look: survivor.

The Thunderbird Invitational. Las Vegas. The only place there was any notable number of Jews walking the course, any notable number of Jews in evidence, period. Not a private country club sponsoring a tournament for fine young White Anglo-Saxon Protestant boys.

In Las Vegas there were Jewish tourists, proud to cheer on this son of the Diaspora, the Golfer Jew.

My head was in the tournament. Still, I was aware of this reduced little man, looking for all the world as if he couldn't walk across a room, walking tee to green, tee to green, keeping up, though none of his ambulatory parts seemed to work in synchronism with the others.

It wasn't until the back nine that I realized he had changed his position. Now he was always abreast of my father where my father customarily walked – several steps behind me and to my right – or where my father customarily stood when I set up to hit each shot – straight out from me ten to fifteen yards, where I could see him if I wanted to, but not so close as to distract me once I locked on to the ball between my feet.

Finally, as I was leaving the eighteenth fairway, swept up by the tournament officials and well-wishers, I saw the old man point a finger at my father, as if to say 'You!' and my father glanced at me. Did he regret that he had to talk to this old man and therefore couldn't be with me in the moment of victory as I headed for the tent to sign my scorecard – *or* did he look at me to see if I had seen this old man raise this finger at him; this finger that seemed to recognize my father and, more, to accuse.

You!

Who was that old man, Poppy?

Who knows? Some schnorrer *who thought I reminded him of someone.*

Did that happen, or was it only happening now as I invented it for a play I hadn't written?

Couldn't be sure.

Believe me, selling someone a good pair of shoes that fit properly is just as satisfying as performing a good surgery.

Did he ever say that to me?

I have the right to be new!

Who was that?

Leslie Ann.

Margaret and Motke.

Who *were* they?

Just some old schnorrer *who thought I reminded him of someone.*

In the night you called me Pop.

I had a drunken vision of me between Margaret and Motke on the front seat of Motke's old Caddy convert, driving cross-country, singing old songs, my arms around their shoulders.

No mommy, no daddy, no brother, no you. Unfinished person with nothing but unfinished business.

No way she went skiing in the Sierras with Howard and not to Honolulu.

No fucking way.

Still, before rehearsal, I asked Skip Donner, the artistic director of the American Southwest Rep, if he knew a director in Los Angeles named Davidoff.

'Gregory Davidoff?' he asked, indicating by his tone, the eminence of the man.

'That's him,' I said.

'Only one of the most powerful beings in the theater.

He better not be trying to snake this play out from under me.'

Armed with the number, I called Davidoff's theater, told the person who answered that it was crucial I get in touch with Leslie Ann Masterson, who was rehearsing Lady Macbeth in Mr Davidoff's production of *Macbeth*.

I was informed that Miss Masterson was no longer with the production.

When I asked why, I was told I couldn't be told.

15

Within the next few days, the mysteries of my father and of Leslie Ann took a backseat to thoughts of murder.

Here were my reasons for wishing Diane Newbury dead:

1. She could not rehearse a scene without crying, irrespective of whether tears were appropriate or not.

2. She could not do a scene without falling into the depths of depression wondering what her character's *subtext* was, even if what her character was feeling on the surface and what her character was feeling underneath were perfectly clear to everyone else in the room.

3. She could not do a scene the way I wrote it, even when she was through crying and Howard had given her a subtext. She seemed to have, in fact, some beast in her that could only be mollified if she transposed my dependent and independent clauses or if she used colorless synonyms for my most colorful words.

4. She didn't like any of the other actors – not, I was convinced, because they didn't like her (which they didn't), but because she thought them beneath her talent or was convinced they each thought she was beneath theirs and hated them for being wrong (though secretly she was terrified they were right).

5. She had a thing about fluorescent light bulbs. They

sapped her energy, gave her headaches, exacerbated her menstrual pains.

6. She never had her own pencil. Each morning D.W. gave her a new one; each ensuing day Newbury required a new one.

7. She had a mustache that reminded me of Charlie Chan's, longest at the outside edges.

8. She had hammer toes with hair on them and wore the same open-toed sandals to rehearsal each day.

9. She ate Clorets incessantly – but surreptitiously; she didn't want anyone to suspect her breath might be susceptible to the same odors the rest of ours were.

10. She did some secret thing to her hair on the top that made it look like an awning, then spent a great deal of time crushing it downward, as if trying to implant the free ends in her forehead.

11. She bit her fingernails and used the little scissors on her Swiss Army knife to snip the cuticles after her carnivorous attacks. During notes or discussions of the text, the snip snip snip of Newbury's tiny scissors performing surgery on her cuticles became part of the aural landscape, like the incessant wheeze of an asthmatic.

12. *She wasn't Leslie Ann.*

In the men's room during a break in rehearsal, I wondered if there was any way I could have her killed and not get found out.

Howard braked into the urinal beside me.

'I want Leslie Ann, Howard. I want to get rid of Newbury and I want Leslie Ann to do the role.'

'What's the matter with Newbury?'

'I hate her.'

He tapped his forehead tiredly against the wall in front of us (he didn't want to be having this conversation now

– he was working). 'Everyone in the arts but actors,' he said, 'retain part of the child in them and grow into adults of sorts, okay? Actors borrow the adult in other people and remain children. And usually the little twits you despised when you were a kid. We *all* knew and despised Newbury.'

It was odd to hear him say something direct and unfettered by profanity. But then it also seemed that he was taking the doing of my play with extraordinary seriousness, keeping me acutely aware that he had a dream beyond this place and that the vehicle for his getting there was me.

Nevertheless I said, 'She's terrible. I want the person in the role I wrote it for.'

'Give her a call and see if she can get here in the near future, say sometime before we *open*, so she can rehearse this very different version of your piece-of-shit play a time or two. Where is she – got her number on you? – let's both call her.'

He looked at me, raised his eyebrows. He knew I had no idea how to find her.

'It'll be there on the night,' he assured me.

'What night?'

'Opening night.'

'What'll be there?'

'*It*. A performance by Newbury that'll blow your mind.'

'Couldn't I have my mind blown sooner than opening night?'

'Not likely.'

'Could I blow my own?'

'Up to you. Use a small-caliber revolver with hollow-point shells.' Howard shook, sending a droplet of urine flying through the air from his urinal onto my wrist.

'You just flicked piss on my arm, Howard.'

'So, what is it – little acidic yellow water. Concentrate on the big stuff, Landau. Life's too short.'

Howard checked for nose hair in the mirror over the sink while I scrubbed his urine off my wrist.

'Remember the day Leslie Ann came to your apartment and asked you to piss on her?'

He didn't pee on me. I told him I was playing a joke on you.

'How could I forget the inception of the fabulous urination scene,' he said. 'Maybe we should put it back in this version. Brilliant piece of playwrighting.'

'What was the liquid you and Leslie Ann used to make me think you'd really pissed on her?'

'You jest,' he said, and exited the men's room, his whole, fixed attention reverting to the work at hand.

16

D iane Newbury asked me to have coffee with her during a break in rehearsal the next afternoon, as Howard got ready to work the climactic scene in the play, in which he had decided to have Daphne rip her clothes off – that is, to perform the scene nude, in rebirth as she was at her original birth.

In the run-throughs I'd seen the last several days, the scene had been 'marked.' That is, Diane mimed tearing her clothes off and remained in her rehearsal outfit.

In the Green Room, she went to the coffeepot. Her back to me, she popped a Clorets from the stash in her shirt pocket.

'You want some coffee?' she asked, looking my way.

I shook my head.

'I don't want any, either,' she said. 'After eleven in the A.M., it makes me feel ookie.'

She smiled in the spirit of someone sharing intimate information with a new friend. I nodded and smiled, leaving open to interpretation the possibility that I, too, was susceptible to caffeine-induced ookiness after eleven in the A.M.

She indicated the Naugahyde couch. 'Sit down, Landy.'

In one of the quaint affectations of Show Biz, everyone's name was reduced to a diminutive, implying almost unbearable closeness and warmth. Thus I had become Landy, the very good-size Artistic Director

Skip Donner (who was playing Warren) was Skippy, the actor playing Michael, Rob Davenport, became Robbie, Diane was Dee-Dee, D.W. Cashbaugh became Dubbie. Only Howard remained Howard, never Howie, and utilized the diminutives only when he *really* wanted something from someone and was pretending he had any earnest, human feeling for the person from whom he was trying to get it.

I sat beside Newbury on the Naugahyde couch.

She picked at a small crack in the leatherlike material of the couch as if at a scab. I found myself playing with my wedding ring, turning it round and round, sliding it forward and back. White gold inside yellow gold; twenty-six vertical, equidistant harsh marks in the white.

'Can I be honest with you?' she asked.

'I doubt it,' I said. 'But we're here, give it a shot.'

Her pale eyes skittered around my face like a little windup ladybug my sister had when we were kids. The residue of memory reminded me that I had wanted that ladybug and she wouldn't give it to me and so I had smashed it with a paddleball racket.

Diane Newbury arranged her lips in what was intended to be a very sweet smile. 'For a second there,' she said, 'I thought you were serious.'

I laughed. 'Get real,' I said.

She tried to laugh, but it came out a cough. She covered her mouth, cleared her throat, and popped a Clorets with a surreptitious little swipe across her mouth.

I can't stand her! For all the reasons above and more. She's just so *at the mercy of.* Yet, someone in me touched her gently on the arm. Her skin was sticky to the touch. I felt myself getting erect. Inside, I shook my head in awe at the wondrous, complex *simplicity* of my manhood. 'Go on, please,' I said to her.

She stopped picking at the Naugahyde scab but couldn't handle this without some sort of prop, so she half disappeared headfirst into her cavernous purse and exhumed her Swiss Army knife. Like Captain Queeg, she began to turn the knife in her hand.

'When I accepted the role of Daphne in your play, there was no nude scene.'

'Mm-hm.'

Newbury turned the knife in one hand, picked at the scab with the other; she moved her Clorets from one cheek to the other.

We could be here a long time.

So I said what she wanted to say for her. 'But now that we're at the moment of performing the nude scene *nude*, you don't think you can do it.'

She'd come to me in search of an ally, hoping I'd go to Howard – whom we both knew was really in charge – and get her out of doing a scene I'm sure he had told her with suppressed glee both in rehearsal and in the privacy of their home that she was goddamn well going to do.

I wished I liked her better – or at all – so I would feel disposed to help her out. I would like nothing better than to have a good reason to have a cataclysmic argument with Howard, undermine the production of the play before I had to find out if I'd actually made it better.

'At first I didn't think we needed the nude scene; but Howard convinced me it could be stunning as a statement of Daphne's rebirth.' And in fact, I *had* come to believe that, much as I didn't want to because Howard thought it up.

Since finally she was an ordinary actor, I could see the wheels turning in Diane Newbury's head; she debarked from this flight, connected with another, and embarked toward the same destination via a different route.

'Jacob, you're a Jew – a Jewish person, I mean – '

'And those are actually very similar, Diane. Many Jews are also Jewish persons.'

'I'm sorry,' she said. 'Some people don't like being called Jews.'

'To the contrary, *many* people don't like being called Jews. But that's another discussion. Let's get to the point of this one.'

Even with my eyes riveted to hers, I could see her nervous hands endeavoring to open the Swiss Army knife in her lap. 'Though you are Jewish, Landy, I think you can understand if I tell you' – she looked around the Green Room; no one else was near – 'that I'm born again. And I'm afraid God Jesus will not look favorably on my doing a nude scene in this play in front of hundreds of strangers.'

'God Jesus won't.'

'No.'

'I'm a little confused here, Diane. Are we talking about Jesus or are we talking about God?'

'They're the same,' said Diane Newbury with just discernible trepidation.

'That depends to whom you're talking, doesn't it?'

With what passed for aggression, Diane Newbury finally managed to snap open the little scissors on the Swiss Army knife, and she said, 'I'm talking to *you*, Landy.'

With what would never be mistaken for anything *but* aggression, I said coldly, 'Then they're not the same. To me, Jesus is not God.'

'No, of course not. As a Jewish person, Yahweh would be your –'

'Excuse me – not Yahweh, either. If we're speaking of the white bearded gentleman in the Old Testament – that Yahweh – he was a fucking sadist and certainly no one to credit with something as luminous and puzzling as the creation and maintenance of the world.'

What had my father called old Yahweh?

A hedonistic, arbitrary lunatic.

'So who is God, Landy?'

'Me. You. Sammy Davis. Tricky Dick. Folks.'

Blood rushed like an assault team to Diane Newbury's cheeks, armoring her against these blasphemies.

'Oh, no,' she said, 'believe me, that just can't be, Landy.'

'Believe me, I don't like it, either. Especially Sammy.'

She began to compress and depress the little scissors. Snip snip snip. 'Then who is Jesus to you, Landy?'

'Some guy, probably of questionable sexuality, who had some none-too-novel ideas but a nice way with people.'

Beneath the flesh of Diane Newbury's face, a virtual red corpuscle stampede was in progress. The snipping stopped. 'You're kidding, right?'

'No, no, I'm not. And the nude scene stays. Do it or get out while there's time for us to replace you.'

We could put an ad in those trade papers in Los Angeles: 'Leslie Ann Masterson! Your role is calling! Please contact Jacob Landau at . . .'

I started back toward the rehearsal hall, past Rob Davenport, who was immersed in a daily ritual in which he decided which of the candy bar slots to pull in the candy machine. As each of the six slots was filled with Snickers, I assumed location was everything.

'How come you do that, Rob?' I asked him the second time I watched him do it.

'Karmic transmigration,' he'd said.

I was pretty sure all these people were certifiably full of shit.

That I was here with them, I was pretty sure, was a message I should open, peruse, and digest.

Newbury grabbed me from behind, pressed me around the side of the soda machine, out of Rob's hearing, and told me this: 'I have small boobies.'

Fleetingly I thought: *We've just jumped a huge hunk of connective tissue in this discussion – God Jesus to tits with no segue.*

So at this moment, when I ought to have been sensitive to Diane Newbury, I said instead, 'Someone who's born again shouldn't say "boobies," Diane. I would think someone who's born again doesn't *have* boobies. She has mammary glands, maybe, but not "boobies." That aside, though, Daphne, who isn't born again, *should* have small boobies. In fact, it's the one thing she really *ought* to have. Little teeny tiny pathetic boobies.'

Newbury pointed a quavering hand, clutching the little scissors, at me angrily. 'You're not being very nice!' she said.

'Frankly, Newbury, I wasn't all that fond of you to start with, and now this God Jesus business has just really pissed me off.'

Newbury burst into tears, and it was half an hour before Howard could calm her sufficiently to get her into the rehearsal hall to work the scene.

When Diane Newbury got around to taking off her

clothes, so childlike and sad was she in her nudity that I had to leave the theater.

17

I was wrestling toward inebriated sleep when the knock on the door came. I had no idea who it was or why I did this, but, though it was after one A.M., I felt guilty being asleep when whoever was at my door was awake, so I threw some script pages around, grabbed a pencil, and opened the door with the edge of irritation I figured a writer ought to convey when he was interrupted at middle-of-the-night work.

'Howard threw me out,' she said.

'Why?'

Newbury shrugged. 'He said he didn't have to tell me why. If I couldn't stop him, he said, he could just do it because *he* knew why.'

'Interesting concept,' I said.

'He masturbates.'

'No.'

'Even when I'm not having my period.'

'Unbelievable.'

'Can I come in? I'll only stay a minute. I need someone to talk to.'

'And you selected *me* – after I was so terrible to you today?'

Newbury shrugged deep into her shoulders – my behavior didn't seem germane – and she smiled a not quite unsexy smile and waited.

I didn't want her to come in.

And I did.

That confusion aside, if I sent her away, where would she go and what would she do? I didn't know her well enough to know how close to genuine despair her self-indulgence ran. If I had no sympathy for her as a person, I had a lot of concern for her as a third of the cast of my play.

'Sure,' I said, and gave way in the doorway.

She left her body there, angled her neck, introducing only her head into the room, where her eyes surveyed the terrain. Satisfied that whatever she feared might be inside wasn't, she entered.

I closed the door behind her.

'This is where you live?'

'No, I live next door. I just come in here to answer the door.'

Diane Newbury was either someone devoid of a sense of humor or I wasn't the amusing person I thought I was.

'I meant it's so depressing.'

I looked at the room. It was spare and unencumbered and smelled of old hotel. In fact, now that I had adapted my body to the dunes of the bed, I was comfortable in the room. Its lack of particular personality freed me simply to do my work without concern for furnishings or ghosts.

Diane lifted the straight-back chair under the small desk up and out, turned it toward me, sat demurely, leveled me with her eyes, and waited.

Though *she* needed someone to talk to, it appeared she expected *me* to initiate the conversation. She reminded me of the several female students who had come to my office after my first classes at UNM – both supplicant and sightseer.

Were you good? Sandra had asked.

You bet. I kept picking my nose with my ring finger.

It suddenly struck me that someone always trying to be 'an amusing person' could become really tiresome. I tried to speak the truth simply to Diane Newbury.

'I don't want to sleep with you, Diane, so you can get even with Howard,' I said.

'Sleep with me so I can . . . What on earth makes you think I have the remotest interest in – '

'It's late,' I said.

She thought about whether she wanted to tap-dance further, decided she didn't and came right out and asked, 'Because you're his friend?'

'No.'

'Because I'm ugly?'

'You're not ugly,' I told her.

'Cross your heart and hope to die?'

'Yes,' I said.

And then my mouth made one of those sporadic utterances that just surprised the hell out of me. 'You ever really not want to do something you were really tempted to do?' I asked Diane Newbury.

'Sure,' she said. 'I mean, I'm not sure. I think, but what exactly do you mean?'

'I mean I'm tempted to sleep with you, but I really don't want to commit adultery. My wife is stupid enough to trust me. I hate her for that, but there it is.'

The reason these words surprised me was I meant them: I wanted to keep my marriage vows.

Why?

'I understand,' Newbury said.

'Do you?'

'No. But could you just hold me?'

'Sure.'

She opened her arms.

I went to her and she rose to meet me.

First touch of a new person. Surprisingly, she was malleable against me, her shape shaping itself to me, corners to corners, crevasses to crevasses. In the distorted mirror behind her back, we bled into each other, some two-headed, bisexual hominid.

We lay down on the warped bed, rolled toward the weak side, I grabbed the brass headboard, we shuffled in the other direction, bounced, rolled, balanced, and she tucked herself in against my chest.

She popped a Clorets.

Now, I thought, *I'll kiss her and within minutes I will have vacated this absurd impulse toward fidelity.*

Newbury looked up at me, all subterfuge gone.

She looked defenseless and sweet.

Pretty in the way something utterly unadorned can be pretty.

But, looking at her, I not only had this mystifying urge to remain pure in marriage, I wanted to go all the way back to innocence and come forward again.

Wanted to dream the woman of my dreams from scratch.

What, I wondered, would be the fundamental traits of that woman, given the benefit of recent experience?

I kissed Newbury's forehead and pulled her close.

We fell asleep.

18

Howard cornered me between the Coke machine and the water fountain.

'It took me a while to figure it out, but she was with *you*. Wasn't she?'

Both a lie and the truth made themselves available to my lips. Before I had to choose, he sped on.

'How was she? You like that gentile, born again, shit-for-brains cooze? Oh, Jesus Jesus Bubby Bubby Bubby Jeeeeeeesus!'

'She came to my room, she was unhappy, I held her, we fell asleep.'

'I thought you didn't like her.'

'I don't. But as it turned out, I didn't find that a deterrent to holding her.'

'Don't talk in sentences like that, you hyperliterate son of a bitch!'

He made Diane do the nude scene three times, inviting all the tech people in the last time to watch under the guise of discussing lighting and sound concepts for the scene.

According to D.W., Diane spent the dinner break in roiling hysterics in the women's dressing room while Howard went out for the ziti special at Dino's with Sharon Postum (Postie), the assistant stage manager, whom Skip Donner, in our boy huddles, had nicknamed 'Zeppelin pelvis' for the reputed size of her landing and hangar areas.

I had spent the dinner hour in the office, rewriting a scene, which was now being mimeographed.

I went backstage to the dressing room and knocked.

'Come in,' said Diane Newbury in a clear, strong voice.

I opened the door to find her perfectly composed.

'You okay?'

'Actually, I am,' she said. And then: 'Thank you.'

'For?'

'For what didn't happen last night.' She smiled a simple, uncomplicated smile, toothsome and adult.

'You're welcome,' I said. 'I feel pretty good about it myself.'

This was ridiculous, but the actor who rehearsed Daphne that night was a much better, a much more grounded, believable one than the one who did it that afternoon.

At one point Howard leaned over me from behind, startling me, and said, 'You swear on your mother's life you didn't sleep with her?'

'Yeah.'

'You did *something* to her.'

Managing not to sound amazed myself, I said, 'I didn't abuse her.' But then, in my current spirit of probity, amended, 'Or only a little bit – verbally.'

'Fuck you, Landau, and I really mean it.'

And he continued down the aisle, his notepad rammed into his armpit, riveted – as I was – by what Newbury was doing onstage.

Toward the end of notes D.W. leaned over me. 'Sandra's calling from the airport.'

'Who?'

'Your wife.'

'What airport?'

'Orly. Paris.'

'What?'

'Ours. This one.'

'Oh, Jesus.'

'Did you forget to pick me up?' Sandra asked when I picked up the phone at the stage manager's station in the wing.

'No, are you kidding? This is incredible, but I was on my way out there and the car I borrowed blew a tire and I just got back here to get another car and you're already here.'

So much for the spirit of probity.

D.W. peered at me in a new light. The Artist Semi-Exemplar as Pedestrian Liar.

'I hate to make you come all the way back out here,' Sandra said. 'Can I get a cab?'

'I really wanted to meet you,' I whined, repelled by the sound of my voice and, more, by my lies.

'Don't be silly, I don't mind.'

I forgot my wife was coming!

I knew it last night and this morning and even into the afternoon. But then I became engrossed in rewriting and in the change in Newbury and what it did to my play and – Jesus Christ, what a terrible thing to do to this person who believes I don't lie to her all the time.

'Should I come to the theater or should I go directly to the hotel and slip into something comfortable?'

Sound focused, sound interested: 'Come to the theater. I want everyone to meet you. We'll go to Spaniel's. Then we'll *both* slip into something comfortable.'

When I hung up, I looked at D.W. 'I didn't forget because I don't want to see her or anything like that.'

'I didn't say anything.'

'I just don't want you thinking less of my wife.'

'Don't know the woman.'

'It just slipped my mind because of what was going on here this afternoon.'

'Right.'

'I'm fucking serious!'

The ferocity of my outburst startled both of us and drew the attention of everyone in the wings.

I went back to my seat in the house, feeling foul, unable to fasten back on what was going on onstage.

Where they were Making Art.

19

S o,' Howard said to Sandra in Spaniel's, 'what do you figure the attraction is?'

'Which attraction is that?' Sandra asked. She smiled at Howard, attentive, anxious to be liked by this group of aliens.

'Him to you, you to him,' Howard said, 'start wherever you want.'

The logic of Howard's obvious and instantaneous attraction to her was abundantly apparent: she looked wonderful. She'd let her hair go wild; it fell in soft, loose sable coils about her face, accentuating its delicacy.

And I don't think I was imagining that she held herself differently. For as long as I'd known her, there had been something about Sandra Pollack that said 'Don't touch!' This Sandra Landau didn't invite liberties, but she did seem eminently approachable.

Sandra looked at me for a signpost.

'He's flirting,' I said.

'Oh,' she said.

Assuming from my attitude that this was all in fun, Sandra said, 'I guess the attraction is that we just like each other.'

'That's an *answer*? You just *like* each other? What new science is this?' He leaned close. 'Hasn't it hit you yet that you're totally mismatched, and haven't you wondered what perversities were at work when you found yourselves together?'

Sandra looked at me. I sipped a Jack Daniel's and RC Cola. And continued to assure her wordlessly that I would protect her here.

My first outing as willing husband.

Or whatever I thought I was.

Because I was thinking about Leslie Ann, wondering why, really, she'd permitted herself to be treated as she did by Howard – 'meat,' 'Tits,' 'Nips.'

Was she actually inviting what she thought she merited, or was her indulgence somehow part of what her father described as 'that love which passes all human comprehension'?

Was it possible to rise above what Leslie Ann had experienced?

And why was she no longer rehearsing Lady Macbeth?

'So,' Howard said, 'tell us something about yourself. Your husband hasn't said a word about you.'

My eyes told Sandra that was a lie.

Though it happened to be the truth.

'He told me a lot about her,' Newbury said helpfully.

Sandra glanced at Newbury. At me. I smiled a smile at her that said 'There, see?'

Newbury flicked her eyes at Howard, didn't like what she saw, coughed, and got out her Swiss Army knife.

'So,' said Howard, 'you preggers yet?'

'We're going to hold off on that a while,' Sandra said.

'How come?'

'We both have things we want to do.'

I put a supportive hand to my wife's back and was startled to feel through her jersey turtleneck the absence of the usual ridge of reinforced fabric against my palm.

Sandra Pollack Landau was not wearing a brassiere.

'Got a lover?' Howard wanted to know.

'Just my husband.'

Sandra looked at me. She knew I'd noticed the hair, the posture, and now the absence of a brassiere.

I was conscious of D.W. watching from the bar.

'Little piece of advice: Get a vibrator.'

'Why? He's only been gone a week,' she said. 'We stockpiled before he left. Nuts for winter – that sort of thing.'

Sandra sipped her Vodka Collins and waited for Howard's next foray.

Though not much taller than she, Howard seemed to hover over her from his chair. It took me a while to realize he appeared to hover because he was on his knees so he could close the distance separating him from his quarry across the table (and, I assume, appear taller).

'Trust me,' Howard said. 'A hard, plastic marital aid is the ticket.'

'And why is that?'

'Because all that sexual energy he's currently expending on you's gonna go into his typewriter, onto the ole page. Orgasms by the score.'

'I think I'm beginning to see.'

'Unless, of course, your husband, as I personally suspect, turns out to be one of those playwrights who comes to hate the theater and quits because he can't stand being part of a collaborative process where he pretends to be the most important cog but knows he's really number three behind the director and the actors.'

'If he's so inconsequential, why would he want to do it?' Sandra inquired of Howard with a sensual little smile at the edges of her mouth and a tiny toss of her new hair.

She really was a *very* attractive woman.

'Because he's one of those people who're afraid to try to make art on his own. Can't operate alone. Gotta have other people sustain him.'

Like a gas tank filled to its limit, Sandra's tank spilled over. 'That's bullshit,' she said. Everyone at the table was zeroed in. At the bar, D.W. edged our way. 'Jay was a great golfer. He lived a very isolated kind of life.'

Howard cupped his ear as if he were having great difficulty hearing, even though Spaniel's was notable for nothing if not its quiet, voices rarely raised, the stereo on its nightly, muted journey through *The Well-Tempered Clavier*. 'He was a great what?' Howard asked.

'Gol-fer,' she said, ventilating each syllable, though she knew Howard heard her the first time.

'Golfer?' Howard seemed profoundly puzzled. 'Like in hit the ball, go find it, and hit it again?'

'That's the one. He was famous as a golfer as a teenager.'

'Famous as a teenager? As a *golfer*?'

'You got it,' she said. She shot her eyes at me. She was not asking for help; she was wondering how long she ought to put up with this out of politeness . . . or how long I was going to permit it to go on out of whatever motive lurked behind the smile on my face.

'But now he's pushing thirty,' said Howard, 'and he's *not* famous as a golfer. The number of people who think of him as a famous, isolated lonely-guy golfer are *none*. He's not famous as *anything*. He's an aspiring playwright dependent for his prospective fame on us.' He pointed around at the assemblage and then added pointedly, 'And especially on mine own self.'

Sandra shot her eyes at me again.

I kept my smile intact and remained silent.

And began, distantly, to wonder why.

Maturity? Curiosity? Or something more? Something not good.

And why was Howard treating Sandra so differently from Leslie Ann? Because Sandra was not an actor – not 'meat'? (I couldn't imagine that Howard viewed any woman as anything *but* meat.) Because he assumed Sandra was a Jewish Princess, with all the privileges appertaining thereto, chief among which was the birthright to be treated with exhaustive civility by members of the male gender? (In fact, for Howard, he was being exhaustively civil.)

'Like to dance?' he asked Sandra.

She glanced around – never mind that we were listening to Bach; there was not only no one else dancing, there was no dance floor. She shook her head. 'No,' she said, 'I don't believe so, thank you.'

Howard was already getting off his knees and onto his feet. He was caught in midrise and looked very short.

To me Sandra said, 'I'm really tired, Jay. Can we go?'

I thought about that for a moment. My suspicion was that I really wanted to stay to aid this by my silence to move onward toward a cataclysm of some sort; yet I said, 'Sure,' and I drained my drink, rose, and went to the bar and paid our tab.

'Odds are still that he inseminates her before the weekend's up,' D.W. drawled, 'but she did good for an amateur.'

When I returned to the table to collect Sandra and

bid everyone good night, in Howard's eyes there was indeed the promise of a challenge unfinished.

20

Outside Spaniel's, Sandra said, 'What's wrong with that man?'

'Wrong with him?'

She whistled a note of contempt. 'Voracious,' she said. 'Why didn't you say anything?'

'Why do you think?' I asked.

'Because you wanted to prove to me that I could show up here and handle myself.'

I smiled on her paternally.

She pressed my arm in hers. Pressed her head to my shoulder. She felt good against me.

In fact, I had missed her.

'You trust him?' she asked.

'With what?'

'With your play? As a person?'

'With my play, yeah. As a person, no.'

She took a handful of the flesh of my arm into her fist and squeezed hard. 'Good.'

We walked, silent, feeling each other, and then she stopped. Looked up through yellow streetlight into my face.

'I'm jealous – I need to get it out.'

'Of?'

The actress with the bug eyes.

'I don't know. Everything. I'm an outsider. There's this gang, this team, these friends, and I'm the playwright's wife.' She made the appositive sound dirty.

'You'll get to know everyone.'

Why would she want to?

'Next time,' I said, 'you'll come with me from the start.'

Next time? So, are we saying more plays, then? Certainly not if this goes into the crapper again – no way.

'And I didn't need to see how that woman was looking at you.'

'What woman?'

'The actress with the frog eyes who you supposedly told a lot about me.'

'How was she looking at me?'

'Like she was really thrilled I'm here.'

I gave my wife my learned-professor-to-immature-student tone. 'You have a vivid and paranoiac imagination, Sandra.'

'Do I?'

'I would say so, yes.'

'I have nothing to worry about?'

'Nothing.'

'You've been good?'

'I've been perfect.' I stroked her face, ran my fingers down the tip of her nose in a gesture I realized was part of our life, but the derivation of which escaped me.

'I like it,' I said, nodding at her hair. 'This, too.' I pressed the back of my hand gently against the softness of the jersey, the softness of her breast.

'Do you?'

'Very sexy.'

'Yeah? I was so scared. I thought everyone would notice and laugh. Or call my mother.'

She took that fistful of my arm again, squeezed hard.

A new gesture. It struck me that it was both a sign of affection and of anger.

We walked.

'I'm sorry I said "frog eyes." She can't help that.'

This was all new. Jealousy. Of what I do. And whom I do it with.

'She's been called worse things,' I said.

She hugged my arm. 'Really? Tell me some.'

She had never expressed any jealousy of the coeds in my classes, the graduate TAs I hung around with in the Faculty Commons Room. Perhaps because we were both away from home, the separateness of our lives and the dangers inherent in being separated were suddenly illuminated by an hour in a bar.

'When you went to pay, he asked me if I wanted to go to temple with him in the morning.'

'Howard's going to *temple*?'

'Is that bad?'

One of the few bones of contention between us – or one of the few, in any case, that we spoke of to each other: being Jewish. And, more specifically: being Jewish in the Southwest.

When we arrived in Albuquerque in August, Sandra discovered that there were actually about nine Jews in town and that they had a synagogue, complete with a Conservative rabbi. She asked me if we could join the congregation. Sounding as ecumenical as possible, I said I couldn't, but she certainly could. She said she would feel strange going to services and bar mitzvahs and especially the High Holy Days without me. I told her I had last been to temple when my mother's father died when I was seventeen, at which time it struck me sitting there staring at the parabolic splendor of Beth Sholem's dome that organized religion – ours and everybody else's — was the most prodigious crock of shit in the history of a species surely to be memorialized, above all else, for popularizing a multitude of shit crocks. She said I was showing off, being more cynical than I really was, but that was all right, she would join without me.

She joined the synagogue and had actually attended Friday night services the last five weeks, plus services on the High Holy Days.

Feigning disinterest, I never failed to ask with interest what the young rabbi's sermon had been about when Sandra returned home on Friday nights.

Once, I had dreamed of going to Israel. When was that? Before the Six-Day War or after? Definitely after *Exodus* and after I had fantasized in high school of disappearing from my failed adolescence and showing up on TV and in the newspapers as Fidel Castro's new white, Jewish right hand from the Beach.

Left to right: Che, Raul, Fidel, and El Grande Rojo Yack it up around the campfire over lox and bagels in the Sierra Maestras.

There was definitely something in me hooked on what I tried to dismiss as *Er-etz Yis-ra-el*, mocking its syllables in the same way that comics mimic evangelists turning Ga-wa-duh into a three-syllable laugh word. *Er-etz Yis-ra-el* — that arthritic finger length of desert over there at the top of the continent of Africa in which more and more Jews were politely rounding *themselves* up this time so that another seven million could be wiped out in one fell swoop one of these days.

I suspected that amid my education to the historic ebb and flow of savagery from way back then (the pharaohs) through the Inquisition to the Third Reich to the current frivolity in the Middle East, somewhere along the educational line, at a point of departure I couldn't name, I had become a secret Zionist.

The thought boggled my mind. I couldn't drag from the murk what that was about.

'What is it,' Leslie Ann had asked me somewhere in her tour through Orthodox Judaism and her methodical destruction of that student in *The Lesson*, 'to know that no matter where you go, what you achieve, who you become, you'll always be viewed in millions of secret hearts as a greedy, grasping, undeserving kike? You'll always be misunderstood. A lot of times on purpose.' Looking me in the eyes, she had said, 'I should have been a Jew.'

'What are you thinking?' Sandra wanted to know on that dark street in Austin.

I was startled to find her beside me, our bodies connected at the elbows. I was used to being alone this time of night, on this street.

'Two Jews,' I lied, 'alone in the outback of Texas.'

She hugged my arm hard to her.

'You should go with him to temple,' I said.

'You don't mind?'

'Certainly not. A good Jew is a good Jew even if he's a viper.'

She looked into my face. She sensed, I think, that I was willing to lose her. But then she said, 'Boy, I'm horny as the proverbial hoot owl.'

'On the Sabbath, San?'

'Boff our way to atonement, darling.'

'Sounds excellent to me.'

21

And it did.

But back in my hotel room, in this characterless place where I had lived a solitary, monastic life (with the exception of last night) for a week, and where I had orgasms by the dozens daily into a typewriter, Sandra did a lewd striptease, the effect of which was peculiar.

She was a terrific dancer. I remember thinking when we were in college that she invested her dancing with a great deal of sensuality she had learned to subvert in her normal life as a Jewish American Princess from the Beach.

At twenty-five, braless in a pair of panties in Texas, she wiggled and jiggled salaciously up to my crotch.

But: nothing.

I smiled at her gratefully, the smile intended to let her know I really appreciated this, and boy, it was really sexy, but I might be *so* tired that I lacked the requisite energy to make love.

Unfazed by my muted enthusiasm, she hied herself into the tub.

I hoped the sight of her naked in the old bear-claw bathing apparatus would do the trick.

She smiled at me.

I smiled at her.

She blew me a quartet of what she called her 'fishy' kisses.

I blew a quintet back.

Nothing so far.

I got in bed and tried to arouse myself with my hand, so that when she came to bed, I'd have the means to make love with her and avoid the pressure of knowing I owed her.

I couldn't get an erection, though – not thinking of her on her knees in front of me, not thinking of Newbury onstage in the nude scene last night.

Finally I turned to Leslie Ann, a usually surefire method of launching an erection.

But what sprang to mind was the image of Leslie Ann Masterson standing on the grass of the amphitheater at Stanford University the day she told me she was pregnant, asking me what I wanted to do, and remembering the hatred and love I felt for her.

Sandra washed her hair in the shower, dried it, came to bed with wild hair, makeupless, skin sparkling, smelling faintly of lavender (from a soap she was having manufactured exclusively for her store by a soap person in Santa Fe).

The twisted symmetry of the ancient Death Valley mattress, on which I had learned to balance, was destroyed by her arrival. I shifted, slid, sank in declivity where normally I rose.

I told myself my lands were being invaded by hostile forces, and I had the right to be resentful of her arrival in this arena in which I was slutting after immortality.

She touched me at the hip, slid her hand horizontally, skirting the crack between my buttocks, making her way groinward.

Balancing precariously among the dunes of the mattress, I pretended to have fallen into exhausted, leaden sleep when her fingers took my limp lingam in her hand.

Finding me unavailable, she freed me to seek ominous rest.

22

Fortunately, I awakened each morning with an erection.

During the night, however, my mind obviously fucked with my member.

Today I awakened with a tiny link sausage between my thighs.

I slipped from the bed, took a leak, tried to abuse an erection to life.

Zip.

I escaped to the typewriter to do the rewrites Howard would expect me to arrive with at rehearsal.

By the time I became conscious of Sandra, she was dressed, having awakened and gone to the toilet, put on her makeup and clothes as she always did – in such a way as not to disturb the Great Me, whether I was preparing for class, reading and grading papers, or – as now – playing nursemaid to the Muse.

Making frigging Art!

When I arrived back in this galaxy and took notice of her, she hugged me so as not to wrinkle her silk blouse and remarked, 'You're getting a gut.'

Talk about postnoncoital depression!

I scrambled in front of the full-length mirror on the back of the bathroom door. 'What gut?'

The funhouse mirrors in the Travis had obviously been specially crafted to make all its guests look as if they had elephantiasis. I had protrusions and distensions, goiters, tumors, and blobs everywhere.

'Gut?' I demanded.

'I didn't mean it as criticism,' said Sandra.

And in fact it hadn't sounded like criticism, but what else did a gut imply if not disapproval?

Should I tell her I'm terrified I find her attractive and apologize for last night and this morning?

Did she know about last night and this morning?

She patted my tummy. 'It's cute,' she said.

'Flab is cute?'

'It makes you look settled and less imposing.'

The phone rang.

Howard was downstairs.

'Now, for Godsake, don't worry about this, all right? You've got enough on your mind with the play.'

'This' meaning just my gut, or was there also the limp lingam implication?

'Promise?' she asked. 'Say I promise.'

'I promise,' I said without conviction.

She didn't have time to deal with my lack of conviction. She kissed me good-bye so as not to disturb her lipstick and went off to worship with the only person I knew who I could conceive had more to atone for than I.

In her absence, the first thing I did, needless to say, was scrutinize myself microscopically in the full-length funhouse mirror, trying to compensate for its inherent distortions to accurately gauge the particulars of my putrefying flesh.

I had always eaten copious amounts of food and never had any trouble maintaining my weight – for several years because I swung a long club with a weight on its end thousands of times a week and walked eighteen holes of golf five, six, seven times a week with a twenty-pound pack on my back; in college because I was poor; and in graduate school because, initially, I couldn't afford to eat and then because Leslie Ann severely circumscribed my tendency to eat crap and the problems with her and the play and the pains in my chest drove me toward anorexia.

Since Sandra and I had gotten married, though, no one was marshaling my intake. And we were both enjoying her efforts at cooking.

And we were drinking a lot.

And I was getting no exercise.

And she was right. Flesh that could only rightfully be called 'flab' was festooning out from my middle.

I hit the floor for fifty situps.

Managed eleven.

23

'How was temple?'

She kissed me briefly on the mouth. She tasted of wine. 'He speaks fluent Hebrew,' she said. 'Did you know he went to the Yeshiva for a year – he was going to be a rabbi.'

I hadn't had to deal with a situation where Sandra tried to make me jealous – not in either incarnation of our relationship. Thinking back to the haze of college, she could be outrageously adorable, and though she wouldn't dance on tabletops, she was a wonderful dinner and party guest, especially fueled by a couple of drinks, at which time the long-lost remnant of her southern accent would surface and she would become a Jewish Scarlett O'Hara, though her family had emigrated from Atlanta to Miami Beach when she was in the second grade.

But now that I thought about it, she seemed scrupulously to avoid at the several faculty parties we'd attended any conduct that could be mistaken for flirtatiousness. Whether out of respect for me and the sanctity of our relationship or out of fear of reprisal from me or of unleashing some beast imprisoned by civility in *her*, I couldn't say.

Now, though, I had the feeling she was trying to make me jealous, and although I didn't think I *felt* jealousy, I did feel an obligation to appear as if I did.

'So what kept him from the rabbinate?' I asked. 'A desire to serve *all* of mankind, regardless of creed?'

'He said he knew he'd want to be an Orthodox rabbi, but that he also knew he wouldn't have the fortitude to adhere to the dietary or moral tenets of the Orthodoxy.'

'Why not become a Reform rabbi, then? Eat what you want, no yarmulke, *schtup* members of the congregation.'

'He said he wanted to be something that demanded enormous discipline.'

'So he became a theater director? In the hierarchy of required discipline, that ranks just above a glutton at a buffet.'

'You're jealous,' she said.

Good job!

'I'm what?'

'Jealous.'

'Jealous?'

'I think you are.'

'Ever occur to you he's just trying to seduce you? You didn't go for vulgarian last night, he opts for fallen cleric today. The guy may be psychopathic, but he's not stupid. I'm not thrilled about him trying to put the make on my wife.'

Now we're cooking!

'He's just a very interesting man.'

'You stop for a drink after a tough morning of religious worship?'

'We just had a glass of wine at the reception afterward.'

Turn it up a notch. 'Look, Sandra, I have a lot on my mind here! I would appreciate it if you would try not to complicate things right now, okay?'

On her face was something powerful: she felt desired. 'You have nothing to worry about. What are you getting so upset about?'

'I'm not upset!'

'Yes, you are. Okay, so, now.' She sat on the edge of the bed, fixed me at the desk.

' "Okay, so, now" what?'

'What about this Diane Newbury?'

'What'd he tell you?'

'Nothing.'

'Then why are we back on her?'

'It's what he implied so that I couldn't miss his implications.'

'What'd he imply?'

'What do you think?'

'What am I supposed to do now, San, incriminate myself? Manufacture evidence for a crime I didn't commit?'

'He implied there was something going on between you.'

One of the things that amused me about some of the couples I knew at Stanford who were involved in the Movement was their belief in the so-called Open Relationship, in which each partner could do as he or she pleased sexually but was honor bound to confess everything he or she did. What havoc that kind of honesty tended to reap!

So why did I have this irresistible impulse to be open with Sandra Pollack Landau?

'Howard mistreats her,' I said. 'She thinks I'm her friend. She came to me the other night; he'd thrown her out; I let her sleep here. I held her. No kissing, no sex.'

Sandra stared at me, ran the fingers of one hand easily through the soft coils of her liberated hair.

'If I'm going to be guilty for what I didn't do, Sandra, then I might as well have done it, you know what I mean?'

She stared *into* me, then went far away and came back. She nodded. 'This is going to be very hard,' she said.

'What?'

'This,' she said, indicating me, the desk, the typewriter, the building next door, and by extension, I assumed, the world of Show Biz beyond. 'Trying to make a lifelong relationship work between two real goddamn dissimilar people.'

24

She asked me if I wanted to comparison shop the fashions of downtown Austin with her. It was not until after I had declined politely and she was gone that I wondered if, in fact, she was going to comparison shop fashions or guys.

And it was then that a notion hit me that only a few days ago would have struck me as genuinely bizarre: What if I was not pretending to be jealous, but *was*.

I hurtled into the street, looking into the doorways of women's shops for my wife. As I passed a sporting goods store, however, I was seized by an even more powerful impulse than that to circumscribe my wife's freedom: the impulse to buy a pair of running shoes and to start very seriously exercising.

In the store, trying on running shoes herself, was D.W. Cashbaugh.

She saw me. And ignored me.

How had I offended *her*?

'How you doing, Dub?'

She looked at me, said grudgingly, 'Don't tell me you're actually taking my advice.'

What advice? Had she given me exercise advice?

'Damn right,' I said. 'Need a pair of running shoes – what do you recommend?'

'Running or jogging?' she asked.

'What's the difference?'

'What's the *difference*?'

'I just said that,' I reminded her. I gave her my killer smile – slight tilt of head, hooded eyes, all hundred and ten teeth full front.

She was obviously not smitten. 'Big difference. One you run in, one you jog in.'

'Could you be a little more specific?' I suggested.

'Sure. You gonna run the hundred, the four forty?'

'No.'

'You gonna run distance?'

'Yes.'

'Slow or fast?'

'Slow.'

'Then you want shoes that are good for jogging long distance, don't you?'

I didn't answer that question. Something was obviously amiss – she was even colder than usual. I had a distant sense of what might be at issue here.

'What brand?' she wanted to know, knowing of course I'd have no idea.

'Does Cheerios make a shoe?'

She didn't bite.

'You decide,' I said.

'How much you want to spend?'

'Whatever you think.'

Her look said this was not a responsibility she relished having dumped on her. She located the salesman, a Y-shaped guy – obviously a body builder – across the store with a customer shopping basketballs.

She walked over to the Y shape, said something. He must have told her she could go into the back and get some shoes. I assumed they knew each other – presumably from a gym.

D.W. was wearing shorts, and for the first time I saw that her legs were slightly bowed at the calves and her ass looked like sculpted rock inside the close-fitting shorts. She was also wearing a tank top; her breasts looked more like a man's than a woman's, with just a hint of cut pectorals visible at the armholes – probably from lifting weights.

Out the front window of the store, I saw Sandra come out of a store, alone; she slipped down the block a ways, stopped and took a small notepad out of her purse, made several hasty notes, and walked on.

I felt a mishmash of relief and regret that Howard wasn't with her.

D.W. returned with several boxes of shoes and crouched before me on her haunches, her long thigh muscles flexed tensely below her shorts.

'You work here in your spare time?' I asked.

'What spare time?' She dropped her eyes to my feet. 'Used to work here – before the theater opened.'

Like Sandra's new hair, D.W.'s seemed to make a specific statement: it was very black and regimental and brushed briskly to the side in a style popular among women who seemed to want to send a warning to men that even male hairstyles weren't safe from the ongoing liberation of the female of the species. The part in her hair revealed an amoebalike birthmark on her scalp.

Before I could think not to, I reached down and touched her head, tracing the line of her part down over the birthmark with my index finger.

D.W.'s head snapped up. 'What the hell're you doing?'

'My father owns a shoe store,' I said.

'Your father owns a shoe store.' With brimming sarcasm, she was trying to make this non sequitur connect. 'And that's got something to do with molesting me?'

Her lips were slatted across her teeth. Small teeth, the right front one a cap, just slightly different in its whiteness from the real one beside it, a thin black line at the top of it where it just failed to meet her gum. Decay? Accident? Someone hit her? Asian? American? Stranger? Parent?

She was waiting for an answer. 'Birthmark,' I said. 'Wanted to touch it. Call the cops.'

Instead of doing that or inviting me to leave the store, she simply got on with the business of fitting my shoes, settling for a small shake of her head to suggest some people were really weird.

'So. Tell me everything you know about running that I need to know.'

'Heel toe. Warm up, warm down.'

'Concise – almost pithy in its simplicity.'

She yanked the laces of the shoe tight enough to cut off circulation to my toes; as she did this, she flexed her lats beneath her snug tank top – or, perhaps more precisely, her lats flexed themselves.

'How do I lose weight?' I asked her.

'Don't eat,' she suggested.

'Where does the jogging come in?'

She yanked the laces of the other shoe tighter than the first. 'That's for your cardiovascular system. Heart, lungs.'

'Is that what cardiovascular means?'

She flicked hard eyes up at me from where she knelt at my feet. 'Are we being contentious here or what?' she wanted to know.

'No,' I said, 'we're flirting.'

She gave me a smile that twenty-five or so years of those short teeth had fine-tuned to happen with her lips rigidly sealed. 'Not likely,' she said.

'How come?'

'How come? 'Cause I can't stand men's how come.'

I was relieved to know it wasn't simply me.

'I don't suppose I can really blame you,' I said.

She flicked her eyes at me. Just past her head, I glimpsed someone familiar.

Outside the sporting goods store, my wife passed, notepad in hand, glancing into the window directly at me. Without a shred of recognition, she continued on.

'And if I was interested in men, I sure as hell wouldn't be interested in anybody who was involved with Diane Newbury.'

Ah, I thought.

Ah what?

Ah, she's heard the Newbury-Landau rumor and she's . . . Evidently not jealous. So if not that . . . what?

D.W. stood up, stepped back. 'How do those feel?'

I got up and took several steps. 'Snug.'

'Tight? Or snug? Tight's bad, snug's okay.'

'Then they're okay, because they're not tight. They're only snug.'

'You want them or not?'

'You want me to have them?'

'Has anybody told you recently you're not nearly as adorable as you think you are?'

'Not for a really long time – no.'

She gave me the no teeth smile; my time was up. 'Want to wear them out?'

'Why not.'

She reached for my loafers. Her trapezius popped up like sentinels.

'You work out with weights?' I asked.

'Yeah – you wanna say something cute about my musculature now?'

'I don't do musculature jokes.'

She didn't deign to look at me. She went behind the desk and bagged my loafers.

I handed her my MasterCard, and she took an impression.

'You worked out once upon a time,' she said.

'How can you tell?'

'Residual tone in your shoulders. Flex your delts.'

'Delts, delts,' I said, glancing over my upper body. 'I know they're up here somewhere.'

She flexed her shoulders and upper arms. I flexed. She gave my delts a cursory feel across the counter. Her hands were rock solid.

She looked at the credit card imprint on the receipt to make sure it was clear.

'You should start by walking a quarter mile, then run a half. Warm down by walking another quarter. Do that a coupla days, then up it gradually. And you should start doing at least moderate weight work. Not to put on mass, just to get the tone back.'

'I don't have a lot of time,' I said, knowing as I said it that time wasn't the issue. Nor was desire. I had no doubt that I had to do something about my gut – the thought that two women now had told me in euphemistic language that I looked like shit was intolerable.

So what was keeping me from asking where the nearest gym was?

A radar scan of my psyche quickly picked up a sizable blip: the notion of working out in a gym with a lot of hard-bellied, Y-shaped twenty-year-old students was intimidating.

Intimidating? It was revolting!

Approaching thirty!

'Any suggestion where I might start working out while I'm here?'

'You only have a week left.'

'A week's a week.'

Indeed, she did have a suggestion where I might work out and, further, agreed to meet me there the next morning at six-thirty sharp to help me set up a program, 'if,' she said, 'and only if, you promise to stick to it when you leave.'

'How're you going to know?'

'I won't,' she said. 'I'm just going to have to trust you.' She gave me a smile that disclosed a tiny bit of slightly snaggled incisor.

25

In a show of magnanimity that I could only imagine was motivated by his desire to bang my wife, Howard invited the three actors and Sandra and me to go stomp dancing and have a couple of drinks on him after rehearsal that night.

The six of us piled into Newbury's mortally wounded Datsun and headed out I-10 to a western dance hall.

Howard drove; Newbury sat on the bucket seat beside him, nibbling a fingernail. Sandra sat on my lap in the back; next to us was Rob Davenport, and squashed into the corner was the good-size Skip Donner. We were all neutralized in our efforts to be the Most Compelling Person in the Car by Howard, who held forth the entire trip on the growing nuances he was seeing in rehearsal and their potential ramifications on the ensemble and how those nuances were vastly more interesting than the nuances he managed to coax out of the playwright or the actors in the play's rudimentary original production.

Was he doing this to pump up the confidence of this current company, or was he obliquely criticizing Leslie Ann for my benefit, to punish me for some ongoing if generalized sin against him?

I could see Howard's eyes in the rearview mirror look our way, and I assumed this presentation was as much for Sandra as it was a boost for the three actors and/or a slap at me via Leslie Ann.

Sandra listened intently. I imagined her thinking: *So articulate. So in charge.*

The dance hall was a gigantic corrugated warehouse with a football field-size dance floor and a bar that ran the entire length of one side of the place. Crushed to the other walls were a hundred or so wooden tables.

The decibel level of the five-piece band was too high for conversation, leaving nothing to do but get stinking drunk and dance till you dropped. When we arrived, the University of Texas students and the local cowboys had a big head start on us in both areas.

The bodies were dense and the roadway to a table was full of treacherous turns and blinds. I felt it incumbent on me to lead the way, an indication somehow that I was still a formidable and Real Man, even though I was a guy approaching thirty sporting a rubber tire around my waist whose wife was being seduced by a garrulous midget. I took Sandra's hand as, single file, we headed for the distant wall and a small homestead I could make out through the darkly gelled lights and smoke.

To my relief, she held my hand firmly.

We arrived unscathed and unchallenged under my leadership and took seats, Howard managing with little effort to stake out the chair on the other side of Sandra.

Newbury, clearly, was not pleased with Howard's choice of seat.

Howard ordered popcorn, peanuts, and two pitchers of beer, and then asked Sandra if she wanted to dance. She agreed, and they navigated their way onto the dance floor.

Newbury sent signals my way. I pretended not to notice. She took out her Swiss Army knife, got started on some cuticle snipping.

The others at the table, whatever else they were doing, were tuned to the seduction in progress on the dance floor.

Howard sober was a very good dancer, had somewhere learned to stomp dance (the appellation given to western dancing) – in this case the song was a polka – and he moved Sandra through the herd of bodies on the floor with great ease and style.

For her part, Sandra was such a good dancer that she could even follow me, who had never been noted for his grace on a dance floor.

I felt a hand on my thigh.

'You want to dance with me?' Newbury asked.

I removed the hand.

'Come on,' she said, 'dance with me.'

Sandra and Howard were sailing counterclockwise amid a roiling polka circle, dipping, rising, turning. My wife's face was slashed with a smile. Though I couldn't hear her or read her lips, she was burbling something happily.

Some twisted form of logic told me that better than dancing with Newbury at this time would be to ask the date of some monstrous cowboy to dance. As I scoured the room, I knew what I anticipated happening in that process: I would get the shit kicked out of me by a card-carrying shit kicker and would feel better about many things, in addition to forcing my wife to pay a lot of attention to me.

Across the room at the bar sat the very attractive, blue-eyed, unfinished-nosed, Asian, man-hating stage manager D.W. Cashbaugh. On her left sat a very large human being in a felt cowboy hat and a pair of boots that looked like they'd kicked a good deal of shit.

So, I thought, *maybe the man-hating part was only a ruse to keep me from acting like a male.*

I knocked off the last of my beer, told Newbury I had to go to the bathroom, and headed for the bar.

Halfway there, however, Newbury caught me, grabbed me by the scruff of my neck, pulled my ear to her mouth. Her musty rehearsal breath banked off the side of my head and seeped around to my nose. 'This isn't helping me get ready to open your play, Landy.'

Newbury's fingers were wrapped into the long, curling hair at the nape of my neck. They were blunt against my skin, so short had she sheared her nails with her teeth. 'What isn't helping, Diane?'

'Your wife doing whatever she's doing with Howard. That story about going to temple today . . . !' She didn't bother to complete the sentence, so preposterous was the notion they had actually done that.

I unloosed Newbury's fingers from my hair, keeping her hand in mine. Over her shoulder, across the sea of bodies, at the bar I made eye contact with D.W. Cashbaugh. She shook her head disparagingly.

I peered down at Newbury. 'What will you do if I don't make her stop whatever she's doing, Newbury?'

No dummy, Newbury decided to take a middle ground and see where it led. 'I won't rehearse with my usual ease and confidence.'

Usual ease and confidence?

'You know what I think, Landy?'

'No idea. You're pretty well out of my league thoughtwise, Newbury.'

'I think you want him to sleep with her, so that'll lessen your guilt about wanting to sleep with *me*.'

At the bar, D.W. watched me. 'I think you may be semiright, Newbury.'

'You do?'

'Yeah. But what I think I think more than that is that I don't want him to sleep with her a lot more than I do.'

So I should certainly not continue on to where D.W. Cashbaugh and the behemoth with her sat at the bar. I should turn back in the other direction and go woo my wife, convince her that what didn't happen with Newbury didn't happen because of her.

I turned and looked over the dance floor.

The band was into an up-tempo tune now, a beat to which the stomps danced a dance similar to what we used to call the Lindy.

I started along the edge of the dance floor, looking for an opening to make my way to Sandra and Howard. Newbury followed like a stray dog.

The up-tempo tune ended when I was still twenty feet from Sandra and Howard, and the band started a slow ballad. The current stomp vogue in slow dancing was for the man to just go right on and cup his partner's ass in his hand. As I approached, Howard followed the vogue, and my wife stepped back and gave him a look that could melt Kryptonite. She took his hand and placed it at her waist where she wanted it and rested her head against his shoulder. Howard settled for this, and they danced slowly.

As Newbury appeared in my arms and took my hand and put it on her ass.

Before I could stop myself, I grabbed her by the shirtfront and snapped her up on her hammer tiptoes. 'Cut it out, Newbury.'

'Well, gosh, Landy, you don't have to get *mad*.'

My eyes met my wife's as she caught this sudden act of violence close to her. Howard's eyes followed Sandra's. I put my arm politely around Newbury's waist and moved her the last few feet to our mates.

'Here,' I said to Howard, and pressed Newbury in his direction, at the same time holding out a hand to Sandra.

Which she declined with what passed for cute – rather than mean – haughtiness. 'I'm dancing with Howard, Jay. You'll have to wait your turn.'

With that she took his hand, put it back at her waist, and pressed her head discreetly to his shoulder.

Howard swept her away in a rondure of glitzy turns.

Newbury let out a sob and headed for the bathroom, bouncing off bodies and chairs and tables en route.

26

Outside the hall, the moon was a sliver in the long Texas sky. The light from billions of stars arrived in my eyes, having left home millions of light-years earlier.

Millions of light-years earlier.

I had one of those momentary attacks of anxiety that have come periodically when I've looked up and contemplated the utter lack of consequence of life on earth measured against the infinite and inexplicable universe.

But, I asked my father as we came off the eighteenth green at Normandy Shores just after dark one star-filled night, *how can the universe not end if everything has to end?*

Ishcabibble, said my father.

What does that mean, Poppy?

That means some things you can't explain.

Yeah, but —

Yeah, but that's the best I can do, Rusty. Ishcabibble.

I hadn't discovered in the years since anything that made much more sense than that.

Ishcabibble.

I started walking toward town, following the Evening Star, wondering if it was just possible that everything that had ever happened in the history of this unlikely species had happened as a result of boys wagging their cocks at one another and yelling, 'Look at mine! Look at mine!'

Although such an assumption made a certain amount of sense, it seemed an incredibly anticlimactic revelation for these millions of years of evolution.

A car, unbidden, stopped beside me. I was tuned in to some evolving revelation and, though it was miles to town, turned to say I didn't care for a ride as an electric window whirred down and a woman's face came into focus, the eyes detached and distant thanks to booze and cannabis.

'Give you a ride, cowboy?'

She was alone in the Olds Cutlass with the open sun roof.

'What happened to your friend?'

'What friend?'

'The behemoth sitting next to you at the bar.'

'Just some guy trying to find a way into my drawers. I got no friends, bronco – just like you. Let's go, you gettin' in or not?'

I knew this woman was not altogether cohesive or coherent at this time and that, therefore, I should not get into her car with her.

So I got in, and before I could close the door, she floored it, sending up a tornado of Texas dirt and pebbles behind us. We fishtailed across the center line, and she whipped the wheel right as the big car straightened onto the road that disappeared into flickering Venus and the sliver of moon above. I managed to get the big steel door slammed before I flew out of the car and became one with the earth.

The mind is an amazing apparatus; before my door was closed, it was already concocting reasons to succumb to this woman who might or might not like men and rationalize the legitimacy of such a fabrication in any of the following ways:

Boys will be boys.
My wife is asking for/inviting/demanding it.
I want to.
If she doesn't like men, I'll persuade her to start, thereby enhancing my currently jaundiced and diminished view of myself.
I'll hurt her feelings if I don't. And I must stop hurting people's feelings.
And, finally Ishcabibble.

'Want to smoke a joint?'

'Uh-uh.'

'Why not?'

'I don't do drugs.'

She looked at me with what wasn't quite disdain but exceeded simple wonder by a couple of clicks. 'Jesus, you're a real pansy, ain'cha? Knew the minute I read your play – a wimp trying to write tough.'

The car drifted to her side, forcing her to overcorrect the steering just before she went off the soft shoulder to her left.

'I just smoke some grass, pop some uppers,' she said. 'Drink some vino, some Scotch, some malt and hops. No biggie.'

She looked cockeyed at me. The car drifted left. She snapped it back more or less on course.

'But, hey! Never when I'm working. When I'm stage managing the ole rehearsal, I'm straight as your proverbial arrow.'

'I'm supposed to meet you at a gym tomorrow, and you abuse your body with – '

Finger to lips: 'Sshh, shut it, nix, *nyet!*'

From here, I could look up and see the stars through the open sun roof, or I could look at the speedometer and see she was doing just a mile shy of a clean century.

I was about to tell her to slow down when the notion hit me that this might be a nice way out of it, leaving a veritable banquet of guilt behind me.

If only I had danced with him . . .

If only I hadn't tried to seduce his wife . . .

If only I hadn't complained about what his wife was doing to me . . .

D.W. tried to focus sideways at me, missing me by a scant inch or two. 'That's why you went running off into the night back there. 'Cause you're a wimp. Little wifey making you look like a butthole extraordinaire. 'Cause she knows you porked Newbury.'

'I didn't pork Newbury.'

'Buuuullshiiiiit.'

She smiled at my section of the dashboard. The car was too cumbersome for her hard, lanky body, her delicate Asian face. It fit only her Texas accent and those cold blue Teutonic eyes.

Her struggle to keep it on the road continued. The speed held steady.

She had a bottle of beer jammed down between her seat and the console. I took it, swigged from it.

'Good for you to get put down now and again,' she said.

'How do you figure?'

'Hell, bronco, you got to feel rejection and jealousy and anger and all that cockadoo occasionally, don't you, boy, or how you gonna write about all those feelings?'

We swerved onto the far soft shoulder.

She overcorrected the steering with a vengeful twist

and initiated a little change of pace in the conversation. 'You wear underwear?' she wanted to know.

I looked at her. She tried to look at me – her eyes banged off my door.

'Question too tough for you?'

'Yeah, I wear underwear.'

'Wimp!' she said. And then, 'I don't. Under here' – indicating her ankle-length denim skirt – 'I'm wearing no undergarments.'

'Hmph,' I said.

She eyed the dashboard in my direction coyly. 'You think I'm going to invite you up my skirt?'

'D'know,' I said.

She turned toward me and her breath wafted past me, sour with beer and sweet with cannabis. 'Uh-uh, I'm not.'

Soft shoulder. Sudden shift left. The road seemed to extend endlessly until suddenly the illuminated body of Austin appeared out ahead of us another couple of miles.

Something mean was in the air and I wanted out of the car, but I didn't want to ask her to stop and *let* me out.

'You know what I *do* have under my skirt, though?'

'A teeny, tiny surgically implanted penis?'

The car swerved wildly to my side, hit the soft shoulder, went down into the gully beside the roadway, swooped left, hit the tarmac, fishtailed, straightened out.

'Guess again,' she said through gritted teeth.

'The usual female accoutrements would be my second guess.'

'What else?'

'I give.'

'Come on, what's the matter with you, Landau? I saw the way you were looking at me in the shoe store, right down there just where you wanted me between your legs. Well, here we are, just you and me, one wearing underwear, one not. So what else, go on, guess — female accoutrements and what else?'

I flipped my hands palms up to indicate I was out of ideas and kept myself poised to grab the wheel.

'Like to see?' she asked.

I assumed she was going to produce a joint or a pharmaceutical of some sort. Maybe even a syringe.

The speedometer eased back to ninety-two, and her left hand, which I noticed now for the first time was down below the level of her left thigh, came into view and lifted lazily toward me.

Now that the moment had arrived, it seemed I had been awaiting it for years: a gun in someone's hand aimed at my head — or, in this case, at my crotch.

Death by violence.

And at the hands of an irate female.

Except for the fact that I was scared shitless, it was comforting. Both hands gripped the beer bottle between my legs. As coolly as possible, I lifted the bottle to my lips, sipped, returned the bottle to my lap.

'Take your clothes off,' she said, 'and throw them out the window.'

'Why?'

'*Why?*'

The car swerved left. She hurled it back. 'Because I *said* so. Don't you know how to play this one, bronco? I'm gonna dump your smarmy naked ass out on the highway here and let you think about what a rotten shit of a stud you are for diddling Newbury.'

There was certainly an appeal to that — lonely road,

naked, having to try to get to the hotel, through the lobby, up to my room. Or decide which unknown car to step in front of – naked – and from which to seek understanding, cover, and a ride.

The gun was pointed across her flat chest directly down into my lap from a distance of about three feet.

'You hear what I said?'

'Yes, I did,' I said, 'but hearing what you said is not a sufficient reason to *do* as you said.'

'You think I won't shoot you?'

Before I could respond, she fired the gun. The bullet went out the open window to my right, so close to my nose that I felt a shift in the gusting air as it passed. The smell of gunpowder burned the flesh of my nostrils.

D.W. Cashbaugh flicked her eyes at me, getting real close to making contact, and smiled.

'Now, you take your goddamn clothes off, bronco, before I – '

We used to play a game at the Fifth Street Gym the summer long ago I took boxing lessons. One of us put his hands palms down on the upturned palms of another. The object of this hand speed drill was to see if the person with his hands underneath could slap the hands of the person on top before the top hands could be removed. Of the fifteen of us taking lessons that summer, only one of the Cuban kids was faster than I was.

Whether that exercise came into play now or whether it was simply a matter of D.W. Cashbaugh being whacked out of her head and me semisober, I don't know; but I flipped the beer bottle in my hands to the floor and had the muzzle of the gun in hand and turned toward the windshield a millisecond ahead of her response. The bullet went through the windshield, leaving a perfectly symmetrical spider's web of splintered glass. Then I pronated her wrist down sharply. I heard her elbow joint crack, she cried out, and the gun was in my hand.

The grip was hot and wet, and my heart was pounding in my jaw. I had never been so frightened in my life. For the first time in months, that old fist took hold of my throat and furiously compounded the fury in my jaw until I thought I was going to scream.

I put the urge to cry out into words. '*What're you — nuts? Are you out of your goddamn mind?*'

'Give me that gun back!'

'*Right! Why don't I do that?*'

She threw the wheel to the right, pulled onto the soft shoulder, slammed on the brakes. We careened sideways, coming to a stop perpendicular to the roadway, dust enveloping us like a shroud.

'Get out!' she ordered.

'No,' I said, '*You* get out.'

'What?'

'You heard me.'

'You can't make me get out of my own *car*.' Her eyes pranced defiantly around the very vicinity of my own terrified orbs.

I needed to grab my jaw, I needed to hit it, to rip it off my skull.

Her face swam before me. 'I said, get out of the goddamn car.'

She rammed her chin at me. 'And I said – '

I reached over and grabbed the handle of her door, yanked it inward, and shoved the door out. Then with my foot I shoved her out of the car onto the tarmac. She landed on her drunk, ripped ass, her skirt flying up

over her underwearless thighs, giving me a broad view
of her shaved twat.

I ripped the door shut, hopped the console into the
driver's seat, threw the car into drive, and floored it. In
the rearview mirror, under the sliver moon and the star-
light, I could see her sitting there, screaming after me.

'*You cocksucking cockless Jew faggot!*'

I slammed on the brakes, threw the car in reverse,
floored it backward. In the rearview mirror, I watched
her scramble to her feet and head into the scrub oak
at the side of the road. I slammed on the brakes, threw
the car into park, got out.

'*What'd you call me?*'

Nothing.

'*What . . . did . . . you . . . call . . . me?*'

Nothing.

I fired the gun in the air.

From the foliage came her disembodied voice. 'I
didn't mean the Jew part. Just the rest.'

'That was the only part that offended me.'

'I apologize for that part.'

'All right, let's go home.'

'Where?'

'Home – let's go.'

'You promise?'

'Yeah.'

'No reprisals?'

'No.'

She appeared out of the shrubbery.

'I'll drive,' I said.

'Good idea,' she said.

In the car she seemed a good deal more sober than
when I last saw her. I breathed deeply and slowly, trying
to placate the fist.

'You okay?' she asked.

'Yeah.'

'How come you're breathing like that?'

'I have a pain in my chest.'

'Oh, shit, you having a heart attack?'

'No.'

'Feels like it, though. Pain right up here.' She pointed to the point at which her throat met her neck.

I nodded.

'Esophageal spasm,' she said.

'How do you know?'

'Get them all the time something awful.'

She reached onto the backseat, came up with a battered canteen.

'Here, drink this.'

'What is it?'

'Sulfuric acid! What do you think it is? Water. Best thing for an esophageal spasm. Drink water. Always have water close.'

In fact, now that I thought about it, I was conscious that she always had a large plastic Disneyland glass with water on her stage manager's table in rehearsal.

I drank slowly, watching the road with one eye, hoping I was safe from D.W. on my blind side. The fist released slowly.

'Never met anyone else with them,' she said.

I handed her the canteen. Didn't say anything. Didn't feel like sharing psychosomatic manifestations of neuroses with her just now.

'You threw me out of the car.'

I looked at her. She was smiling at me.

'You threw me frigging right out of my *own* car.'

'You shave your twat.'

Her eyes bounced off things all around me. 'Yeah –
so what?'

'So I just want you to know I know.'

I pulled up in front of my hotel, put the Olds in park,
and got out. I took the gun out of my belt, fumbled the
cylinder open, emptied it of its three remaining slugs.
Held the revolver and the bullets out to her.

She climbed across the console, plopped an elbow on
the rim of the door. 'Still on for tomorrow morning?'
she asked. She took the revolver and bullets, dropped
them on the other bucket seat.

When I was slow to answer her question, she said,
'Just forget what happened tonight. It was a mistake. I
can't drink *and* take uppers *and* smoke dope at the same
time. It just really makes me erratic. What do you say?
Get you in shape, after your wife dumps you you'll still
be able to attract something won't make you puke.'

'Sure,' I said, 'see you in the morning.'

And I turned for the entryway and managed to walk
into the hotel with every hair on my head tingling
with anticipation, imagining her reloading, aiming, and
putting a bullet into my spine.

Bang!

Sandra came in, bumped into a chair, bumped into the dresser, tittered discreetly, bumped into the bed, made a small sound of pain.

I pretended to sleep.

Clothes fell, urine hit water, faucet went on, toothbrush scraped teeth. Rinsing. Spitting. Faucet turned off. She hit the chair, said, 'Shit,' hit the bedstead, said, 'Jesus H. Christ,' and collapsed finally safely beside me, sending the bed into chaos.

I shifted, fought for balance, and kept my previously occupied territory.

Sandra belched. And then I could feel her above me; she was looking down, peering at my face.

'Oombie oombie oombie,' she said, and then fell back and soon snorted and snored in unconsciousness.

I was up before Sandra – probably hours before she would awaken with a racking head – and I was torn between staying here to deal with her when she did awaken or going to the gym, there to deal with D.W. Cashbaugh and to be surrounded by a lot of young, intimidating male bodies.

I opted for the gym.

Where I found myself surrounded not by many twenty-year-olds at all, but by a great many men and women of varying ages and body shapes – some stunning, some wrecked, some merely on their way to wreckage like mine.

I was met by a sober, dressed-for-business D.W. Under the fluorescents and in tank top and leotard, she had a suppleness that was just short of grotesque.

Why would a woman want to make her body look like a man's? Because she hates men and wants to be the male object in a female-female relationship?

Or was it conceivable that, just as I'd once been interested in golf, she had become interested in the sport of body building?

Like a parent, she lectured and led, explaining that on three days I'd work stomach and legs and run; on three days I'd work upper body and run; and on the seventh day, I'd only run.

We 'spotted' each other, and we didn't talk about anything much unless it was related to what we were doing. After forty-five minutes of light weight lifting, we walked briskly to the UT track and then slowly jogged a four forty, walked a four forty, jogged another one, and then walked briskly back to the gym.

Only after we'd showered and met in the lobby and started in the direction of the hotel and the theater did she say, 'I'm sorry about the way I acted in the store yesterday.'

'In the store? What about last night?'

'I'm not sorry about that.'

'You're not sorry about last night when you fired a *gun* at me, but you're sorry about the store where you were merely unpleasant?'

'Yeah, 'cause for you to stoop to competing with someone like Bellman just plain chaps my ass.'

'Where's Howard fit into this?'

She considered whether to tell me or not. Decided to spill it. 'Donner wanted to hire me as your scenic and lighting designer. I went to meet with Bellman, showed him my portfolio, even had a damn good model of a set for your play. He turned me down.'

'How come?'

'How come you think?'

'Because you weren't available for him to boff, I suppose.'

'You suppose good.'

'If that's the case, how come he's letting you stage-manage for him?'

'Donner already had me hired for the season. No way little Howie could get rid of me.'

'Maybe he just didn't like your work.'

She swept her short black hair from her forehead and peered at me with her blue eyes, the hood pulled over them. She knew I knew that wasn't it.

'Is that why you decided to be nice to me?' I asked her. 'Figure I might do you some good sometime?'

She smiled at me. Then the smile was gone. 'Don't let that little sloth come on with your wife or I'm gonna lose the little bit of respect for you I'm currently nursing. Especially on top of having an affair with a douche bag like Newbury.'

'I am not having an affair with Newbury!'

She searched my eyes for the truth, seemed to accept my declaration of innocence. 'Come on,' she said, 'I'll buy you a muffin.'

She made a sharp right turn into a health food store.

Seated at one of the three tables at the back of the store over a whole-wheat muffin and coffee, I tried to fathom what I was feeling about D.W. Cashbaugh. Not anger about her behavior toward me. Not even any resentment of the fact that she'd actually pulled a gun on me (now that it was over and I'd lived, I was thrilled about that). Not a need to woo and win her romantically. Something else.

She carefully divided the muffin and handed me half. She licked her blunt-ended fingers with their neat, short nails.

My sister.

'Let's talk about your drug usage,' I said.

'Forget it. I'm not in the market for a daddy. I had a really lousy one to start with.'

Daddy? I'm not that much older than she is.

She tapped her mug of coffee gently against her lips, testing the heat. Took a sip. 'And where do you come off talking holier than me where booze is concerned? Bartender at Spaniel's says you get started most days at noon. Least I don't start till dark.'

Before I knew I was going to do it, I had her free hand

in both of mine. 'Tell you what – we'll both at least stop drinking to excess and you quit abusing yourself with drugs and I'll make you a deal.'

She looked at the commingling of three of our four hands. She didn't retract hers.

'Let's hear the deal.'

'We both get ourselves under control, and if I write another play, you'll design it.'

'You haven't seen my work.'

'I'll take the chance.'

'Chance, my ass! My work's *fine*!' She gave me some air space to challenge that assertion, and when I didn't she said, 'What if you don't write another play?'

'We'll both have a far more lucid view of our unhappiness.'

She looked at me a long moment. Then said, 'Deal.'

Jesus, I felt so mature!

29

I was only half as exhausted and crippled as I expected to be when I returned to the hotel. It was eight-thirty and I found Sandra still asleep. In the shower I conjured a fantasy rife with D.W. Cashbaugh's sweat and stink, tense musculature and sunny-side-up breasts.

Nothing.

So I called on Leslie Ann – replayed a night returning from *Shrew* when I'd slid my hand under her skirt as she drove us home and we'd made love in the garage of our building on the backseat of her DeSoto, her skirt around her chest, my pants around my ankles – and managed to exit the shower with a passable erection.

Bearing it quickly to the bed, I awakened Sandra hastily (under the guise of ravening hunger) and without preamble (due to the same hunger) managed to initiate sexual intercourse with my wife. She was leaving the next day and not returning until the opening a week hence, at which time I'd worry about a repeat performance.

Inside her, my erection hardened, and, certain it was there for the duration, I slowed down and tried to concentrate not just on boffing Sandra, but on wooing her.

Being better than the person I assumed she hadn't slept with but might be contemplating sleeping with.

But now she seemed to have awakened to the reality of where she was and with whom. Her hands suddenly pressed up against my shoulders, and she said, 'Don't. Stop.'

'Don't stop?' I asked stupidly. I'd heard the punctuation between the two words, but I was flummoxed.

'Do,' she said. 'Do stop.'

I did.

'Get off,' she said. 'Now!'

I slid out of her, flipped over beside her on the lopsided bed, grappled for the head board and balance.

'You can't just jump on me, Jacob.'

'I didn't. How do you think you woke up? Foreplay.'

'I was awake,' she said. 'I heard you come in. I thought if I pretended to be asleep, you'd start writing and forget I existed, so I could get dressed and be ready to go before we had to talk, and certainly before the onus of having sex arose.'

'The *onus* of having sex?'

'I'm sorry – rewrite it however you want.'

'But the point is you don't want to have sex with me.'

'Not right now. And certainly not like this.'

'Where were you going to get dressed to go?'

'I was going to have breakfast with Howard.'

'What if I say I don't want you to have breakfast with Howard?'

She looked up at me. 'Jacob, do you ever wonder what on earth we're doing together?'

No! I thought. *Not now. I can't have this conversation and rewrite this play simultaneously.*

'No,' I said, 'I never wonder that. Why would I wonder that? I love you.'

'Do you know when the last time was I felt that?' She got up on one elbow and stared with real wonder at me.

'No,' I said, 'when was the last time?'

'Weeks ago,' she said. 'Before the store. When you

weren't threatened by me having a life of my own. When you could project that my life was and would remain totally and only your life.'

I truly believed she was wrong, that I thought her having her own life was a terrific thing, and that I had communicated that over the past several months. But the fact that she represented her version of my attitude with such conviction made me wonder if maybe she was right.

'Just having Howard flirt with me has made me realize how long it's been since I felt butterflies.'

'Butterflies?'

This new thing: her fingers ingesting the flesh of my arm into her fist. Squeezing. Hard.

'Last summer, I used to feel butterflies every time you touched me. Now, when you touch me, though, you don't touch me long enough for the cocoons to hatch.'

Oh, Jesus, lepidopteran metaphors now!

She pressed her hand to my cheek. The flesh was soft and warm against my skin. I pressed my hand over her hand.

'Make it feel new again, Jacob.'

'How?'

'I don't know. Take time with me. In our meals and in our walking from place to place and in our lovemaking – or what used to be lovemaking.'

I bent to kiss her. I wanted to make butterflies again, if that's what she wanted. Wanted to not only because her lack of butterflies reflected badly on me, but because she was . . . because she was living her only life with me and she was really a very nice person.

She turned her face away.

'But not like this. Not just now. Later. Soon. You'll know.'

She patted my cheek, squeezed her lips together in a melancholy smile, and got out of the bed, leaving me rolling on a gentle sea. As she headed for the bathroom, I watched her buttocks quake gently as her feet padded across the floor.

'Are you still going to breakfast with Howard?'

She nodded and closed the door.

After three months, she still couldn't pee with me in sight.

I blessed the door and Sandra within.

Pee in peace, Sandra Pollack Landau.

30

S andra and Howard sat down at Howard's end of the
table in Spaniel's that night, he in his accustomed
position, back to the wall, on his knees.

I sat at the other end of the table.

Midtable, Newbury popped Clorets and snipped her
cuticles.

Without looking, I knew beside me D.W. Cashbaugh
had her eyes dialed to the continuing drama.

As for the others – Rob and Skip, the designers and
crew – who knew? The company gossip wire was pretty
swift and comprehensive.

The climactic moment came early on.

'Are you sleeping with me or not?' Howard whispered
to Sandra.

I couldn't hear the actual question, but I knew that
was the gist of it by Sandra's just audible response.

Which was: 'Stop asking me that. I told you, no, I'm
married.'

What Howard said to her next that I couldn't hear
was something like 'He cheated on *you*.'

What Sandra answered, again just audible even though
she was facing away from the rest of us toward
Howard, was something like 'He says he didn't and
I believe him.'

Howard glanced at me, leaned in closer to Sandra by
feigning great interest in Spaniel's cheap wainscoting,
and said something like 'He's lying.'

Sandra's eyes found mine, bounced off D.W.'s, and lighted on Newbury at midtable.

She called down the table to Newbury, 'Did you have sexual intercourse with my husband, Diane?'

That question allowed everyone to quit pretending they weren't watching what was going on at Sandra and Howard's end of the table.

Newbury's eyes bounced off mine, off the table, off the wall, off Howard; she couldn't imagine that question had been uttered aloud, let alone directed at her. 'What?'

'You heard me.'

'No, I did not.'

'No, you did not hear me?'

'No, I did not have sexual intercourse with your husband.'

All eyes moved as if we were at Forest Hills at match point of the U.S. Open.

'Did I, Landy?' Newbury inquired of me.

'Don't ask him; he already gave me his answer.'

'What'd he say?'

'Never mind – I'm asking you. What did you do together the night you slept in his room?'

Newbury flicked her eyes at me. At Howard. At her Swiss Army knife. Then, to her eternal credit, she met my wife eye to eye and said, 'I was scared. He held me. On the bed, under the sheet. We slept. In the morning, I thanked him and I left.'

The game with Howard was over. Sandra knew it and I knew it and each of us knew the other knew it . . . and so we stood simultaneously and said our good-nights.

Hand in hand, we walked the block back to the hotel.

31

She lay face toward me, and I realized the strange styptic smell in her mouth had disappeared at some point since we got married.

Her hand wove itself into my elbow and consumed a hunk of the flesh of my upper arm. This fierce gesture, it occurred to me, was an affirmation.

Of passion. Appetite.

Of life.

It went, somehow, with her hair and the absence of a brassiere.

She went to the bathroom, flipped off the light by which we'd made love, returned to the bed. We teetered, readjusted.

In the dark, we had this conversation:

'Can I ask you something?'

'Please,' I said.

'You won't laugh?'

'Can I hear the question first?'

'Sure. You hate my boobs, right?'

'Who hates your boobs?'

'You.'

'I don't hate your boobs – who told you that?'

'No one told me. I'm with you when you fondle them, I can tell.'

There was something wonderful and endearing about having passed through the Howard/Newbury crucible to this in a matter of an hour.

I pulled her close. 'I don't hate your boobs.'

'You hate my nipples.'

'There's a difference,' I said.

'See, you *do* hate my nipples.' She tried to pull away.

I wouldn't let her. 'You said I hate your boobs. Boobs to me refers to the entire apparatus. And I don't hate your nipples.'

'You don't exactly like them, though. If you were going out to pick a set of nipples for your wife's boobs, you wouldn't pick mine. True or false? And don't lie.'

'True.'

The boy, dreaming his dream, would have put them side by side, naked — Masterson, Pollack — and never known the pleasure of this conversation because he would have dismissed Pollack out of hand because of her nipples.

'Okay,' Sandra said, 'so what I want to know is, would it be ridiculous for me to have nipple augmentation?'

'Say again.'

'Okay, see, they do this thing with silicon. You know silicon?'

'Well, I don't know him personally, but I know his derivative.'

'You're very funny.'

'I think we established that many years ago.'

'I can have it done in Albuquerque.'

'Nipple augmentation.'

'Yeah. Are you laughing?'

'Definitely not.'

'Should I?'

'Definitely not.'

'You swear they're okay?'

'On my life.'

'What if the baby can't get a grip?'

'We'll bring in a surrogate . . . What baby?'

'I mean, when we have one.'

'There's this new concept called bottle-feeding that many women . . . Do you want to have a baby?'

'Do you?' she asked.

I rolled toward my bedside lamp; I teetered, tried to compensate, failed, and hit the floor.

'You all right?'

I got to my knees, found the lamp, turned it on. She had rolled to my side, our faces were inches apart, she on the bed, me on the floor.

'Do you?' she asked.

'What about the store?'

'There's this new concept called hired help. Do you want to have a baby, Jacob?'

'Yeah. You?'

'Yes.'

'Are we pregnant?'

'I have a doctor's appointment when I get back. I'll know by the time I come for opening next Friday.'

'Jesus,' I said.

'If it's a boy,' she said. 'Mary if it's a girl.'

She smiled.

What if I *had* had an affair with Newbury and Sandra found out and she *was* pregnant? She'd be going back to Albuquerque to pack to go home to her parents, seek legal counsel. . . and, if she were pregnant, to get an abortion.

Garbage in the Universe.

But wait a minute.

Yes, I want a baby.

But do I want a baby with my wife?

Yes.
Yes?
What does that mean?
Ishcabibble.

32

At the airport at dawn the next morning, I put my palm to Sandra's belly, kissed her gently, and said something that I thought I just nearly meant.

I said, 'I love you, Sandra.'

33

'Y ou're late,' D.W. said.

I looked at the clock on the gym wall. It was six thirty-two.

Rather than addressing the implication of being two minutes late, I simply said, 'Sorry,' and took on the countenance of someone ready to change his life.

Got to get in shape for a baby.

Little bimpsker, little ootchky, little hunsacker . . .

Where did those names come from – nonsense names of love for a small child?

They could have come only from memory, from Flossie and Morrie the Bear.

She led me through the free weights toward the incline boards. 'What's with you?' she asked.

'What do you mean?'

With mock distaste she said, 'You look happy.'

D.W. Cashbaugh assumed my good humor had to do with her, so I gave her a comradely rap on the shoulder and followed her lead onto the incline board, where she commenced to put me through an hour of the worst physical torment I've ever known.

In my hotel room, after a shower, I looked at myself naked in the funhouse mirror. Though I still bulged grotesquely, though I knew the mind inside the mongoloid head was still the brain that retained the memories of my ten thousand idiocies, I felt differently about myself today. I was, I believed, a notable improvement both physically and morally on the person who had left Stanford five months ago and married Sandra Pollack three months ago.

An improvement even on the person who had come to Austin, Texas, ten days ago.

Despite the unsightliness of the figure in the mirror, I was harboring intimations of hope for him.

Some impulse had made me bring Gertrude Stein's underwear with me to Austin. I felt so furiously full of goodwill and possibility today that I wore them to rehearsal.

34

The next night there was an urgent message to call Sandra when I returned with D.W. from the dinner break (we each had a piece of trout, small salad with oil and vinegar, three glasses of water; no alcohol).

Shaking, hyperventilating, I placed a collect call to our house. The operator let it ring ten times before she informed me it appeared no one was at the number.

I looked at my watch. Her Business Law class in the Extension College began tonight.

I started to place a call to her parents but told the operator to forget it: she wouldn't tell them before she told me, no matter how excited she was.

I sat through rehearsal paying scant attention to the play, fantasizing various versions of the conversation we were going to have in two hours, then an hour and a half, then an hour; finally a half hour, fifteen minutes . . .

And then I was placing the call again and the phone was ringing in Albuquerque again.

But again, she didn't answer.

I looked at my watch. She'd had ample time to get home from the first class.

If she were pregnant, she'd have nobody to celebrate with, so I figured she'd come home to wait for my call. Therefore she wasn't pregnant. She wasn't pregnant and she was upset, so she was driving around or sitting somewhere picking at a hamburger or something.

From Spaniel's another hour later, I placed the call a third time.

This time she answered.

'Hello.'

Not her voice. Disembodied.

'Hi,' I said.

Breathing.

Then she said, 'Jacob.' As if to a stranger.

'Not pregnant, huh?'

It seemed a long time before she said, 'No.'

It's gone.

You went without me.

I didn't want to have to deal with your feelings and mine, too . . . It was gone like that.

'Tried to call you a couple of times earlier,' I said to Sandra.

'I had class.'

'I remembered. Go out driving afterward?'

Breathing.

'Yeah. Figured you wouldn't call till after rehearsal.'

'I was anxious to know, so I called earlier.'

'I'm sorry.' Disembodied again. Not her voice.

'That's all right.'

'I'm sorry,' she said.

'It's not your fault. I mean, we know how babies are made now, we can try again, huh?'

Breathing.

'I'm not sure,' she said.

'About what?'

'That we should have a baby now.'

'Why not?' I asked.

'I just think maybe it bears more thought.'

'You're upset. We shouldn't talk about it now.'

'No,' she agreed, 'we should wait.'

'You okay?'

Breathing.

'Yes,' she said. 'You?'

'Disappointed. But sure, I'm okay. I wish I were there with you, to hold you.'

Breathing.

'Me too,' she said.

'Big day.'

Breathing.

'Yes. I'm going to go to bed.'

'Okay. I love you.'

Those words again. Just right there on the edge of feeling *meant*.

Breathing.

'I love you, too, Jacob.'

'I'll talk to you tomorrow after the first preview.'

'Okay. Good. Good night.'

' 'Night.'

And we hung up.

Standing at the pay phone in the hallway between the rest rooms at Spaniel's, I knew that something very wrong had just happened in our lives – or, more specifically, in our life together, that the period of growth that I believed had just begun, which I sensed was about to take flight, had been sharply truncated.

I felt empty and angry.

And newly adrift.

And I wanted to hurt someone.

The only viable candidates for injury I could think of were Sandra and myself.

FRITZ 'N' FRANZ

1

After the first preview, I made my way backstage.

As I came into the backstage corridor, I hit a wall of well-wishers and theater staff. For just a moment, the sea of bodies parted and I glimpsed Howard at the other end of the corridor, just outside the Green Room.

He was talking to a beautiful young woman with radiant eyes and shimmering raven hair.

The woman was extremely pregnant.

Assuming my mind was playing tricks, I wedged a casual path toward the Green Room.

Hands reached out, voices stroked or offered urgent, brittle advice, and I tried to be both polite and slippery, and not stop as I pressed on toward Howard and the woman.

I was almost close enough to be heard, to say her name, when big Skip Donner rose up in front of me, blocking my view.

'So, *nu*?'

Skip loved to say 'So, *nu*?' He thought it made him Jewish.

'Good,' I said, trying to slide around him.

He blocked my egress. The word *good* standing alone wasn't what he was looking for.

'It was a hell of a first shot,' I said, patting him, nodding, and trying to get around him.

'To me, it felt strictly *farblondjet*.'

'No, no way.'

Farblondjet? I didn't even know what that meant.

'It'll be better tomorrow night, *chas vesholem.*'

I nodded, patted Skip, hit my passing gear, and went around him.

And saw the woman go out the fire door and into the alley.

The president of Skip's board, Preston Forbes, blocked my path. He was with his wife and a man about my age. 'Jacob, there's somebody Bess and I would like you to meet.'

'Good, great,' I said. I stuck my hand out at the man with Mr Forbes and his wife. 'Listen, I don't mean to be rude, but . . .'

Before he could shake my hand or we could be introduced, I lunged through the fire door.

There were half a dozen people in the alley, none of whom was Leslie Ann Masterson.

I ran down the alley to the street, looked both ways. No one who resembled her.

A car pulled away from the curb halfway down the block. It was a big old American car.

Her DeSoto?

I ran down the street. My right calf muscle seized, cramped, tripped me, sent me crashing to the pavement. When I dragged myself up, one of our local winos was inspecting me.

'You see that car?'

He looked in the direction I pointed. He nodded.

'Was that an old DeSoto?'

'Excalibur,' he said. 'Nineteen and twenty-seven. Got any spare change?' He belched and, extempore, the belch was followed by vomit, splashing against the wall of the hardware store next to the theater. I dug in my pocket and shoved a dollar bill into his coat – felt guilty, found a five, added it to the one – and beat it, limping badly, back into the theater.

The cast was gathering for notes in the Green Room, and Howard was just about to go in when I waylaid him.

'Who was that pregnant woman?'

'What pregnant woman?'

'The pregnant woman you were talking to.'

'Some pregnant woman.'

'Obviously.'

'She liked the show.'

'What was her name?'

'I didn't ask, she didn't volunteer. Some woman.'

'Not Leslie Ann.'

He looked at me as if I were nuts. 'Masterson?'

'Never mind.'

He tucked his chin into his chest, raised his eyebrows. 'You really got a little problem where that broad's concerned, you know what I'm saying?'

'I said *skip* it.'

'You smell terrible – what'd you do, puke on yourself? Get some rest, will you, please? Go home, come back Friday night. I need you before then, I'll call.'

'Look, let's just do notes, what do you say.'

'That's what I was about to do.' He snorted dismissively. 'Leslie Ann Nippleface – here. Wouldn't I love that – let her see a real actress play the role.'

A wild-eyed Skip landed on us. '*Oy gevalt*,' he said through his teeth. 'Don't be obvious, but you see the guy with the Forbeses?'

I took a casual look. The Forbeses were down the hall a ways with the young man Mr Forbes had tried to introduce me to.

'Mm,' I said.

'Yeah?' said Howard.

'Rich young investment banker from New York who would like to talk to Landy about' – Skip took a deep breath – 'optioning the play for' – he exhaled a lot of air – 'Off Broadway. His family bought an old theater on the East Side, renovated it; now they're looking for a show to put in it immediately.'

Now Howard began to hyperventilate, the two of them exhaling shallow, sour breath at me from two directions.

'Has to be a joke,' I said.

'How do you figure?' Skip asked.

'How'd he get here? Who told him about the show?'

'Preston, obviously.'

'Yeah, but New York producers don't just show up in Texas and take plays to –'

D.W. stepped into the group. 'Ready?' she asked Howard.

'When I'm ready, you'll see me in the Green Room and I'll be talking.'

'I'm letting them go in twenty-eight minutes.'

'When I'm ready, you'll see me in –'

'Twenty-eight minutes. Union rules.' D.W. walked away, back into the Green Room.

'He wants to talk to you alone,' said Skip.

'Alone?' Howard demanded. 'What do you mean, *alone*?'

'He wants to talk to Landy solo.'

'You sell us down the river, Landau, we'll kill you,' said Howard.

'Sell you down the river how?'

'He'll want the play with none of us regional amateurs attached.' Howard glanced at the Forbeses and the young, ostensible producer. The dementia behind Howard's irises was gurgling.

'Leave him alone, Howard,' said Skip. 'All you have to do, Landy, is listen. Do what's best for you.'

Howard, almost a foot shorter than Skip, now bellied up to him belligerently. 'What're you, nuts?' He swung around on me again, grabbed my hand. 'We're in this together, Landau, we're a fucking *team*.'

'Howard, go start notes,' Skip said, 'I'll be right there.'

Skip unloosed me from Howard's rabid grip and ushered me over to the Forbeses and their guest, a beautifully dressed, rail-thin young man with watery eyes, hollow cheeks, and a top ten Jewish nose, whom Preston Forbes introduced as Jerry Katzendorf.

'Congratulations. And thank you for this evening. My wife wasn't feeling well and went back to the hotel, but she's with me one hundred percent in what I'm about to propose to you.'

I could feel Skip's trembling hand against the small of my back.

Jerry Katzendorf had an American accent that aspired to be British. The result was I understood every syllable he said.

'To get right to the point,' he said, 'my wife and I would like to option your play, put up thirty thousand dollars, and open it Off Broadway as quickly after it closes here as we can get it moved.'

'Thirty thousand dollars?' I asked. 'Your own?'

'If you're concerned about carrying the burden of all that money on your back, let me just say if we didn't have it to risk, we wouldn't. After what we've been through, my friend, nothing scares us.'

What did that mean? Was I supposed to ask?

Down the hall, Howard eyeballed us from the Green Room doorway.

'This cast and director and designers,' I said, 'go to New York to do it there, of course.'

Jerry Katzendorf's eyes bounced off of mine to Skip's to Preston Forbes's, back to mine. 'Well, I think you and my wife and I will want to sit down and discuss whether all the elements are as strong as we can make them.'

Before I could weigh the ramifications, I said, 'No. It can't be up to you and your wife and me. It can only be up to me.'

'It doesn't work that way, Jay,' said Skip, his eyes scooting guiltily in the direction of the Green Room – Howard, the cast, the designers.

'Why not?'

'Because it doesn't. The producer has the money in it, he has a big say in what happens, who does what, and so forth.'

I didn't know whether I was trying to scuttle any future I might have in the theater or making an enormously important decision for a future toward which I was about to embark, but again I said, 'No. The fact is, I don't care whether the play goes to New York or not.'

Nobody believed that – me chief among them – but they politely let the remark pass.

'I'm not saying I won't listen to reason, but unless I can have the final say, I don't think I'd be interested in doing business with you, Mr Katzendorf.'

Jerry Katzendorf nodded his head to a beat I couldn't hear. Three, four, five beats. His eyes searched for a message on the beige, enamel wall opposite. Evidently found what he was looking for.

Because he offered his hand and said, 'Done.'

Beside me, Skip resumed breathing.

'Okay,' I said, 'what happens next?'

'Your agent and I negotiate a proper contract.'

'Agent?'

'You have an agent?'

'No.'

'You don't have an agent?'

'Yes, I don't have an agent.'

'I'll make a couple of calls and get you one.'

'You'll get me someone to represent me against you?' I shook my head, turned to Skip. ''What do playwrights' agents do, exactly?' I asked him.

'Negotiate contracts, circulate your work to the regional theaters, deal with publishers; control amateur and stock rights, hold your hand.'

'You need someone,' said Jerry Katzendorf, 'who's not afraid to make enemies to protect your interests.'

'I have an agent.'

'I thought you said you didn't,' Jerry Katzendorf said.

'Mistake.'

'Fine,' said Jerry Katzendorf, 'excellent. What's his name?'

'Her.'

'Her name, then.'

'My sister — Susan Landau.'

'Susan Landau.' Jerry Katzendorf riffled a Rolodex in his head, thought he found her. 'Oh, yes, at William Morris.'

'No. At Bi-Rite.'

'Bi-Rite? That one of the West Coast agencies?'

'Bi-Rite Shoes on Washington Avenue, Miami Beach, Florida.'

Skip tensed anew, and Jerry Katzendorf looked at Preston Forbes uncertainly.

'Guys, guys,' I said, 'I'm kidding. She used to work for my parents. Now she handles most of the acting and writing talent in Miami and What's-his-name, the big mystery writer down there.'

I didn't know what I was talking about, of course, but neither did Jerry Katzendorf or Skip Donner.

'Oh, sure,' Jerry said, 'the guy who wrote . . .' He waggled his fingers, imploring forth the well-known title.

'Oh, yeah,' said Skip. 'What's-it.'

'That's him,' I said.

2

While Howard finished notes, I went up to the pay phone in the lobby.

Though Susan and I hadn't spoken since I left, my parents and I spoke every Sunday morning, thanks to Sandra Pollack Landau, who spoke to *her* parents every Sunday morning and got me into the habit of speaking to mine by dialing the number herself, filling my parents in on the news of the week, and then handing me the phone for the wrap-up.

It was all relatively painless.

My father and my mother picked up extensions simultaneously tonight. Neither said hello. My mother simply said, 'So, how did it go – the preview? Good, please God?'

My father had wanted to spend five hundred dollars to fly the two of them to the opening, but I had convinced them it just wasn't that important ('A play opening in Austin, Texas?').

Now I said, 'It went pretty well, I think. I mean, I think people were stimulated by it.'

'What kind of talk is that?' my mother wanted to know. 'Not moved, not touched? Stimulated?'

'Okay, listen, there's this guy and his wife, and it seems they want – '

'To put it on in New York,' said my mother.

Totally unable to subvert the smile that twisted my face, I said, 'Yeah.'

'Are you serious?' my sister said, eavesdropping from what I assumed was the extension in her garret.

'Yeah.'

'Ah, my boy,' my father said very quietly, 'my boy, my boy.'

'Susan,' I said.

Susan didn't answer; her intrusion had been a slip, she was incommunicado again.

'Susie,' said my mother, 'speak to your brother, for Godsake, before I come up there and kick you in the *tuchus*.'

'What?' said my sister.

'How'd you like to be my agent?' I asked her.

'Be your what?' asked my father.

'Agent,' said my mother.

'Who be his agent?'

'Susan,' said my mother. 'Morris, be quiet.'

'Aren't there about ten thousand of them in New York and Los Angeles?'

'I think,' said my mother, 'your brother is offering you a partnership, Susie.'

No one spoke.

Breathing.

I waited.

'Is that what you're offering me?' my sister asked.

'Yeah,' I said.

Breathing.

Waiting.

'What would I have to do?' she wanted to know.

'Just the sort of stuff you'd be great at. Mainly ball busting.'

3

The Forbeses, Jerry Katzendorf, the audience, the company gone, I sat alone in the theater, terrified by Jerry Katzendorf's offer and wondering if I'd conjured Leslie Ann Masterson just to complicate things a little.

On one hand, it would be fitting that she show up on the night a producer offered to take me to the next step in pursuit of The Big I – Immortality.

But I had to be imagining it was Leslie Ann.

Because if she'd been here, why wouldn't she speak to me?

Couldn't be Leslie Ann. The woman I saw was very pregnant.

Or looked pregnant.

Of course, Leslie Ann could have gained a lot of weight, could have worn a voluminous caftan kind of thing to hide the fact that she'd eaten herself into obesity pining away for . . .

She was an actor, she could impersonate any character she cared to. Build a fat suit, pretend to be pregnant in order to . . . what?

What month was this?

October.

She was five weeks pregnant when she had the abortion in April.

If she *hadn't* had the abortion, in mid-October she would be in her seventh month.

Why *wouldn't* she have had the abortion?

If she *hadn't* had it, that in itself would be one hell of a reason why she might not speak to me.

4

At Spaniel's I knocked off a shot of Jack Daniel's, took a can of Tecaté, and headed toward the cast and staff, knocking off half the can en route.

Newbury stepped into my face. She was already drunk – or, by the look of her eyes, drunk and stoned. 'Were you really pleased?' she whispered.

'Yes,' I said absently, 'yes, I was.'

'But am I as good as the other girl?' Newbury wanted to know.

'Yes,' I lied.

'You're lying,' she said. 'Howard said I could never be as good as her. She was an artist, he said, and I'm a mechanic.'

'He was just challenging you to peak performance.'

Newbury puffed a mouthful of doubt through her lips, moistening my cheek. 'I think he just basically despises me,' she said with equanimity. 'Would you punch him real hard in the face for me?'

'Maybe, yeah.'

'But not unless I tell you, okay? Where is he?'

'Isn't he here?'

'If he was here, he'd be doing all the talking.'

She had a point. I didn't hear his voice.

I raised my hand toward the bar for another Tecaté. D.W. caught my eye. I hadn't had a drink for two days, since she quit. She wasn't happy I was drinking tonight and she wasn't. I didn't care. I'd told her we wouldn't drink to excess, not that we had to become teetotalers.

Why was I rationalizing? I had a drinking problem. So I was drinking.

'Can I go home with you and you'll hold me and make me believe you're not lying that I'm as good as the other girl?'

'Don't whisper, Diane. Share!' Howard was beside us. 'You know how interested we all are in your every insight.'

'Hi, lovebug,' Newbury draped herself drunkenly across Howard's face.

He wiped her away like sweat.

He looked like he'd smoked a log since I last saw him.

As we moved around the table to sit with the company, Howard reached for D.W.'s bicep, squeezed it, said, 'Big guuuuy!'

'Don't do that,' said D.W.

'What'd you say?' he asked her, and before she could answer, he repeated the question to me, 'What'd she say?'

I moved Howard onward toward his corner, wondering, as Newbury did, just where he'd been.

I took the chair beside him as my fresh Tecaté arrived. 'Where have you been, Howard?'

'Where am *I* supposed to sit?' Newbury wanted to know.

'Sit over there,' Howard said, pointing to an unoccupied table some distance away.

Newbury gave Howard a look that was supposed to wither him. It served only to provoke him. 'Sit over there.'

'Okay,' said Newbury, 'I will.' Petulantly she headed

into exile, peeking back once en route at me in search of help that was not forthcoming.

I put a hand on Howard's shoulder.

'I asked you where you've been, Howard.'

'That an existential or geographic question, Jaker?'

Down the table, I was conscious of the fire in D.W.'s eyes.

Men!

Howard whispered, 'When's the meeting with the prospective moneybag and moneybagette?'

'Tomorrow.'

'Mr Dinero like my work?'

'He didn't say.'

'Didn't say? Who the hell does he think made the piece of shit work?' He poked me in the chest. 'Do not sell me down the river, Jaker.'

'Where you been, Howard?'

He flashed a Baggies at me from a pocket in his ancient tweed jacket. 'Scoring some weed.'

He started to lean away from me, toward Sharon Postum on his other side. I wrapped his upper arm in my fist and held him in place. He offered me his blasted eyes to try to read.

'That's my arm, Jaker. What the hell's the matter with you?'

The matter with me is I'm hallucinating. Must be. Couldn't have been Leslie Ann.

I let Howard go and moved down the table to where D.W. sat. I put my hand on her arm. Her muscles rose up to meet my hand tensely, ejecting it off.

I drained my Tecaté, raised my hand for another.

'Why don't you have a couple of beers?' she asked.

'Why don't you take care of yourself?'

'That's what I'm doing, bronco.' She sipped her soda

water. 'So,' she said, 'what's the next one going to be about?'

'Next one?'

'Play.'

'Jews who hate other Jews,' I heard myself say. 'And hate being Jewish. And hate themselves.'

'What kind of set am I designing?'

'Two sets,' I told D.W. 'An abstract space of some sort and a pier.'

'Where?'

'Miami Beach.'

'What's it look like down there?'

I couldn't think to answer her question. 'What do you think it looks like?' I asked her.

She thought about that a moment, then said, 'Okay,' and told me.

Though I didn't really hear her.

I was conjuring a scenario in which I was Leslie Ann. I went to get an abortion. Entered an office, was put in an examining room, told to undress. Doctor entered, thrust my legs up in the stirrups, came at me with a stainless-steel instrument for scraping away life . . .

Eventually D.W. must have finished telling me what Miami Beach looked like because she said, 'We going to do it here?'

'Yeah,' I said. 'Next season.'

So I'm doing a play here next season.

Hmph.

'Who's directing?' she asked.

'Not Howard,' I said.

So Howard's not directing.

I wonder who is.

WHO CARES! I want Leslie Ann to be here! I want her to be pregnant with our child!

*And, equally, I DON'T want her to be here and I
DON'T want her to be pregnant with our child.*

BECAUSE THAT WOULD REALLY COMPLICATE
MY LIFE!

My Tecaté was set down. D.W. looked at it. I
looked at it.

I willed myself not to drink it.

And drank.

And in the next several hours challenged myself to see
if I could drink more than I had ever drunk before in one
sitting in my life.

In addition to smoking my first joint in a year and a
half in the ladies' john with Sharon Postum.

Who gave me the two Nembutal she said would be
required to neutralize my indulgence so I could sleep
and the Dexedrine tab I'd require in order to reverse
the effects of the Nembies so I'd be ready for rehearsal
in the early A.M.

5

Tapping. Barely audible. Insistent.

Thought I was dreaming I was awakening.

Didn't know where I was.

Head orbiting my neck and thrumming from deep within. Spun dizzily back down some narrow, corkscrewing passageway toward unconsciousness.

Knew I had to go away for hours before I could come back and feel unlike this.

Tapping persisted.

Clock. My eyes wouldn't focus. Just a luminous dial; could only tell that the hands were to the right of the median. So: middle of the night.

My head filled the room, compounded by that insensible state reached by being jolted from an hour or so of deathlike, drunken, drugged sleep into massive nausea and even more commodious guilt that it was I, alone, who was responsible for my current state.

'Who'zi?' I said – or thought I did. No one answered. Maybe I didn't speak loudly enough to be heard.

Walked into a wall, thinking I was heading for the door. What room was I in? Thought I knew.

Felt my way along the wall through the dark toward the tapping. Door. Opened it.

Dim bulb lighting the hallway.

Woman – backlit. Silhouette.

Sandra.

She'd forgotten her key.

I collapsed back onto the bed, clinging to the head-board for balance with one hand. Other hand tucked in.

Drifted down fast.

'Oh, Jacob,' she said, 'are you drunk?'

I tried to deny I was anything but sleepy; the words were a jumble.

Tried to sleep.

But she hit me. Hard. On the side of the head.

And now her fists rained down. Fast. In turn. Bone against bone.

Wham! wham! wham!

I ordered my fingers to grasp her wrists. To stop the blows. Grappled for her pounding fists.

'I'm so disappointed in you,' she hissed against my ear. 'I came to congratulate you, to explain to you, to make our peace and part like adults, but you – '

She let out a bestial cry that set my head to vibrating. She tried to tear her fists free, but I clutched them now and took her powerfully in my arms.

Felt her belly against me – big and fat with our baby.

Instantly aroused, I engulfed her.

'Oh,' I cried, 'my *love*.'

And she went loose in my arms. And our mouths were on each other, our tongues digging in the other's mouth.

Seemed a long time since I'd felt the density of her flesh, the sweet taste of her lips – those above, those below.

Thought I would explode, all of me disintegrating through my penis, and she turned me and climbed on top and slid me into her. Inches and inches of me. Feet!

Then she went stiff and cried out, not in pleasure.

Pain.

'What? What, baby, what? What is it?'

Her breathing echoed in the room – hard, fast, in, out. She was off me. I reached. I couldn't feel her. I tried to open my eyes. Thought I did, but couldn't see her.

Silence, stillness all around me but for my panting and quaking.

When I awoke again it was morning and Sandra was already up and dressed and had gone to work.

My head still felt as wide as the room.

Shower. Take a cold shower and jolt my system back to . . .

Up and dressed and gone to work?

Whoa!

Sandra was at home in Albuquerque.

I had been dreaming, of course, and of course it wasn't Sandra I'd imagined coming into my room, with whom I'd made love. It was the pregnant Leslie Ann I'd imagined visiting me in the night.

I looked at the clock. Six oh-eight.

Twenty-two minutes to get to D.W. Had to be on time.

I headed for the bathroom but caught my distorted reflection in the funhouse mirror. My face and chest and groin were mottled red. My first thought was that it was an accident of morning light striking the glass.

I went close and looked.

An accident, maybe, but not of morning light.

I was covered with blood; it was crusted around my nostrils like hard sugar.

Whose blood was all over me?

It's conceivable I could have had a bloody nose *and* a dream.

Six-ten. The phone rang. I snapped it up, the hundreds

of loose parts in my head thundering against each other.
'Hello.'

It was my mother. Happily even joyously – she sang,
'Good morning, good morning, I've called to say good
morning.'

I made myself laugh, tried to say 'Good morning' back
to my mother with a joy equal to her own.

She told me Susan was en route. She'd taken a red-eye
at four; she'd be arriving via Houston at ten-twenty.

And now I had the urge to cry out to my mother, to
ask her to grab the next flight, come to Austin herself
and be my mommy.

'This is going to be the beginning of a wonderful time
in your life,' she said, 'you and your sister. Enjoy.'

Standing here covered with blood, I had my doubts,
but I agreed with her, thanked her, and came within an
eyelash of saying 'Iloveyou.'

But didn't.

I jumped in the shower.

In there, I scrubbed myself clean of my blood and
thought this: As a kid, from the time we had a television, I remember the family watching the evening
news – Douglas Edwards till Walter Cronkite came
along – every night before we sat down to dinner.
That way, my sister pointed out, we could always eat
depressed. And in fact, looking back, that time of day
– dinnertime – had a palpable feel to it, and the feeling
was one of despondency at the endless stream of bad
news that abounded in the world because of our basic
ineptitude in living mannerly lives within the confines
of twentieth-century civilization.

When Eisenhower occupied the Dominican Republic,
my sister and I were able to understand only that we
were sending soldiers somewhere real close to us and

that it wasn't good. I was not yet the little boy who thought of himself as Big Red Landau, and I was scared to death that I would end up going to war. I had screaming nightmares for nine days.

On the tenth day my mother suggested that we eschew the evening news and that she and my father watch the eleven o'clock news in our absence – after we had gone safely to bed.

'No,' said my father, 'it's important they know what one human does to another, and what one nation does to another nation, so that perhaps when they are in charge of this stinking world, they will fix it.'

I didn't even read the news anymore, didn't watch television at all unless it was a sporting event. I no longer knew the details of what was going on in Vietnam, Laos, in the Cold War. Oh, I knew Nixon was going to China, *but I didn't care.*

Okay, so assuming, as I did, that there was no Supreme Deity – Bearded Male, Big Black Female, Blue-eyed Christ, or Swedish-Cherokee Christa – what was there to believe in . . . if not the notion that when people cried out for help, we should at least *try* to provide it?

6

Roger, the night man, was just heading out when I came through the fire door into the lobby.

'Hey, Rog!'

He waited for me, letting me know as he did that he was doing so against his will.

'Roger.'

'Yes, Mr Landau – what? – I said yes.'

'Pardon me, Roger, but you didn't say yes; you didn't say anything. You just waited.'

'Well, isn't waiting like saying yes?'

'Perhaps in this part of the country, Roger; however, as a visitor here, I am not acquainted with all of your arcane customs and idioms. And, just for the record, Rog, it's Doctor, not Mister. Dr Landau.'

Roger revved his engine in waspish silence, waiting for me to get to the subject of my intrusion into his off hours.

'Did you see a woman with black hair, mid-twenties, about five seven, green-and-yellow eyes – you see her come through the lobby early this morning?'

'I don't keep track of all the hookers who slink in and out of here, *Dr* Landau.'

He gave the 'Doctor' just enough puff adder to make it poisonous.

'This wasn't a hooker, Roger. This was a beautiful and refined-looking woman, so beautiful that even a screaming faggot like you couldn't help but wish you looked like her. Now, does that ring a bell?'

I expected Roger to turn and exit in a huff – in which case I would have to detain him forcibly. But he cocked his head, showed me a nice selection of teeth. Maybe he liked a little abuse. I thought fleetingly I ought to introduce him to Newbury – they could start a support group.

'She came down at two twenty-eight.'

'Not two twenty-seven or -nine?'

'No. She asked me to call her a taxi, and I always log the exact time I call for a taxi.'

'Do you tell the cab company whom to ask for when they arrive? Like cab for Miss So-and-So?'

'Sometimes I do, sometimes I don't.'

'How about in this case?'

'In this case, there was no name.'

'Know where she was going? An address?'

'First she said Fremont Street.'

'Where's Fremont Street?'

Roger pointed east through one of the walls of the hotel. 'But then she said the hospital.'

'Hospital?'

'Hos-pit-al,' said Roger, enunciating all three syllables. 'Now, may I go, *Dr* Landau?'

'Of course. Thank you, Roger.'

'It's my pleasure to serve you here at the Travis, *Dr* Landau.'

Roger started across the lobby.

'Roger!' I called after him.

With a sigh fraught with martyrdom, Roger stopped and waited, his back to me.

'*Yes*, Dr Landau.'

'Was she pregnant?'

'Either that or a repulsively obese female.'

I ran to the pay phone in the alcove off the lobby, called University Hospital, the nearest one.

'Do you have a Leslie Ann Masterson or Landau registered? She would have come in early this morning – three A.M. or so.'

The operator checked, said they had no admissions at that time and no one by that name.

'How 'bout Emergency?'

She could connect me with Emergency and did. When someone answered I asked, 'Did a pregnant woman, twenty-six, black hair, green eyes, did she come in this morning – about three A.M.? She may have been experiencing some bleeding.'

'I'll check for you.'

Breathing.

'Are you a relative?'

Jesus, does that mean she was there?

'Yes, yes, I'm her . . . I'm the husband of her child. Father, I mean! I'm the father of her . . . Look, please, is she there?'

I probably sounded like someone the nurse perceived as dangerous to the pregnant woman in question, maybe the person who had made her bleed in the first place.

Yet the woman's voice was calm and forthcoming. 'Sir, I wish I could help you, but I don't see anything to indicate the woman you described was here during the night.'

'Okay, thank you,' I said. 'Thank you very much.'

I called Michael Pollack's house. Carol said he was at the hospital. Try the office in an hour or so. Could she help me?

No, no, nothing important.

Nothing important.

7

I hustled into the free-weight area six minutes late.

D.W. barely looked at me. She motioned to me to get on the floor for warm-ups.

'Look, my mother called, I couldn't just – '

'Oh, armadilloshit, Landau. You make a pact with me not to drink, said you'd be here at six-thirty, you show up late and wasted. Get on the floor.'

I got on the floor.

'Man,' she said, 'you disappoint me. I mean, are we going to have a relationship in which we play straight with each other, or are we going to screw each other around in the usual fashion? Tell me now, because I want to know!'

But before I could, she said, 'Christ, man, if you're going to presume to tell us how we should all treat each other in your frigging *play*, don't you have to show the frigging *way* by example?'

She whacked me across the shoulder, sending shock waves through my wide-load head.

'Listen, where's Fremont Street?'

'What's that got to do with what I just asked you?'

'Nothing – but I'm not available for an ethics quiz right now. Where's Fremont Street?'

'I live on Fremont Street.'

'Long street, short street?'

'Cheap street. Jesus, man, you look awful!'

'Hey, you don't look that great yourself!'

'Hey,' she said, 'I had a houseguest last night. She woke me up at five this morning dragging in. You tell *me* why I did *him* a favor?'

'Who?'

'Little Howie.'

'What do you mean, what kind of favor?'

'The Howitzer had an outta town guest at the show last night; guest needed a place to stay. Good ole Dubbie could put her up, right? Sure, Howie, anything for you. Guest said she might be in late. No problem, I said, I'll leave the door open. I thought she meant like twelve-thirty, one o'clock. Frigging five A.M.'

'Pregnant?'

'What?'

'Was she pregnant?'

'Yeah.'

'She still there?'

'¿Quien sabe?'

8

My hand trembled as I held the screen and D.W. unlocked the front door to her ramshackle duplex.

Inside, the two rooms were empty.

What remained of her guest was the faint scent of Tabu.

D.W. drove me to Newbury's.

Howard answered the door. He looked very much like I looked an hour ago: deranged from booze and drugs and interrupted sleep.

'Oh, Jesus – what?'

'Where is she?'

'Oh, for the love of God, Landau, who do you fucking think you are? She's fucking sleeping, you fucking idiot!'

'Here?'

'I'm not sleeping,' said Newbury from behind Howard.

'Not her,' I said. 'Leslie Ann.'

'He said I was better than the other girl,' Newbury said, 'so you don't have to bash him.'

'Okay,' I said to Newbury, 'then I'll just do it for my own pleasure. Where's Leslie Ann, Howard?'

'Who?' asked Newbury.

'Diane, please,' I said, 'I'm saying this nice, okay? Don't ask any more questions after I ask my questions, okay?'

'Go to your room, Diane,' said Howard.

'Do I have to?'

'What'd I just say?'

'Go to my room,' said Newbury, and went there.

Howard looked at me through the one eye he was able to keep open.

'Where is she, Howard?'

He squinted out the door at D.W. sitting in her Olds Cutlass. 'Slept at young Miss Biceps', I thought.'

'She's gone.'

'Well, she ain't here, Jaker.'

I moved slightly, trying to block the sun from Howard's eye, thinking incongruously that I wanted his sight unhindered when he answered the following question.

'It's my baby, right?'

One-eyed, Howard said, 'Yours, mine, the business guy's – who knows?'

'Did you ask her?'

'No, Landau, I pretended not to *notice*.'

'What'd she say?'

'That it wasn't mine – what *would* she say?'

'If it was yours, why the hell wouldn't she tell you?'

'She hates my guts.'

'She allowed someone she hates to impregnate her? She's got problems, but I don't believe they extend quite that far, Howard.'

'Whatever you say, Jaker. So how 'bout I return to sleep now so that come eleven o'clock I am physiologically able to lead us, one and all, onward to glory. Whudduya say?'

'Because that's what's important here, right?'

'Certainly is to mine own self.'

'Why didn't you tell me it was her last night?'

'She asked me not to.'

'And you always try to accommodate other people's wishes.'

'Well, that and the fact that I just love to piss you off.'

And now I was out of gas. I didn't know what to do next.

Though I knew I couldn't continue to stand here.

So I walked down the stoop, across the walk, got back in the Olds.

'Now what?' D.W. asked.

I glanced at my watch. 'I need to pick up my sister at the airport at ten-twenty.'

D.W. put the car in gear and, for Howard's benefit, shrieked away in a cloud of rubber, setting off sirens throughout my head.

'You going to tell me what's going on – or am I just your servant?'

'Listen, you know anything about pregnancy?'

'Happens to heterosexual women a lot, I think.'

'Everybody's funny in this group. You notice?'

'I'm sorry – what?'

'Woman's in her seventh month – she can't have sex, right?'

'I'm not sure.'

'And she doesn't have her period.'

'Definitely no period.'

I nodded.

D.W. waited. 'And?'

'And what?'

'And what's all this mean?'

'I'm sorry,' I said, 'but I can't tell you.'

After I'd showered and while I waited for D.W. to come back for me, I called Michael Pollack's office.

'Doctor Snakeski.'

'Micker, I'm sorry to bother you.'

'Please – bother me, I'm up to my elbows in vaginal fluids. Everything okay?'

'Yeah, listen –'

'Play open tonight?'

'Tonight's the night – *Michael*.'

'Shoot.'

'I'm researching a new play. I need some medical expertise.'

'If it's got anything to do with poon, I'm your guy.'

'A woman seven months' pregnant – can she have intercourse?'

'Oh, sure. Preferably on top and not with mindless abandon.'

'What if there is some mindless abandon and some blood?'

'A little blood isn't unusual. You might notice a little spotting in her underpants, say, if you want your character to discover it.'

Most of the blood could have been from my nose, from her pounding it with her fists. On the other hand, a lot of it could have been from her.

She didn't go to the hospital. The baby must have been fine.

Unless she didn't want to hear what they had to say.

'What if there was more?'

'In her seventh month. Is there going to be a *lot* of bleeding?'

'What if there was?'

'You want the baby to be alive?'

'What do you mean?'

'You want the baby she's carrying in her seventh month to be a live fetus?'

'Well, yeah, I mean, who wants someone to be carrying around a seven-month-old dead fetus?'

'Overly active sex – a man, say, with a penis just slightly longer than the woman's vaginal canal – could cause a rupture. If she's bleeding heavily interuterine and she's seven months pregnant, probably looking at a placenta previa or an abruptio placentae – in either of those cases the baby could be fine – or she could be carting around a carcass.'

9

Susan had a contracts book in hand and was wearing a dress, complete with hat.

We embraced. We kissed. And as we headed for baggage claim, she held my hand. Hers was damp.

D.W. moved lithely at my side, taking it all in.

'Thank God Pop has books in all and sundry fields,' she said of the contracts book, talking at a speed much greater than normal. 'I slammed just enough jargon into my head to be dangerous. I also picked up a *Writers' Market*. They have a section on something called the Society of Authors Representatives, so now I know what my ethics are. I figure for now, though, anything they offer, I decline and let them keep coming back until I figure they've made their last offer.'

'Sounds intelligently capitalistic.'

'What about the outfit?' she wanted to know.

'I like it.'

'I decided I need a trademark. Hedda Hopper's dead – I'm going to wear hats.'

'Hats are good.'

She turned to D.W. 'Good or not good?'

'Personally,' said D.W., 'I like it a lot.'

'Okay, take me to these people before it hits me how improbable this is and I come apart.'

In the car Susan leaned forward from the backseat, pulled my head to her roughly, kissed my cheek, and said, 'Thank you, big brother.'

D.W. dropped us at the elegant Alamo Hotel, gave us both a hug, and wished us merde.

'You okay?' Susan asked me in the elevator. 'You seem more nervous than I do.'

I wanted to confide in someone.

'I'm fine,' I assured her.

When we stood outside the Katzendorfs' top-floor suite, Susan filled her lungs with air, expelled it, and knocked with purpose.

Jerry's wife, a pretty, slender woman with wide shoulders, opened the door, wearing the most gracious smile I'd ever seen on a human face. For a moment I imagined that I was looking at Darlene Delvecchio, standing before me in expensive grown-up clothes – no crutches, no lisp, no impending death – and briefly I wondered if life could, after all, heal as well as wound.

'Jacob,' said Jerry Katzendorf's wife, 'God, it's good to see you.'

Mrs Katzendorf smacked her lips resoundingly against mine, then held me at arms' length.

'Dust to dust, my ass!' she cackled.

'I was scheduled to decline into complete incapacity,' Darlene said, 'and Jerry was scheduled to die of a brain tumor. So we became friends last summer through our hospice group as we waited patiently and courageously for the end, but my MS and his tumor both went into remission and we still liked each other anyway, so we indulged ourselves in an inordinate amount of great sex and got married October first. We've inherited a theater in New York and an ungodly amount of money between us, and we want to do something useful, so we're starting an arts foundation and a scholarship program for disadvantaged kids. When Maggie wrote that the play was being done here, we decided if it was any good, we'd go into the play-producing business, too. I owe you, Jacob.'

'No, you don't.'

'Learn to accept gratitude, Jacob, when it's meant. Believe me, I owe you.'

Darlene and I sat knees to knees, hands wound together, alone out on the terrace of their suite. Inside, Jerry and Susan were laughing about something.

'Thank you,' I said.

She nodded her lovely cherub's head.

'How did Leslie Ann know the play was being done?'

'She read it in the paper.'

'In Los Angeles?'

'New Mexico. She wrote me at my parents', sent me an

article from an Albuquerque paper. She was very proud, figured I'd like to know.'

The English Department had done a release that was in the *Journal*. 'But how'd she read an article in the *Albuquerque Journal*?' I asked.

Darlene's eyes consulted something past my shoulder, against which she waged a debate.

'I was asked not to say anything.'

'She was there – in Albuquerque?'

Darlene nodded, as if this were not literally 'saying anything.'

'What was she doing there?'

Darlene looked at me, torn.

'How long was she there?'

Torn.

'Come on, Darlene – do I have to guess and you'll nod or shake your head? Eventually you'll confirm everything and we'll have wasted a lot of time.'

'She was very confused. She said she felt like a lunatic, but she had to see you, see your wife, and "hoped she'd know, amidst a lifetime of wrong choices, the right thing to do."'

'Those were her words – "hoped she'd know, amidst a lifetime of wrong choices, the right thing to do."'

'And she said she'd given up acting and was trying to figure out what she wanted to be when she grew up.'

'Given up acting? I knew she quit her acting class ... But she was rehearsing Lady Macbeth in a big production in L.A.'

'She dropped out. Quote: "It's not fit work for a responsible adult. This idiocy, this acting" – underlined three times – end quote. My dad used to say Margaret was on a different page than the rest of us; you knew you could look at the page, but you couldn't decipher the language.'

'No communication since that letter?'

'Nope. Don't know how long she was in Albuquerque. Don't know where she is now. There was no return address on the letter.'

Leslie Ann, hanging around Albuquerque. Following me. Maybe following Sandra.

Did she go up to Santa Fe to visit her ghosts?

So alone.

'She's here,' I said to Darlene. 'And she's pregnant.'

'How could she be pregnant if she . . .'

Darlene stopped in mid-sentence; she knew the answer before she finished the question. 'Creates an interesting dilemma for you, doesn't it, Jacob?'

Jerry Katzendorf called from the living room of the suite. 'Hey, how about we do this!'

Seated in the living room, Jerry looked at me, looked at Susan. Said, 'So.'

'So,' said Susan Landau, sounding properly agentlike, 'what sort of financial arrangement do you have in mind?'

'We're a little new at this, so whatever you usually do,' said Jerry.

'Or,' said Darlene, 'break new ground, set a fabulous precedent for playwrights of the future to profit from. We don't care.'

They looked at us so openly and warmly that Susan had little choice but to say, 'I've never done this before.'

'Oh?' said Darlene.

'Yeah, that's right,' said Jerry, 'Jake said you just handle actors and that terrific mystery novelist down there.'

'What wonderful mystery writer?' Susan asked.

'What's-his-name,' I said.

'You know,' said Jerry, waggling his fingers.

'No, I don't,' said Susan. 'But it doesn't matter. The fact is, until yesterday I was keeping the books for our family's shoe business in Miami Beach.'

'Oh,' said Jerry.

'That's wonderful!' Darlene said without missing a beat. 'You'll come home to New York with us, we'll go to some hotshot agent and make him teach both of us the ropes.'

'Are you serious?' Susan asked.

'Honey, I may walk and talk like a regular person just now, but I haven't gotten confident enough in my future to waste time screwing around.'

11

The sight of Sandra at the arrival gate filled me with tenderness and guilt.

I held her so tightly she coughed.

'My goodness,' she said.

D.W. drove. I made Sandra sit on the front bucket seat on my lap. I wished for the courage to tell her everything, but she seemed withdrawn, stretched, and that gave me an excuse to wait.

Knowing if I did, I would in all likelihood continue to deceive her.

When we got up to my room in the hotel, she told me she'd been with the contractor and painters at the store all day; she needed to take a bath. I lay down on the bed, trying to convince myself to disappear into sleep for a while.

Take a little nap.

But all around me I heard doors opening, slamming, characters streaking in, out.

I felt I'd awakened this morning into a door-opening, door-slamming farce by Feydeau out of Kafka.

Pregnant dream woman enters from door left, exits bleeding through door right as ... dying friend appears healed and with money to grease the hero's future as ... estranged sister arrives ... mere moments before the young, unpregnant wife struggling for her place in the life of Our Hero arrives to find her husband whirling center stage like a centrifuge.

I thought I heard Sandra whimper.

I went to the bathroom door, was about to step in, kneel on the floor, touch her, but something about the attitude of her head, the stillness of her body, stopped me.

'You all right?'

She didn't seem to hear me. From above and behind her, I could see her hands clasped beneath the water between her thighs. She was staring at her kneecap.

'San, what's the matter?'

She turned. Her eyes were misted over. It seemed to take a moment for her to place me.

I sat on the edge of the tub. She didn't move her hands.

'Sad about the baby?'

She shrugged.

I reached a hand out to her.

After a moment she took one of her hands from between her legs and put it wetly in mine. Squeezed her eyes and the hand shut fiercely.

12

Before the performance, Sandra and Susan met in the lobby.

Sandra knew, of course, that Susan wasn't wild for our marriage.

Susan knew this was time for reconciliation.

When the stiff amenities were out of the way, Susan said, 'All right, so listen, I know I've never treated you with – '

'I never liked you, either,' Sandra said. 'Who knows why. Or cares. I'm willing to start over if you are.'

My sister looked at me, looked at Sandra. She said, 'As far as I'm concerned, Sandra, life began anew, right here, today.'

Sandra smiled a small distant smile, said, 'That's nice, Susan.'

After a little confusion concerning whose arms would go where, they embraced each other.

13

Skip Donner spoke first, thanking the audience of wealthy Austinites for their faith and support, and then he slipped backstage to prepare for the official opening performance of his new theater. Then Preston Forbes, the President of the Board, spoke, dwelling on the importance of the evening and of beginning this enterprise with a new play by a new American (and 'southwestern') writer.

Beside me, Sandra hyperventilated so badly that she had to put her head between her legs.

I stroked her back.

The brassiere was back.

At first she tensed against me. But then she relaxed, and one of her hands reached over to grip my thigh.

Preston Forbes made his exit to the enthusiastic applause of this packed house of corporate and individual sponsors, and Sandra sat up as the house lights dimmed and someone I didn't know seated behind me patted my back.

I watched the play from a distance as my mind slipped away – to Leslie Ann, wondering for the thirtieth or fortieth time today what to do about her should she give me the opportunity to make a decision.

Then I was thinking about what she wrote about acting in her letter to Darlene. *It's not fit work for a responsible adult. This idiocy, this acting.* Surely the same could be said about writing for the theater.

Yesterday I had found myself thinking about returning to New Mexico, to the university, had even prepared the opening remarks for my return to my classes: 'I have returned to catapult your minds onward into space you never thought you could inhabit and experience. Who's ready?'

Trepidant hands rising throughout the room.

I had been surprised to realize I wanted very much to get back to the classroom.

Yet what if this play did actually move to New York and what if it was successful there?

How would I feel then about returning to the classroom?

Who was I kidding? I'd give my firstborn to be a successful (New York) playwright.

But what would Leslie Ann do if she didn't act? Who would she be?

I was dimly aware of the moment when Newbury went through Daphne's abreaction with her fist, forced myself to surface again for her big scene with the two men – which was met with gasps by several of the wealthy Austin matrons around us who could never imagine telling two erudite and attractive men to go screw themselves while you writhed in front of them naked, then set off on your own, crippled and penniless.

The applause at the end was strong and sustained – though nothing like I'd dreamed (the entire place on its feet, going berserk).

Truth be told, though, the play didn't deserve people on their feet going berserk. It was pretty much getting what it deserved: a respectful and respec*table* response.

Sandra embraced me and said quietly, 'Oh.' Grateful for the pride and generosity uttered in that one syllable,

I embraced her in return and said against her ear, 'Thank you.'

Skip stepped forward at the curtain call, silenced the audience, told them in spite of their financial largesse, ultimately the evening happened only because someone sat down at a typewriter and put words on paper.

He called me to the stage.

I received a polite standing ovation, one that occurred because the Forbeses, in the second row, stood up, forcing everyone else to follow suit.

From where I stood and thanked the audience for their generosity in making Skip's dream and therefore my opportunity possible, I could see Howard in the back of the orchestra pointing at himself, indicating that I should bring him up there, too.

'Howard,' Skip whispered to me through clenched teeth.

I pretended not to hear him.

I knew Howard should be invited up; yet I took pleasure in ignoring his gesticulations.

I took a bow with the company, and we exited into the wings, Newbury's fingernails locked into my arm like tines.

'Oh, Landy, I was good, wasn't I?'

'You were great, Newbury,' I told her. 'You were perfect.'

She crushed her lower lip in her teeth to keep from dissolving in tears.

'We probably should have invited Howard up,' Skip said as we hugged each other. 'I said something, but I guess you didn't hear me.'

'Where was he?' I asked.

'In the back of the house.'

'Oh, gee,' I said.

Skip shrugged. When all was said and done, he was as willing as I to pretend we playwrights and actors had done this pretty much on our own, without any appreciable help from some director.

Backstage, in the men's dressing room, a livid Howard bellied me into a corner.

'I really want to thank you for asking me to join you onstage, Landau.'

'Skip said nice things about you before the show started, Howard. I don't feel your contribution was ignored.'

'You just can't stand the fact that I'm a sleazeball who nevertheless has contributed mightily to your life, can you?'

'I'm having some difficulty with that, Howard, yes.'

Unprepared for the truth, there was a little lurch in what Howard had planned as a smooth, indignant exit.

When I turned around, I was face to face with my sister.

She put her hands in mine and said, 'Living with me all those years, you actually learned something about women, didn't you, Big Red?'

My sister peered up at me. 'We're going to own the world, Jacob.'

But not, I knew, with this play.

But I didn't say that now. Instead I let the currents around me sweep me away.

14

L ate into the night, I sat in the Katzendorfs' suite with Darlene and Jerry, Sandra and Susan, Skip and Howard and Newbury.

Skip said we didn't want the review in the *Austin American* to be *too* good. 'The New York critics have to feel they discovered us. That they invented us! We don't want them to love the play but feel they can't agree with some simpleton from Austin, Texas, who's already pronounced the play a masterpiece.'

He was serious.

'Positioning now,' he said, 'is everything.'

I didn't know what that meant but didn't really care to ask.

For myself, I knew the review would be good enough to confuse me about just how much I had really improved the play – whether sufficiently or just a lot – and whether I really had a future as a playwright.

The review arrived. Jerry read it aloud. The review was cautious to the point of feeling constipated – as if the reviewer might have had a conversation with Skip Donner and didn't want to put us in a bad position with the New York critics.

Skip confessed that, indeed, he'd 'coached' the reviewer a bit, but he 'read between the lines,' letting everyone know that the reviewer was really saying he loved the play, the production, the future promise of the enterprise.

Together, all those gathered in the room dreamed dreams about our impending ascension to the rarefied world of the Big I.

As Sandra and I left the hotel with Skip and Howard and Diane (Susan and Darlene and Jerry had stayed together to 'stretch this incredible day,' as Susan put it), Sandra clutched my hand in hers, and having had entirely too much to drink, she sang a loud, rollicking version of 'Give My Regards to Broadway.'

Skip Donner accompanied her by thrumming his fingertips against his lips.

As we passed out of the empty lobby of the hotel into the night, the noise they were making was overcome by the sharp report of a car backfiring, making everyone jump.

Except Howard.

Who was hurled backward into my arms, knocking both of us to the sidewalk.

The first thing that went through my head was this: *They've killed my director!* Not the extraordinary incongruity of holding someone who'd just been *shot*, but a paraphrase of Jacqueline Kennedy's words (*They've killed my husband!*) when JFK was assassinated.

But Howard wasn't dead. At least not yet.

'Oh, fuuuuuuuuuuuuccck!' he cried. 'Oh ow, oh wow, ooohhhh, Jeeeeesssuuuus!'

Newbury, insentient with alcohol and dope, began howling hysterically. Skip lunged back into the lobby. Sandra screamed, recoiled to the doorway, but then came to my side, making me conscious of the choice she'd made, making me wonder if I weren't *buried* under Howard, if it were she out here and me free to hide in there, whether I would have left cover to come to her side.

My scalp tingled. I peered across the lighted street into the darkness of an alley for a glint of metal that would tell me all of us were about to become statistics, but something in the silence told me the assailant was gone.

I tore Howard's shirt open. The wound was not on his chest, not around his heart, not in his abdomen.

'Owwwwiieeee,' Howard moaned, 'owwwiieeee, owwwiieeee.'

When there were no more shots, Skip crept from the lobby and knelt beside us.

'Call an ambulance,' I told Sandra.

She ran into the lobby.

Newbury's caterwauling was piercing my brain like a knife.

'Go do something to Newbury,' I told Skip.

He took off, and moments later her voice receded into the hotel.

I pulled Howard's leather sports jacket down off his shoulders. He was bleeding profusely but evenly below his left collarbone. I eased him over. The bullet had not passed out his back.

I yanked off my sports jacket and pressed it to the flow of blood. When I looked at Howard's face, he was staring into my eyes with dilated pupils. With Howard, that could be shock or it could just be the result of his pharmaceutical excesses.

Sandra ran back out, knelt beside me again. 'Get his legs higher than his head,' I said.

She sat at Howard's feet and put his legs up on her lap.

I put one hand under his head and my other one to his forehead.

'It's okay. It's not an artery, you're not losing that much blood.'

'Owwwwiieeee,' he said quietly, 'owwwiieeee, owwwiieeee.'

'Jesus,' I heard someone say, 'that Feydeau, that Kafka.'

'What, Jay? What'd you say?'

Evidently the someone who had spoken was me.

I patted Howard's head, stroked his forehead.

He said something. I lowered my ear to his lips.

'Didn't hear you,' I said.

'Dying word,' he whispered. 'Just in case.'

'Dying word?' I asked. 'Just one?'

He nodded. I waited.

'Hunger,' he whispered. 'Put it on my tombstone,' Howard said.

The first siren was audible in the distance.

Newbury materialized at my shoulder. Her body was whipping like a flag in the wind. 'Is he going to diiiiiieeee?' she cried.

'No,' I said, 'no such luck.'

I may have imagined it, but I thought I detected behind Newbury's eyes just a twinkle of disappointment.

Two sirens now, coming from different directions.

Howard mumbled again. I leaned close. 'I just figured it out.'

'What?' I asked.

'You arranged it,' he said against my ear.

'To have you shot?'

He raised his eyebrows.

'Why would I do that?'

He aimed his eyes past me. To where Sandra knelt.

'You knew you were losing her to me.'

Was he serious? Did he actually think I arranged to

have a piece of metal propelled through the air and into
his body, threatening his very life?

Yes.

And except for the fact that I happened to know I
hadn't arranged it and knew who did, it made perfect
sense that I might have.

'Talk to me, Jaker,' said Howard.

'What was Feydeau's first name?'

'Feydeau?'

'Yeah – you know his first name?'

'Oh, sure,' said Howard, 'Fritz.'

'Fritz Feydeau? I don't think so.'

'Yeah, definitely.'

I remembered now that it was Georges.

But I liked Fritz better.

'Fritz 'n' Franz,' I said.

'Had a pastrami and Swiss on a hard roll there just
ten, fifteen years ago,' said Howard. 'Fritz 'n' Franny's.
We were only kids then, Jaker, you on the road to being
a famous lonely guy golfer, me to being Colonel Chaim
Bellman, Israeli tank ace.'

He smiled into my eyes. 'Talk some more, Jaker.'

I was about to tell him about Israeli Tank Captain Jake
Londovnik when a wave of pain slammed Howard's eyes
shut and he puffed like a sprinter at the end of a two
twenty.

An ambulance and a police car howled to a stop at the
curb, and two cops in blue and two Emergency medical
attendants in white descended on us and took over.

The medical guys put Howard in the ambulance and
packed the hysterical Newbury in with him.

By the time Sandra, Skip, and I finished with the
cops and arrived at the hospital, packed in Skip's VW
bus with Susan and the Katzendorfs (who came out

with most of the other guests in the hotel when the sirens stopped below them), Howard was in surgery and Newbury had been tranquilized.

We waited the forty-five minutes it took them to remove the bullet and send Howard up to intensive care (just as a precaution, we were assured).

Then Skip dropped Susan and the Katzendorfs at the Alamo and Sandra and me at the Travis before he took Newbury home.

I had Howard's blood on my hands and clothes (two days in a row, someone's blood on me), and I stood at the sink and washed myself with a washcloth, thinking that for all the sympathy I felt toward him on the street back there, I would not have regretted Howard Bellman's death.

Beside me, Sandra took the washcloth from my hand and turned her face up. Opened her mouth to me.

I bent to meet her lips, remembering that it had been a while, maybe a long time, since she had offered herself to me with any real desire.

I slid my hand up under her short skirt and slipped my middle finger around the edge of her panties. And stopped.

'I can't do this now. I have to go somewhere.'

She stared up at me, the bloody rag against my chest where she was huddled. 'Can I go?'

Between her legs, against her pubis under the edge of her panties, my fingers were warm. It was with real regret that I removed my hand. 'No,' I said.

'Why not?'

'Trust me.'

She thought about that a moment before she said, 'Okay.'

15

I took a cab to D.W.'s. When she opened the door, I banged her in the chest, sending her careening across the room onto her couch.

'Are you crazy?' I demanded.

'Who you hitting? Don't hit me!'

'*Are* you? Huh? Nuts?'

'What're you talking about?'

'What do *you* think I'm talking about?'

'I got no idea. But I'm warning you, don't come in here and – '

'Where were you an hour and a half ago?'

'Here.'

'Can anybody corroborate that?'

'What are you – the cops?'

'Consider this practice for the real thing.'

'What happened?'

'Do we really have to play this out? What happened is you *shot* Howard Bellman.'

'Did I kill him?'

'No,' I said. 'You wounded him in the shoulder.'

D.W. snapped her fingers in regret. Then something cut loose in her face, came at me as concern. 'You're serious.'

'Yes, I am, I am serious.'

'Somebody shot Howard?'

'That's right.'

'With a gun?'

'Correct again.'

'Wasn't me. If I'd shot at him, he'd be dead.'

It wasn't her. Unless she was a better liar than I thought she was.

'Unless you just wanted to scare him.'

'Wouldn't bother. You can't scare people like him. You gotta kill 'em.'

Definitely wasn't her.

'What's the prognosis?' she asked.

'He'll be fine.'

'That's really too bad. You tell the cops it was me?'

'I told them I had no idea who might have done such a thing.'

'So, you thought it was me and you protected me. That's nice.'

16

The elevator in the Travis smelled of Tabu.

Instead of getting off at my floor, I went back downstairs.

'Roger.'

'Yes, *Dr* Landau.'

'Stop calling me *Dr* Landau, Roger.'

'I thought you wanted me to call you *Dr* Landau.'

'I want you to call me Dr Landau, not *Dr* Landau.'

Roger pretended to be baffled by the distinction and waited for me to tell him what else I wanted.

'Remember the woman who had you call her a cab at two twenty-eight yesterday morning?'

'Yes, I certainly do.'

'Does that woman happen to be staying here tonight?'

'I'm not at liberty to dispense information about guests of the hotel, Dr Landau, without their permission.'

'So she is staying here.'

'I couldn't say.'

'What if I want to call her room on the off chance she *is* staying here. If I picked up the house phone, for instance, and said, "Would you ring Miss Masterson's room?" what would you say to that?'

'I'd say there's no Miss Masterson staying here.'

'Miss Carmine.'

Roger shook his head.

'Any other Landaus here tonight, Roger?'

'Just you and the missus.'

'Is the woman who asked for the cab last night here tonight, Roger?'

'I'm not at liberty to say, Dr Landau.'

'If I offered you money?'

'How much?'

'Twenty dollars.'

Roger smiled.

'Fifty?'

I didn't *have* fifty.

'I'm afraid not.'

'How much?'

'Five thousand.'

'A little steep for me.'

Roger shrugged. 'I have to do the books, Dr Landau. So if you'll excuse me.'

I took the elevator to the second floor. I walked the halls, sniffing.

I did the same at floors three through nine.

They all smelled to me of Tabu, which, I assumed, had more to do with my nose than with Leslie Ann's whereabouts. She had probably not laid down a Tabu trail throughout the hotel.

I went back down to the lobby. Roger was just visible in the office behind the desk. I got on my knees and crawled past the front of the desk, around its edge, and behind it. I knew the Travis had an old-style register. I figured Roger was working from the little cards on which they kept individual room and phone charges. The register, I thought, just might be . . .

Where I found it. On the first shelf just under the top of the front desk.

I looked toward the office. I could see only Roger's feet from here. He had his shoes off. He had a hole in one sock, his big toe protruding; the toe had an extremely long nail. He rubbed his feet against each other like a cricket, making the sound of Orlon against Orlon.

I slipped the register off the shelf and onto the floor, where I was perched on my knees.

It took me all of fifteen seconds to find the name she was using, Lorna Greene (in tribute to *Bonanza*'s Lorne, obviously), and to discover that she was staying in the room next to mine.

Upstairs, I tiptoed down the hall, past my room to the next.

For a moment I thought we were in the midst of an earthquake.

Then I realized my entire body was trembling.

What am I going to say to her?

Play it by ear.

Action. Reaction. Behavior.

I shook my hands hard, as if that would stop their shaking, and turned the knob cautiously, anticipating that it would be locked, that I would have to then decide whether to knock or go through Sandra's and my room onto the ledge and climb one room over and hope the window was open.

Clearly, little with Leslie Ann Masterson was as it should be, though.

And therefore I found the door unlocked.

The trembling intensified, and the tanks appeared magically in my chest.

I breathed deeply, evenly.

And I opened the door as quietly as the age of the hinges would permit, which is to say not that quietly.

I stepped inside.

The bathroom door was cracked an inch. By the strip of light coming from within, I could see the brass double bed in the room was empty, had not been slept in that evening. I crept to the bathroom door and, with a forefinger, poked it open.

Empty.

She was gone.

Where?

D'know.

What did I do now?

Hang out with Fritz and Franz. Watch all doors.

17

Sandra was in the shower.
It was after four in the morning.
There was a sealed hotel envelope with my name on it on the bureau just inside the door.

I recognized the handwriting instantly.

Inside the envelope was a folded sheet of stationery. I opened it.

The note said: 'I was aiming at you.'

I tore the note in half, into quarters, dropped it in the wastebasket on my way into the bathroom.

Where I poked my head around the edge of the shower curtain. Sandra's eyes were closed. Ice-cold water bombarded my face. 'You all right in there?'

'Sobering up,' she said, 'and trying to have a revelation.'

'Ah,' I said. 'What about?'

'The future.'

'The world's?' I asked. 'Ours?'

'Ours,' she said.

'How's it coming?' I asked.

'I haven't had an epiphany yet.'

I was aiming at you.

'No epiphany yet, huh?'

'None yet.'

'I'm sure, at an appropriate moment, it will epiph,' I said.

I just learned that someone had tried to kill me, and I was being cute.

Sandra opened her eyes. Bored holes through me with them.

'What?' I asked.

She turned off the cold water knob and pushed the curtain back.

I held out a towel. She took it.

But made no move to dry herself.

'Kneeling together over someone *shot*, with a *gun*, in the *street*,' she said. 'Then wanting you inside me.' She shook her head. 'Talk about inappropriate.' She seemed to consult silently with someone off her shoulder. 'It's such a shame to live a lie when life's so precarious.'

'What lie is that, San?'

'This. Us. I came here in a panic, carrying a message for you.'

'Message from whom?' I asked her.

'From me,' she said.

'What's the message?'

And she said, 'That I'm having an affair and I don't know if I want to stay with you.'

I laughed.

She smiled.

My laugh was fatuous, her smile was sympathetic; behind my laughter was doubt; behind her smile was the truth.

And so I understood why she was staring at her kneecap earlier in the bathtub.

She stood naked, glistening in the shower, towel held demurely to her breasts, and she looked me in the eyes. 'I went home from here last Sunday very confused about you and what it looks like you may become and how I fit into that; and I went to the doctor hoping I wasn't pregnant. But when he told me I wasn't, I started crying and couldn't seem to stop. Even in my class, the first meeting of my Business Law class, it was obvious I was a mess, and the professor asked me afterward if I was all right and I said no, I wasn't, and he asked me if I wanted to have a drink, and I said sure . . . and we ended up at our house having sex. In our bed — yours and mine. I was there when the phone rang the first time.'

She traced the line of a small scab along her collarbone with a fingernail. She'd started doing her own fingernails every other week now, keeping them shorter than before, covered only by clear polish.

'I wanted to start getting even, I guess, for all the sins I assumed you were going to commit against me over however many years we managed to stay married to each other.'

Oh, Fritzy! Oh, Franz!

You tummlers, *You clowns!*

Do you guys know how to thicken up a plot or what!

She raised her palms to me. It was my turn.

To react.

Behave!

I was immobilized. I was furious and mortified and certain I'd gotten what I deserved, and I loathed her for giving it to me — she, my wife standing naked and unapologetic before me — and I thought by some birthright I was permitted to bash her in the mouth, and thinking I would do that now, I heard myself preface the punch with these words: 'I forgive you.'

'What?'

What!

'I forgive you.'

'No, you don't.'

Face tight with fury, I said, 'I do!'

'How can you?'

'I don't know, Sandra – I just do.'

'Then why are you shouting?'

'Because I'm so angry I can hardly see.'

'Then you obviously don't forgive me.'

Like a chill, the anger passed. I shook my head in awe at what I was about to say. 'I think,' I said, 'that I'm falling in love with you.'

'You think you're . . .'

'Yeah, yes – what I said. What I said is what I meant – I meant what I just said, Sandra, now don't get me really pissed.'

I was frightened. Frightened of the doors opening and closing in what was, in fact, not a Feydeau-out-of-Kafka farce, but my only life.

I spun around on the wet floor and went into the room, dumped myself on the bed. Rolled. Balanced.

The towel around her, Sandra stood over the bed.

'You weren't in love with me before?'

'No, no, I definitely wasn't in love with you before.'

She sat on the edge of the bed. 'Why'd you marry me, then?'

'Same reason you married me.'

'Why was that?'

I raised a hand to her face. To her cheek. Soft and strong and vulnerable against my palm. 'D'know,' I said. 'Mostly bad reasons. But I know right now we're even. We start from scratch.'

'How do you mean, even?'

And I told her about Leslie Ann Masterson, up to and including the night before last and the contents of the envelope that was on the bureau when I came in the room fifteen minutes ago.

When I was finished Sandra got off the bed, the towel pressed around her, and stood by the only window in the room. She stared into the alley below. Quietly she said, 'I know we're supposed to be in the midst of a great sexual revolution and that people are having children out of wedlock all over the place, but, Jesus, Jacob.'

'I told you, I'm not sure it's my child.'

'What was she doing in your room, Jacob, on top of you, why did she try to *shoot* you, if it's not your child? I'm trying to understand this, Jacob, but I'm having a hard time being as open-minded and mature about it as you seem to be.'

She turned her eyes heavenward. Closed them. Her shoulders dropped. 'I'm too tired for any more of this now.'

'Want to sleep?'

She nodded.

She put on her silk shorty pajamas, turned off the bathroom light. Felt her way back to the bed. Lay beside me.

We didn't touch.

It was a while before she said, 'I can't sleep next to you. Whoever's the guiltier should go sleep in the chair.'

'I figure that's me.'

'I figure it's probably a toss-up, but I'm too tired to argue.'

I slid off the bed and went to the small armchair next to the desk.

I sat there.

Soon I knew Sandra slept.

Above somewhere a door slammed.

She didn't stir.

GARBAGE IN THE UNIVERSE

1

Wherever I went in Albuquerque, I looked for her.

Partly out of concern for my life; more, I thought, out of concern for hers and her baby's.

If I saw her, though, what would I say to her?

First I would confirm she was carrying *my* child.

And then what?

D'know.

I was only certain that she haunted my days and nights and that, despite the fact she'd shot at me, my first feeling when I dwelled on her was tenderness, the second anger.

The anger, I thought, as always, came equally from her actions and my inability to comprehend and deal with them.

I believed somewhere in me that she was struggling to find *amidst a lifetime of wrong choices, the right thing to do.*

Maybe I was kidding myself.

Maybe I was nuts.

Not fit work for a responsible adult. This idiocy, this acting.

My mind wandered a hoary psychological trail, projecting her father and Big Vince Carmine into the role of Macbeth, her mother, her stepmother into the role Leslie Ann found herself endeavoring to play in a sympathetic manner.

Thought this: I could see where a person whose father had abused her, whose mother had been both 'perfect' and in all likelihood a silent accomplice in the father's abuse, wouldn't want to play Lady Macbeth because, just as she'd told me on the phone, 'She's an awful person.' Was it possible at the most elemental level that Leslie Ann, for all her ability to disappear into other people – roles – even right there on the brink of becoming the actor she dreamed of becoming – that she wanted above all else to be a sane and solid version of herself living in the real world?

Be a mom who could provide for her child the one thing that, ultimately, wasn't provided for her: safety from harm from within her family?

If I'm the father – if Howard or Big Vince is the father – how do we help provide that safety?

My initial thought was this: We're too selfish, each of us, to do that by our presence, and so we could best do it by our absence.

But, of course – if it was my child – that might not be the best way; only the easiest.

Maybe I was missing the most obvious answer: She had 'become' Daphne, the character I had created with her. Locked into a marriage with a man unequal to her needs and a past she couldn't escape, she had seen no alternative but to contrive – with me – to destroy her marriage relationship and to assert her 'independence'; yet, now outside the role, alone, pregnant, she was sick of 'becoming' other people, she was frightened and . . .

The goddamn woman made my brain hyperventilate.

Jesus, I was confused about everything. Leslie Ann and the Thing in her belly. Sandra. Our marriage.

I really wanted to have at least a peek at Sandra's Business Law professor, but she asked me to let it go, and so I didn't go to see him and I tried to let go of that too.

Didn't do very well.

Starting even, Sandra and I decided, was a commendable idea. And as easy to talk about as it was difficult to achieve. We would hope, in the six weeks until the play opened, merely to hold steady, and then when we knew what fate held in store for the play, we would move forward, if forward seemed the appropriate direction.

For the next four weeks I tried not to watch Sandra for signs of inconstancy, for lies.

Tried not to feel watched myself.

She slept in our bed, I slept on the couch.

Until she came to get me one night and told me to come into the bed with her. Where we touched, at first, like strangers. And then with an intimacy way beyond what we'd experienced with each other before.

She didn't try to explain it.

Neither did I.

And yet, her body warm and protective against my back, her arms circling my waist, I imagined Leslie Ann with her bulging belly in her position in our bed in Palo Alto, tucked safely into my chest and hips, hands drawn in, my arms around her, she, her child protected from wolves, me enclosed front and back by the three of them.

Someone stuck this, typed, to my door one day: 'Me only cruel immortality / Consumes; I wither slowly in thine arms, / Here at the quiet limit of the world.'

My first thought was Leslie Ann. But something said no, wasn't her type of poem. Too explicit.

Therefore, someone in the department.

Thus, the classic academic's panic struck: I didn't know whose lines those were. And I was embarrassed to go to anyone else in the department who might know, for fear of being held up to ridicule. Realistically, I knew that someone with a Ph.D. in Literature wasn't expected to know every line of everything written by everyone who'd ever taken pen to paper.

But that was reason talking. And what did that have to do with behavior?

So I closed the door to my office, pretended to be immersed in class preparation, and spent three hours searching my *Norton Anthology of Poetry* for the goddamn lines.

Didn't find them.

Knew all day every day I was there that I was being wished ill by someone in the department who doubtless smiled to my face.

A curious conceit – to feel disposed to become someone I wasn't sure I wanted to become so I wouldn't have to face the satisfaction of those who didn't want me to become that person.

In restless sleep at night, my fantasies were more nightmare than dream.

I sent rewrites to Howard in Austin; he rehearsed them into the show with the three actors, who waited there with him, tending, stoking, champing.

Waiting for the weeks to pass so we could get on with it.

I looked out the window of my office. Since I'd left and returned, the grass beyond the English building had turned brown. In the fall afternoon students sat in singles and twos and little groups. Others passed left and right.

As a matter of habit now, I looked into the corners, the doorways and shadows.

On my door: 'I asked thee, 'Give me immortality.' / Then didst thou grant mine asking with a smile, / Like wealthy men who care not how they give.'

In what I told myself was at least a modest act of maturity, I took both snatches of poetry to Dr Joel D'Amico's office before our weekly faculty meeting. I managed to resist pretending I knew who the lines were written by and was merely quizzing him, and simply asked, 'Who the hell wrote these?'

Dr Joel read the first snatch. Read the second. Read the first again. Held one under the other. Looked at me. 'Little thoughtful for Coleridge. Not passionate enough for Keats. Heck if I know.'

Dr Joel carried both snatches into the faculty meeting, was discreet enough not to hold me up to potential ridicule by connecting the unknown lines to me. Votes went as follows: Matthew Arnold, 2; Coleridge, 3; Edward Fitzgerald, 1; Robert Browning, 1; an unknown graduate assistant, 3; abstentions, 11.

The next morning there was a note on my door on departmental stationery. Different typewriter. 'Tennyson. "Tithonus." If you want to say you figured it out, I'll never say otherwise. A Friend.'

At first I thought, *What a nice gesture*. Then paranoia took over: *Why not sign his or her name, let me know who my friend was?*

Because I take the advice, announce at the next faculty meeting I figured it out, this person stands up, says Bullshit, tells the story. Humiliation! Scandal!

I locked my door, got out my *Norton*, found 'Tithonus,' read it three times, dwelling on these lines, packing them away for future use in the event I came home in

December bearing with me the wrath and indignity of the New York critics:

> Let me go; take back thy gift.
> Why should a man desire in any way
> To vary from the kindly race of men,
> Or pass the goal of ordinance
> Where all should pause, as is most meet for all?

And then I wondered whether Leslie Ann was the responsible party, after all, and had assumed I would find the rest of the poem and understand she wasn't just taunting me but crying out for herself as well ('take back thy gift'), telling me in some dizzy, tortuous way that she was inviting me to 'the goal of ordinance,' to be husband and father to her mother and wife 'at the quiet limit of the world.'

Quiet limit of what world?

Not this one!

Why not come forward, stand at the door in place of Tennyson, at least recite the goddamn words to me herself?

Because!

Because, though in my infinite, analytical, interpretative wisdom I couldn't explicate the son of a bitching sense of it, I knew it made sense.

Leslie Ann sense. Complicated, loony, human being sense.

Sun of God sense!

She couldn't stand in my doorway because she couldn't.

Blessedly, the future arrived and I got to leave for New York and the pick-up rehearsals that would lead at least to a definitive and final verdict about this play I started writing to impress the woman of my dreams.

On the plane, I walked the aisle, front to back, looking for her.

Not there.

2

Thanksgiving week I was staying at the Algrove, a small apartment hotel on West Seventy-second Street between West End Avenue and Columbus, when Sandra, Neddie and Ernie, Michael and Carol, and my mother and father arrived.

My mother and father were prepared to move into Susan's just rented, barely furnished, postage stamp-size apartment in Greenwich Village when Ernie insisted that everyone move into the Plaza on him, Sandra and I, and Michael and Carol sharing a three-bedroom suite with Ernie and Neddie, my parents in a spacious double.

There was no way my father could accept this.

And no way he could turn it down.

So the trick was to come up with a way to accept the offer that didn't sound as though he were doing it because there was no way he couldn't do it.

Sandra solved the dilemma. She whispered to my father and my mother, 'Jay would feel much better knowing you were close.'

'Ah,' said my father.

'I know Sandi's right,' said my mother.

And my father accepted this offer from Ernie Pollack, which made him froth at the mouth with resentment but, at the same time, allowed him the comforts of the Plaza. And the best part, as Ernie put it, 'the whole fam damily's together for this mitzvah.'

Standing in one of the corner minarets in the Edwardian living room the next morning, looking far down, I saw a pregnant woman, bundled against the November freeze, her long black hair swirling about her face in the wind. The woman stood beside the fountain in front of the Plaza, almost seeming to look up at where I stood.

The hard winter sunlight bounced off the concrete around her, making walls, an eerie oubliette, down into which my eyes peered, trying to read in her blazing eyes madness or enlightenment. An imaginary hand left my side, traveled below, through the stories of air, into her prison to her cheek.

And in my ever evasive, disordered soul, I heard a voice say, 'Don't be my child.'

And another say, 'Do!'

The hand that touched the woman's cheek stroked . . . then punched. Stroked. Punched.

Feeling foolish but unable to resist satisfying the foolishness, I told Sandra I was going over to the theater.

'I thought they didn't need you this morning,' Neddie Pollack said.

'So he's going anyway, Mother,' said Sandra.

'Have you heard of being nervous, Nedra?' asked her son, Michael. 'The word *anxiety* ring a bell?'

Sandra nodded at me, reassuring me that on the day before my first New York opening, a little eccentricity was perfectly acceptable.

Michael Pollack asked if I minded if he walked a ways with me.

3

By the time we had ridden the elevator down and come out the revolving doors on the east side of the hotel, the woman was gone.

I need to talk to you, Leslie Ann.

I looked back up toward our corner suite. It was impossible to distinguish anything in the windows from here.

Michael and I set out north on Fifth Avenue along the park.

'Don't say anything until I'm finished,' Michael said. 'Okay?'

I nodded.

The sidewalk sloped slightly uphill before us.

Clouds of frigid air fired out of our mouths in measured bursts.

'I want to get a divorce,' he said. 'Move out to Los Angeles, practice a little medicine, but go into business with you. Susan told me at dinner last night you'll probably go into the movies – that's what the big agent guy who's teaching her told her happens to playwrights as soon as they become successful in the theater. I'd be a damn good producer. I have a million story ideas. I have an excellent business mind. That's what I want to do so bad I can't tell you. Don't let me down, Snake.'

Michael Pollack leaned into the slope of the sidewalk. He waited.

'First of all, Michael, I haven't become a successful

playwright.'

'But you will.'

'You don't know that. And second of all, I have no idea how to write a movie.'

'So how'd you write a play?'

'I don't know. I guessed.'

'*So?*' He laughed – was anything simpler than this?

'Michael, I can't talk about this now.'

'Okay, okay, you have the opening on your mind, I understand. But you'll think about it, okay, and you'll give me an answer in a couple of days when you can remember there are other people in the world who have aspirations, too.'

I was going to defend myself by saying I had more than the opening on my mind, but for whose benefit would I be telling him? His?

What'd he care? He had something really important on his mind.

Himself.

'What about Carol and the children?' I asked.

'Screw 'em,' said Michael Pollack.

'I couldn't do that.'

'What are *you* doing? They're *my* family.'

'I couldn't be part of your dumping them. If the opportunity were to arise and I *could* help you, you'd have to take them with you.'

Michael's big face filled with blood, looked like an overinflated balloon. He lurched to a stop. We formed a dam on the sidewalk. 'You're saying you won't take me with you to Hollywood if I won't stay married? Do you know how pretentious that is?'

'Feels really pretentious.'

'So you're kidding about putting that stipulation on the deal.'

'No – you're right, it's pretentious, but I'm not kidding about doing it.'

'Well, screw you, forget it, then, I'm not going with you.'

Michael aimed himself back toward the hotel. Then yawed. Looked back at me where I stood watching him, implored me with his eyes to call for him, retract the rider. When I didn't, he stomped his foot on the sidewalk and motored briskly south, limping slightly from the force of the blow he'd just delivered his ankle.

I continued north.

After Susan raised the movie issue last night, Sandra and I discussed it in our landing strip-size bed at the Plaza, her one foot across my ankles, her head against my shoulder.

And she asked one question – with its inevitable preface. 'If we're together, would we have to move to Los Angeles?'

'I don't know,' I said. 'What if we did?'

In the living room of the suite was a fake Edwardian grandfather clock. It was six ticks of that clock, audible through the wall of our bedroom, before she said, 'I don't know.'

'You don't think you'd like it there?' I asked.

'I'm just about to open my store, you just started teaching. Seems . . .' She shook her head against me. Her still longer, curlier, wilder hair tickled my shoulder. I resisted scratching because I didn't want her to feel I wanted her to move.

'Seems what?' I asked.

'Seems too easy. Moving there, being swallowed up into that world – seems like we'd stop learning about the real world. Just this – being here – Manhattan, this hotel, the theater, an agent, producers – I don't know, it doesn't seem real. Seems like childhood again. Protected. Expurgated, if that makes any sense. And the movie life seems like it would be even more protected than this. I'm afraid we'd just be rich and complacent, like if we'd stayed in Miami Beach and the jewelry business. It wouldn't be a sufficient life.'

She took my hand from her buttock, examined it like a palmist. 'But at this point, ' she said, 'I think both of us have to decide what we really want for our*selves*.'

There was no unkindness in this. Only conviction.

As I was about to turn east toward the theater, a hand startled me out of myself and I swung around, my heart instantly pounding in my throat, anticipating I would be facing Leslie Ann Masterson, frightened and excited to learn what we would say and do to each other.

Michael Pollack was apoplectic and out of breath. He'd run all the way back.

'It occurred to me,' he said, 'that you might've thought I wasn't serious. I am. I want to change my life.'

'I understand, Michael.'

'Okay. Just wanted to make sure. Great. See you later.'

4

Howard and Newbury turned onto East Seventy-fourth from uptown as I turned from downtown.

They were staying in Howard's mother's apartment on Fifth and East Eighty-fifth.

Howard's shoulder was still mending, and he wore a sling, another constant reminder to me of the gunman.

I was aiming at you.

On impulse I asked Newbury if she'd mind walking ahead of us a minute.

'Why? Oh, no – what?'

'Nothing about you,' I said.

'Then why can't I hear? Oh, God – what?'

'Will you shut up, dumb-cluck,' Howard said, 'and just do what he said.'

Newbury dug up her Swiss Army knife from deep in her purse, prepared to snip some cuticle, and forged ahead of us.

'But not ahead of us,' Howard said. 'Behind.'

'Why not ahead, lovebug?'

'Because I don't care to look at your ass, that's why. Behind us, you can always stab me if you feel like it. Now *move!*'

'Okay, you don't have to get *mad*.'

'Then don't *make* me mad. Then I won't *get* mad.'

'*Okay*.'

Newbury let us pass. Howard set a brisk pace,

swinging his free arm in a long arc. He turned back to glance at Newbury. 'Too close,' he said. 'Lag. Lag.'

Newbury lagged.

He looked at me.

'Do you know if Leslie Ann is here?' I asked.

He thought about what sort of answer he would give me for some seconds before he said, 'Haven't seen her, Jaker.'

'Okay,' I said, 'it's important that I know if the following assumptions are true: The baby's mine, she didn't sleep with you, you didn't urinate on her, she didn't go to the Sierras with you.'

'Oh, Landau, you are so tiresome.' And indeed there was a weariness in his eyes – the journey from where we'd begun to where we were had been long.

But, despite his mouth giving lip service to his old venom, the shooting had at least slightly diminished the agitation between us.

When he said, 'Okay, you want the truth?' I assumed, however grudgingly, he was paying me off for kneeling over him on the street outside the Alamo Hotel that night.

'Yes,' I said. 'I do.'

He looked at his watch as if that would dictate how much truth he told me. 'I didn't urinate on her, though I'd have been happy to had she not opted for OJ instead. We didn't go to the Sierras together. In fact, I never had the pleasure of formally introducing my lingam into her yoni; therefore, the issue of her womb probably is yours, unless it's the business guy's.'

We stopped at a light on Seventy-eighth and Park. Howard glanced at Newbury. 'Stay,' he said.

Newbury stopped short of the crosswalk.

'You know for a fact she was sleeping with the business guy?'

'I'm an imagination guy, Jaker, what do I know from facts?' Howard kicked a beer can out of his way; the can clattered over the edge of the sidewalk and into the gutter. 'Actually, I only saw her with him once. Right after the play opened at Stanford. Took my car in for service. She was in the parking lot, talking with the guy in a Mustang. Realized I'd seen the same guy at the play the night before.'

'Big guy. Graying. Curly hair.'

'You got him.'

'Ever occur to you, Howard, that maybe that's all they did – talk.'

'About *what*? Guy's a fucking *businessman*.'

The light changed. We crossed. Howard glanced behind us. 'Okay, walk.'

Newbury walked.

'Do you swear to me that's the truth?' I asked.

Howard gave me his crooked smile, for a moment making me doubt everything he said. But then, easily, simply, he said, 'That's the truth as I know it.'

'Didn't you feel guilty lying to me? Misrepresenting her?'

Howard shrugged. ''Not particularly. Maybe a little.'

And now Howard had other things on his mind. 'Long as I've got you with me,' he said, 'I'm thinking we need to take a little tuck in scene four of Two. Noticed some ass rustling about the time Michael launches into his umpteenth mea culpa.'

5

M y child – no question.
    Had to find her.
Them.
How?
I made the cut Howard requested and tried to sit in
rehearsal.

Couldn't.

Walking back to the Plaza, I found myself thinking
about my bar mitzvah.

Why?

D'know.

Figure it out.

I wore a borrowed blue suit because my father thought
it was ridiculous to spend seventy-five dollars on a new
suit I'd wear once and never again. I did get new shoes,
of course, from the store. But surely that wasn't why I
was thinking about my bar mitzvah.

My father, though, was in the ballpark.

Because this is what it was: *My father said to Rabbi
Oscar Lerner, I would prefer not to make a prayer in
which I thank God for his goodness. I would like simply
to speak words that my son should grow up to be an
able man.*

Did he then – or ever – define an able man for me?

I checked the message desk in the lobby each time I
came in, hoping Leslie Ann would leave a message, ask
to meet.

Nothing.

Upstairs I found only Neddie Pollack.

'Where'd everybody go?'

She weighed the cost of responding. Took a large breath – a speech of some length was coming. 'Michael's asleep. Carol went somewhere. Ernie's cost shopping at Tiffany's and Cartier. Sandra got a call from somebody and went out. And I'm about to take a shower.'

Having said that, she headed for the bedroom she shared with her husband.

'Who called Sandra?' I asked.

'Couldn't say,' said Neddie.

Not couldn't say, but wouldn't.

Neddie closed the door to the bedroom. In a moment I heard the TV, then the shower.

I went into my room. Closed the door.

Would Leslie Ann have called Sandra and asked to see her?

You don't know me, but I'm carrying your husband's child. You're in the middle. I'm sorry.

Gun out, pointed . . . fired.

Or they could have flipped a coin – loser gets stuck with me.

Who else would call Sandra here? Old high school or college friend.

I stood at the window of the minaret in our bedroom and looked down. The fountain across the entryway was virtually deserted except for Leslie Ann Masterson, sitting far below, looking up.

I wrestled with the lock on the window, forced it to turn, threw open the window, stuck my head out into the freezing wind.

'*Leslie Ann*,' I called.

Twelve floors below, she looked up. I could see her

breath coming at me, dissipating, disappearing.

'*Stay there! I have to talk to you! Will you wait? Please!*'

She stared up.

I grabbed my jacket.

My mother and father were getting off the elevator as I jumped on.

'Where are you going?' my mother asked.

I pointed in a southerly direction. The doors closed.

By the time I got to the lobby and out the door, she was gone.

'*Goddamn it!*' I screamed.

A dozen cab and limo drivers, several bellhops, and fifteen or twenty guests ignored me.

I asked the doorman if he'd seen the woman at the fountain. He had. Real pregnant, he said. Had he noticed which way she'd gone?

North, he said, into the park.

6

I walked into the park. Past the Children's Zoo.

And then it hit me. Would she have done the same thing she did in Austin?

Stay at the same hotel!

As I had nothing else to go on, it was worth a shot. Which one first?

She headed north.

The general direction of the Algrove. The hotel I'd been in until two days before.

The eyebrowless, corpulent woman who managed the hotel with her bushy, single-browed, corpulent husband looked up at me with a disingenuous smile, recognized me, and stopped smiling. 'Forget something, Mr Landau, when you moved to a fine hotel?'

She was being ironic and hurt. I pretended not to notice. Today she had managed to pencil in both eyebrows at approximately the same elevation, which wasn't always the case.

'It's Mr Landau, Ricky.'

Her husband, Ricky, looked up from the *New York Post* X-rated movie section. He didn't remember me. He sucked his teeth. His eyebrow looked like it came from the floor of a barber shop – thousands of randomly compressed hairs slammed into his forehead.

'I forgot what room my cousin Miss Masterson's in.'

'Masterson?' Mrs Ricky had never heard the name.

'Greene, I mean – what'd I say – I meant Greene?'

She flicked her eyes at Ricky. 'Greene, Ricky.'

Ricky sucked his teeth, lifted the *Post* to run his eyes beneath it at the current Algrove roster. 'We got a shitload of Greenes – who we talking about? Sergeant and Mrs Felix, Alan and Natalie, or Lorna?'

Jesus Christ.

'Lorna,' I said.

'Three Greenes at the same time,' said Ricky, shaking his head. That was right up there with UFOs and the Abominable Snowman.

'What room, Ricky?'

'Four sixteen,' Ricky said. 'You want I should ring?'

'Na, she's got my chess board, I'll surprise her,' I said.

Chess board? Always trying to impress somebody.

I took the elevator to the fourth floor. The place, now that I'd moved to the Plaza, smelled badly of old hotel, needed a lot of replastering, some new carpet. At four sixteen I knocked. No one answered. No one stirred within.

Down the hall, a maid's cart sat outside a room. I walked down to the open door. Inside a Latina woman had the TV on and was changing the bed.

'My wife must've gone out. I came up without a key. Do I need to go all the way back down or can you open four sixteen for me?'

'I thought ju was up on eleben?' the Latina woman said.

'That was yesterday. We moved.'

She opened the door for me, and I entered Leslie Ann's hotel room.

The smell of her was unmistakable; the energy of her, even in her absence, filled the room.

On the dresser, a few neatly arranged cosmetics. In the

top drawer, folded in her precise manner, a few pair of panties, a bra, a pair of athletic socks.

An envelope. In it: a quarter inch of hundred-dollar bills and an uncashed check made out to Margaret Mayes from the Wilson Bushyhead & Anna Leslie Mayes Trust for five thousand dollars.

A ballpoint pen sat on top of the beaverboard desk. I opened the top, side desk drawer.

Box of .32-caliber shells and a small, aged leather holster with the initials *WBM* embossed on it.

When she was preparing to do *The Lesson*, she said she went to a shooting range, shot a .32.

She suggested we should have a gun in our home.

When I asked her why, she said, 'The challenge of not using it on each other.'

The gun she fired at that shooting range was probably the one not in this holster. The one that had shot Howard Bellman instead of me.

And probably belonged to her father.

In the next drawer: bottle of multi-vitamins; bottle of long-acting vitamin C; bottle of Super Calcium; bottle of combination fish oil, kelp, and vitamin E.

She was taking good care of herself.

Opaque prescription bottle in the name Leslie Landau. Refillable. I popped the cap. Cotton packing. Under the cotton, only two capsules. I replaced the pills, the cotton, the cap. Looked at the label. Dalmane. From an Albuquerque Walgreen's.

Dalmane, as I recalled from wherever information like this came from, was a sleeping pill.

A person who can't sleep, I thought, must remain awake.

With herself.

Or haunting other people.

What was I to do about this person?

What was I to do for this person?

And how did I approach doing whatever I was going to do when she had a gun she was willing to use?

She was dangerous.

Or was that bullshit? Because, inside where I believed, at least intuitively, I knew her, didn't I believe she wasn't trying to kill me?

Yeah, I did believe that. What that bullet had been was a less lyrical cry for help than Tennyson had been.

Following which illumination, I thought: If you're wrong, you're potentially in a lot of trouble.

It struck me that this portion of me who decided to wait here until she returned was somewhat more noble than the rest of me.

Nevertheless, I sat on the edge of her bed. Got up, turned the desk chair around backward, sat. Got up, laid on the bed, pillows propped up, casually crossed. Got up, stood against the wall beside the dresser.

Okay.

Waited.

As it turned out, the wait wasn't long.

Because a key slipped into the other side of the lock on the door of the room and I turned to face Leslie Ann.

Ricky and Mrs stepped into the room.

'How'd you get into Miss Greene's room?' Mrs Ricky wanted to know.

'She let me in. She had to run out a minute.'

'She just came in downstairs. We told her her cousin, Mr Landau, was here.'

'Ah.'

Mrs Ricky cocked one painted eyebrow at me. 'She said you were in her room uninvited.'

'Where'd she go?'

'I don't think that's really the point here.'

'What is the point, you figure?'

'The point,' said Ricky himself, furrowing every hair in his extensive brow, 'is whether we should call the cops or not.'

'Is that what *she* wants you to do?'

'She didn't say what she wants us to do,' said Mrs Ricky. 'So I guess it's up to us. Do *you* think we should call the cops?'

'No, no, I don't. I think the police would be an enormous waste of time and just further complicate an already very complicated situation. What if I were to offer you tickets to the opening night of my play and we just let this go?'

'Tickets to a play? We got a *hotel* to run, Mr Landau,' said Mrs Ricky. 'So how about you just get the hell out of here and don't come back.'

'Sounds good. But let me write a note – would that be all right – I write a note?'

Mr and Mrs Ricky consulted each other briefly before Mrs Ricky said, 'Sure, a note would be good.'

I sat at the desk, opened the top drawer, took a sheet of stationery and the ballpoint pen on the desk beside the phone, and wrote quickly: 'Please talk to me. Please.'

I put the note on the bed as I said to the Rickeys, 'Listen, if she – Miss Greene – if she does anything peculiar, will you call me at the Plaza?'

'Oh, hey,' said Ricky, 'you bet. *She* does anything peculiar, what we'll do im*med*iately is we'll call *you*. At the Plaza.'

I took a cab back. In the lobby I went to the pay phone and called the Algrove. Imitating my father's accent, I asked for Miss Lorna Greene.

Was informed she'd checked out fifteen minutes earlier.

7

All the Pollacks and Landaus went to dinner at a steakhouse in the theater district.

Outside the restaurant afterward, while my father tried to convince Ernie Pollack to let him pay half the check, my sister took me aside and whispered, 'Who's the guy?'

'What guy?' I whispered back.

And instinctively, before my sister said the words out loud, I heard them in my head: *the guy your wife* . . .

'The one Sandra's having an affair with?'

Fritz 'n' Franz do Manhattan!

Not wanting to appear the ignorant cuckold, I managed to say in what sounded like a reasonably serene voice, 'Where'd you see him?'

'Christ, big brother – in the restaurant. Sitting a couple of tables away, off your right shoulder.'

Eye contact with wife across table from me. Wife's eyes bounce left.

I'd thought her behavior peculiar only in light of the conversation we'd had in bed last night. Concerns unspoken and half-spoken about the future. Eye contact that deflected because the business of the future was so complex and threatening.

My back was to the big plate-glass window that stretched across the whole of the front of the restaurant. I scratched the side of my nose, which didn't itch. 'Can you see him from here?' I asked Susan.

'Move to your left a couple of steps and turn your back.'

I did as instructed.

Susan turned easily to the others, said, 'Give us just a minute here – one quick piece of business,' then turned her back so that the two of us stood side by side facing the restaurant.

She didn't have to tell me who he was. I tracked from where I had been sitting to a man several tables away I realized I knew.

How?

Dark, handsome, about my age – Italian, maybe. Dressed differently from the others in the restaurant, the others he was with. Jeans, snap-button workshirt, sheepskin jacket slung on the back of the chair; legs crossed, worn cowboy boots visible.

Not Italian. Latino. Or Indian.

Adrenaline torpedoes fired through oceans of blood, miles of veins, rushing toward my head. The torpedoes hit my eyes. Exploded.

The party we threw to announce the store several weeks ago. Saw him there, standing in a corner of the empty shell that was now almost *Felicity.*

But somewhere else.

Newspaper. His picture in the newspaper.

Two couples with him in the restaurant. New Yorkers. Professionals.

'Know him?' my sister asked.

'Oh, sure. He's the guy from Albuquerque my wife's having an affair with.'

'Hey,' Susan said.

'Yeah?'

'Let's go to Hollywood and make movies. It's time to grow up.'

In a flash I knew why I'd been thinking earlier in the day about my bar mitzvah. Not just my father's words to Rabbi Oscar Lerner about becoming an able man. Those were, after all, the days when I was becoming a golfing prodigy, when my father and I secretly envisioned a life on the links of epic magnitude. His fingers at the four-in-hand knot I had labored long to tie myself, he'd said, 'As you become supposedly a man, you know the most interesting thing I have learned about being this supposed grown-up person?'

I, of course, shook my head in the negative.

'Other people,' said my father, the periodic sage, 'are going to live their lives even as you are living yours. Isn't that amazing, my boy? Sometimes, even at cross purposes with yours.'

I'm sure I nodded as if this made a great deal of sense to me, was something that would be a heck of a springboard into Manhood, but the truth was at thirteen, the apple of my father's eye, the star in the Landau firmament, I had no idea what my father was talking about. Other people were going to live *their* lives at the same time I was living *mine*?

Get serious.

8

Sandra and her parents and mine were going to see *Sweet Charity*.

I was supposed to go see the preview of my show.

They were late now, as Sandra had been late when she'd returned that afternoon to our room in the hotel.

'Where you been?' I had asked, hoping to seem breezy and genial.

'Oh,' she'd said, 'a friend of mine from college called. Bonnie Braunstein – you remember her. We met in the Palm Court.'

'Didn't see you there,' I said.

I checked her eyes, her mouth, for any telltale wavering or twitching. I did dimly remember a Bonnie Braunstein from the University of Florida.

'I saw *you*,' she said.

'Oh?'

'Well, I caught a glimpse of you at the message desk before you went upstairs.'

If she'd met someone she was having an affair with, surely she wouldn't have met him in an open restaurant in the middle of the hotel we were all staying in.

As we parted on the street outside the steakhouse, I said to Sandra, 'Are you okay?'

'Yes, do I seem not okay?'

Her father told her to move it.

She kissed me. 'Concentrate on what you have to do right now. Day after tomorrow, we'll talk about us.'

I didn't really know this woman, but it didn't strike me as inconceivable that she could marry outside her faith, outside her race, or simply live with a Latino or Indian and operate a clothing store in Albuquerque, New Mexico.

And be content.

Other people are going to live their lives even as you are living yours.

Watching her walk away, I wanted very much to go after her, catch her, hold her.

Keep her.

By the time I walked across town to East Seventy-fourth and Second and the theater where *Who Stalk the Tiger* was playing, the first act was almost over.

The theater was about half-filled — a hundred and fifty people or so — most of whom were here on free tickets that Jerry and Darlene had spread around town. We had no stars, and neither the playwright nor the director had any reputation that would have influenced anyone but the most inveterate preview goer to buy a ticket.

I looked across the heads in the orchestra, searching for Leslie Ann.

Went up to the balcony. Several dozen people. She wasn't there.

But the cowboy from the steakhouse and his four New York friends were.

Slick.

That's what he'd called me when we'd met at the party announcing the store. It was odd, I'd thought at the time, that he would pick that name.

He couldn't have known, of course, that at our house once upon a time I was known as Slick Menscheim. Coming out of his mouth, it had seemed innocuous;

people out west, I noticed, often threw generic nicknames at each other – Bronco, Slim, Bubba; yet, on
reflection now, there was something disquieting about
it. Diminishing. A real westerner calling a pretend
westerner a cowboy name.

Slick.

He could have sensed in me wiseness, I suppose,
canniness. On the other hand, he could have sensed my
callowness, my slimness . . .

I stood at the top of the stairs when they headed out
for some air at intermission.

The cowboy's eyes hit mine and skidded away. He and
Sandra must have practiced that technique together.

I went downstairs and outside.

Howard materialized in an agitated state at my side.

'Newbury's psychotic. According to her, someone in
the second row was purposely coughing on all her
sibilants from scene three to the end of the act. She
was *terrible*.'

I took some steps down the sidewalk, looking for the
cowboy among the audience standing on the street, quietly
passing judgment on the issue of my imagination.

Howard followed me. 'So you going to dump Sandy-
Wandy-Wingo as soon as the play opens?'

I looked at him.

'Well, you're going to want to be with Masterson,
right? Her and your little bambino.'

'You figure I'll dump Sandra, you dump Diane, you
claim Sandra on waivers.'

Howard raised his eyebrows, smiled. 'How's that
sound to you?'

Skip had already slotted my new play for next season,
though we'd agreed not to say anything to anyone until
after this play opened here. Despite his telling me the

truth about his relationship with Leslie Ann, I wanted to hurt Howard, wanted to tell him he wasn't going to direct the new play; yet what came out of my mouth was, 'Why don't we stop doing this, Howard.'

'Doing what?'

'Picking at each other like carrion birds.'

'Jesus, you literary guys. Can't you just say "quit fucking each other around" or something like that? "Picking at each other like carrion birds"? What the hell are carrion birds?'

'Birds who eat shit,' I said.

'Because they have to,' Howard wanted to know, 'or because they like to?'

The lights blinked, indicating the end of intermission. Howard headed inside before I could answer the question – to which I didn't really have an answer.

Though it was certainly an interesting question.

The cowboy and his friends passed, and in a blink I knew who he was.

Not the newspaper. Hadn't seen his picture there.

Faculty newsletter. New faculty. Right next to me alphabetically. I even remembered his name.

9

I stationed myself outside the theater during the curtain call.

As they came out and turned toward Third Avenue, I stepped away from the wall and into their path. He looked at me, figuring me for a panhandler because he reached for his pocket – although I suppose he could have been reaching for a gun or knife, which I assumed most real westerners had the good sense to pack back east.

Then he recognized me.

And then pretended not to and started past me.

'I know you,' I said, sticking my hand out, first as a barrier, then in greeting.

The cowboy shook his head – he didn't think so.

'You're Fernando Lamontagne, you teach Business Law at UNM. I'm Jacob Landau, I teach English.'

'Oh,' said one of the women in a heavy New York accent, 'that was undoubtedly one a the best things I've seen in years.'

None of the others agreed or disagreed with her.

'Thank you very much,' I said, fixing Fernando Lamontagne again.

My hand was still out, and he took it now. 'Of course – how are you, Jay?'

Jay?

In Albuquerque I was Jake or Jacob (or Slick). No one there called me Jay.

Except my wife.

'I didn't recognize you for a second. Don't think we've ever met in person, actually, but we've probably seen each other around campus.'

'Actually, I think we met briefly at a party my wife threw a couple of weeks ago to announce the opening of her clothing store – you mistook me for someone named Slick.'

This didn't seem to ring a bell for him.

'My wife's a student of yours,' I said helpfully. 'Sandra Landau.'

'Of course. Sandra's your wife.'

I nodded, turned my palms up. Small world. 'Yes,' I said, 'she is, she's my wife. Sandra. What are you doing in New York?'

'State of New York's trying to extradite a client of mine on income tax fraud. Had to come up, see what I could do about keeping him home.' Fernando Lamontagne looked around. 'You alone?'

No, Sandra's over there, bent over that Buick, skirt flipped up over her ass . . .

'Yeah,' I said, 'I'm alone.'

'Like to have a drink with us?' asked the woman with the accent.

'No, I don't think so,' I said. I looked at Fernando Lamontagne. 'But when we're both back in Albuquerque,' I said, 'maybe you and I should get together. Have a talk.'

Fernando Lamontagne was a big guy. That swarthy, satin-skinned, Mexican Indian mestizo look; very long hair – hidden behind his head in the restaurant – tied in a ponytail with a leather thong; ebony eyes that kept their counsel.

A devilishly handsome guy. Man.

I felt pink and repulsively Anglo.

'We ought to do that,' he said, and stayed right with me.

He knew I knew. He was willing to let me lead. This deep into The New Morality, did cuckolded husbands still take swings at the guys who had sex with their wives?

Somehow that didn't seem to be the point – my shame, my honor.

So what then?

'Sure,' I said, 'let's do. I'll call you.'

Fernando Lamontagne's friends said their good-byes, I said mine. They moved on.

So: he was just filling a void, so to speak, I had created.

10

Susan found me backstage during notes, tiptoed to my side, whispered, 'This Warner Brothers production vice-president saw the preview. He said he couldn't believe it. He said it was a home movie of his marriage. He's waiting for us.'

'I can't.'

'You have to. I said I'd deliver you.'

Norman Feingold was waiting at a table at a famous French restaurant you couldn't get into without a reservation made months in advance. Some instinct told me he'd gotten in by arriving at the door and making eye and hand contact with the maître'd'.

I knew the moment I saw him that it was possible to spend the rest of my life in the presence of men I could easily empower with the ability to diminish me.

After the requisite strokes and the introduction of Norman Feingold's date (a young woman – girl, really – who couldn't be older than nineteen and whom I had assumed as we approached the table must be his daughter), we ordered drinks (club soda for me; I hadn't had alcohol since Austin).

'Jake, you *tsetummelter*, are you ready to come to Lotusland and become extremely rich writing movies?'

'The thought's crossed my mind,' I said.

'I'll bet it has!' Norman Feingold laughed the big, easy laugh of a man on top. 'Whose mind hasn't it crossed!

We're about to move into an era in which *everyone* obsesses about celebrity.'

Norman Feingold must have been forty years old, the number two man at a major movie studio. His body was lean and hard; and it was evenly pecan-colored, I would guess, right down to his buttocks. His hair was obscenely abundant and perfectly coiffed to look totally untended. His jeans and boots, his yoked shirt, turquoise bolo tie, and tweed jacket bespoke not only wealth but disgustingly good taste.

He was even more attractive than Fernando Lamontagne, and I felt not only unattractive across from him, but badly dressed, unworldly, and hopelessly at his disposal.

Let's go to Hollywood and make movies. It's time to grow up.

'Let me just tell you this, Jake,' Norman Feingold said. 'Much has been written about Hollywood, about southern California, about movie people. How superficial it is and we are; how stultifying the atmosphere, how seductive and destructive the ease. When I got out of college and went out there, I thought, The generalizations about the place can't be fair, they have to be exaggerated. And I was right. Fact is, the whole place was much worse than anything I'd heard. And within months I was a deliriously happy part of it.'

Norman put his hand gently to the teenage girl's cheek. 'You hungry?'

She both shrugged no and nodded yes at once. 'Na, I guess sorta – you know.'

Norman seemed, indeed, to know. To us he said, 'Forget the menu,' and crooked a finger at the captain.

'Oui, Monsieur Feingold.'

'Tatie, tell Jacques to poach us whatever's fresh and

steam us some vegetables. And tell Simmy to bring us a bottle of that chardonnay I had with Mickey and Jan last month.'

Entrusted with these instructions, the captain bowed backward from the table.

I tried to resent Norman Feingold for his confidence in ordering for everyone without bothering to ask if either Susan or I hated poached whatever was about to be poached.

But it didn't work. It only made him more attractive.

Made being part of his world more attractive.

'Listen to me,' Norman Feingold said, sighting me down his slender, un-semitic nose. 'Your sister says you don't know if you want to write movies. You want to know what I say to that? I say that's caca, it's just *spilkes* that you won't be good enough at it. Trust me – you will. I know. I saw that tonight. You want to know what'll happen? You come out there, within ten days you're dreaming of a Ferrari, three-hundred-dollar cowboy boots, hundred-fifty-dollar workshirts with western snap buttons and yokes embroidered by a Vietnamese refugee named Tran from Burbank who'll throw in a blow job for another thirty. Designer boot jeans that hug your ass like paint. A house in the hills of Beverly with a cook housekeeper with a Slavic accent and a private security company that guarantees armed response within four minutes of an alarm. Locked-in tables at certain closed-to-the-public restaurants. A limo service for the airport, with your own steady driver named Hal. You're going to love Lotusland, Jake. Screenwriters live a charmed life. Collect a big paycheck and suffer no responsibility.'

'Writing a screenplay isn't a responsible undertaking?' I asked.

'Oh, well, sure, I mean, it takes work, requires some talent. But you don't have to worry about critics, budgets, temperamental stars, drugs on the set. The onus of responsibility is off the writer and on the producer and the director. Nobody credits you with the failure of a movie.' He put his hand on mine; his nails, like Sandra's, were finished in clear polish; he alerted me with a twinkle in his eyes that a punch line was coming. 'Of course,' he said, 'nobody credits you with the success, either.'

'And you're saying that's all good.'

'Absolutely. Leaves you most of your time for acquiring and fucking.'

It's time to grow up.

Norman laughed his handsome, rich, important-guy laugh, took his hand from mine, and disappeared it onto the thigh of the teenager beside him.

'You married, Jake?'

'Yes,' I said.

Norman Feingold winked at me. 'I want to fuck five thousand women,' he said.

He confirmed that with a nod to Susan.

I didn't know what to say to that or whether a response was anticipated.

Susan, however, inquired, 'How many are you up to now, Mr Feingold?'

'Oh, Jesus — I'm only in the four hundreds. Four fifty-six to be precise.' He nudged the teenager. 'Four fifty-seven if I get lucky tonight.'

The teenager elbowed Norman Feingold.

'Ouch,' he said. 'Make it better.'

She kissed her fingertip, touched his side.

'Know how many women I'd planked when I left college?'

This was to me, and I said, 'Uh-uh.'

'Two. That's a lot of planking since I got out.'

'A lot,' I agreed.

'You think I'm lying, right,' he said to Susan, 'four hundred and fifty-six?'

'Why would I think you're lying?' she asked.

Norman suddenly turned back on me. 'You don't approve of me, do you, Jake? You write for the theater and that's kosher; I make movies out there in Tinseltown and that's *trayf*.'

'I'm not passing judgment on you. In fact, I'm sitting here envying you.'

'Why don't I believe you?'

'Maybe because you're projecting on to me what you feel yourself.'

Norman Feingold smiled at me, he smiled at the teenager, he smiled at Susan. 'I could save three hundred dollars a week at the shrink if I had you out there with insights like that.'

What was I doing here? I should go back to the hotel to attend to my wife, my marriage. I needed to watch the fountain outside my hotel in anticipation of the delivery of my first child.

Yet I didn't move.

The sommelier arrived with the wine. He showed the bottle to Norman Feingold.

'No, not that one, Simmy – the other one.'

'Oh, but of course, Monsieur Feingold,' said Simmy in his heavy French accent, and he headed back to the wine cellar.

Norman Feingold spotted someone he felt obliged to acknowledge. With the smallest of movements, he lifted his chin at whoever it was somewhere behind me.

'So, Jake, you got any movie ideas?'

'Not really,' I said.

'I can give you fifty. I want to fly you out next week, we'll spend a couple of days spitballing. In the meantime, you think about areas that might interest you.' He lifted a finger, stopping me from embarrassing myself by disclosing those areas of interest precipitously. Leaving the manicured finger in the air, he used it and the three others connected with it to enumerate the following: 'Couple of hints. Nobody's interested in Vietnam. Someday. Not now. Everybody's pretending it didn't happen. Hippies are a bad joke. Black people are on their way back into the tapestry. Love stories concerning people of differing sexes are no good unless they end badly.' He was out of fingers; he put the hand back on the teenager's thigh. 'So what does the public want?' He looked at Susan, he looked at me. When neither of us was forthcoming with an answer, he told us. 'Tits and ass. And they want to see money and they want to see karate and real blood from real guns, preferably shooting Hispanics. Combine the above ingredients into a movie that grosses fifty million and you'll never have to work another day in your life.'

After our poached salmon with Norman Feingold, Susan cabbed over to the Plaza with me. She and Norman had almost single-handedly finished a second bottle of wine.

'So,' she said torpidly, 'you dump your wife, we move to L.A., and we sell out, right? Make some money while we prostitute ourselves and get ready to do something we'll be proud of in middle age.'

When I didn't respond readily, Susan said, 'You're a salable commodity, and there are thousands of women out there needing to be fucked and counted. Get wise, big brother.'

11

It was almost midnight when I came through the east-side door of the lobby of the Plaza Hotel.

And stopped. And stood.

Because I had no idea where to go.

Should I go upstairs and talk to my wife about the affair she was having with Fernando Lamontagne?

Should I go upstairs and tell Michael Pollack, 'Sure, divorce your wife, Hollywood's available, let's buy a Mercedes and do a Seventies, cross country, rich kid version of *On the Road*?'

Norman Feingold wants to fuck five thousand women.

I'm in love with two.

One of whom I could pack up and take to Hollywood with me – if I could find her.

Should I start calling every hotel in New York and run by their desk clerks any and all names Leslie Ann might be registered under?

But now I imagined this. I would turn toward the message desk and all conjecture about where she might be would become moot.

Because she would be standing at the entrance to the Palm Court.

Her massive belly protruding before her, she would look more beautiful than I remembered – even in my naive boy's dreams.

My eyes would be drawn magnetically to her belly,

where there lived a child I believed to be some mysterious commingling of our two legacies, going back who knew how many generations.

We would exchange greetings. Simple, brief: 'Hello, Jacob.' 'Hi, Les.' She would smile a small, uncertain smile, and she'd ask me if I wanted to have a decaf and a Napoleon in the Palm Court.

I would feel obligated to say something clever. I might ask, 'Are you armed?'

Her smile would disappear. 'It's a mean city,' she might say. 'I have a passenger. But I promise I won't shoot at you again.'

So we would sit in a corner, away from the string quartet playing Mendelssohn, and she would explain herself to me to my satisfaction, so that the decision I had to make as to what to do with my life would be easy.

'I was just trying to scare you when I shot,' she would say calmly, reasonably. 'I was never good with a gun. As to following you, well I know it seems obsessive but . . .'

Forget it. She would never explain herself.

Action. Reaction. Behavior.

No fear.

I felt that somehow I was guiltier in this mess than she was, that somehow I should've been smarter than she, able to overcome the nutsiness of both of us and create order.

I remembered when she was in her Orthodox Jewish period, she asked me one day if I would be her 'rock and her redeemer.'

I told her that was an Old Testament reference to God.

She said, 'What can I say, pal – I guess that's the role I'm auditioning you for.'

12

I needed a lawyer.

Providentially, my wife was having an affair with one.

Sandra lay in bed, reading *In Ole Virginia* (she was reading along with the graduate students in my Southern Lit seminar).

'Boy,' she said, 'is this boring.' She held the book my way, accusing me of some vague sin that may have had to do with Thomas Nelson Page's book or may have had to do with the hour and what I assumed was her vague supposition – if she was foolish enough to stay with me – that I would begin to disappear regularly into various nights just like this one with a succession of threats to her well-being. 'Where you been?'

'Susan dragged me to dinner with a guy from Warner Brothers.'

'Really? How'd it go?'

'Fine, good, I'll tell you about it later. Where's your friend staying?'

'What friend?'

'I need some legal advice.'

She turned her eyes to her book again, and for a moment I thought she was going to return to reading as if I hadn't spoken. 'How'd you know?' she asked.

'I didn't. I was dumb enough to think when you said in Austin it was over that it was over. Susan pointed him out to me in the restaurant tonight.'

'Susan pointed him out? How'd *she* know?'

'She's always been a keen observer of anything that portends great human suffering.'

'I want you to know I didn't invite him here.'

'He followed you.'

'Yes.'

'Against your will.'

'Yes.'

'It's a free country.'

'We never got to discussing it in constitutional terms, Jay. He just presumed I didn't mean it when I told him it was over.'

'He's continued to thrust himself on you.'

'He's tried.'

'But you haven't capitulated.'

She closed the book, placed it on her belly. 'Once,' she said. 'When we got back and we weren't touching. It was the day we found out the play was definitely coming to New York. I had class that night. I was feeling very confused and insecure.'

'So you slept with him again that night. And then you told him again it was finished.'

'Yes.'

'But he was doubly dubious now.'

'I guess.'

'But you're not sure it *is* over, because you're not sure of us.'

'Yes.'

'I'm not, either.'

'Why should you be? You're facing the prospect of living a unique life. Why would you want to settle for an ordinary one?'

'There's a lot to figure out, San. And I'd like us to do it together, openly, if we can.'

She looked down at her lap and for a moment I couldn't see her face. I didn't know whether she was going to cry or laugh or scream her confusion in my face. When she finally looked up though, there were no tears, no smile and the words were almost without inflection. 'We can certainly give it a shot.'

'Good. But right now, I really need a lawyer.'

13

We met at a deli on West Fifty-sixth Street, sat upstairs in a corner.

I explained to Fernando Lamontagne only that I wanted to be able to see my child. Beyond that, I figured none of it was any of his business.

Sandra looked radiant, illuminated by the friction the two of us sent across her at each other.

Her two hands, trembling just noticeably, were folded together on the table, equidistant between Fernando Lamontagne and me, and I wondered if he was wondering, as I was, if either of us had the right to reach over and steady those hands – I because I was her husband, he because at least twice she had chosen him over me.

'You looking to make a case for custody?' Fernando Lamontagne asked me. 'You want the child – you and Sandra – is that the idea?'

Fernando Lamontagne glanced at Sandra, asked with his eyes whether she cared to become the adoptive mother of this about-to-be-born child and remain the wife of the child's father.

Sandra didn't respond.

'No, that's not the idea,' I said. 'I just don't want to be cut off from my child. I want to know what the legal options are, and I want to do whatever needs to be done quickly – before she can disappear with the baby.'

'I understand. I'll do some research this morning,' said

Fernando Lamontagne, 'as soon as I can get out of court on this extradition matter.'

Extradition matter – Christ!

I wanted to scream at Fernando Lamontagne, 'Just tell her you came here solely because she's done something to your heart!'

'To keep her from disappearing,' explained Fernando Lamontagne, 'we can force her to go through the clinical aspects of proving fatherhood. That should give you the opportunity to work your magic on her and straighten her out.' He raised his palms to me, indicating that was it; he was available to represent my interests in the matter if I cared to retain him.

I must have assumed I was now free to change the subject, because I asked him, 'Do you want to marry my wife?'

And my wife said to him sharply, 'Don't answer that.'

'I don't mind,' said Fernando Lamontagne.

'But I do,' said my wife. She turned fully to me, sunlight from the windows behind her irradiating the spools of her hair. 'Whatever happens between you and me, Jay, can't have anything to do with what Fernando wants. From my point of view, what's going on between us has to do only with us. If we split up, it won't be because I want to be with someone else.'

14

In the early afternoon, Fernando Lamontagne called.
'I retained co-counsel on the bar in New York on your behalf,' he said. 'We're on the docket for two-thirty tomorrow afternoon in district court. Any clue where this Masterson woman might be?'

I didn't like the sound of 'this Masterson woman'; it seemed to do something to Leslie Ann I was pretty sure I didn't want done to her. But I told Fernando I had no idea where she might be except around, close.

'We got to have her served before noon tomorrow.'

'Served?'

'Subpoena ordering her to appear.'

'Well,' I said, 'my hope is she'll surface sometime tonight – at the opening, the party, around the hotel . . .'

'I'll have to have the process server follow you around then. He'll identify himself to you. When you see the woman, point her out to him.'

'What's the matter?' Sandra asked when I replaced the receiver.

I shrugged.

'What?' she asked.

'He referred to her as "this Masterson woman." '

She nodded, waited.

I shook my head. 'I have to be fair to her, Sandra. Does that make . . .' My throat constricted and I waited, hoping Sandra would press me to her, say something really sensible and authoritative.

'I have to get out of here for a while,' is what she said. 'I'm sorry.'

My back to her, I nodded and, momentarily, heard the door open, then close.

Mormons, I wondered, certain Middle Easterners – polygamists – did they marry the second wife simply because they wanted someone new? Or was it possible to love two women equally . . . or so nearly equally that you didn't want to be without either of them?

Fine for the guy.

Look at mine!

Real unequal for the women.

15

E ighteen inches, uphill, left to right, against the grain.

Sink it, your life goes one way.

Miss it, it goes another.

The curtain went up. The actors did what I'd written and they'd rehearsed.

The critics — faceless, nominative nomenclators (the *Times* Guy, the *Daily News* Guy, the CBS Woman) — sat in the dark, judging.

I had stood across the street from the theater with Fernando Lamontagne's process server while the audience filed in. And if I had seen Leslie Ann, she would have been served with a court order. Our incipient adult lives would be taken out of our hands and put in the hands of the government. The government would decide the disposition of our child.

Maybe this was wrong. Maybe it would be better in the long run for our child to know only the constancy of its mother. Was it, above all, selfishness that decreed I had to be able to see my child? This unborn being, about to be thrust against its will into a world he or she would find difficult enough without the added burden of an occasional father.

Then why was I waiting out here? Why hadn't I told the guy to go away?

Because I wanted her found. Had to see her and speak to her.

My parents and the Pollacks had arrived, and I realized my father's eyes and mine had met and deflected
half a hundred times in the last several days.

I want to write about you, Pop.

There was still that road to walk down.

My father stepped beside me close and whispered,
'Okay.'

I looked at him. Instinctively I knew what that one
word meant.

'You want to talk,' he said, 'fine. First this, then the
other. You'll know, and if you'll write about it' – he
shrugged his massive shoulders high up into his equally
massive neck, leaving his head with its dark, fathomless
eyes perched precariously atop his trapeziuses – 'okay.'

Soon then, that, too.

Feydeau and Kafka, my instincts told me, were merely
an advance guard. My father and the woman of my
dreams were the two forces I sensed had converged
here this week to push me to the next plane of my only
existence.

I stood now at the back of the house. I looked
down to the fifth row where all the Pollacks and
Landaus sat. Each sat ramrod straight, reminding me
of schoolchildren attentive to something interesting,
something different from the everyday course of events.
With their various feelings, they were here to witness my
talent on trial.

My eyes settled on my father, overfilling his seat,
dwarfing my mother, his back rising and falling hard.

He cared a lot.

To dream of immortality, Jakey, is so selfish . . .

And my mother – her hands clutched to her sternum.

Cared a lot.

My sister.

Cared a lot.

My wife . . .

Complicated.

My mother and father-in-law, my brother and sister-in-law.

Complicated.

I found that I wasn't angry that part of some of them wished disaster on me.

Once the actors settled into the first scene, I went into the lobby. I had told the house manager when I went in to keep his eyes open for a pregnant woman, and I had described Leslie Ann. He told me no one had come in fitting her description.

I told the process server I was going for a walk. He said he'd wait there in the lobby.

I left the theater and started south.

Margaret and Motke accompanied me.

Did you do something, Pop, something you're so ashamed of that it's affected every moment of your waking life since?

Margaret – what about you?

I knew now that during the last two days I had thought a number of times distantly of that old man at the Thunderbird Invitational in Las Vegas, following us, finally pointing a finger at my father: *You!*

I recalled again the way my father looked at me, to see if I had seen the old man raise that finger at him that seemed to recognize my father and to accuse him.

Had I not ever asked my father the right questions because in some way I was protecting him?

From what?

Or was it possible, that as with Leslie Ann, it was, finally, *me* I was protecting? Was it possible that I knew the right questions to ask but didn't because I didn't want to be bothered having to try to deal with the ramifications of the answers? Or knew I *couldn't* deal with those ramifications?

As I walked away from the theater, I understood with the opening of *this* play, there was *that* one to write.

Next.

Now.

Chuck the one about Miami Beach — the solipsistic monologue, the thing on the pier.

And write that one.

My father and Leslie Ann.

Margaret and Motke.

The one I told my father I wanted to write about him.

Where did Leslie Ann come in?

Somewhere. Intimately.

I wandered into a bookstore in the East Sixties on Third Avenue and started perusing the latest in Continental poetry for a course I was to teach next fall.

Next fall.

A year away.

And standing there, I knew I had to stop dwelling on myself — in life and art.

I left the bookstore, went to a pay phone on the street. Called Information and got the number for the Polish diplomatic mission in New York. Standing in the freezing wind on Third Avenue, I dialed the number.

It rang a long time. I told myself to hang up but didn't.

Finally, a heavily accented man answered. I told him I was an American citizen and a Jew (somewhat more vehemently than I thought I felt) and inquired whether there was any reason I couldn't travel to Poland and, once there, around Poland.

He said he was a soldier on guard duty and couldn't

give me an official answer but offered this: To his knowledge, there was no reason I could not travel wherever in Poland I cared to, as long as I applied for a visa, had a current passport, and was not an agent provocateur of a foreign government.

I told him I wanted to go to Auschwitz and inquired whether it was still there.

He said simply: 'It remains.'

16

The process server shook his head. No Leslie Ann.

I sat on the floor in a corner of the lobby, the camel overcoat Ernie Pollack had lent me bundled around me. From inside I could dimly hear the accusations and denials of Act II of the play I had written, which was having its official, commercial opening this evening.

In New York City.

The capital of theater in America.

And on notepad I printed: 'MARGARET & MOTKE.' Crossed it out.

Then I wrote 'THE GOLEMS.'

Then I wrote: 'Did you do something, something you're ashamed of?'

Then I crossed out 'THE GOLEMS' and wrote 'DINNER AT AUSCHWITZ.'

Dinner at Auschwitz?

I crossed it out.

But wrote it again.

'DINNER AT AUSCHWITZ.'

I had no idea what that meant. Didn't matter.

I blew cloudy air from my lungs into the glacial air of the lobby of the theater.

In a few hours, millions of New Yorkers were going to be reading about my play, receiving instructions whether to ignore what I'd invented or to rush to their phones to pledge their fourteen bucks per ticket to witness the issue of my imagination.

Inside I heard applause. The official opening night performance of my first play in New York City had ended.

I had asked my relatives not to call 'Author, author!' so they didn't. And neither did anyone else.

I tried to convince myself it didn't mean anything. Was only partially successful.

I slipped into the back of the orchestra. The process server followed me.

I looked over the house, head by head, searching for her.

I knew she was here.

But now, as the applause was about to die, it crescendoed again, and two voices from the orchestra I recognized unmistakably as Susan and Michael's rose above the applause, calling, 'Author, author!' The cry was picked up – whether out of duty or admiration I didn't know; in either case, momentarily I was onstage with the company, embracing Skip and Diane and Rob.

Frightened to speak because I had no clue what I would say, I felt myself raise my hands nevertheless, heard the theater come silent, felt two hundred and ninety-nine sets of eyes on me from the dark.

'Being in this theater,' I said, 'watching this play being performed in front of you represents the end of an incredible journey for me. For us. Because theater is a collaboration. These three actors and I are among the partners in this enterprise. But there are people at Stanford University, especially one extraordinary collaborator there, and there are folks from the American Southwest Repertory Theater in Austin who should be

up here with us. In the stead of those who aren't here,
I do want to bring one other person onstage with us,
because the truth is without him, none of us would be
standing here. The man who's directed all three of my
play's productions, Howard Bellman.'

Howard fairly ran down the aisle and up onto the
stage. He lifted his one functional arm over his head
and then wrapped the arm ferociously around my waist,
pressing his forehead to my chest. Even against the
applause, I could hear him say, 'Oh, Jaker, thank you.'

Beyond him, up in the balcony, as he embraced me,
I saw a very large woman in a voluminous man's
wide-shouldered overcoat stand, her hand to her mouth
as if, perhaps, she were weeping, and head for the exit.

I jumped off the stage to go after her but was
there swept up in the hands and arms and words of
well-wishers.

17

The entire company and their relatives and friends and friends of friends who'd been invited to make up the two hundred and ninety-nine people at our New York, Off Broadway opening went to Sardi's to await the reviews.

Disclaimers were as thick as the air in the upstairs ballroom itself.

HOWARD (in private to me): They were off. Jesus, they were so off I could've killed all three of them.

ROB: I just didn't get there. I had to fake it. Any critic worth his saltpeter's going to know it.

JERRY: Was that an audience full of tongue amputees, or what? Who can tell me, who saw their IDs? Did they ever hear of *laughing* at things that are *amusing*?

SKIP: It's a first play. People don't know how to respond to a new voice.

DIANE: I think my tits probably did us in.

SUSAN: What we've got from it as it is, is more than sufficient for our first crack out of the box.

D.W.: Fuck 'em!

Only Darlene (and I) said nothing.

I saw her looking at Newbury, and I knew she was remembering and comparing.

Skip Donner materialized in front of me. He told me something in Yiddish that he found funny – and I didn't understand – and told me to enjoy the evening, then gear up for the Miami Beach plays next season.

I told him I didn't want to do the Miami Beach plays next season, that I wanted to do a different play the season after.

Why not the *mishpukah* plays? he wanted to know.

Whackin' off, I told him.

He told me to think about it. I told him I would so we could stop talking about it.

Word had spread at the theater about Norman Feingold's visit last night (as it had Monday and Tuesday about the other movie and TV people), but Susan must have conveyed something special about Norman because Newbury whisked me away to a corner.

Her skin looked like parchment. It appeared she'd been dead for some time.

'You have to get me in the movies,' she said, 'or onto a series. Howard says the theater's dying and if I don't become a star in the next two years, I never will because I'll be over thirty. Women don't become stars over thirty. And I can't become a character actor till I'm forty or fifty and how am I going to live that long if I don't become a star now?'

My mother hovered. I excused myself from Newbury with an all-purpose upper-arm squeeze.

'Do what I can,' I said.

Newbury kissed my cheek wetly and popped a Clorets.

'So?' my mother said. 'It's out of your hands. Relax.'

I pretended to go limp, becoming a heap on the nearest table. My mother laughed.

Flossie.

There were no questions, no doubts, in her eyes — only love.

'Slickguy Menscheim,' she said. 'Huh — remember?'

'Sure,' I said, 'you named me that. Wore his guns

backward like Guy Madison, rode a big palomino
named Milt.'

'In the play, when they talked about who they
didn't become as adults that they dreamed of being
as children, I thought of him. Slickguy.' She smiled,
floating far away on some private reservoir of
memory. 'You would rescue the Rosenblatt and the
Bialenki girl and bring them and your sister home
to your house to recover from what you had rescued them from, and you would personally make
them a PB and J sandwich or cut a nice selection of
melon to serve with a Dr Brown's cream soda.'

Jake the (Good) Snake did that?

'No,' I said, 'I didn't do that.'

'I beg to differ with you.'

'I served refreshments?'

'You were the only cowboy rescue guy with a nice
domestic touch. That's why I called you Slickguy
Menscheim.'

I had no recollection of Jake the (Good) Snake in this
light. 'Slickguy Heroman because I had a nice domestic
touch?'

'Heroman?' said my mother. 'What Heroman?
*Home*man. Slick,' she said. Her smile let me know
she remembered those days with great warmth.

Now I was really confused. 'What do you mean,
*Home*man — where do you get that? "Mensch" is human
being, right?'

'Right.'

'And *heim* is hero.'

'Who told you *heim* is hero, I never told you that.'

'Pop. Pop told me Menscheim meant human being
hero, so Heroman.'

'What your father knows about German and Yiddish

I could put on the tip of a shoelace. *Held* is hero. *Heim* is home.'

It seemed a little ridiculous, but I was irked. 'All that time, galloping around the neighborhood, I thought you thought of me as someone named Slick Heroman and all the time it was Slick *Home*man?'

My mother laughed from her belly, from deep in the past. 'You would tell the girls that someday you would finish saving everyone from all the evils in the world and you would come home and marry them and raise a family.'

'Marry both of them?'

'You were a little mixed up about the legal part, but your motives were nice.' The past filled my mother's eyes. 'Slickguy Menscheim,' she said, 'what a guy.'

My mother put her hand to my cheek. I took the hand, pressed its fingers to my lips.

She cocked her head at me just like Leslie Ann and said, 'What an extraordinary thing to do.' She looked at the spot I kissed.

And I pressed my mouth to her ear and heard my lips form audibly these words: 'I love you, Mom.'

A small sound escaped my mother. It bespoke what I can only call relief.

Susan swept Flossie Landau away to meet a famous someone, and I found myself eye to eye with Ernie and Neddie, far enough away that if we cared to speak words to each other, someone would have to close the distance between us.

I made my way through a dozen bodies to where they stood.

'A nice affair,' said Ernie Pollack.

I nodded.

'Neddie got to meet that actor – What's-his-name – from her show.'

Ernie nodded at a cluster of people across the room. I had no idea whom he was talking about. But then neither did he nor, by the vacant look in her eyes, Neddie.

Yet, as if to belie her unavailability, Neddie tilted her head in my direction and bounced her eyes off my lapel. 'Short,' she said.

'What's that?' I asked.

'Lot of short men go into acting. Would you agree?'

I had come to them, I gathered, to be gracious, so I felt disposed to answer her question, since it had been asked; but what I said was this: 'I hope you're proud of what you saw tonight. It would please me a lot if I thought you were.'

Ernie turned his palms up. 'Proud?' he asked. 'Are you kidding me or what? I couldn't be prouder if you were my own – '

'Small,' said Neddie with a fluidity and ease that seemed to still not only her husband, but all the sound around us. 'So many little, teeny, tiny people,' she said, and set out with painstaking resolve for the bar.

Ernie Pollack ignored his wife's departure; he leaned close to me, gripped a fistful of my arm in a manner not unlike his daughter's, whispered passionately, 'I envy what you can become.'

And my wife's father, my father-in-law, kissed my cheek and headed obediently for the bar in Neddie's festering wake, leaving a gap through which I caught my father's eyes on me from a deep corner of the room. He sent me through the air the most imperceptible of nods.

You!

I made my way to where he stood, driven by an

impulse to give him a Yiddish lesson. But instead I said, 'What'd you think of the play, Pop?'

My father lifted one of his huge hands. 'For young people to be so tormented by doubt. To be so angry at what they have failed to become. Why does everyone think he has to be such a big man? Why can't we accept being just regular?'

Obviously my play had sent my mother and my father to a similar landscape of memory and factoring.

My father waved a hand across his face, in effect saying he didn't care to say more on this subject of childhood aspirations and adult compromises.

At the same time, I wasn't sure whether he was complimenting me, criticizing me, or giving me a piece of advice he simply considered germane at this time.

But then his eyes grabbed on to mine and he said, 'I'm very proud of you, Jacob – what you've written, where we've come tonight to be with you.'

'Thank you, Pop.'

His eyes flinched, peered at a barrier between him and the several hundred other people in the room.

And I said, 'Pop . . .'

Did you do something, something you're ashamed of?

And staring at that invisible barrier, he said, 'Not here.'

'Where?'

'We'll have a talk.'

'When?'

He consulted the barrier for several earnest seconds. 'Tomorrow. In the morning.'

I followed my father's eyes across the room.

There my mother and sister were staring at us. They smiled, lifted hands toward us.

Then beside my sister the incredibly sensual, muscle-bound D.W. Cashbaugh emerged out of the crowd, her hands holding out a glass of wine to Susan, another out to my mother.

My father gripped my arm with his wiener-size fingers; he leaned in close, and I leaned in to meet him. He too was going to say something warm and supportive, and I would say: 'I love you, Pop.'

'Your sister,' my father said quietly.

'What about her, Pop?'

'You and me,' he said, 'we were her he-man role models.'

He patted my shoulder and lumbered away, down the wall, heading for another corner.

Susan had called me in Albuquerque to ask if I'd mind if D.W. shared her apartment with her while we waited to see if the play was going to run, whether D.W. was going to need a residence in New York for the foreseeable future.

'Why are you asking my permission?'

And then the reason had come to me.

'You hate me?' she'd ask.

'I could never hate you,' I told her.

'Disapprove, then. Disappointed? Revolted? Reviled? Talk to me,' my sister said.

'I have no right to pass judgment on you.'

'Should I tell Mom and Pop the truth?'

'Jesus,' I'd said from Albuquerque, 'no. Never.'

Now, tonight, I could tell her, 'Pop knows.'

But my mother didn't. And my father would never tell her.

Morris Landau stood at a distant window, looking out onto West Forty-fourth Street, looking at the New York

Times building, trying to divine, perhaps, the fate of his son's play.

And I sensed at this moment that my father believed he got only what he deserved, no matter how distasteful what he got was.

You and me, we were her he-man role models.

18

I took refuge in the men's room on the second floor of Sardi's. As I stood in front of the bank of urinals trying to decide if I needed to use one, Michael Pollack lumbered in.

'Kid playing me even looks like me, Snakey. I was a handsome kid. Hell of a lot better-looking than you. Before hair over the ears came in, you were dead meat. You were Dumbo, man.'

I laughed.

'So,' said Michael Pollack, fixing me with eyes dropped to half-mast from dread and booze, 'you think I'm that weak and vain a guy, Snakinski? Don't answer that.'

'I wasn't conscious of writing about you, Michael. I was just writing about myself, or some version of me.'

Michael looked at himself in the mirror, checked both shoulders of his jacket for loss of hair. 'But listen, hey, it's important to me that you know how proud I am that you frigging made something of yourself somebody can be proud of.'

'Michael, you're a doctor, for Godsake. You're a healer.'

'Please don't speak to me about healing, Snakey, okay? Certainly not in a major Show Biz rest room when you know I just want to go to Hollywood and meet a starlet who can give me a hard-on.'

Jerry Katzendorf stuck his head in the men's room. 'Reviews coming up in five minutes.'

An esophageal spasm struck my chest. I bent to a faucet, drank slowly, water trickling down the side of my neck into the top of my shirt collar. The spasm released. I took a linen towel from the pile, wiped my face, patted my collar.

Michael Pollack stood at a urinal now, his *schvontz* in one hand over the top of his red, overstuffed bikini briefs; in his other hand he clutched the baloney around his waist, tried to wrestle it into submission. He threw his hand off his gut, leaving there on his reverberating flesh the imprint of his wrathful fingers.

'Snakey,' he said, 'Carol's a nice lady. She's never done anything but try to support me. You think I don't know she wishes she'd been better-looking, had better teeth, so she could have attracted someone better than me?'

Michael whipped his head side to side as he stuffed himself back in his bikini briefs and zipped. 'Okay,' he said. 'We have children. I should want to stay with Carol for them, right? I mean, they're my *children*.' He turned frantic eyes on me, beseeched me with clenched fists. 'But, see, the thing is, they're not a reason to live.'

'Christ, Michael, are you threatening to kill yourself if I don't take you to Hollywood?'

'I might! Or I might just ruin all the lives around me by living a really mean life.'

'Here's a reason to live a decent life, Michael, okay? Live a decent life because your children will never forgive you if you destroy their lives before they have the chance to do it themselves.'

I sounded like my father.

And before I knew it I would be my father's age and

my father would be gone, and what would I have made of my life?

And with whom?

'Okay, here's what I want you to do, Michael. I want you to get a good night's sleep, get up in the morning, and then really think about what you want to do. And then tell me, okay?'

'Sleep, get up, think.' Michael Pollack nodded acquiescence. 'And what I decide, you'll respect.'

'What you decide, I'll accept.'

Michael gripped my hand. 'Dr Snake, fixer of lives.'

'I haven't fixed anybody, Michael. I'm only endeavoring . . . I'd just like to be able to . . . Oh hell, let's get out of here.'

I kissed Michael Pollack on the forehead.

Jerry walked back in as my lips met Michael's flesh.

'Let's go. It's time. History awaits.'

19

At ten to midnight Parker Granger, the agent the Katzendorfs had arranged to append Susan to for her apprenticeship, guided Susan, Sandra, Darlene and Jerry, and my mother and me (my father was nowhere to be found) upstairs to a small conference room where we would have bestowed upon us *The New York Times* and *Daily News* reviews.

'If they're devastating,' Parker Granger said, 'you can at least be mortified in relative privacy.'

Parker was a big, dapper, gay gentleman who was an agent of legend in the theater, on whose fringe I waited to discover if I would be permitted entry, that I might set out toward becoming a legend myself.

In the conference room, Parker lit up a Fatima. Jerry opened a window and stuck his head out into the raw night air.

'Dear God,' he screamed heavenward, 'what do you say, Big Guy, have mercy on the folks in this room. Thank you and amen.'

Sandra sat shaking under my shaking hand.

Susan nibbled at one of her perfectly manicured fingernails (the first manicure of her life).

My mother held her hands prayerfully in her lap and stared at me as if we were in intensive care, me the one in the bed.

Darlene stood just inside the door, watching the rest of us like a momma bear with her cubs.

All these women.

I got up, went to the window Jerry had opened. Peered out into the night, looking for the woman who was missing.

Why does everyone think he has to be such a big man? Why can't we accept being just regular?

Could I be content as a regular-size man? A home man?

An able man?

As I wondered what I was trying to communicate to myself, Leo Spellman, the company manager the Katzendorfs had hired to run the show, stuck his head in the door. In his fists were three crumpled tear sheets.

I felt suddenly on the brink of screaming, 'All right, I confess, I care deeply, this matters a whole, whole lot,' not quite sure whether I was referring to the play, to writing, to celebrity, or to something else, boys and girls, men and women, families . . .

'The *Daily News*,' said Leo, 'decrees you're a pervert, and is so adamant about it that he makes the show sound like the sexiest, filthiest, most revolting thing in town. It'll sell thousands of tickets to the thrill-seeking dipsticks who read the *News*.'

'Leo, nobody cares about the *News*,' said Parker, disseminating a cloud of Fatima smoke into the room. 'What about the *Times*?'

I felt my sphincter muscle tighten involuntarily, sending a knife blade up into my sacrum.

Uphill, left to right, against the grain . . .

It wasn't good, I could tell, even before the words began to spill over Leo's lips.

'Measured praise,' said Leo.

I was startled to know that what I was feeling, amid the instant pain and anger, was relief.

Leo held the review at a distance – a man who needed glasses he didn't have with him. ' "A somewhat too facile sense of domestic urban warfare." "Endeavoring to use a handicap to gain empathy for a character we might otherwise find off-putting." "Glibness once too often in place of substance, making us aware that Mr Landau's very fulsome, dark sense of humor was masking a subject somewhat too cursorily investigated." "But a writer to watch, to encourage, perhaps one day even to cherish." '

Around me everyone defended, railed and ranted, postured and threatened.

And then seemed to run out of words simultaneously, and the room was silent.

From below, street noises rose.

The night passed, and somewhere a woman who had given herself to me for life carried our child.

'I think what I just heard is accurate,' I said. 'I'm going to move on.'

20

I sat in the Oak Bar of the Plaza and had a drink.

Being married to Sandra had come to make so much sense. Despite the affair with Fernando Lamontagne, I knew if we wanted to we could make our peace and that there could be, with her, the prospect of years of safety and dependability. We could get past the affair, the threats inherent in a life in Show Business, two careers, and settle into a union of allegiance and calm.

I went upstairs. Came into our bathroom behind Sandra.

Her lovely face was covered in cold cream. Her hair was tied in two pigtails with ribbons.

She stared at me in the mirror, and for a moment the only sound was the clank of the steam pipes as the huge hotel was warmed for the comfort of its guests against the cold outside.

And then Sandra said, 'Darlene called a few minutes ago. She's waiting up. It's important.'

I leaped the distance between the bathroom and the phone, snapped it up. Began dialing.

Sandra closed the bathroom door. I heard the lock turn.

Before the phone had completed a ring, Darlene picked up.

We'd agreed in Austin that if she had any further communiqués from Leslie Ann, she would tell me.

'She came to see you,' I said.

'Called. When we got home. I don't mean to melo-
dramatize, but she wasn't in good shape. She wouldn't
tell me where she was. She said she just wanted to thank
me for what I'd done for you. I told her I wanted to come
and get her. But she hung up.'

Fear tore up through my legs.

'Jerry called a detective buddy of his, told him I
thought Margaret sounded in danger, but of course
the police can't start looking for someone just because
someone else thinks she sounds troubled.'

I thanked Darlene, hung up, ripped open the bottom
desk drawer, hefted the enormous Manhattan Yellow
Pages onto the desk, started searching for the 'H's'
– hotels.

How else to do it? I had to find her.

Sandra stood in the bathroom doorway. 'Now what?'

'Darlene thinks something's wrong.'

'Really? And what was Darlene's first clue that something was wrong?'

I was glad to hear the edge of rancor in Sandra's voice;
perhaps incongruously, I thought, Good, make me angry,
make me dislike you. 'Sandra, I'm sorry, I am, but I can't
placate you just now.'

She laughed a small, nasty laugh. Said, 'You *couldn't*
placate me at this point, Jacob, so you don't have to feel
the least bit guilty for not trying.'

I knew I should turn, face her, look her in the eyes,
but didn't feel I had time. I had found 'Hotels.' There
were pages and pages.

'I can't do this, Jacob.'

I couldn't conceive beginning to attack this list. Had
to come up with a method of limiting the numbers. Start
with those between here and the Algrove.

Sandra had spoken. The words arrived. The edge was

gone; the words were soft, simple. 'Can't do what, Sandra?'

I ran a finger down the 'A's.'

So near the top that it seemed to leap out and smack my face was the Algrove.

I felt Sandra close. Knew I had to turn.

'I can't live with this much drama, Jacob.' Her eyes were directed without malice into mine. 'And because, thanks in good part to you, I have the right to choose, I choose not to.' She put a hand to my tie, moved the knot just slightly. 'You can't satisfy everyone. We both have to do what we need to do.'

And quietly she closed a door between us.

As the phone rang.

I knew instantly it was Leslie Ann, because though I didn't know where she was, she always knew where I was.

I snapped the receiver to my face, said hello.

'Doing?' she said.

'Wondering where you are, Leslie Ann.'

'Can you talk a minute?'

Her voice was clear, but almost eerily without inflection, as if it knew exactly what she had to say but barely had the muscle to perform the task for her.

'Of course. Where are you?'

I strained to hear in the background anything that would give me a clue. In the distance, I heard music, almost indiscernible. Her window at the Algrove faced West Seventy-second. Below, in a corner, there was a restaurant. Dimly I remembered a photo of a quartet in the little marquee box outside the restaurant.

'Maybe I should have told you,' she said.

'Told me what?'

'I kill things, Jacob.'

'Kill what things, Les?'

Sandra stared at me from the bed, over the top of her book.

'Bushyhead. Momma.'

'You didn't kill them, Leslie Ann. What happened to them happened because of them. You were just a child.'

'I wanted to tell you.'

'Tell me what, Les?'

Breathing. In, out. In, out.

Sandra was beside me now. She mouthed, 'Should I do something?'

I shrugged, raised my free hand – do what?

'Talk to me, Les.'

Sandra stayed close.

Did you do something you're ashamed of?

'What did you want to tell me?'

Breathing. Leslie Ann's into my ear, Sandra's coming up from below my chin across my face.

'When I came into the bathroom that afternoon, when she was killing herself in the bathtub?'

'Yes,' I said.

Through the phone now, I heard a sound like a soft siren carrying these words, gouged out of memory where she'd kept them all these years: 'She was still alive.'

Distantly, dumbly, I thought, *Her dead mother was still alive?* 'What do you mean?'

'She was unconscious but she was breathing. Ever, ever so slightly, she was still here. Breathing. I sat there and watched her until she stopped. And then I called the police.'

Instantaneously, because instinctively I knew it to be true, I said, 'You couldn't have saved her.'

'I killed her.'

'You couldn't have saved her, Leslie Ann.'

'I kill things, Jacob.'

'Leslie Ann, tell me where you are.'

Breathing. And then her voice brought her close, brought these words: 'I don't know why certain people love each other, Jacob. I used to look at so many of the characters in books and plays and I'd wonder, What are those two doing together? But then I started playing some of them and I figured it out.'

'What is it?'

'The stupid morons just can't help it.'

I laughed a small laugh.

'I was scared every day we were together because I believed in my heart we could grow up together. And I'm so stupid that even at this very minute, this second, in my heart, I still do.'

I sensed I had one more opportunity to deliver this order in such a way that she would have to comply. 'Leslie Ann,' I said, 'I want you to tell me where you are.'

But her response was a single word torn out of her throat: 'No.'

21

I ran across Central Park West, glancing back every few seconds for a cab.

Off duty. Off duty. Occupied.

I bent my head into the wind and increased the pace.

She had to be at the Algrove. They were protecting her when the operator said she'd checked out.

Different room, maybe, but she was staying there.

On each breath, I exhaled these silent words: *Wouldn't kill herself. Wouldn't kill herself. Wouldn't kill herself.*

Not with that child in her belly!

As I rounded the corner to head up Central Park West toward the Algrove, two black teenagers threatened my life with their eyes from the entrance to the park.

'You want some blow, man?' one of them called.

I shook my head.

'Then what you *lookin*' at, m'fuck!' the other one wanted to know.

Spontaneously, my cerebral cortex unloaded a shipment of gall into my throat. My feet slowed, my body turned, fists closed, mouth opened to expel the bile in my throat at the two boys.

Forget it, forget it, forget it, I said silently to the rhythm of my feet as they picked up the pace again.

The two black kids snorted their disdain at what was to their view my obvious cowardice and walked away in their rolling, fuck-you gaits, glancing back once more as they were about to disappear into the darkness of the park.

I glanced down Central Park West, saw a cab with its light on, and hailed it.

My door barely closed, the cab shrieked away from the curb and up the avenue.

My heart pounded in my throat – from fear of the two black kids and more.

'Whu'd you say?' asked the cabbie.

'What?'

'Thought you said sompin'.'

'D'know, may have.'

'You innerested in some dynamite weed?'

I looked at the cabbie for the first time – white guy, compost heap of hair, my size, maybe a little thicker, phlegmatic eyes on me in the mirror.

The emotion boiling in me sensed its release. My heart, which was still pounding in my throat, picked up pace.

'Are you offering to sell me narcotics?'

His eyes measured me in the mirror, wondered if he'd made a mistake or if I was being playful.

'Seriously – are you telling me you're dealing drugs out of your cab?'

He thought I was kidding. Or at least one side of his mouth thought that, because a small, indulgent smile showed up there.

I leaned forward and peered through the bullet-proof glass at his ID card, affixed to the glove box of the cab.

'What's your name and ID number?'

Now, there was some heavy doubt that this was a rib.

'Hey, take it easy, huh? I just thought maybe you was on sompin' and it whudn't no good – what's yuh problem?'

'What's *my* problem?'

'Guy's gotta make a livin', don't he?'

'You're *making* a living! You're driving this cab!'

'Oh, oh, yeah, right, you figure that pays a guy enough to live the way he wants to, right?'

I was en route perhaps, to try to save two lives, and those lives were in this guy's hands.

Okay, but why was I talking like this to him when I'd resisted a confrontation with the two black kids?

Who knew!

Ishcabibble.

And so I started pounding on the bulletproof glass with the side of one fist.

Behave! Act! React!

'I'm calling the goddamn Taxi Commission and I'm going to report your ass. I got a *baby* about to be born. You think I want my baby growing up in a world full of idiots like you?'

Two things were going on in the cabbie's eyes in the mirror now. On one hand, he knew I had to be nuts or really tripping badly on some awful pharmaceutical. On the other hand, he was afraid I might be just sane enough to ruin his career as a cabdriver.

'I wouldn't make dat call, I was you.'

'But you're *not* me! I don't know who that's luckier for – me or you – but I know you're not me. *I* am! I'm me and I'm phoning your ass in.'

I drove off the seat of the cab with my thighs and brought the side of my right fist from my shoulder with all the force I could muster into contact with the Plexiglas between the cabbie and me and sent a lightning bolt of pain exploding through my body.

So: bulletproof *and* punchproof.

'Are you fuckin' *crazy*?' the cabbie screamed. 'Are you fuckin' *nuts*?'

The cab shrieked to the curb on Central Park West.

I dug my money out of my pants pocket. 'Your license is gone! You're unemployed!'

The cabbie swung around on his seat, and instead of breathing fire, he gave me a periodontist's delight of a smile. 'Okay, okay, hold it, hold it, okay? So look, hey, dis trip's on me, whudduya say. Ferget I said anything, huh, whudduya say? I didn't say nothin'.'

I slapped three dollars into the little metal tray between the bullet- and punchproof glass and me. 'Keep the change,' I said. 'And you said what you said, Harlowe, William S., number B-7436. Have a really nice day.'

I climbed out of the cab and headed for West Seventy-second Street.

I remembered now I'd left Ernie Pollack's overcoat on the back of my chair in the Oak Bar of the Plaza and that I was cold, the hair on my legs beneath the wool trousers of my suit standing rigidly on end.

'Hey, hey, yo, c'mere, lemme talk to you a minute!' William Harlowe opened his door, but I was too far up the block, so he jumped back in his cab and drove after me.

'Hey, will you c'mere for two seconds!'

To my left a line of fifteen- and twenty-story apartment buildings, broken only by cross streets, were almost all dark.

'Yo, pal, hey!'

People were sleeping.

Were presumably safe.

Until morning. When they would awaken to go out into a world populated by desperate, demented, sick, mean, and crazy lunatics like me and William S.

I headed across the north side of West Seventy-second,

the wind from the west piercing my clothing like needles, whipping my very grown-up foulard tie over my shoulder, heralding my assault on the Algrove half a block away like a banderole.

William Harlowe swung to the curb ahead of me and piled out of the cab. 'Hey, hey, you gonna hold on a second or what?'

He had a fatigue jacket. Christ – he'd served in Vietnam. Another reservoir of guilt sprang open, came at me, just as William S. did.

'Listen, palsy, c'mere – two seconds.'

Arms outstretched in a sign of comradely welcome, he approached with what was supposed to be a neighborly smile.

He had peace symbols all over his fatigue jacket. How could I hit a guy who went off to that fucking war and lived through it?

'I want to just give you one little word of advice. You turn me in – Ooooooooffffffff!'

It felt like my fist intruded six, eight, *ten* inches into William Harlowe's center.

Oooooooooffffffff!

He coughed a raspy smoker's cough – phlegmy and pestilential. All the better: a smoker!

I entered the lobby of the Algrove.

'Hi, I'm Jacob Landau.'

'Yes, of course, I remember you.' The night clerk was bespectacled, about nineteen, was reading *African Genesis*, could have been one of my students.

'My friend,' I panted, 'she was registered as Lorna Greene. I know she's here. She may be in danger. What room is she in? You have to tell me.'

'She checked out, Mr Landau. Too bad – I loved looking at her. She's gone.'

The young man was telling the truth.

Then I knew.

'Jesus Christ. The Plaza.'

'What about it, sir?'

William Harlowe was lurking around the corner of the door to the old hotel. He backed off, raising his hands to let me know he just wanted to talk.

'Okay,' I said, 'take me to the Plaza. Don't say *one* word that irritates me and I won't make the call.'

22

In Austin, she had been in the room next to mine.

I stepped to the door next to Sandra and my bedroom, raised my fist to knock, and found it just barely ajar.

What took you so long?

I pressed the door away from the jamb. The only light in the room came from the bathroom, its door barely cracked.

And now I knew where she was and what she was doing.

I threw myself at the heavy old bathroom door, shining under coats and coats of glossy latex paint. It sprang backward, hit the wall.

At first I saw only her gigantic belly rising mountainously out of the tub.

But now I focused on the fact that she was sitting naked in several inches of foul-looking water.

In slow motion, her dying eyes came around at me.

I knelt beside the bathtub.

Scent of her breath, voice barely audible. 'What a nice speech,' she said. 'To thank me.' Dreamily she nodded her head and smiled, her dry upper lip sticking to her teeth, and then she bit her lip, sucked air through her nose.

I put my hand to her belly. A satin rock.

She stared up into my face, a curious witness to the race that was about to begin.

The bottle of sleeping pills lay on the floor.

How could she kill herself with two sleeping pills?

I picked up the bottle.

Different bottle.

I looked at the label. Dalmane. Fifty capsules. Refilled today.

'Stupid *goddamn* woman.'

I ran out of the bathroom, through the room, down the hall, and into our suite.

'Help!' I screamed, and experienced a ridiculous moment in which I hoped to hell I'd screamed the word loudly enough to wake somebody up, that I hadn't said it softly out of fear of looking foolish or weak.

I burst into Michael Pollack's bedroom. He lay on top of the bed, dressed as I had last seen him when we returned from Sardi's. Beside him, his wife had been startled awake by my cry.

I shook Michael.

'Wha'zi?'

'There's a woman having a baby. She took a bottle of sleeping pills.'

Michael babbled, 'Go 'way,' and shoved my hands off him.

'She's *dying*! Let's *go*, Michael! *Now!*'

Michael Pollack peered at me with not a shred of recognition.

He was unavailable for a house call.

There's another doctor.

That realization propelled me into the living room. Sandra was on her way out of our room, as were her parents out of theirs.

'Leslie Ann – she's trying to kill herself. She's having the baby.'

I was speaking to Sandra, of course; her parents had

no earthly idea what I was talking about. Ernie looked terrified. Neddie, even in motion, seemed inert.

I didn't have to awaken my father. He was standing in the doorway to the Pollack's suite.

'Pop.'

He didn't know who Leslie Ann was, he hadn't been a doctor in almost three decades, but he said, 'Show me.'

'What should I do?' Sandra asked as she ran behind us down the hall, my mother and Carol behind her, Neddie and Ernie behind them.

'Call room service,' my father told Sandra. 'Have them send up two very sharp paring knives.' He pointed at Carol. 'Get the water in the bathroom running as hot as possible. Florence,' my father called back at my mother, 'call an ambulance and bring me your sewing kit.'

In the bathroom, Leslie Ann's breath sounded as if it were coming up out of a crack in the earth. From the distant outlands of her life, she watched us enter the arena.

My father looked at the liquid in the tub.

Slowly Leslie Ann's eyes turned to the water.

'Out of the tub,' my father ordered, and the two of us lifted her onto the bath mat as Carol started the faucets running.

He looked at Neddie Pollack – hopeless. 'Ernie,' he snapped, 'sheets off the bed.'

Sandra ran in, looked for the first time at the woman in the tub – at her face, her belly.

As Leslie Ann's head turned slowly toward Sandra.

And for a moment their eyes came together and the race stopped.

And resumed.

'Sandra,' said my father, 'towels.'

To me: 'Jacob, give me a glass of warm soapy water – quickly.'

Like the others, I did as I was told. As I sudsed up, I watched in the mirror over the sink as my father checked Leslie Ann's airway, then her pulse.

And she watched me, our eyes locked together in the mirror.

Why would she do this?

'Can you hear me? What did you say is her name, Jacob?'

'Leslie Ann, Pop, this is stupid goddamn Leslie Ann.'

My father took barely perceptible notice over his shoulder of the last part of my introduction and said, 'Leslie Ann, can you hear me?'

Leslie Ann peered at my father. Though behind her eyes someone was clearly paying rapt attention, she didn't respond.

Taking notes, I thought, in case there was theater in the hell to which she assumed she was about to descend.

My father pinched her hard on the shoulder, and she emitted a sharp, instantaneous yip.

Satisfied, my father put a hand to Leslie Ann's belly and after a moment said almost inaudibly, speaking really only to himself, 'She's not abrupting.'

I didn't know what that meant, but it obviously wasn't good.

Roughly, he spread Leslie Ann's legs, looked up inside her.

'She's crowning,' said my father. 'Soon, please, Jacob – the soap.'

I squeezed the mass of foam on my hands into a glass. Added water.

My father moved to Leslie Ann's head, lifted her by the shoulders toward the toilet bowl.

I handed the soapy water to him.

'Swallow this, please,' my father said to Leslie Ann, holding the glass to her lips.

In slow motion Leslie Ann reached a hand to my father's face. 'Motke,' she said.

My father was caught up short for just a moment. In that moment I sensed he understood exactly who Leslie Ann was.

'Drink,' my father ordered.

He was through being polite. He shoved his fingers in Leslie Ann's mouth; she clamped her jaws shut. Swiftly, easily, my father pried her jaws open. He poured the soapy water down her throat and forced her mouth shut.

Leslie Ann gagged, choked, and exploded soapy water out her nose as my father continued to hold her mouth closed. Then she convulsed fiercely and her eyes came at me wide in terror.

It was spectacular to see. I had never really seen her frightened. Not that first night I met her when Howard threatened her, not later when I threatened her. Not when she spoke of her father's abuse or her mother's dying.

Not twenty seconds ago.

Never fear.

But here it was.

She may not have minded dying, but she didn't want to die *this* way.

My father took his hands from her mouth, and Leslie Ann projectile-vomited into and around and beyond the toilet.

When the spasms stopped, my father grabbed several towels from Sandra, spread them, and eased Leslie Ann onto her back again and got between her legs.

'Jacob, Sandra, hold her legs up at the knees.'

Sandra and I did as we were told, kneeling in Leslie Ann's fluids, unfolding her grotesquely before us.

I became aware of the others peering with helpless fascination into the bathroom from the doorway, and I had the impulse to order Sandra and Carol, Neddie and Ernie, and my mother to get out.

But on each face I saw only caring.

We were people doing our best.

So we remained there, all of us, strange supplicants before a stranger shrine.

Unable to say whose hand moved first, I found that Sandra and I wrapped our slick fingers together.

My father pressed firmly on Leslie Ann's abdomen, and he implored the person inside to come forth. 'Come on, little baby, drop for me, yes? Come on.'

He pulled back, then leaned into Leslie Ann's abdomen again and massaged. For a moment, when clearly what he wanted to happen wasn't happening, I glimpsed his eyes skidding across the pages of a long unread manual on difficult births for an answer.

He pulled back, pressed forward. And then he said, 'All right, here we are, it's coming. Florence, try to give me as clean a field as possible.' He nodded at the leakage around his knees, seeping from out of Leslie Ann's middle.

My mother eased herself down beside us with towels and sheets.

To Leslie Ann my father said, 'I need you to push.'

Just perceptibly Leslie Ann moved her head sideways, put her eyes on mine.

'Les, you have to help us here, okay? We're your friends, we care, but you have to help us.'

She was not convinced.

And I thought, *You can't rescue who won't be rescued.*

Sandra leaned forward, as close to Leslie Ann's ear as she could, still holding her one leg up at the knee, still holding my slick hand. 'Just push like you're having a bowel movement. Can you do that? Can you push even a little bit?'

Leslie Ann's voice came at us from so far away that I could barely hear it. 'She's dead.'

'No,' I said, 'why would you say that?'

Her mouth trembled with the effort needed to say, 'I killed her, too.'

Leslie Ann tried to clutch my hand to her; there was no strength in her fingers. The words clawed up out of her. 'She stopped kicking this afternoon. When it was time to come and be with me out here. I tried to pretend everything was okay. But she never moved again. She just died inside me.'

'Pop – is that true? Is the baby dead?'

'Sshh – how would I know, I don't know,' said my father. 'I have no stethoscope, I have only . . .'

He left the sentence unfinished. His one huge hand massaged Leslie Ann's belly, his other was swallowed inside her.

'She said the baby hasn't moved since this afternoon. What could have happened?'

'Many things. Sshh, *please*!'

But I sensed he knew the truth.

I felt a surge of idiotic relief that Leslie Ann hadn't tried to kill herself *and* the baby. She was merely in the process of killing *herself* because the baby had died inside her and because she thought she'd killed her mother and father and because because because . . .

I pressed her head to my chest. Her hands came up and she took refuge against me, her breath searing through my once crisp white-on-white dress shirt.

And I knew this was the way it was going to end: the baby was dead, and now Leslie Ann would die. And I would be free to embark on a life of regret and remorse.

Against her burning cheek, I hissed, 'Don't you die.'

Was there something badly twisted about me to feel what I felt for her? Was *I* the one who was disturbed?

No fear!

I was terrified. Terrified that I wouldn't have the opportunity to try to live with her without fear.

'Do you hear me?' I whispered hard against her face. 'Don't you die on us.'

'All right,' my father said, 'finally.'

From here, our faces — Leslie Ann's, Sandra's, my mother's, mine — fixed with reluctance on the event about to take place below us.

From between her legs my father coaxed into this room the child Leslie Ann and I had made.

For a moment I was certain that a child who had endured a journey such as this one had would surely not — could not — come lifeless into the world.

But as the tiny head appeared, it was clear it was only a casing.

'*Oy gut*,' said my mother through her teeth as the rest of the fetus sprang free into my father's hands.

Behind us in the doorway, I heard feet moving away. Mourners in retreat.

My father sucked air in and out through his nose, and again, almost to himself, he said, 'Speak to me, you.'

And he held the inert fetus by its feet upside down and slapped it sharply on the back.

But nothing happened.

My father's index finger slid into the tiny mouth, and simultaneously, Leslie Ann, Sandra and I turned away.

Leslie Ann wailed. With the strength that remained, she dug her fingers into my back and clung as she had the night she'd told me her mother had killed herself.

At the back of her head, against my palm, I felt the ridge of scar tissue where her brother had hit her with the baseball bat.

'Go,' my father commanded his delivery team. 'Go away! Go!'

Sandra stood up, backed off. My mother struggled up off her knees. Behind me I heard their feet on tile, then become faint against the rug on the floor of Leslie Ann's room. I heard a second slap of my father's hand against the fetus.

And again nothing from the fetus.

My father put his face to the fetus, consumed in his mouth the dead infant's nose and mouth. Breathed into the infant's lungs. The tiny chest expanded. My father took his mouth away. The tiny chest fell.

I pressed my lips to Leslie Ann's head. Could feel her lips quivering against my chest.

How dreams change, I thought. *The boy wants a perfect body to fuck, a slave to adore him. Perhaps what the man begins to understand, where human relationships are concerned, is the elegance and mass of* ishcabibble.

And now my father screamed.

I thought: *He's gone back to his own birth and, from that moment, set up a howl of protest at the curses life is going to dump on his head.*

But then I realized that the sound I heard had not come from my father at all. But from what he held in his hands, attached by a cord of flesh back into its mother's womb.

The sound I heard was my daughter's first cry of life.

Like small children viewing some astounding earthly wonder, Leslie Ann and I peered at what my father held.

'Sometimes,' said my father, 'they are reluctant. And who can blame them?'

In his huge hands now he held a tiny, roaring, living being.

Both Leslie and I raised hands toward the shrieking person he held. He laid the baby on Leslie Ann's chest.

And, incredibly, she stilled.

'She hears the heart she knows,' my father said.

Settled there against her mother's chest, our baby breathed.

In, out.

In, out.

And I breathed her breath against my face, took it down deep into my lungs.

Sandra stood again in the doorway with my mother.

As, with a paring knife that had arrived at some point from room service, my father cut the cord.

The baby breathed free.

In, out.

My father knelt between Leslie Ann's legs again; he applied gentle pressure on her belly, pulled gently on the severed cord, and delivered the placenta.

Leslie Ann peered into my face. Perhaps in the power of this moment, I saw more than there could be to see, but I thought I watched a thousand veils fall away from her eyes.

Two men and a woman in white hurtled into the bathroom and, in what seemed like seconds, had secured Leslie Ann to a gurney, one of the men wheeling her out of the room, the other following with an intravenous solution in hand, its tubing plugged into

Leslie Ann's body, fortifying her life, no longer against her wishes.

The baby was wrapped securely in a bath towel in the bedroom. The woman lifted it to her chest.

'Please,' I said to her, 'let me.' I indicated what she carried. 'Just to the elevator,' I said.

The woman handed me the towel and what slept inside.

So small and solid, cradled against my chest in the crook of one arm.

Breathing.

In, out.

The two men wheeled Leslie Ann toward the elevator.

My father walked beside me; the others remained down the hall.

Except for Sandra, who stood just outside the door to Leslie Ann's room.

'I'm going to the hospital,' I told her.

She nodded.

I kissed her cheek. Felt her strong, warm lips against my chin. 'Thank you,' I said.

She nodded against my face.

They were holding the elevator for me. I got on.

The woman in white reached for my daughter. I stepped away. 'Just downstairs,' I said.

The doors closed.

Leslie Ann reached up under my suit coat and hooked her index finger into the back pocket of my pants.

DREAMS OF LONG LASTING

1

The following morning, my father and I walked into Central Park, into the Children's Zoo.

'I brought you here as a little boy once,' my father said.

'You did?'

'Of course. On a vacation won by me for my shoe salesmanship.'

'I don't remember.'

'Unfortunately, as we grow up we tend to remember not so much the good as the bad. It was a nice holiday. We had fun.'

The day was cold but clear, and there were quite a few people wandering the main thoroughfare through the zoo.

It was some seconds before he said, 'Jacob.'

'Yeah, Pop.'

'All that you told your mother and me has happened in this young woman's life, all of that wasn't your fault. No matter how badly you would wish it otherwise, you cannot change the past. You can only try to comprehend it to make for yourself and those you love a better present.'

'I understand, Pop.'

My father nodded. He indicated a bench. We sat. And then my father said without adornment, 'I was a coward.'

I knew these were the words I had anticipated from

my father for many years. I didn't have to ask him to explain. I had only, now, to listen.

'I told you,' said my father, 'that my father made me come to America ahead of him, that he would join me, but then decided to return to Warsaw, implying to you that I would have gone with him had I still been in Lyons when he made the decision not to come here but to go there. That was a lie. He thought we should both go. The Jews had been herded into a walled ghetto. There was talk of detention camps, even incredible whisperings of mass graves. I wove articulate excuses about the consequence of my work in Lyons, gave to myself more value as a scientist in France or America than as a mere general surgeon in a ghetto. But the truth is I was afraid. Afraid that many, many there were going to die; afraid to be among them. Though I was always the biggest boy among my peers, I was the most frightened of others' fists and taunts; and so I was afraid that in the moment prior to my death, I would somehow earn and be held up to ridicule and humiliation. So I did not go and do what I knew in my heart and head I should. My father permitted me my lies – I know he always blamed himself in some way for my softness, my fear – and he left me in Lyons and went to Warsaw. The coward came to America. My father became a part of the resistance movement in the ghetto. The last I heard from him it was a few days before the Warsaw ghetto uprising. Many of the Jews in Lyons who knew us – an old man who once followed us on a golf course somewhere among them, perhaps – they knew the truth about me. Smelled behind my scientist's erudition and hunger to heal the world my cowardice at actually attempting to save lives.'

My father leaned close, at me; he wanted there to be no doubt in my mind about whom he was speaking.

'That is who is your father. So, you see it is no wonder that when that terrible moment came on that golf course when you were fifteen and you needed the support and guidance of a strong man, none was available. But you know what wry truth I have realized over the years, Jacob. It is harder to be a coward than it is to be courageous. Though not having been courageous ever in my life, I cannot be sure of that.'

'Pop . . .'

'Don't speak now. It's not necessary. I am a long time living with who I am. Wait. Think. And then if you would want, so okay, you'll write. I wouldn't try to stop you. Who knows, maybe you can learn something that will help you as a man before you doom yourself, also, to a life of regret.'

He looked past me, over my shoulder, seeming to see there something far away. Then the bell on a hot dog cart down the walkway behind him pulled him back to the present.

'I'm hungry enough to eat the ass out of a golem,' he said, and reached for his back pocket. 'And you – you need strength for what lies ahead.'

When I had returned from the hospital at five-thirty that morning, the door to my mother and father's room was open. They were waiting up for me.

I had told them everything. And then waited for guidance, sitting there next door to a room in which my wife slept, half a mile from where the mother of my child and that child slept.

My father had remained silent. My mother had said only, 'You'll make the right decisions.'

Now my father pulled out his wallet, a slim anteater wallet Susan and I had given him for his fiftieth birthday. Sixteen years later it looked as new as the day we gave it to him except for a slight bend at one corner where his copious tush squashed it day after day. Morris Landau's wallet contained only cash – no credit cards, no photos, no coins, none of the paper testimonials to useless phone numbers and forgotten appointments that seem to find their way into aged wallets.

He took out a twenty-dollar bill, then seemed to debate for some seconds whether to put the wallet back into his pants or not. He glanced over my shoulder again, into that distance, and from the secret chamber behind the money compartment he produced a photograph – two by three or so – and slid it across the bench. It was cracked and faded. I lifted it by one of its edges.

A young man with his arm around a young woman. They were laughing, and the woman stood on one leg, the young man supporting her in a lovely arabesque. There was water in the background. On the white border around the photo, it said 'Gdansk 1936.'

I felt myself smiling. 'When was this?' I asked him. 'When you and Mom first met?'

'Not Mom.'

I bent close. Indeed, the woman wasn't my mother, and had I thought, I would have known immediately it couldn't have been my mother, who was born in Brooklyn and had never been to Poland.

'Who was she?'

'Someone I lost because I did not possess the courage to have her.'

Why did this seem so stunning?

Because of the connection with Leslie Ann?

Because I had viewed my father all my life really only through the prism of the Nazis?

Ah, Flossie!

I put the photo back into my father's hand; he replaced it in his wallet.

A dozen questions collided in my head, but I was hesitant to ask any of them out of some confusing desire to protect my mother.

Yet my father waited, was available, and what came out of my mouth was a question to which I suspected I knew the answer: 'Where is she now?'

He pointed vaguely over my shoulder, toward the distance. 'With my father. My friends. Where I should have gone. Should be.'

I watched myself reach across the distance between us and take my father's hands in mine. 'That's not right, Pop, that's just not right. Because you're here, Pop, and Mom's here and Susan and I are here.'

My father exerted a simple force against my hands, endeavored to retrieve himself, but I exerted an equal force and kept his hands in mine.

Clutching my father's hands, I said, 'There was a day, Pop – I was a boy, we went fishing. You told me, you said that to dream of fame was to dream only of myself. You said a person could be famous in a minute, by one act, or could pursue selfish dreams all his life and never share his life with another living being. Do you remember telling me that?'

'No.'

'Yes, you do. And I asked you if you didn't dream of fame, and you said sure, for a while, and I asked you, okay then, what did you dream, and you said to be the greatest surgeon of all time, and I asked you what you dream now, and what did you say, Pop?'

'I don't remember – I think you have invented this.'

'What did you tell me, Pop? You told me now you only dream the dreams that last. And I asked you what those dreams were, the ones that last. And what did you tell me?'

My father's hands in mine began to quiver.

'Tell me, Pop, what you told me.'

My father took a great gulp of air into his chest and said, 'I told you that dreams of . . .' His voice clutched in his throat, his eyelids slammed shut.

'You told me that dreams of redemption last a long time, but that dreams of love . . . dreams of love, Pop . . .'

'Dreams of love,' sobbed my father, 'last forever.'

And tears spilled down Morris Landau's cheeks. He tried again to retrieve his hands from me, but again I wouldn't let go.

I put my father's hands to my lips.

'I love you, Pop.'

2

As we were walking out of the park with our hot dogs, walking south toward the hotel, my father said, 'I didn't think about this until last night, sitting in the theater, when the main girl made up the funny song. In the ghetto, you know, there were skits in the synagogue on certain occasions. My father was a very fine musician who fancied himself a writer of small musical diversions.'

'Really?'

'Oh, yes. So, what I remembered, I remembered a Chanukah skit he wrote when I was a little boy, in which I and four of my friends formed a quintet. On each of the eight nights of the holiday, at a most crucial moment in the drama, we sang a song, the lyrics for which the author had slaved over for many, many long hours. It was, as I think they say, an *important* song, which urged mankind to stop being nudnicks and embrace all of humanity in a blessed family of man.'

My father was on the brink of laughter at this memory of his childhood.

'The problem was the words to this song changed each night depending on the whim and temperament of our quintet of young singers. As the evenings passed, we became progressively more frightened by our lack of unanimity as to what the words to this important song might be at each performance. And the more we flubbed the song, the greater burden everyone else put on us to memorize it correctly. One night, the song was so diverse in its message that all five of us began to blubber, right there onstage in the synagogue. We had to be escorted away, the song unfinished, mankind, needless to say, unimproved – thanks to us.'

My father unleashed his laughter into the morning. He shook his head in joyous disparagement.

'But then I remember the thing my papa did. He gathered us in the rabbi's tiny bedroom, and he said he would wait until we had stopped our blubbering and then he would tell us a thing that would make us feel so much better we wouldn't believe it. So we stopped our crying, and he told us that he didn't care about the lyrics because, he said, by our passion alone we could change the world. So, for the final three nights of the show, we sang with such fierce conviction that nobody cared that each of us sang to my father's tune his own words.'

We stood at the edge of the park at West Fifty-eighth Street. My father chewed the last bite of his hot dog, remembering his father and his father's little son.

And now my father looked at me. 'So,' he said, 'now I think I have told you everything smart and useful I know. You're on your own.'

But I wasn't and we both knew it.

My father wiped something away from my mouth. 'Mustard,' he said.

He ran the back of one of his big hands along my cheek. 'You know what, though?'

'What, Pop?'

'I still don't know how you missed that putt when you were fifteen. I mean, it was hardly from here to here.'

He held his hands a foot and a half apart before

my face, shrugged his massive shoulders, and crossed to the hotel.

I continued on toward the hospital, where at noon I was to feed a child.